Maria Von Rummelhoff

MAGIC
OF THE
NIGHT

NOCTIS ONUS

Tigger warnings
This book, Magic of the night by Maria Von Rummelhoff, may contain scene that can trigger some readers.

Here are the following triggers: Blood, mention of bones, mention of child death and killing, death, depression, infertility, kidnapping, needles, pregnancy, PTS, Sexually explicit scenes, starvation, violence.

Cover design by: Maria Von Rummelhoff
Translated by: Hanne Utheim Gundersen
Original edit in Norwegian: Heidi Garvik

Illustrations in chapters: Pixabay
Character art 4 drawings: Carol Pisarro
Cover illustrations: Clip studio paint pro

Prologue

The last time I checked my watch it was ten past two in the morning. The cold damp air swept me up like a veil and I was consumed by grey mist. Light spots were dancing before my eyes, and they kept growing clearer. Shadows were dancing slowly in front of me. I reached out a hand towards them, and just like last time, the shadows began to move faster. Twice I got the sense that something caressed my fingertips almost like a light breeze. It didn't feel like a dream. I felt wide awake. For a moment I believed that I saw a hand in front of me and I reached for it. Then, I felt almost certain that something touched my fingers, but the sensation was gone just as quickly as it had appeared. What was this? Whatever it was, it was a wonderful sensation.

Chapter 1
Sleepless night

My expectations had been skyrocketing from the very beginning. Even William had been convinced that this time it would be a completely new start for us. His beautiful eyes were gleaming again just like they had done four years ago when we first met and became a couple. He had already started to prepare for our new life, and he had spent a considerable amount of time talking about the nursery and which colour it should be. That very night I found him on all fours while he was measuring how much space we needed for the cot. What would he say now? I stared at my fingers where I held the little object. My hands were cold and clammy around the little white stick. 'Not pregnant.' I just couldn't understand it. It had been seven weeks since my last period and we'd been paying close attention to my ovulation calendar. Our sex life was close to non-existent. It hadn't been joyful for any of us since our wedding last summer. Sex had been reduced to a job. Something we needed to do in order for me to become pregnant. The hard sound of raindrops hit the window, but I didn't hear it. The gloomy Duluth fall made a proper dent in my mood. My stomach churned at the thought of what I had to tell my husband, and then I heard the car coming up the driveway. Cold shivers ran through my body and

1

instinctively I pulled my feet up under me. The armchair felt uncomfortable and hard. The flames from the fire gave no warmth. The door opened and my husband entered with that beautiful, crooked smile I immediately noticed when I met him the first time. I was out with the girls one night to really let our hair down. A common friend introduced Will and me and that was it. We ended up in his car and talked until five am the next morning. We would talk about anything, and it felt so natural. He had smiled several times, and I was sold.

'Hi babe,' Will said.

'Hi handsome,' I whispered back. I was squeezing the pregnancy test so hard that my knuckles turned white.

'I wish this weather would stop,' he said and shook the water out of his ashen blond hair. His bangs were a little too long and hung obliquely down to the left corner of his eye. Just enough to barely hide the eye. The words took shape in my mouth, but nothing came out. Will turned and studied me for a moment and I could almost hear his heart skip a beat. The sound hit my eardrum and the grip around the test became even harder while I felt my eyes burn.

'Not pregnant.' My voice broke and my lower lip started to quiver uncontrollably.

'But....' Will had gone quiet. I couldn't bear to look at him. My entire body was in terrible pain, and it felt like my chest would collapse. I began to cry.

'Babe,' he said and sat down on the armrest while his hand stroked my head. 'I really believed that we had done it this time. It's not normal to have such a long period of time between periods.' There was concern in his voice.

'I've been so convinced myself. Maybe I've convinced myself so strongly that it has affected my body and my cycle.'

For once I had believed that we finally could get rid of the stupid comments people could make such as 'You have enough time,' 'Don't worry about it and it will happen,' and 'You're still so young.' All of these naive comments were intended to be supportive concerning childlessness. I was 24 and Will was 25 but we had wanted a child for so long. We sat there for a long time and just held each other without words.

The gynaecologist had already informed us about the opportunities and our application had already been approved. We had put it off as long as possible and hoped that everything would sort itself naturally, but we were both aware of what was in store for us now. Assisted fertilization, IVF, and test tube treatment. All the names mean and insinuate the same thing. I was left with a feeling that I'd lost a battle which I was never intended to win. Yet it was hard to give in. I was raised to do my best before I asked for help. Besides, the treatment was expensive! However, if that meant that I finally could become pregnant we'd pay whatever it cost. The wait was not a positive experience either.

There were so many others who waited in line for the test tube treatment so there were several months of waiting time for the first consultation. To top it all off, before we even got there, I had to go through an operation in order for the doctors to figure out what the problem could be.

There loomed an uncomfortable silence over the couch that whole evening. None of us wanted to talk more about the pregnancy test but I assumed that Will thought about it as much as me since he was just as silent as I was. We let the TV fill the room between us with bland shows and Will was almost asleep on the couch when I got up.

'Will, I'm going up to bed.'

'Hm? Yeah, I'll be right there.' He stretched and yawned.

Everything felt like it was moving in syrup and when I finally got to bed Will was already asleep.

Once in bed, my thoughts wouldn't stop churning. My chest ached and a tear trickled down my neck. I felt that Will took everything so much lighter than I did and I wondered if that might be because he knew that the fault didn't lie with him thus the fault had to be with me. It took me a long while to calm down and close my eyes. I floated away towards the cold and comfortable dark. A cloud of black mist consumed me. My arms felt weightless. The mist billowed and I was naked in the moist breeze. I felt unreal and yet so real at the same time. I felt the small hairs on my body move. Far away Will snored, and finally, everything became quiet while the moist mist still surrounded my body. Just then I caught a glimpse of something far ahead of me. It could just be my senses who played tricks on me. I sensed that I wasn't alone. That there were other shadows present in my state of mind. The moist mist slowly blew away and sleep encapsulated me.

I woke with the feeling that someone had hit me in my stomach all night. It was swollen and tender. I had no doubt about what this was, and, in the bathroom, the confirmation stared me straight in the face. The test was right. I felt the tears coming but I didn't want to cry in front of Will. That would ruin his day, so I gritted my teeth and kept my facial emotions in check. We were both quiet during breakfast. Pretending everything was ok.

'I have to get to work now. I've got lots of clients before lunch today.' Will got up from the table and came over to give me a kiss on the cheek. His lips were soft and loving, but they didn't bring much comfort. Will worked as an assistant manager in a real estate company and he enjoyed it. He was very competent and responsible and also often worked late at night.

'I'll call you when I've talked to the hospital today,' I said before he went out the door. The doctors hadn't been able to find any faults on either ultrasounds or tests so the only thing left to do was check if endometriosis could be the cause of our problems. Endometriosis is an illness which is hard to discover and often creates scars and infections in the abdomen which aren't easy to spot on either blood tests or x-rays from the outside. The doctors, therefore, had to enter through a tiny hole to see for themselves using a camera. If they found endometriosis scarring, they'd try to burn it away so that the uterus could function normally, at least for a period of time and hopefully that would be enough to conceive a baby.

Our house was located on the west side of Duluth, and we'd purchased it after our first anniversary. It was just the right size for a family of four. The yard wasn't large but nice and intimate with enough room for the kids to run around and play.

I was home standing in front of the bathroom mirror. My pale face had dark shadows under the eyes while my skin almost looked transparent. My hair reached just past the ears, and it was wet and unkempt. Originally my colour should have been a burgundy-black tone, but my roots were quite visible, and the colour had faded. Nothing was as it used to be, and it had been a while since I was happy with my own reflection. My hair was dull, my skin transparent, my eyes lifeless, and I'd gained at least fifteen pounds. I was ashamed that I didn't even try to look good for Will anymore, but the spark was gone.

It felt nice to have some time to myself before I called the hospital. I made a cup of tea and sat down in the armchair in front of the fire. It was still smouldering and gave off a comfortable warmth. The phone was in the living room, and I picked it up to dial the number of the hospital. After dialling through the menu with quivering fingers until it finally began to ring. My heart was ringing in my ears. A few minutes later the date was set, and I could hang up. A hollow feeling left me feeling like someone had removed all my intestines. The pain in my stomach came out of nowhere and with impeccable timing so did the nerves. My appointment was on November 1st which was just a week away. I felt clammy and my knees were shaking. This was going to be my first operation. What would the results be? Would I be ok?

The night before the operation I struggled with sleep.

'Are you nervous, baby?' Will laid down close to me.

'Yes. I don't feel well. I'm nauseous,' I said turning around to rest my head on his arm close to his chest. It felt safe to hear his heartbeat, steady and calm. Nothing could touch me in his arms. I was safe here.

'You'll be fine. They've said that it is a simple procedure.'

'There might still be complications. They said as much.' My body started to shiver when I said this out loud. Will hugged me closer to him.

'That's the sort of thing they're required to inform about. Don't be a pessimist. It will all be ok,' he said while he stroked my hair and down my naked back. I got goosebumps from his soft touches. We laid like that for a while before I got up on my elbow and gave him a soft kiss on the lips. Then I turned around and pulled the duvet up to my chin.

Will fell asleep quickly but I had a storm of emotions inside me. Again, I lay watching the lights dancing in wavelike motions over the ceiling. My eyes burned as I did everything to keep the tears from flowing which was useless. I was glad that Will was asleep. This would have been so much harder if he was awake. It was difficult for him to talk about difficult stuff. He had changed. He used to have the smile that charmed me beyond everything, his dark-blue eyes which could see straight through me, and his joyful laughter. It was impossible to not be happy when he was around. He still smiled but it was a strained sort of smile, and it wasn't infectious like it used to be. His gaze wasn't shining anymore but shallow and joyless. My thoughts brought back memories of how things used to be when he would kiss my cheek and turn my stomach into butterflies while electric pulses shot through my entire body. He could embrace me and put his hands on my lower back while his fingers slowly moved my sweater up a notch until they barely touched the skin beneath the layers. He used to caress my neck with his lips without kissing me. Just his breath tickling my neck and shoulders. The memory of his breath against the nape of my neck made me tremble even now. Will we ever be good again?

The last time I checked my watch it was ten past two in the morning. The cold damp air swept around me like a wail, and I was consumed by grey mist. Light spots were dancing before my eyes, and they kept growing clearer. Shadows were dancing slowly in front of me. I reached out a hand towards them, and just like last time, the shadows began to move faster. Twice I got the sense that something caressed my fingertips almost like a light breeze. It didn't feel like a dream. I felt wide awake. For a moment I believed that I saw a hand in front of me and I reached for it. Then I felt almost certain that something touched my fingers, but the sensation was gone just as quickly as it had appeared. What was this? Whatever it was, it was a wonderful sensation.

Chapter 2
The hand in the dark

𝕴 didn't mean to scare you babe. I thought it was better to wake you rather than letting that awful alarm clock kick off your day.' Will pulled me close to his warm body.

'I was dreaming. I'm fine now,' I mumbled still quite unfocused. I had been close to the hand in the dream. If Will had waited just a few more seconds, I'd have been able to grab hold of it.

'Are you ready for today?' Will whispered. For a moment I couldn't remember what today was but then it suddenly hit me like a tidal wave. The operation.

'No, but I don't have any other choice,' I said giving a little sigh. It didn't take long before the nausea was back. My empty stomach did cartwheels, and it did nothing to make me feel better.

At the hospital, I just fell into the stream of routines. First, we headed for the lab to do some blood tests and then we moved on to the department that handled surgeries during the day. Walking among endless white corridors reminded me more about movies I'd seen than what I was experiencing. Will waited outside the lab for me when I came out. He put his arm around my shoulders.

'OK?' he asked and kissed my cheek. He looked me straight in the eyes and expected an answer which surprised me.

'Yes,' I said. 'Almost.'

'Come. It's already 8:55am. You're up in five minutes.' Will lead me down the corridor towards the surgery department.

'Ugh, I'm really dreading this now.' My voice was shaky.

'Poor girl. Come, let's sit and wait.'

It didn't take long before the doors opened and a small man with an Indian complexion came out.

'Amelia Godseth?' He cast a glance over the rows of chairs with waiting patients. I froze. My throat tightened making it hard to breathe. I tried to clear it, but my voice failed me.

'Here,' I was able to squeak while my legs were searching for some ground to stand upon. Will followed me to the door where he held me back and put his arms around me in a big hug.

'Good luck, babe,' was all I heard as the doors pulled shut between us.

The man gave me a striped hospital gown and pointed towards a door.

'You can change in there. I'll wait here and then I can escort you over to your bed, if need be,' he instructed me.

I did as he said. The thin gown didn't cover a whole lot of my body and it was very thin compared to the temperature in the room. Come to think of it, this was probably only one of the reasons why I was shivering.

When I came out, the man was waiting for me and waved me through a great metal door. In the next room, there were many hospital beds running down one wall.

'You can lay down in this one, and you can put your clothes over in this one,' the man said and put a plastic box on the nearest mattress. I pulled the duvet aside. The bed was just as cold as the room. The man, whom I now understood to be a nurse, disappeared through a great glass door. I remained sitting and looked around as I wrapped myself in the duvet. When he finally returned, he brought a chair and placed it by my bed. Then he sat down.

'I am Ahmed, and I am the ward nurse here. I'd very much like it if you could answer some questions for me.'

It hit me how strange he was. His hair was only a few inches short except for one single long hair in the middle of his forehead. It was several inches longer than the others and he twisted it around his finger while he gave me information and asked me questions like: 'Have you been eating or drinking today?' and 'Did you shave?' That last question really took me by surprise until I realized what he was really asking me. When my brain caught up with the question and its meaning, I could feel myself blush.

'Yes, I have.' I answered and when I had given the answer, I felt something reminiscing of a smirk cross my face.

'You will now be given some medicine to help you relax, then the anaesthetist will come and talk to you in a little while.'

He went to get a glass of water and gave me some pills. I probably snoozed for a couple of minutes because when the anaesthetist came, I jolted awake.

'Amelia? Hi, my name is Dr. Reesfield. My job is to handle the anaesthesia during your operation.' The man who had materialized next to my bed was lanky, tall, and had a bushy moustache like the moustaches which were fashionable in the 18th century. The sort of moustache with a curl at the end. What hair he had left was shaped like a blond garland with a touch of red in it. It reminded me of a circus clown. He went into detail about what would happen while I was under the anaesthesia but the only thing I was able to focus on was that bushy moustache bouncing up and down under his nose while he was talking.

When 'Dr. Moustache' finally concluded his explanation, they wheeled me into the operation room. The grand, sterile room was furnished with steel countertops containing all sorts of machines. In the middle of the room was the operating table which mostly, to me, resembled a butcher's bench.

'You can lay down over here,' one of the nurses said when they had wheeled my bed close to the bench. I was shaky when I slid my body over onto the bench. My heart was pumping so hard it seemed like my ribs would give in. The panic grabbed hold of me, and I hyperventilated.

'Hi Amelia. My name is Anne and I'm a nursing student.' A beautiful young lady grabbed hold of my hand.

'Hi.' My voice was raspy and dry.

'I'm just going to give you a little pinch in the arm now and then you'll be asleep soon.'

I followed her with a hysterical look, all my muscles tense. A slight burn spread throughout the arm and after that it was like I floated away from the table. Again, I was surrounded by this thick mist just as dark as it had ever been.

I could feel the moist breeze against my skin while I was floating. My weightless state felt wonderfully dazed. The mist grew slowly lighter and the light spots I'd seen in my dream were here as well. I reached for them just like last time but instead of disappearing they opened even more than before and gradually they started playing in front of me. I got the sensation that something was caressing my fingertips. The light spots grew into silhouettes out of focus. In the next second, I could clearly feel a hand close to my fingers. Far away I could hear a woman's voice. I took a deep breath, so deeply it hurt, and then reached with my whole body in a last attempt to touch the fingertips. Suddenly, someone said my name and I felt someone clutching my arm and pulling me towards them. At the same time, everything grew cold. Again, someone said my name and my skin felt like I was being dragged up from warm water. I was dry but at the same time kind of cold and moist.

☙❧

Before I knew it, I fell with my full weight and landed flat on my stomach against a big hard surface. The fall knocked the wind out of me, and it took a little while before I came to myself and realized that I was lying on the floor of a big room. My gaze stiffened when I saw a stranger's feet right by my side and realized that someone was standing over me. I wheeled around on my back. Two slightly unfocused figures looked down at me. The room was filled with the loud sound of pounding. When my eyes had gotten used to the surroundings, I saw a grown woman in a long pale dress with a tight braid at the nape of her neck. Her hair was brown with some grey areas and her face was kind.

After a while in this pressed silence, the pounding started up again and the echo of sound created a song around me.

'Amelia. My name is Mirini. Before you ask, we must get away from here!' the woman said seriously with a hushed voice. Right next to her, there was a man dressed in a brown garment tied with a white rope around the waist. It wasn't until I moved my gaze to look closer at him that I realized that I was lying on the floor of a church. There were great gothic stone columns rising above me and they met in sharp arches by the ceiling. The beams made of stone were decorated with grotesque monsters who looked down on us from above with their wings spread and their fangs grasping their plinths. They sat quietly screaming at their own shadow.

Mirini grabbed my arm and pulled me up. I saw straight into a gigantic mirror with the strangest surface I had ever seen. It was like I was looking down into dark restless water which made the reflection almost unrecognizable. It almost seemed like the reflection showed both the depth within and the reflection of the room I was in at the same time. It was only when I had looked into the mirror for a while that I realized what I saw on the surface. Straight in front of the mirror was a naked woman's body. The picture moved in harmony with my own movements but the woman in the mirror had a slenderer figure and hair to the waist. She seemed familiar yet she was a stranger, and it took me a while to realize that the woman I saw in the mirror was me. I was unrecognizable even to myself but at the same time several similarities began to show and then, amidst all these realizations, I also realized that I was completely naked.

Before I was able to cover myself with my hands, Mirini had thrown a big garment at me, just like the man was wearing. The pounding around us was still strong but when I listened more closely, I picked up some muffled shouts over the pounding.

'Take the back door!' the man, whom I assumed was a priest, whispered.

'Who is that? Where am I? Who are you? What is happening?' I hissed at them.

'Not now, Amelia. I promise that I will answer all your questions later but if you don't want to die within the next two minutes we have to hurry. Now!'

I could hear the anger in her voice. My feet felt glued to the floor while this scene in front of me moved through my head. This could under no circumstances be real but on the other hand, it felt just as real as a normal day at home. This had to be the strangest dream I had ever had. What a nightmare!

Mirini put an arm around my back and led me resolutely towards the altar which was in the shadow of the mirror. Next to the altar on one side there was a massive wooden door which led into a narrow dark corridor decorated with paintings of old, and what I assumed, dead priests.

The small door creaked when it closed behind us. The priest remained on the other side. At the end of the corridor there was another door and Mirini pushed it open in front of me. The door led out to a dark cobbled street. I couldn't see much beside the light from the stars shining above us.

'Hush!' said Mirini and held a finger to her lips while she peaked around the doorframe. She stood quiet for a little while and looked towards something I assumed to be the front of the church. Curious as I was, I leaned carefully around her and saw that the doorway we were in exited the long side of the church. Far down, at the end of the church, where I suspected the main entrance to be, I could see small stone houses in epic style which stood closely together just across from the church. In between the houses and the church was a great cobbled square which seemed to be full of people. As far as I could see, there were lights dancing on the house walls, just like there was a lit fire in front of the houses. In the distance we could hear angry shouts. Suddenly I realized where the pounding sound in the church had come from. Someone was trying to tear the door down by force.

'Who...?'

'Hush!' Mirini broke me off again. She took one step out of the doorway, then she leaned her back against the wall to make herself as small and invisible as possible.

'Come,' she commanded me and waved me on after her towards the back of the church. I obeyed and attempted to imitate her light steps. We stopped at the corner and looked back towards where the voices could be heard. There was no longer any light at the front of the church and the voices had gone quiet.

'Don't blow our cover now, Benedikt!' she mumbled to herself. Then she was quiet for a few moments before she hissed; 'God damn it. When will he learn to keep his mind to himself!'

Suddenly, everything happened so quickly that I barely had the chance to breathe before she grabbed my arm and pulled me behind the church. I felt uncomfortable. My thoughts had all but disappeared, so my head felt rather empty. What was I supposed to believe about all this? I could feel neither fear nor anger. This could not be real. This could not be anything but an inexplicable dream or rather a nightmare.

18

MAGIC OF THE NIGHT

We were standing in an ancient church yard which made me giggle sarcastically to myself. Of course, there couldn't be a nightmare without a dingy churchyard during the night. What would be next? White sheets and zombies grabbing at our feet? I could already hear the cliché retort in my head: 'I want to suck your blood.' The zombies would say it in Count Dracula's voice with a broken Transylvanian accent. The whole situation was almost comical.

Looking at the state of the church yard, it couldn't have been used in the last hundred years or so. All the bushes and trees grew wild and had almost consumed the tombstones. Some were so well hidden that they were only visible as small lumps in the yellow grass. The contour was still clearly visible in the strong moonlight though. One of the trees looked like a giant hand which was about to dig up a tombstone from the ground. The perfect scene for a horror movie.

'Over here,' said Mirini. She ran behind the great trees with hanging branches and came back with a big horse. I stopped dead in my tracks and looked amazed at both her and the horse. Goodness gracious, where am I? Really? I thought to myself. Were we going riding?

'Come here and I'll help you up. Put your foot on my knee,' said Mirini.

'Are you nuts? I can't ride.'

'Come on. There's a first for everything.' She took on her commanding voice again, and I understood that there was no time for discussion. I took a deep breath and did as I was told. It wasn't until I lifted my leg to pull myself up by her knee that I realized that I was

19

barefoot and rather cold. In the distance, we could hear a rumbling noise which quickly grew louder.

'Damn it!' Mirini's voice was louder and angrier than before. She pushed me up and put her own foot in the stirrup. Then she jumped up behind me, grabbed the reins and dug her heels into the horse's side. With a strong jerk the horse moved on in a canter between the tombstones and out through the open iron gates.

The little gothic church was the town's centre point. The cobbled streets stretched out around it as they moved on between the houses. Behind us I could hear the rumbling noises of many hooves and angry yells from their riders. The seriousness of the situation was about to hit me. There was someone following us, and they were coming closer by the second. A cold shiver ran through my body. The horse increased its speed dramatically as if it was urged on by fire.

We came to an alley between the houses, and it was so narrow that I could touch the walls on both sides of the horse. The alley was very dark, and I could barely see a hand in front of me. Lights from some windows down the alley were our only source of light. The sound of the riders following us kept coming closer, but they weren't on our heels just yet. Ahead of us I could barely see an embankment which was just low enough for me to see over it. Mirini kept a steady and firm pace towards the embankment and the horse moved in small leaps up it. I grabbed hold of the horse's mane and closed my eyes as we came to the top of the embankment and moved down the other side. Ahead there was a moat which seemed to surround the entire city. The water was so dark that it made me think of oil.

'This is going to be cold,' said Mirini and lead the horse towards the water.

'Are you nuts? It will be ice cold. Do you want me to freeze to death?' Thankfully, I was able to keep my wits about me just so that I wasn't screaming at her.

'If they catch us, the temperature in the water will be the least of your concerns,' she replied.

The water was rising against the horse's legs and steadily up ours as well. The shock of being lowered into the ice-cold water made me struggle with my breathing. It felt like being cut with a thousand razors against my shins and it was unbearable. The horse stretched its neck to keep its head above the water. I stopped breathing when the water enclosed around me, and I was wet and cold to the bone.

The horse continued up the other side of the moat towards the dark forest which was denser than any other forest I'd seen before. We stopped a good way in between the trees and slid down from the exhausted horse. The embankment was barely visible between the trees and the alley we'd ridden through. Now, it was ablaze with the light of torches. I could see the top of someone's head, but their faces remained invisible in the dark. They looked around and talked agitated amongst themselves, but we couldn't hear what they were saying. The light from the torches faded away down the alley and it all grew quiet.

While we followed our pursuers' retreat, we'd stood still. Then, I turned towards Mirini where she stood short of breath right next to me. My whole body was shaking but this time it wasn't from the cold.

'Tell me what is happening. NOW!' I demanded.

Chapter 3
Grimmer

The dark forest presented as darker than before since I was focusing so hard on the sopping wet woman next to me.

'You are in Grimrokk,' she said.

'That doesn't give me anything. It's not good enough! Try again!' I hissed angrily between my teeth.

'Grimrokk is simply a different place, a different reality than the one you already know.' Her explanation was meaningless to me.

'That's not a good answer! Why am I here and who the fuck are you?' My head had started to spin.

'I'm Mirini and why you are here is a question I do not know the answer to.'

'Alright? Well then, who were the people following us?' I was so angry now that I was almost spitting with every word. I took a better stand to gain balance.

'The Myrthing Clan. They don't like people coming here so they try to do everything in their power to stop it.' Mirini looked questioningly at me furrowing her brows.

'Well, I can't say that I disagree with them. I don't fancy being here much either.' I was starting to get dizzy.

'Get back on the horse. The operation is almost over and they're about to wake you.'

How could she know that? My head was spinning, and my legs wouldn't support me. Mirini grabbed a hold around my waist and guided my foot into the stirrup, then she pushed me onto the horse. She jumped up behind me to keep me steady. With a jolt the horse began to canter into the dense forest.

'What is happening?' I could not focus on anything around me anymore.

'You are done with your operation and are about to wake up. Nobody can be in two places at once. Don't tell anybody where you've been. That is important.'

I wasn't quite able to understand what Mirini was talking about.

'You will wake up here again and when you do you will get the answer to everything. Batist will be with you when you wake up.'

My body became heavy. I did not manage to keep my eyes open anymore. Nothing of what Mirini said made any sense and what I had just pondered slipped away from me just as the rest of me did the same. The last thing I heard was;

'Don't tell anyone where you've been.'

CR8O

Suddenly there was someone who pulled me quickly from the dark. Then the pulling stopped, and I floated for a moment. Far away I could hear a distant voice and could barely see a weak light which was moving closer and closer.

'Amelia? Amelia?' It was the surgical nurse, Anne. I tried to look at her, but everything was spinning both inside and outside my head until I realized where I was.

'Amelia, your operation is over now, and everything went fine.'

'Dim you fhint anyphing?' My speech was slurred due to the drugs I had been taking. The question which could determine our family's future and the question I had been wondering about every minute of the last few days.

'Yes. We found endometriosis behind your uterus and a small spot on your left ovary before we removed it all. Now you can start with clean sheets.' Anne smiled mildly at me.

I was moved over to my own bed again and fell asleep before they had had the time to wheel me out of the operation room.

'Amelia? It is William.' I felt his fingers brush over my hair and his warm lips against my cheek. His voice was comforting and soft. My eyes were as if glued together and I struggled to open them. The work to keep them open was almost too much.

Through the narrow slit I saw William smile down at me.

'There you are,' he said.

'Hi.'

It was lovely to see him. It was clear to me that he had been worried, no one could question that. He was pale and his hand shook slightly as it brushed my hair. The nurse in the recovery room supported me when I sat up. My stomach was noticeably ready for food and water, and it didn't take long before the apple juice and bread with ham stood in front of me on a little tray. Never had bread as dry as this appealed to me. It was wonderful to eat something after almost 24 hours without sustenance.

Not long after this meal we were on our way home and I was snoozing with my pain relivers in one hand and a can of soda in the other. I felt like I'd just sat down in the car when Will woke me announcing that we were home. Out of habit I stretched both arms and legs in front of me so almost my entire body was tense and then my stomach abruptly began to hurt making it almost impossible to get up. Will did his best to help manoeuvre me out of the car and just like a stooping old grandma I stumbled towards the house half hanging onto Will's arm.

'Babe? Shall we go to bed? You do look a little weary still.' Will whispered into my ear. I'd slept away the day and now I was snoozing in the armchair.

'Yes. That is probably a good idea. You do look a little bit tired as well,' I said while I met his tired gaze.

'I'll help you up.'

He bent down towards me and put his hands on my hips. I put my arms around his shoulders and then he pulled me up gently. Our walk up the stairs felt like it took forever but Will was patient during every step.

The bed looked inviting, but it wasn't easy to lay down without help. Will helped me out of my sweatpants and hoodie and every movement took forever. He laid me down the same way he had supported me up the stairs.

'Are you ok? Shall I get you something?'

'No thanks, I'm fine,' I said. I was touched and very tired.

'You must wake me if you need anything. Promise me that you'll wake me?'

He looked me in the eye while he leaned over me with his bangs brushing his forehead. That look had always made me weak and even now my body responded to it.

'Yes. Yes,' I said but it was a lie. Will turned off the light and came and lay down next to me. He was quiet for a while before he turned towards me.

'I don't like that you're in pain. I wish I could take some of the pain for you.' He wrinkled his brows in a worried frown.

'Don't say that. I'm not in a whole lot of pain when I lay still like now. I just hope the operation was worth it, so I didn't go through this for nothing.'

He sensed that I was lying again. The pain would be the same whether he worried or not.

'If this isn't the root of the problem then I don't know what I'll do. We've tried and tested everything else, and everything is ok.' The desperation in his voice was obvious. For once Will let it out.

'One thing at the time. We can't give up now.'

I was trying to calm myself down just as much as I was trying to comfort him. He leaned over me and kissed my lips softly;

'I love you babe. Sleep tight.'

'I love you too handsome. Sleep well,' I said.

My body was in more pain than I wanted to admit to Will and my stomach was very swollen. I couldn't fall asleep right away, so my thoughts wandered back to the operating room and the narcosis. The dream was the weirdest one I'd ever had but what struck me as even more weird was how real it had seemed. I had even had cold feet and felt Mirini's hand grip my arm. I'd felt the cold water of the moat against my skin. To try and find a logical explanation I tried to remember a place where I'd been that could remind me of the little village. After all, dreams are supposed to be the workings of experiences you've already had but that didn't help me either. Everything in the dream had been foreign. My eyes finally grew heavy, and the darkness engulfed me. I felt featherily light again and for a moment I was floating but I could sense the moist mist and the cool breeze wasn't there now. After a little while the light grew brighter, and I felt sleep escaping me. I stretched carefully and opened my eyes.

CR80

The room I was in was utterly foreign to me. I looked around and it appeared to be a little wooden hut with a tiny kitchen in the corner and another corner for a fireplace with two worn armchairs in the front. In the middle of the room there was a roughly made dining table with four different chairs. The walls were strangely decorated. Stuffed animals, tools and shelves which were flowing over with bottles and jars in all shapes and sizes. The contents varied from illuminating green stuff to moving, slimy stuff which were twisting and turning slowly, and others contained what I assumed to be herbs. A bed was in the corner next to the door. The room was so quiet that I was sure I was alone but then I realized there was someone sitting in one of the armchairs. The chair had its back to me so I could barely see above one of the armrests. A couple of legs poked out resting on a little stool. Across the armrests I could see a hand with a hot beverage.

'Hello?' I said so quietly in order to not frighten the person.

'Look at that, you are awake. How marvellous.'

An older, chubby man got up from the chair. He was wearing green felt pants and a half-length jacket which lay down below his hips. He put the mug down on a little table between the armchairs and came smilingly over to me. His short hair was grey and so were his eyebrows.

'Where am I?' I asked a little guarded.

'In Grimrokk. I am Batist,' the older man said, and his smile faded.

'What?' I burst out a little too loudly. 'Am I here again?'

'Yes. Don't be scared. It's not so bad, really.' Batist stopped a little way away from the bed with a slightly desperate look in his eyes.

'This is the craziest dream I've ever had.' I could feel my heart hammering and my hands were cold from sweat. 'Why am I here?'

'That I do not know. Mirini felt that you were on your way and decided that we should greet you.' He tried to calm me down by quieting his voice while his hands were moving in a calming gesture in front of him.

'Felt that I was coming? Is she psychic or something?' My tone was sarcastic, and I could hear it.

'Not psychic but she can read minds.'

Before he could add anything else to this statement, I loudly said to myself.

'This is a bit too much for me. I'll probably wake up any minute now.'

'Amelia, you are awake. Let me explain. It isn't easy to comprehend, and I understand that.'

Batist gestured with his arm to the armchairs as if to ask me to have a seat. I stood still for a moment while I thought about all my questions and the answers they required. After some thinking I noticed that I wasn't wearing any clothes and quickly grabbed the blanket I'd been sleeping under. Batist turned away just as quickly out of politeness and headed towards the kitchen. With the blanket wrapped around me I took a deep breath and went to sit down in one of the chairs by the fire.

'Here, this is Imaginari-tea. It helps the thinking process. Be careful, it is warm.'

He handed me a mug and with a sceptical look I accepted it. The content was clear as water and the warm steam didn't contain any noticeable odours.

'What did you say this was?' I asked.

'Imaginari-tea. Think of your favourite hot beverage,' he smiled carefully.

I wasn't quite able to grasp what he was saying since I was so preoccupied with the green vapor rising from his own mug.

'It isn't dangerous. What is it that you like to drink?' His gaze tried to catch mine.

'What? Oh, ehm hot chocolate,' I said and shook my head in an attempt to become more focused.

'Think about hot chocolate and take a sip,' he smiled.

I thought about the lovely slightly bitter hot chocolate I used to order at the cozy cafe in town and then I smelled the content of the mug again. The aroma was amazing. I took one careful sip. The chocolate flavour was amazing, and I could almost taste the chocolate rolling around in my mouth and playing with my tastebuds.

'Yum! This is absolutely delicious! Thank you!' I was baffled.

'It's you who knows how it should taste, not me.'

'You're the one who made it though,' I said still a little unfocused.

'Making Imaginari-tea is the simplest thing in the world. It's the ingredients who does the trick and the person who conjures the flavour with its mind of course.' He laughed a careful little laugh.

'Does that mean that your content doesn't taste of chocolate?' I felt like an idiot.

'That's correct.' He confirmed. 'My mug tastes of currants and rhubarb with just a touch of mint which is my favourite.'

How could this be? Two tea mugs with exactly the same ingredients but tasting differently? It did not add up.

'There will be a lot of things that are foreign to you, but Grimrokk is nothing different from other places you've been. Here, there's a lot that will marvel you. I can tell you what I know first and then I'll answer your questions later.' He waited for my response.

'That's fine,' I nodded.

'The mirror in the church, do you remember that? It is one of very few portals or doors to Grimrokk. That exact mirror is the only door within weeks distance. When you sleep in Gaia, there is a big chance that you....'

I interrupted him. 'Gaia?'

'Yes, the reality you come from is called Gaia. In order to come over to Grimrokk you need a portal, and you came through the mirror. However, did it occur to you that you arrived here today without a portal? When you've first entered Grimrokk you'll enter again when you go to sleep like normal in Gaia. Grimrokk is a different reality, Amelia. Just as Gaia but different. You're not dreaming. If you die here for example, you'll be dead in Gaia too.'

He stopped to catch his breath and ensure that I was paying attention.

'Grimrokk is a great place when you get used to it. Take the Imaginari-tea for instance. It's an elixir. I've mixed many different ingredients, and everyone can make the mixture but for the mixture to become magical you need special powers like I've got. Only

32

magic can bind the ingredients together to a symphony of your wishes. It is my gift or special quality if you wish. Mirini has her own gift: She can hear thoughts. It isn't as frightening as you might think. She can only do it if you are open to it and if you are open to it, it doesn't matter where you are. She can hear you anyway. Yet, you'll never be able to hear hers in return.'

Batist took a sip of his mug and leaned back in his chair and scratched his forehead.

'There is something you should know,' he said, 'and that is that everything that exists here, all the myths, the legends, and what you call superstitions in Gaia has its roots here. It exists creatures here that you'd never believe existed. Further, you must know that very few people find their way to Grimrokk. Nobody knows why that is. In other words: You will most likely never meet someone from Grimrokk while you are in Gaia. Yet, it isn't impossible and if you were to recognize anyone you cannot make yourself known. There is a curse between our two parallel realities and the curse states that if anyone under any circumstances makes themselves known for another Grimmer, you'll never be able to pass between the realities again. Normally you and the person you've been exposed to will one be locked in Grimrokk and the other one in Gaia, one on each side.'

Batist took a sip of his tea and gave me a questioning look.

'Do you understand any of this?'

I nodded my head mainly to keep him talking.

'Everyone says that the body they have in Grimrokk and the body they have in their other reality isn't the same thus it does take some effort to meet and recognize each other. Still, you must take the curse very seriously because it could, possibly, cause you to never see your family again. That's one of the consequences of forgetting its existence and its rules.'

He looked like he was thinking about something sad and had to collect himself before he started to speak again.

'You see, both Mirini and I were born here just like many others. Grimmers find love here and have done so for thousands of years and their children don't know any other reality.'

Was all this supposed to be true? How could this be real? I didn't understand anything even if I'd paid close attention. Everything Batist had told me seemed crazy. He was right at one point, however; this did not feel like a dream. The woollen blanket covering me was itching and the embers of the fire warmed my toes where they stuck out at the corner of the blanket. No dream had ever seemed so real. Not even my worst nightmares.

'Who was the priest at the church?' It suddenly hit me that I had no idea who he was.

'Father Benedikt. He is the priest at Wargborough and guards the mirror that forms a portal.'

'And the others?' I asked and meant the people Mirini had called 'Myrthing' and had hunted us from the church. Batist gave a sigh before he began to explain.

'Those who hunted you and Mirini at Wargborough are of the Myrthing Clan. They work for Knuiw Myrthing. He is an evil man who does not like other Grimmers entering Grimrokk. When it happens, he tries to catch them before we get to them. Everything Knuiw Myrthing wants is power and it has resulted in him awakening the worst creature Grimrokk has ever seen.'

Batist stopped to take a sip of his tea. His face went pale, his eyes narrowed, and it seemed like he was holding something back.

'I believe that that is enough for the moment. There isn't much to add before we know more about you.' He looked directly at me with an almost expectant gaze.

'Know more about me? There's not much to know,' I said shaking my head.

'Oh yes, I believe it is. You probably don't know everything about yourself yet, but I believe you'll see soon enough that there is more to you than you think,' he gave a light-hearted laugh.

My stomach began to rumble, and I realized that I was hungry.

'I know just the cure for that. If there's anything I pride myself on it is to quieten the hunger of my visitors.'

Batist rose and went to the kitchen where he hummed to the sound of pots and kitchen tools at work.

'You don't have to make a fuss just for me. I can take something simple. An apple or something like that.'

'There are no apples during the Frostpace. There won't be any fruits until the Long Warmth comes back.' He continued with the food which gave off a wonderful smell in the room.

'Frost what was it?' I'd never heard the word before.

'Sorry, I completely forget myself. You haven't been here all that long. Frostpace is the coldest period of the year when snow, ice and frost cover the landscape. The Long Warmth is the time where it is warm and the flowers bloom. I suppose you call it summer and winter in your reality?' Batist came back with two plates and gave me one of them.

'My specialty. Pine needle pancakes with meadow sorrel gel with coarse sourdough bread covered with blackberry and chocolate mint.'

'Sounds exotic,' I said politely, and tried with all my might to sound enthusiastic. The first bite was really good, and I automatically became more enthusiastic, the smell was amazing. The flavours were delicious while they also gave way for great summer memories. It was magical.

'These are the best pancakes I've ever had.' I didn't care that I was speaking with my mouth full. After all, I was complimenting the chef and I had to talk with mine full in order to continue eating the delicious meal.

'Thank you,' he said and laughed. 'We should find you some clothes. I've got some clothes left over after my daughter in my wardrobe somewhere. We can see if it's the right size.' He pointed towards a wardrobe between the door and the bed.

36

The possibility that Grimrokk was a real place started to sink in. I could not understand or explain it, but the thought gave me a strange sense of calm. It was also very nice to get away from daily life for a little while. Here, no one knew me. Maybe this could be a blessing instead of just an uncomfortable visit.

'Do you have a daughter?' I asked.

'I had a daughter. Silva.'

He didn't continue and I felt really stupid. Was she dead? Batist got up from the chair to clean away the empty plates and mugs. I used the uncomfortable silence to find something to wear. The wardrobe was full of clothes and blankets. Some had to be Batist's own but at the bottom to the right I found some smaller clothes. The clothes were unusual, like a summer fashion collection inspired by the forest and landscape. I chose a wide brown woollen sweater which was too short around my waist so to avoid walking around with a bare stomach I needed something to wear on the outside. Next to a pair of pelted boots was a corset in a dark green velvet which was a perfect fit over the sweater. I tightened it firmly at the back and pulled on a pair of light suede pants. For footwear I took the pelted boots. They reached me to my knees and two leather straps made it possible to tighten them all the way up. I took in my appearance in an old photo frame. My hair was a big mess and I tried to comb through it with my fingers. I hadn't had long hair since I was a child. I looked around for something to tie it up with. Next to the wardrobe there was a collection of leather cords. I tied the first cord in a high ponytail before I braided the rest and tied it with a second cord. On a hook in the wardrobe there was a grey-blue cloak with a hood made of woollen felt. I took it out, put it over my shoulders and wondered whether this was the appropriate attire. I heard a gasp behind me from the kitchen and turned around abruptly. Batist looked at me with an open mouth and surprise in his eyes.

'What is it? Have I done anything wrong?' I asked worriedly.

'No, you look perfect. For a moment you looked like Silva. She used to wear that exact outfit.'

He looked at me for a while before he turned and changed the topic.

'We need to leave in a little while. The horse won't be able to carry both of us and the bags.'

'To Mirini? Why do we need bags?'

Were we staying with Mirini long? I was still quite dazed from all the information I was trying to process.

'We stay there until we go on to the festival. The Rim Gorge is at least an eight-day ride away and we need to pick up some other people on the way,' said Batist.

He wandered around finding and packing things he needed for the trip, but I suspected he also did it to think about something other than Silva.

'Festival? What kind of festival?'

I didn't know whether I should look forward to it or be worried. There was a great chance that there would be a lot of people who were completely foreign to me.

'It's a festival where you compete in different games, buy elixir ingredients, meet people you haven't seen since last year, and best of all: celebrate Christmas.'

'Christmas? Do you celebrate Christmas?' I was surprised.

'Of course! Where do you think Santa comes from?'

'I don't know. It's just a silly story we tell kids, so they behave all year, isn't it?' This was meant more as a question than a statement.

'Santa is a kind man who's always given a lot of himself. He used to travel to Gaia earlier in the day but the intention with Christmas disappeared alongside the hospitality and happiness of giving so he just stays here now during the Christmas season. Normally he stays by himself at The Snow Top.'

Batist had packed three leather bags which were now standing next to the table while he hung a great forest green robe over his shoulders.

'Then we are ready to depart,' he said.

I took the initiative and carried two of the bags towards the door. He looked at me and gave me a happy nod.

We saddled the horse and began the journey into the forest. It was so cold that the frost had left its mark on everything around us. For the first time I was able to see the nature surrounding me in daylight and it was truly magical. The sky was cloudy with a hint of grey and in the silence surrounding us you could hear a pin drop. We walked on a narrow path covered in frosty dirt. From time to time, I got the impression that my ears were playing tricks on me, and I thought I could hear whispers from the deepest darkest parts of the forest. I also felt the familiar sensation I often got when it was dark that someone was watching me even though, now, it was light out.

'This is too chilly for me. Spring and summer are more my type of seasons.' I tried to start a conversation to break the silence from the forest.

'You'll most likely never experience spring here,' said Batist and shook his head.

'What do you call spring here?'

I had understood from what he said before that summer and winter had different names, so I had just assumed that spring and fall had other names as well.

'No, you misunderstood me. We do not have spring at all. Frostpace turns into The Long Warmth overnight.'

'What? Does everything bloom in one night?' This couldn't be true. It sounded so ridiculous that I laughed a little.

'Just wait until you see it. It is the most beautiful experience there is. All the odours and the gorgeous colours. I get giddy with excitement every time it happens.' Batist smiled dreamily. His eyes were glittering at the thought of his fond childhood memories.

'When does it happen?'

'Nobody knows. A year doesn't have a specific number of days here. It varies every year.'

'How can you celebrate Christmas if you don't know how long Frostpace lasts?' This was all very confusing.

'Christmas is celebrated 42 days after the first day of Frostpace. It has yet to happen that the Frostpace has been shorter than a hundred days. We do not make any calendars before the year is over.'

I took a moment to question whether this man had lost his marbles. If that was the case, there would be a logical explanation for it. In the next moment I felt bad for even thinking about it. He had made a solid attempt to make me feel welcome and comfortable.

The forest opened ahead of us, and a great farmhouse appeared. A stone house in a classic Victorian style with pillars and distinct details. The windows had bars made of iron but most of the panes were damaged or missing glass. The house was still very beautiful, and I took myself in daydreaming a little while we headed for the door.

The house had definitely seen better times. Several of the roof tiles had moved out of position. Some were on top of one another while others had fallen into the flower beds. The garden was just as beautiful as the house with rose bushes and hedges carrying the impression of being well kept although they were now covered in frost. The fence surrounding the estate was made of stone blocks spaced out evenly and in between the blocks there were iron spears a foot a part. Some of the spears were missing and some were a little crocked but with some imagination I could see what it once had looked like. A duke would have no problem fitting in. Servants and housekeepers had probably been common in the house once.

'Does Mirini live here?' I was full of admiration.

'Yes. Isn't it grand? This farm belonged to her husband's family. They were very rich, but Mirini doesn't have the strength to care for the farm after her husband died ten years ago.'

We entered through the beautiful grand gate which was decorated with wrought iron rosettes and followed the row of linden trees covering the road all the way to the door. The door was wide and had a railing made of iron. At the top of the stairs there was a great double door made of mahogany with brass handles and two door hammers shaped like lionheads. While we were still standing at the foot of the stairs the door flew open and Mirini smiled proudly down at us from the stairs where there were three other people in the background.

Chapter 4
A perfect symbiosis

ehind Mirini stood two boys and one girl. They didn't look to be the same age, but they were all young.

'Hello. There you are finally. Lunch is ready and waiting. Come on in.'

Mirini moved a step back while reaching out with her arms beckoning us to the door. We took one step over the threshold and stopped.

'This, Mia, is my children. May I call you Mia? I thought it would be more suitable. Grimmers normally use a different name to cover their identities.'

I noticed that Mirini seemed stressed. Maybe they didn't have guests that often.

'Mia is fine. I've been called that before.' Christina, the daughter of some of our friends, used to call me Mia so I was rather fond of the name.

'Great! Mia, this is Theodor, who also goes by Teddy. He's the man of the house.'

The boy she referred to was maybe fifteen years old and had black ridged hair and sharp pale blue eyes. He was tall and slender with a charming smile. He wore a red velvet jacket, short black pants and black shoes with big buckles. However, even though his clothes were fine they were way too small, and the shoes had to be inherited from his father, which were two sizes too big.

43

I assumed these were his best clothes and that they hadn't been used in a while.

'Good day Miss Mia. It is an honour to make you acquaintance.'

He took my hand and kissed it. I was immediately charmed and imagined that Mirini had given instructions to remember the proper etiquette ahead of our visit.

'Very nice to meet you too Teddy. You'll probably break a lot of young women's hearts.' I winked at him, and he blushed red.

'This is Antoinette.'

Mirini pointed towards the lovely girl standing next to her. Antoinette curtsied and smiled. I estimated that she was about thirteen years old, and she had long black hair which curled over her shoulders. She had the same pale blue eyes as her brother and had a slim figure over which were draped a long white dress that reached her to her ancles. There was no waistline just a pink ribbon which was tied together right under her breasts.

'Good day Miss Mia. It's a pleasure. You can call me Nette, everyone else does.'

'Lovely to meet you Nette. I'm not used to such grand manners. This will be a change. I have to say that you are a beautiful young lady.' Nette blushed just like her brother and gave a shy smile.

'Finally, this is our farm hand, Sebastian. He lives in the forest behind the house. He is a wonder who helps around the farm, and he has become a part of the family.'

Sebastian was skinny and pale with skin like porcelain with thick ashen blond hair hanging down into his green eyes. He was a gorgeous boy and he bowed elegantly with both hands behind his back. His suit was grey and worn with brown buttons. He and Teddy were the same height and probably around the same age.

'Good day Miss Mia,' he whispered with his gaze locked on his dusty shoes, obviously shy.

'Another charmer for the young ladies?' I smiled.

Mirini led us into a big cold hall. There was a great elegant staircase which parted into a left and right passage before they met on a balcony on the second floor. I could envision people standing on the balcony looking down into the hall. The steps in the staircase were worn and probably hadn't been oiled in a while. The walls were decorated with rosette printed wallpaper in beige, gold, and red and along the walls hung portraits of earlier generations. I assumed they were the family of Mirini's deceased husband, and this was later confirmed. The floor was made of polished marble which gave the impression of dancing flames from the candelabras on the walls. It was enchanting.

'We'll be here in the salon. Teddy will take your coats and Sebastian will take your things to your rooms. I hope you are hungry and ready for some soup and freshly baked bread.' Mirini pointed towards a room to the right and smiled happily.

'Soup sounds great right now. I'm a foodie you know. Not that I need to point that out.' Batist laughed and patted his round belly. I laughed too.

The double doors were open and revealed the beautiful salon behind them. The walls were covered in the same wallpaper as the hallway, but these had a different colour combination. It was cooler and was a mixture of grey, silver, and blue. In the middle of the room stood two salons facing each other with a coffee table in the middle. The drapes were heavy in blue and grey with solid fringes and a rope with tassels holding them in place beside the windows. This could have been the house of a king if it hadn't been so worn. Batist sat down in the salon, and I did the same.

'Mia, you must excuse me for not serving you in the dining room, but I keep it locked. I've decided that no one is to enter the room before I'm no longer here. My husband didn't like to mix elixirs in the kitchen. He thought it too risky. Therefore, he used the dining room to make his elixirs and spent most of his time there. I must admit that I haven't entered the room since the day he poisoned himself and left me alone with two young children. I'll probably forgive him one day even though I know it was an accident.' She sighed heavily and looked away.

It was clear that she had not recovered from her loss. How empty would my life have been without Will?

'I'm so sorry to hear that. You have my sympathy, and I am very content with dining in this beautiful salon.' I didn't know what else to say.

'Thanks Mia. Go ahead and help yourselves.'

Mirini shook the memories away and opened the soup terrine. The wonderful smell wafting from it made my nostrils flare. She served everyone around the table. I was served first, and I was so hungry after our long journey that I grabbed my spoon and ate the entire portion even if the flavour didn't quite agree with me.

When lunch was over, Mirini and Nette cleared the table and I offered to help but was rejected. Not long after, the table was set again with cups and saucers, pots, and a tray of cookies. The colourless brew in the pots made me think of Imaginari-tea.

'That's right Mia. Has Batist already served you Imaginari-tea for breakfast?' asked Mirini and looked over at me. I hadn't said a word. I had thought of the question, and she had answered me which was a little uncomfortable.

'It's what you thought right?' she smiled knowingly.

'Yes, I'm just not used to this.' My face gave away more than I said.

'You've got nothing to worry about. I would never spill your secrets or private matters. It's not how it works.' She cocked her head while she said it as if she was trying to comfort me.

'It's ok. I don't think I have so many secrets,' I said.

'I wonder what your ability is?' Batist looked at me as if he could guess simply by looking.

'Ability? I don't think I have many of those.'

I could neither cook nor play an instrument. What ability could I possibly have? Doing cartwheels? Juggling? No, I'd never been that much of an impressive person.

47

'Everybody has at least one ability. That's just the way it is,' said Mirini and took a sip of her Imaginari-tea. What sort of flavour did she think about when she drank the tea I wondered. I was still thinking about hot chocolate.

'Black elderberry tea with cinnamon and lemon balm,' said Mirini and gave a little laugh.

'Don't do that. It freaks me out,' I said with a distressed smile.

'Sorry. It's not easy to stop. You ask questions in your mind all the time.'

Batist laughed.

'Tomorrow, I think Mia and I shall take a walk in the forest and see if her ability doesn't make itself known.' Batist looked at Mirini who nodded in agreement.

'Where are we going?' I wasn't very tempted to go for a walk in a strange forest.

'To Huldra. If there's anyone who can bring out your ability it's her,' said Mirini in a serious tone.

'To Huldra?' I had almost convinced myself that this was all real but now my concern came rushing back.

'The hulder's lives in hiding and they're not always in the mood to help. It's important to show them respect and they will give you the same in return. Huldra, the hulder's leader, has always been good to us and given us advice and support when we've needed it.' Batist gave me a pat on the shoulder and then got up.

'How do I know if she wants to talk to me? She doesn't know who I am! Can't I just wait and see what happens? I've been doing rather well without any special abilities thus far!'

'In times such as this it is better to stay ahead of the game. There's been stuff going on recently which makes it troublesome to go anywhere,' said Mirini. I think she mainly said it to calm me down, but it had the opposite effect.

'I'm not going anywhere! If it is dangerous to move about around here, then it is out of the question to go far into some unfamiliar forest and almost ask for trouble.' I had no doubt in my soul about my decision.

Batist were walking in circles on the floor.

'You won't have any trouble in Huldra's forest. You have my word. We will accompany you to the forest entrance,' he said.

'Am I to put my faith in a human being I've known for only one day?' My stomach was twirling.

'I promise you that it will be alright. I shall listen for you,' said Mirini while she got up and moved over to the salon I was sitting in and put her arms around my shoulders. 'Huldra is good to you if you are good to her. It is quite simple.'

'What if I get lost? I don't even know where Huldra resides.' I shook my head vigorously.

'The forest knows where you are going. It will get you there. You are not the first person to seek her advice and most of them were younger than you.' Teddy chimed in.

This was the first time he entered the conversation and my tone seemed to have upset him.

'What do you mean by younger?' I confronted him. He didn't answer but looked at his mother.

'Normally, Grimmers are about the age of ten when they enter this reality for the first time. Here, we've always wondered why that is, but we've noticed that those who do come are experiencing changes in their lives, a tragic accident or a difficult daily life. It is when you look for liberation that they find their way into Grimrokk. At least that is our theory.' Mirini looked me in the eye. 'What has opened your way in here Mia?'

It didn't seem like she already knew. What was I supposed to tell them? That I couldn't have children? For once, I'd gotten away from having that tag visibly hanging over me. At the same time, I had nothing to hide.

'I can't bear children. I've done everything in my power to make it happen, and now there's only one option left.'

There, I'd said it. No way back now. I prepared for the pity in their faces which always accompanied this confession. No one said anything. They just looked at one another with furrowed brows.

'You'll fit in better than you think,' said Batist and left the room.

'Was it something I said? You asked.'

The confusion was giving me a headache. I was starting to grow weary and was longing for Will and our comfortable bed. I missed being in his arms and him hugging me towards his warm body.

'It isn't your fault, Mia. However, I do want you to go and see Huldra tomorrow. It's for the best,' said

Mirini before she got up and followed Batist out of the room.

'This is absurd. It can't be true for fuck's sake!'

If I could get home by going to sleep, I needed to find a bed as quickly as possible. Teddy and Nette looked at me with big eyes as if somebody had been swearing in church. Something I actually almost had done.

'Do you know where my room is?' I asked a bit calmer.

'Yes, let me show you,' said Teddy.

He followed me out but said nothing. It was clear that I had hit a touchy subject since even Teddy had turned sour. How typical of me! Just get out the salat bowl and me and my big feet would stomp right into it until my toes were all green. Teddy stopped outside a door in the corridor at the left side of the staircase balcony.

'This is your room. Sebastian has already put all your stuff in there what little you had with you.' Without looking at me he continued down the corridor.

I was a little out of breath, so I remained outside my door and took a few deep breaths before I opened it. The room was spacious and just as grand as the rest of the house. There was a four-poster bed with a canopy and curtains with fringes. The walls were yellow with big white flowers and there were two big windows with green curtains decorated with white doodles on them in the same material as the bed curtains. I went over to the bed and sat down carefully. I didn't like losing control or that things were not going according to plan. Nothing of what I had experienced that day had been planned or within my control. I couldn't escape from this. Nothing was my own. Not even the clothes I was wearing. I had no money or any opportunity to get back to the mirror in the church. I had no idea where I was, and this made me feel alone and vulnerable.

My head steadily became worse, and my high ponytail didn't help the matter. I loosened the strings keeping it up and massaged my scalp with my fingertips. I headed over to the window where I could see the linden trees. It was starting to get dark and quiet outside.

The atmosphere had been tense when Batist left the room in a hurry, and I felt bad. There was something stirring beneath the surface, something I didn't quite understand. Why had no one said more about the clan that had been hunting us? What was this creature their leader had unleashed? Nobody in this house seemed to want to give me an answer to my questions so I had to get them from someone else. Could Huldra possibly know the answers to my questions?

അഅ

I awoke with a jolt and sat straight up in bed. I was surprised by the intense pain in my stomach. It felt like my muscles were being torn apart. I could hear myself scream.

'What is it?' Will had jumped out of bed in shock.

'I forgot myself. I didn't remember that I've had an operation.'

I was short of breath from the pain. Will put his arm around me for support.

'Careful,' he whispered.

'It's ok now. Can you help me up? I have to go to the bathroom.'

I attempted to breathe through my nose in order to calm myself down a little. Will got up and leaned forward towards me with open arms. I put my arms around his neck and grabbed a hold while he got up slowly. He was there, close to me and it felt nice. I had missed him so much in Grimrokk and now I felt him close to me again. I put my feet down and they carried me so Will supported me down to the bathroom.

After four movies, with small breaks for food and bathroom visits, I was no longer able to stay awake. I looked over at Will, who was doing what he always did at this time of day, sleeping in his chair. He had been running around playing nurse all day and I felt a little bit bad for him. I managed to gather enough balance to get myself up into bed. Several times during the day, my thoughts had wandered to Grimrokk which had started to become an intriguing and interesting place for me. The beautiful landscape, the friendly people I'd met there who had been kind and aimable from the start. I was experiencing a strange sort of longing. The atmosphere when Batist had left the room was bothering me even though I didn't quite understand what had upset him so. I wanted to make it up to him but how? Batist was friendly and hospitable that much was clear from how he had opened his doors for me. It was impossible not to care for the good old man. However, there was something about him, something sensitive that he didn't want to talk about, and I didn't know what that was. I allowed myself to wonder about everything in Grimrokk, which might be a good idea to forget as well. It was with pleasure that I closed my eyes and let my muscles relax.

CB∞

Before I awoke properly, I knew that I wasn't home in my own bed anymore. I could smell the old woodwork and the duvet which hadn't been aired out in a while. Still with my eyes closed, I stretched my arms so my muscles would awake. It was a huge relief to be rid of the stomach pain. A positive side to Grimrokk for sure.

I looked around while I still lay on the hard mattress. The lights from the window told me that it was a cloudy day. The house was quiet, but I wasn't the only one awake. There was a smell slowly wafting through the air. It was the familiar smell of Batist's pancakes! The thought of pancakes for breakfast and Imaginari-tea made me jolt out of bed. I was in my clothes, or Silva's clothes to be precise, before my feet even touched the floor. I ran through my hair with my fingers, so it didn't fully resemble a bird's nest but more of a cool 80's hairdo. I was hungry and couldn't be bothered with the thought of doing my hair more than I had to. The chance of me grabbing some scissors one of these days was increasing. In Gaia I had short hair, and it was so wonderful to maintain.

The door slid closed behind me as I walked towards the staircase. Breakfast smelled so wonderful that I was really looking forward to having a seat and getting started. It wasn't hard to find the kitchen. My nose led me towards a revolving door which I pushed gently open. The kitchen was quite big with old cupboards of different sizes, the walls were decorated with small shelves filled with jars, bottles, and bowls. On one of the longer walls there was a small open fireplace. Right above there was a window towards the backyard where I could barely see another building, probably a stable or barn. This was the only window in the room, and it was framed by a cabinet with a deep porcelain basin underneath.

A wrought iron furnace was placed along a shorter wall a short distance away from the rest of the other kitchen fixtures. The short wall on the opposite side was covered in tiny drawers, there had to be at least a hundred of them. Every drawer had a brass frame with a handwritten note inside. It looked a lot like an old pharmacy. In the middle of the floor was a massive dining table made of wood with room for twelve people. Now there were only two people present, Nette and Batist, who each had a plate of pancakes in front of them. Teddy had placed himself in front of the fireplace with a mug and was turning the pages of a book.

'Good morning,' I said carefully.

Everyone looked up and said, 'Good morning!' in unison.

'Hi Mia. Did you sleep well?' Mirini turned around and smiled at me.

'Yes, I think so,' I said and stifled a yawn.

'You must be starving. How many pancakes would you like?' Mirini was doing a little dance around herself while she found plate, cup, and cutlery for me.

'Yes, I am. I think two will be enough for now. Thank you.' I went over to her to help but was quickly turned away and shown to the table.

'You're our guest, dear. Just have a seat and I'll bring the food over.'

'Are you ready for today's mission? It will be a long day ahead you know.' Batist pulled out the chair next to him.

'Ready isn't exactly the word I would use since I don't know what to expect but I suppose I have to be ready?' I took a deep breath, but it felt like the room didn't contain enough air for me to breathe in.

'It is important to figure out what your ability is. It might take some time before you learn to use it properly.'

Batist met my gaze as he was talking. I scrutinized him to see if the bitterness from last night was still there, but his gaze seemed honest and genuine.

'When do I have to leave?'

'It is probably best if you get going as soon as possible so you can be back before dark. We don't want you wandering alone in the forest around here during the night,' said Mirini while she approached with two pancakes and a cup of tea.

How far did I have to go? What was so scary that even the locals didn't like the forest during the nighttime? I knew now that Mirini probably had heard my thoughts, but she refrained from answering. There was something she wasn't telling me.

The pancakes tasted as well as I had hoped, and the Imaginari-tea still tasted wonderfully of hot chocolate. Yet, all this wasn't quite enough to get rid of the lump of anxiety luring in my stomach. Mirini had found a leather bag she was now packing food and drink into. She also put in a little blanket for me to sit on.

'Mia, don't worry. You'll be fine. Just be polite and kind. It is only the people who wish to harm the hulder folk who get unpleasant surprises,' she said when I got up to leave the table.

'Also remember, that if you do see Huldra's tail you must not stare at it or talk about it. Just tell her that her petticoats are showing,' Nette said eagerly.

'TAIL?!'

'Yes, but like I said don't comment on it. She doesn't like that,' Nette continued.

The thought of this capricious Huldra made the knot of anxiety grow.

'Nette, you're scaring the wits out of her,' Batist laughed.

'I'll be fine.'

It wasn't intended to calm Batist down but myself. I had never been a coward so this Huldra could be as scary as she wished. She wasn't going to scare me away before I'd tried talking to her.

I prepared myself as best I could. I left my things in my room, which wasn't much, just a couple of woollen socks and an extra-large scarf Batist had packed for me. I went downstairs to meet Batist and Mirini who were both dressed and ready to go. Mirini had my bag hanging over her arm and she gave it to me.

'Ready?' Batist asked scrutinizing me.

'Ready.' I confirmed with a nod that probably could have been more convincing.

'Take this. It is an elixir. If you have to hide or need to get away in a hurry, you just throw this away as hard as you can.'

I pretended to understand what he meant and put the little flagon in my bag. Then I hung the bag over my shoulders. I put the cloak over my shoulders and pulled the hood over my face to hide it as much as possible. Mirini opened the door and together we stepped into the cool winter day, or rather the weather of Frostpace.

Mirini and Batist walked next to me towards the beginning of the forest at the end of the big garden. My heart was hammering, and my knees were shaking. I didn't know what I could expect once I'd entered the forest and that was the worst thing of all, the not knowing. If I had known that in ten minutes, I'd meet a four-meter-tall spider I'd be better prepared. Then I could have made the choice to fight or run. Not knowing was definitely worse.

I took a steadying breath and tried to focus. It was pointless. What was wrong with me? Come on, Amelia, you can do this! For a moment I thought I could see

Mirini smiling at the corner of her mouth. She had probably heard my weak attempt of a peptalk.

The beginning of the forest was closer than I had anticipated and when we stood below the first tree my heart skipped a beat.

'How do I find my way back? When am I done?'

I had no idea how long this would take nor where I was going or how long it would take to get there.

'Like we said, the forest knows the way.'

Mirini put an arm around my shoulders and gave them a squeeze. It didn't make me feel any better knowing that I was moving forward alone.

'Someone from the hulder folk will meet you on the way.'

Batist put his arms around me in a warm hug. I gave an awkward wave before I turned around and walked into the forest. My steps were unsure and hesitant as I moved into the unknown forest. It grew more and more unfamiliar the further in I got and around me there were dark trees bending over like giants in all directions. They were covered in frost which shone and crackled in all the colours of the rainbow. The icicles sounded like they were playing carillon every time a breath of wind moved the branches. There was something that resembled a song in the distance. I could hear it and it grew more distinct the further into the forest I went. Suddenly I saw something moving ahead of me. I froze on the spot mid step and held my breath. Out of the dark bushes came an unknown figure.

Chapter 5
The Grange Warden

melia, you've come a great distance. Come with me.'

It was a tall slender man. He was unusually attractive with big chestnut brown curls, smooth pale skin almost like silk, and a serious face with a flush on his cheeks. His clothes were made of dark grey linen, and I was surprised to see how well dressed he was when I suspected that he spent a lot of time in the forest. His presence was surprisingly calming even though I was still nervous.

'Thanks. Could I see Huldra, please?'

I stuttered amidst my nervousness. How did he know my name? I'd never met him before.

'She is expecting you,' he said in a mild tone and turned around.

He walked back into the forest, and I followed a short distance behind him. We moved through the trees and bushes for a few minutes before we reached an opening surrounded by tall trees. The branches sparkled and a soft blanket of frost mist covered the ground making it look almost magical. In the middle of the opening, there was a big silver-grey tree without leaves. It was surrounded by moss-green mounds of soil also covered in frost. The beautiful man stopped and turned towards me.

'Wait here,' he said, still very serious although his voice remained mild.

I remained standing and looked at the little wooden door he'd disappeared through in one of the soil mounds. What sort of place was this? It was incredible that someone lived all the way out here. The way the man looked; I'd expect him to belong in a castle somewhere. Despite all my insecurity, I felt a nibbling urge to follow him. I shook my head in an attempt to focus and stop daydreaming.

Out from a different mound came a female figure. She had voluptuous curves just like a Renaissance sculpture of Aphrodite and she had to be the most beautiful thing I'd ever seen. The hair, which reached down to her lower back, was big, curly, and blond. To top it all off it shone like there were frost crystals sprinkled all over it. Her clothes were rather boring compared to her beauty, but she still carried her green linen dress perfectly. I thought frantically about how I should introduce myself in a proper manner when I suddenly remembered what my great-grandmother had taught me. Back in the days girls used to curtsey and smile. It seemed a bit silly, but I couldn't think of anything better to do. I bowed my head an inch and curtsied, something I hadn't done since I was five years old. The lady did the same.

'I know you seek my advice.' Her voice seemed to sparkle and dance around her when she spoke. This had to be Huldra.

'Yes madame,' I said trying to figure out if I had approached her in the proper manner.

'Come. Sit down.'

Hudra pointed to an overturned tree stump by the beautiful silver-grey tree. I sat down carefully on the cold stump an arm's length away from her.

'This is incredibly beautiful.' I was enthralled by the surroundings and had to focus so not to gape like a fish out of water.

'Thank you, and you are right. No forest is quite like this one. What can I do for you?' Her lips curled in a little smile.

'Mirini and Batist said I needed to know what kind of ability I possess and told me that you could help.' My voice shook and the silence felt unbearable until Huldra began speaking.

'You try to hide your ability unconsciously. You possess an ability we thought to be lost because no one has seen this ability for over a hundred years.' A new silence followed this. 'You have the ability to petrify and, in some situations, to kill.' I looked at her in utter bewilderment and repeated dumbfounded.

'To kill?'

'In your voice, there is a tone which only becomes audible when you focus. Have you ever noticed that when you speak of something you're passionate about others turn quiet?'

Huldra scrutinized me thoroughly while awaiting an answer. I thought about it, and it hit me that I'd never thought about it like that before. I did win more discussions than I lost. I couldn't remember ever losing one.

'Yes, I guess that's right.' My eyes were staring ahead but I couldn't see anything.

'That ability, or power, needs to be honed and practiced in controlled and calm surroundings. The petrifying isn't permanent, but it can take time for the petrified to return to normal if they survive. There's been such a long time since anyone has possessed this ability that it is unknown how it will affect the object. It might vary from person to person. The last one who possessed this ability was the queen of Libya. Her history is both a sad and grotesque one which doesn't tempt repetition. She fell in love with a married man, Zevs. They met here in Grimrokk and appeared to be the happiest of all Grimmers in Grimrokk. They were so in love that they told each other who they were in Gaia and decided to seek each other out there as well. She loved him more than any other man and it didn't take long before she was pregnant with his child and gave birth, twice. In the end, his wife, Hera, found out about the affair which had been going on right under her nose. With all the strength and power invested in her as a goddess she threw a horrifying curse on the queen, so she became cursed to eat her own children and live with the pain, loss, and consciousness forever. No matter how much she tried to fight the urge to eat the children she had to cave in, and the taste of their blood made her lust for more. Continuously the increasing pain of having eaten her own children gave grounds for a jealousy to grow in her and in the end, she was incapable of other people's happiness when it came to children, therefore, she killed every child she encountered. All of her dreadful actions came alive again in her nightmares which haunted her every night and made it impossible for her to sleep. Zevs, whom she still loved very dearly, felt so sorry for her that he gave her the ability to detach her own eyes, so she didn't have to see the grotesque pictures anymore. Not until then was she able to feel some calm during those restless nights. The queen's appearance and personality changed and kept on changing. After a while she was able to smell a pregnant woman many miles away and the unborn children suffered the same fate as the other children before them. For every unborn child the queen consumed her body changed. She had always been the most beautiful creature one could envision but as the time passed and the hunger for children tore within, her body started to resemble a snake more than a human. The soft brown skin became scaly and hard, pale and lifeless like the colour of muddy water. She lost the ability she had possessed, she was neither dead nor alive and her existence was only alive in Grimrokk. After all this, there were several sorcerers who worked together in order to create a spell which would prevent those who revealed their identity from ever travelling between the two parallel realities ever again. It could never happen.'

Huldra's story scared me. If you could encounter such folk in Grimrokk I'd rather be somewhere else.

'What does this have to do with me?' I asked. My muscles had fallen asleep on the cold stump, I was hyperventilating, and felt quite lightheaded.

'You see, Lamia, which is the creature's name, is still here in Grimrokk. Hera's curse were made to last forever but Knuiw Myrthing and his clan awoke her bloodlust again a little while back after she'd been in an enchanted sleep for hundreds of years. He, Knuiw Myrthing, has been threatening both people and creatures all over Grimrokk to either join his ranks or become Lamia's next meal. This will be your challenge. You've been given the same ability as the queen so it is a given that you are the only one who can help us. Nothing but that powerful tone in your voice can finish her off. Since she possesses the same ability as you this is her only weakness but remember; This weakness is also yours. You have to help us find her. Grimrokk may not meet its end today or tomorrow but one day there will be nothing left if this keeps up. Myrthing thinks that he can control her just because he harbours so much power, however, it was the twelve sorcerers of Grimrokk who enchanted her into a deep sleep the last time. Myrthing will never be able to win her over and she keeps growing stronger. Lamia doesn't possess an ounce of logic, only instincts.'

Huldra stared ahead of her. Her eyes empty as if she was far gone down memory lane and the gruesome tales the memories carried with them. I felt a hate slowly growing inside me with every word. Lamia was the curse in Grimrokk which endometriosis was for me in Gaia. The illness took away my ability to choose and instead gave me horrific pain which all the time kept me from getting pregnant. Childlessness was my nightmare. Yet, in my wildest imagination I couldn't understand how I could be the one who would stop Lamia, even if I found this tone Huldra had spoken of. If twelve sorcerers had struggled to capture and enchant Lamia, how could I, just one single person, be able to do the same? Tone or no tone it seemed rather hopeless.

'I'm just one person though. I don't know what Lamia looks like and I don't know how to find her!'

My desperation made my mind spin in all directions but at the same time a new feeling was sneaking up on me. It almost felt like an eagerness, an eagerness to hunt her down and capture her. I felt my gaze flicker around as if I was looking for her already. My gaze stopped at Huldra's feet. Without thinking about it I stared at something poking out of the hem of her dress. I realized that it was the end of a tail resembling that of a horse a little too late. I'd already been staring at it for too long. Huldra cleared her throat.

'What is it?' she asked in a humorous tone.

This was what I had been warned not to do. I became a little panicky but then I remembered what Nette had said.

'I'm sorry but your petticoats are showing under the hem of your dress.'

I pointed and attempted to make it seem like a friendly gesture. Obviously, I had failed since I was still staring at the little piece of tail showing.

'Oh, thank you!' Huldra said smilingly. 'I can't answer as to where Lamia is but I do know that she is not in this forest so you must move on. Go to the forest pond where you'll meet Nicor. Sing to him until he decides to play along. I hope he can give you the answer you seek. You've shown me your honesty and respect and for that I am grateful. As a parting gift I'll give you a huldersong to carry with you. Sing it when you approach the pond because if you don't, Nicor will pull you under. He will try to trick you, so be on your guard because he is strong. Nicor has eyes and ears in the underworld, and he will be able to tell you where Lamia is hiding.'

Huldra's gaze was again lost as if she were in a trance and then she began to sing the most enchanting tune which made all the treetops in the forest sing. The magical song danced around me and before I knew it my mouth opened, and the same tunes came out and blended in with Huldra's in a beautiful harmony. The words were incomprehensible but there was a language there somewhere, an old and almost forgotten language. The melody played on my heart strings all the way into my soul and the experience gave me goosebumps. When the song was over, I remained seated and stared in wonder at the forest around me which seemed to be holding the last three notes. Huldra looked at me in a way that told me that this conversation was over.

'Thank you. Which way do I go to find the pond?'

Why was I asking this question? Should I really go and see a creature who could drown me? On top of that, should I sing to him?

'You can go in whichever direction that pleases you. The forest knows where you are going and will show you the way. Just promise me one thing; You must help everyone who crosses your path whether it be human or animal. Everyone here is protected by us, and you are our guest so do no harm. When dusk comes, you'll find the pond. Follow the advice that I've given you and you will be rewarded on your journey. Go now and remember what I've told you then you'll be safe.'

Huldra got up and opened her arms towards the forest surrounding us. I said goodbye, curtsied, and turned to walk into the forest. The day was still young but the thick clouds covering the sky made my surroundings dark. When I walked it felt like there was someone keeping an eye on me in the darkness. It was so quiet around me that I could hear my own heart hammering and my heavy breathing. The forest grew darker and tightened around me making it hard to breathe. I could hear creaking from beneath the trees and I could hear twigs breaking. Steps turned to stomps and soon the ground was vibrating below me. I turned around but saw nothing but trees, bushes, and darkness.

I panicked. I started running as fast as I could and the stomps behind me increased their pace. The branches on the trees slapped against my cold skin. Suddenly, I reached the side of a mountain and threw myself against it to climb up, but it was wet and covered in moss. My fingers couldn't get hold of anything, and my feet kept slipping. As I was sliding down the stomps behind me came closer. What was it that was coming to attack me? I thought about what I'd been told about Lamia, and I could feel a cold sweat breaking out.

I placed my back against the wall where there was a little clearing and investigated the trees further away. Something was hiding in the darkness of the trees, and it was moving closer. I was shivering and struggled to see what it was due to my fear my eyes were tearing up because of my fear. The stomps quietened and turned into steps while the tears kept running down my face.

'Who is it?' I called but no reply came.

The steps stopped for a moment before they continued towards me. I could barely see the figure in the dark. The sweat was now covering my back. In the clearing, a figure came into the light. It reminded me of a big black horse; however, it was missing a front leg, a neck, and a head. It stood quite still. I thought to myself that it wasn't ugly or foul even thought it was missing some body parts. The body was just made like that. Muscles and skin covered the areas where the bones and head should have been. The creature took a hesitant step towards me and kicked out with one of the back legs. A thornbush appeared to be stuck around its hoof and the thorns had cut into the skin. I took a few steps closer to the horse and reached out a hand. It jolted and I jumped backwards in surprise. I took a deep breath and repeated the words 'Don't be afraid' several times.

'Easy, easy. I'll help you out,' I said probably to calm us both down.

The animal came closer and stopped just a few armlengths out of reach. I reached out my hand again and moved slowly towards the horse. I put my hand on its shoulder and felt the smooth fur. It gleamed like silk, and it was the smoothest surface I'd ever touched. My heart was hammering, and I could feel it in my touch when I stroked the horse. I couldn't understand how this horse could be alive since it was missing both mouth and nose. I stroked the backside of its hind quarters and down the leg where the thornbush was stuck. The bush had wrapped itself tightly around the leg and it wasn't easy to remove it without the thorns hurting me as well. That's when I noticed that even if I touched the thorns, they didn't hurt me, but it did hurt the animal. I did everything I could to be gentle, but it was useless. What I needed was a knife but that was one of few items I didn't carry in my bag. Annoyed at myself, I tore the bush apart with my hand until it loosened from the hoof.

'There. Now you're free of the bush. You can go now.' My voice felt like it was booming in the silence.

The horse moved a few steps away then turned to look at me as if to say thank you. I remained standing where I was looking at the animal for a little while before the strange horse turned around and trotted into the forest. It wasn't until everything had turned quiet that I noticed how much my hands were shaking.

I sat down on a big rock at the foot of the slope. Since there had been so many thorns on the branches there should be some cuts and rifts on my fingers, however, it wasn't which surprised me very much. Some of the thorns I had removed from the horse still lay next to me so I picked it up and stabbed myself in the finger to see what would happen. It didn't hurt at all and there was not a single drop of blood in sight. Next to my legs there was a sharp rock and I picked it up. With some hesitation I held on to the sharpest end and pulled it down alongside my finger. The cut wasn't deep, but it did bleed a sizable amount and in contrast to the thorns this actually hurt. I remembered what Huldra had said about helping someone and that I'd receive a reward for my good deed. While I sat there thinking I took out the food Mirini had packed for me that morning. It was wonderful to eat something. I had calmed down again after my meeting with the horse and was now enjoying the quiet surroundings. When I'd eaten it was already getting dark, so I wrapped up what was left of the food, got up, and brushed moss of my cloths before I moved on.

It didn't take long before the forest opened in front of me. In between the trees I could see the pond glimmering in the final rays of sunlight. The water's surface was surprisingly free of ice despite the cold that was creeping in. The pond was the size of a football field and was encapsulated with yellow reeds which had dried in the fall sun. A tree, lonely and abandoned, was leaning over the water while its roots were clinging on for dear life on the shore.

My steps made crackling noises in the frost covered gras. At a safe distance, and for the first time alone, I opened my mouth widely and just like when Huldra had shown me, beautiful tunes came out of my mouth. The tune made a beautiful sound at the edge of the forest like clear droplets of pearls, and it wasn't even strenuous to perform it. After a while, ripples started to show at the water's surface and the disturbance reached the water's edge. Besides my song one could hear weak music which followed the disturbance on the water surface. It was music like I'd never heard before and it grew stronger by the minute. Suddenly there was a ripple at the surface, and I saw what resembled a bushy assembly of moss on top of what I assumed was a head coming out of the water. Two big round eyes appeared, and the music was now stronger than ever. I continued to sing but it felt like something was dragging me towards it and I became sleepy. My body enclosed on the water and the figure came closer. I could now see the pale green skin and that the creature was holding a fiddle under his chin. Without myself being aware of it I was about to be lured into the water by the music. Nicor was playing stronger than before, and I couldn't resist the water surrounding me. I was almost incapable of singing the tunes Huldra had given me. I sank deeper and deeper into the water, and it wasn't until the water reached my chin that I felt the panic. I was about to drown, and I tried my best to think of the song Huldra had given me and that I had to sing it. Without knowing how, the tunes were flowing out of me and drowned the sound of the fiddle. The water rippled and soon Nicor was playing the same tunes that I was singing. Not until then did I come to myself and was able to take a few steps back towards the edge of the water. Nicor stopped playing and removed his fiddle. I now felt safe enough to stop the singing. The water reached my knees. It was cold and my heart was hammering. Nicor moved towards me. Only three or four steps were between us. He looked me up and down while he held his fiddle behind his back.

'Huldertones you sing making all my water swing. The one who causes me to rise shall feel the whip with their demise. I'll take you down into the deep where I'll make sure you'll creep,' said Nicor making the water shake.

'I've come to ask your advice. Huldra sent me. She said you kept an eye on the underworld.' My voice was shivering from cold and fear.

'Who do you think me to be? I know not all of thee,' he said indifferently.

'I believe you to be Nicor,' I said almost in a whisper.

'Yes. What can this to me mean? Since you Huldra already have seen, I`ll be kind. What is on your mind?' he said in a lower voice, but he still sounded horrifying.

'I need to find Lamia. She wants to kill all children and women who are expecting. All of Grimrokk is afraid.' I tried to gain some sympathy from him.

'What do you want with her?' he asked absently.

'Make an end to her existence' I whispered.

'Nobody has managed to make her cease. What can I from this increase?' He looked at me waiting.

'You've lured many people into your depth with your fiddle, haven't you? If she continues this way there won't be any more to lure into the water with your music because there won't be any left to entrap,' I yelled, annoyed now.

'On the Myrthing Clan's family graveyard you need to look, there you'll find her like a dog gnawing the bones she took,' he said.

'Where is it?' I asked.

'By the Myrthing castle she can claw, where the meat is still raw,' he continued in a dark voice.

'Thank you for your help. I believe I should leave now so I can find her before she slaughters more people.' I backed away towards the edge of the pond as fast as I could. He followed me with small steps.

'Oh no! Now it is too late to leave! Down into the deep you shall proceed.' With a wicked grin he took out his fiddle again and put it under his chin.

'No, you said you were going to help me! Why...?'

Nicor was playing that beautiful music again and cold shivers went down my spine. I felt how my body was drawn unwillingly towards the water yet again. The music from the fiddle engulfed me like a net engulfing a struggling fish. Nicor went under the water's surface while he continued to play. The sound rang through the water, and I felt the water engulf me. It was up to my shoulders and closing on my neck. I knew what awaited me down there. I would slowly suffocate while the music danced around me. The water continued to rise, and my tears were washed away by the water in the pond. The ground left my feet, and I was sure that my final moments had come. I wasn't ready for this. Was I supposed to die without having given birth to a child? Without saying goodbye to Will? To not feel his warm, loving body again or hear him telling me that he loved me? His babe? In front of me, Nicor was moving towards the deep while he played. My chest was aching and paralyzed with fear. I looked around for something to grab onto, but I couldn't see anything. I could barely see the sunset on the water, and I stopped struggling and just sank downwards.

Suddenly, something grabbed hold of me, and I was pulled towards the surface. Someone hoisted me up with my shoulders and feet. When I came to, I coughed so much that I vomited. I tried to open my eyes and through a small slit I could see that it was a man who carried me through the forest. I could barely see his features in the dark, but I wasn't frightened by them. He was big and muscular with a variegated pelt around his shoulders and his hair was very short. He held me in a solid grip and before I noticed anything else the world turned dark.

ॐ

'Amelia, Amelia, you're dreaming.' I could hear a worried voice, Will's voice, and I opened my eyes. William was standing right above me.

'You're covered in sweat. Is something the matter?' He put his hand carefully on my forehead to feel for a fever.

'No, just a nightmare,' I said and smiled. He wouldn't have believed me if I had told him what I had just experienced. It was better to just pretend that it was nothing. The sun was out and warmed my face when I sat on our front steps and enjoyed the fresh breeze while my thoughts wandered to big men wearing pelts carrying me through the forest. From our neighbour's backyard I could hear children's voices and laughter. A wonderful sound I hoped would come from our backyard in the future as well.

'Hi Mia,' a small voice said, and I could see a tiny hand and a blond head with pigtails barely poking over the freshly planted bushes.

'Hi Christina. Are you enjoying the nice weather?' I got up carefully and went over to the bushes.

'Yes, we'w cweaning,' said the beautiful little creature who wore a big red overall and matching pants making her look like a big and cute cherry.

'You're cleaning? Wow, you're all doing a good job!' I laughed back at her.

William and I had become great friends with our neighbours, Aleksandra and Peter, who were the parents of this lovely little angel. Christina had just turned two and hadn't quite cleaned up her speech yet. She had made names for William and I which respectably were Iam and Mia. William came out on the steps. He smiled when he heard Christina's voice.

'Is it Christina who is paying us a visit?' he laughed.

'Yes, we'w cweaning,' she repeated.

'Is mom and dad cleaning too?' William asked with an excessive facial expression just like you tend to have when you speak to children.

'Yes, om on,' she said and waived us with her to show the way. We walked around the corner and saw two grownups working on last year's leaves and moving yard furniture.

'Hi. We were invited over,' said Will and smiled as he picked up Christina.

'Look who we have here. How are you?' Aleksandra smiled.

'Painful but doing good. If that makes any sense,' I said.

'Do you have the energy to be out and about? Don't you have to rest?' Aleksandra looked at me while she collected leaves in a heap.

'Yes, I do but I need fresh air. I'm starting to grow weary of my own walls so it's wonderful to be outside.'

We had talked a great deal with Aleksandra and Peter since they'd tried to become pregnant for a while as well without any luck. I had to remind myself that it wasn't good for people to struggle but at the same time it felt good that we weren't the only ones in this situation. I usually tried to write down words and thoughts that gave me comfort on my laptop. It served as a kind of diary. I felt like my head was about to explode with thoughts and feelings these days, so I felt the urge to put something down. However, it wasn't Grimrokk that were on my mind. It was the thought of our first attempt of test tube impregnation wasn't that far away and I really felt that this was our last option of becoming pregnant.

To myself,

There are pregnant women everywhere. Every lady I see on the street, at the store or on TV appears to be carrying an extra weight around her belly in the shape of a ball which she would love to talk about, show off and let everyone touch. When I was little, I remember that I asked my mother why some people didn't have children. Everyone had to have children since it was the most natural thing in the world. My mother told me that not everyone might want children, and somebody might not be able to have children. I thought about this for a while and always looked closely at those who didn't have any. They were weird people who pursed their lips when they spoke to others who had children. When I think back on this, I see myself and I understand why they pursed their lips. They didn't want to show the feeling of loss and sorrow of their own children and did everything they could to keep their tears back. I've become a weird lady in my mid-twenties who loves to tell people how they should raise their children. Nothing I've done these past twenty-four years has given me any right to express myself in this arena.

I read through what I'd written, and it hit me how bitter I'd become. My daily life was just as negative as my pregnancy tests, and I was tired of the mask I had to put on every day. The fake smile which didn't reach my eyes, my gaze which had lost the spark it once had had, and the joy and happiness which no longer appeared infectious on those around me. This mask which didn't fit had become my daily struggle for people to not show me pity. Because, deep down, I felt shame for not being good enough or being worth enough. The pictures hanging on the wall were of a couple who were happy and looked forward to joy and forever happiness. None of them were recognizable to me. We had put our whole life on hold for a child we desperately wanted but didn't get. There was no happiness attached to this anymore. I just wanted to sleep.

ೞ

Chapter 6
Eight must be better than four

I opened my eyes and looked around in a big room which seemed familiar. I scrambled through my thoughts to remember where I might be. I was wrapped in a thick brown woollen blanket which I pulled aside so I could sit up. I wore a thin petticoat made of cream linen. I was in my room at Mirini's house but how did I get here? I had been to see Nicor and had been pulled out of the water in the last possible second. Who was the man who saved me?

By one of the walls there was a dressing table with a small basin and a piece of cloth. I wandered over to the window and looked out at the sky which was covered in a thick layer of grey clouds.

'Hi, Mia! You're awake! That's good.' It was Mirini who had come rushing in.

'Hi Mirini. Have I been asleep for a long time?' I went over to the dressing table and felt the water. It was lukewarm.

'It's late morning now so you've been asleep awhile. You really scared us but you're here now thanks to Majliv. He was asked by Huldra to keep an eye on you.' Mirini put out a few clothes on the bed and laid a hairbrush next to them.

'Who helped me?' I asked with poorly hidden interest.

'Majliv. He is the grange warden. He takes care of all the animals in the forest and makes sure that we are safe. Get dressed and come downstairs. There's breakfast.' Mirini was gone out the door before I could ask her anything else.

I cleaned up and put on the clothes Mirini had laid out for me. It was a blue dress with a high waistline and black boots with lacing. My hair was tangled so it did take a while to make it look presentable. I braided it and inspected my reflection in the mirror. I hadn't looked this closely at my reflection since that time in the church with Father Benedikt and I barely recognized myself. Why didn't I look like myself here in Grimrokk? Yet, I was so familiar like there was a cousin looking back from the mirror. My body was slimmer, a bit more muscular than in Gaia, and my facial features were more noticeable. My hair was almost black and now that I had braided it, it reached all the way down to my lower back. I had never been very enthusiastic about hair this long, but I supposed that I could get used to it, however, I wasn't quite there yet. I couldn't stand wearing dresses. It had never been a preference of mine to wear things which were billowing around my legs. I could stumble on a bread crumb, if need be, and dresses did not enhance this ability.

I looked around for my own clothes and found them hanging over a stool in a corner behind the door. They were still sopping wet and probably had to dry for a few more days.

'Oh well,' I thought to myself, gritted my teeth, and headed down towards the kitchen where Mirini was making pancakes and tea.

'Hi everyone,' I said while I put on a grimace which was supposed to resemble a smile. Mirini smiled and Teddy nodded politely from behind his mug.

'Hi. How are you feeling?' Nette asked obviously worried. I sat down by the table and was poured a cup of tea by Mirini.

'Good. My throat is a little sore, but I'll survive that.' It wasn't until I'd said the words out loud that I realized that my throat was stinging, and my voice was hoarse. I felt my throat with my hand and as I did so my finger stung. Then I remembered the thorns which had hurt me when I had helped the strange horse. It was difficult to know if it had been a dream or a reality and I shook my head to clear my thoughts.

'You have to tell us what happened!' demanded Nette curiously.

'Nette! Mia has just had a very terrifying experience! Let her come around first before you start nagging her.' Mirini flashed a tense look at Nette but before I could say anything more there was a knock on the kitchen door and a man entered. He wore brown loose-fitting linen pants which were tightened at the waist and solid pelt boots which covered most of his calf. He wore a white shirt which was open at the neck and shaped like a V. The shirt was tied with a loose cord which made his muscular chest barely visible.

'Good morning, Mirini,' he said in a dark yet soft voice.

'Majliv, there you are. Come and say hi to Mia. She's finally awake.' Mirini was busying herself with breakfast preparations and therefore only nodded in my direction.

'Hi,' he nodded without looking at me.

'Hi, nice to....,' I was interrupted when he continued his conversation with Mirini.

'I have to leave earlier than planned,' he said in a cold voice. Who did he think he was behaving like that? I remained seated and gape at his behaviour while I took a closer look at him. His hair was only a few inches long and appeared to be dark blonde. His eyes were deep set in his face and his forehead was tight. His chin was firm and gave his face a very masculine look. His cheekbones were high and marked.

'You'll stay for breakfast at least?' Mirini had stopped and looked at him with an adorable smile in her best attempt to make him stay.

'No, sorry. Somebody has attacked Nicolas at Mr. Vesten and they need help with the tracking process right away,' he said while shaking his head.

'Poor Nicholas. Why can't people just let him be? Well, the deed has been done and it can't be undone,' Mirini said angrily turning red.

'They will keep it up until he dies. I'm quite sure of it.' Majliv's serious gaze met Mirini's.

'I don't think they understand how much he has lost by telling the story. He had a great family in Gaia, and they no longer have a father. He said the other day that he thinks about them every day and he wonder how it must have been for his wife to find him lifeless in bed.' Mirini whisked the contents of her bowl in a severe manner.

'It was a coincidence. He recognized the man and greeted him automatically. It's so easy to slip up like that. Especially when it turns out that it's your next-door neighbour. The neighbour was accidentally at Wargborough travelling through and usually lives a six week travel away from the place.' I was starting to get a grasp of what the conversation was about. A man who had 'revealed who he was' in Grimrokk and had never awoken in Gaia again.

'It was lousy of the neighbour's friends to tell everyone. It was nothing they could do anyway. He has been punished enough. The man has lost his marbles and are wandering around in a dreamlike state. The neighbour still has his life in Gaia,' said Mirini and stopped for a moment.

'It probably isn't that easy Mirini. He has lost everything he's ever known because someone else made a big mistake. Well, I'm running late. Goodbye.' Majliv waved at Teddy and Nette on his way out. I felt like I didn't even exist, and it annoyed me that I'd been given the cold shoulder.

'What a lovely man!' I snapped ironically and rolled my eyes.

'He might be a little restrained, but he does have a good heart,' Mirini said quickly trying to defend him.

'Don't even mention the fact that he is arrogant and rude,' I whispered to myself but not quite low enough.

'He did actually save your life so maybe you should give him another chance,' came a retort from behind the mug in the chair in the corner.

'Teddy, that's no way to behave towards guests. I'm sorry Mia. Majliv is his hero, and he will apologize right now!' she said with a firm look at Teddy who sank down in his chair and mumbled 'Sorry.'

'Glad that's cleared up. Breakfast is ready.' Mirini laid out the prepared food before she left the room and came back with Batist following her.

'There you are Mia! How are you?' Batist asked me in a fatherly manner.

'Good. My throat is a little sore, but it will pass.' I felt that he almost viewed me as a daughter. What had happened to me? There were so many things which were unclear, and none, except for Nette, had shown the least bit of interest. However, I expected it would come out sooner or later.

'Did you speak to Huldra? What is your ability?' Batist asked interested.

'Petrifying and... apparently it can be lethal.' I said.

'Petrifying?' Mirini and Batist looked surprised at one another.

'Yes. There supposedly is a tone in my voice that can petrify things. I'm the only one who's had this ability for several hundred years. The last one who had it was...'

'LAMIA,' everyone in the kitchen said in unison with fear in their eyes.

'Yes, how do you know that?' I was surprised by their reaction.

85

Everyone looked questioningly over at Batist so that he could be the one to explain.

'As you know Mia, I had a daughter not long ago. The topic is still rather touchy. She was your age when she passed. Silva was a good hunter, she made elixirs, and she could dance. I could watch her dance for hours. Some years back I saw and understood that this was a joy I shared with many others. She danced at the Frost festival like she always did but this time she danced with someone special. Someone who had love in his eyes and couldn't look away. Varg was his name, and he did everything to comply with her every need, but she was difficult as always and didn't seem very interested in him. As the time passed, they did get together and got married. They moved into one of the many castles his father owned, and everything was looking good. However, his family got the taste of power and wanted more of it. They wanted to own all Grimrokk. Varg created a group of men whose job it was to force people into following them, but it was useless. The men met only adversity and had to turn tale. That was when Varg's father got the idea to awaken a creature who could ensure there would be no more unwilling followers. He awoke Lamia and let her roam free. What he didn't know was that those many years of enchanted sleep had made her starve and now she couldn't separate friend and foe. Thus, she attacked every child she came upon. In a short time, there were very few children left and she started to attack pregnant women too. She didn't spare any and after she'd finished with the pregnant women, they were barely alive. Varg cared little for his father's actions if they didn't affect him and his family but what he didn't know was that Silva was pregnant with his child.' Batist took a deep breath and lowered his gaze. He took a moment to remember the happiness he had felt.

'One day when Silva was picking herbs in the forest outside the castle she was attacked by Lamia and never saw the light of day after that. Lamia's sense of smell never stops hunting for children or pregnant women. She has a specific ability to smell those who are carrying a child.' Batist dried a few tears on his sleeve. 'Mia, whatever you think about my daughter I assure you that she knew nothing about what Knuiw and his clan was up to. In his disturbed mind Myrthing thinks that he still can use Lamia's strength to make all Grimrokk follow him, but people are resisting now more than ever.' He looked at me with a desperate look.

'I am so sorry Batist.' My eyes were wet.

'I don't want anyone else to get hurt but nobody can rid us of Lamia. She has been cursed to roam the land forever,' he said in despair.

'Huldra said that Lamia's weakness is her own ability and that I am the only one who has had the same ability in a very long time but what am I supposed to contribute with? I'm just me,' I said while I unconsciously shook my head.

'What more did Huldra say?' asked Mirini worriedly.

'Just that I, in peace and quiet, had to practice my voice until it was able to hold a tone. Not that it will help anyone since Lamia apparently is invincible.' I got up from the table and ran towards the door leading out to the hall. My despair was loud in my head and yet again I felt helpless. In Gaia I couldn't get pregnant while in Grimrokk I'd most likely get killed if I became pregnant. When this thought hit me, I thought about William for the first time in a good while. He wasn't here so I wouldn't be able to fall pregnant in Grimrokk. That was it! I just wanted to go home. I sat in my room with my head full of thoughts about my existence in Grimrokk and how my life in Gaia felt so absent. I had become used to this place with its people and the task they had given me. Strange though it was, I didn't want to leave, if it was at all possible. The mystical and dark atmosphere affecting the surroundings had awakened a curiosity inside me. Here I was met with an expectation which excited me even though it was scary. This made me feel alive.

Before I knew it, the day had passed. I collected my thoughts and went downstairs to find the others. They had gathered in the living room around a fireplace. The living room was spacious and furnished with three armchairs, one chaise lounge, and two footstools. Mirini was in one armchair by the fire with her feet on a footstool mending a sock while Batist sat in the other chair with his reading glasses in his hands and rubbing his nose like he'd just been reading. Mirini's children were sharing the chaise lounge and playing chess.

'Hi. I needed to be alone for a while. I hope I didn't offend anyone,' I said, and four heads turned to look at me simultaneously.

'Deary me, no! We understand that this is a bit much for you. Take things at your own pace. I think you're catching on rather quickly,' said Mirini while she finished the touch up on the sock and cut it off.

'Thank you for everything you've done for me. You've been so kind. I was wondering.... what are our plans for tomorrow?' I had to do something. Have a plan. I was going nuts thinking so much.

'Hehe, we're packing for our journey to the festival tomorrow. The day after that we're going to pick up someone who is joining us. The journey will probably take us four to five days. It isn't further than a couple of miles, but Blasen doesn't have the same speed as he used to. His legs are growing old, so we must take it a bit slower for his sake,' Mirini said with a wide grin.

'Who are we picking up?' I asked and put myself in the remaining chair. I looked around and noticed that Teddy was glowering at me with a sour expression.

'My older brother, Siljan, and his two children. Well, they're not kids anymore so his grownup children, Kian and Lynn. I believe they're your age. Yes, Kian is a little older, but I believe that you and Lynn are the same age.' Mirini barely stopped talking when she first began.

'The festival is so exciting! We must find an activity you can compete in. Sling should be just up your alley.'

'What? Compete? What do you mean? I don't even know how to throw a sling?' I could hear that I was getting slightly hysterical.

'Don't worry about it. I'll show you. It's all just fun and games.'

She continued to gesticulate and explain while my face must have betrayed my horror, and my pulse was racing. The freedom of choice obviously wasn't present. I could always feign an illness or hide when the time came. Mirini yawned widely and looked over at Batist who had fallen asleep in his chair and was snoring softly.

'Kids, time for bed. We have a lot to do tomorrow, and you've promised me that you would study Latin before lunch,' said Mirini so crossly that Batist gave a little jump in his chair.

'Yes, but...,' they both chimed together.

'You promised me. No discussion. Finito!'

It was clear to everyone that there was no point in arguing.

Not long after the grownups followed the kids to bed, and I gave Mirini a big hug before I went to my room. When I got into bed, it took a while for me to fall asleep. The ceiling above me was white with spots and cracks but in the soft moonlight I could just glimpse a dark shadow making it appear as the night sky had crept into the room. My thoughts wandered for a while but soon sleep engulfed me softly.

෨෨

I sat in my armchair with my laptop in my lap. My fingers moved quickly over the keys. 'Lamia' and enter. The search engine found a lot of information and I glanced through it quickly. I chose a page which focused on Greek mythology and everything it told me

I'd already learned from Huldra proving this to be true. It was almost scary. I finished reading and did a new search but now I included Grimrokk as a search word. No hits. I didn't know whether to feel relieved or not. I wanted to know more. On the other hand, it made Grimrokk seem more like a fantasy than reality. I remained seated for a while reading everything I could find on Lamia. Some of the content was about a rock band who apparently shared the same name while others referred to ways of looking at Lamia in literature where she could be everything from stunningly beautiful but also turn into the most hideous man you could imagine. The day passed very quickly and when the evening came, I was asleep before my head hit the pillow.

∞

At the breakfast table in Grimrokk the next morning, Batist had made his specialty, pine needle pancakes with sourdough bread and the perfect supplements. Everyone looked forward to consuming the delicious breakfast when there was a knock on the kitchen door and Majliv came in.

'Good morning. I'm not too late I hope?' he asked seriously. The good atmosphere vanished, and I could still feel the cold sensation I'd gotten from him earlier.

'Not at all. Breakfast will soon be ready. Grab a mug with Imaginari-tea from the hearth,' said Batist and pulled out a chair as a sign that Majliv should sit down. With a mug in his hand, he sat down between us.

'Hi,' he said modestly in my direction.

'Hi,' I mumbled without looking at him.

Mirini kept on chatting all the way through serving the meal and filled the room with stories of her brother, how long it had been since she'd seen him, and that he had been taking care of the kids after his wife passed of pneumonia. I didn't catch everything she said, because I had my entire attention on the person sitting next to me. When Mirini, who until now had filled the room with her chatter, became quiet and everyone along with her, I looked up and saw that everyone was staring at me.

'Hm?' I said surprised.

'We had completely forgotten that you don't have your own clothes. It's getting colder, so we all need to pack as much clothing as possible. You don't have any money to shop with either I suppose? No, of course you don't. What am I saying?!' Mirini answered herself without me having a chance to do so and scratched her head.

'Mia and I can make some elixirs she can trade for clothing. We probably won't be able to both make elixirs and go to the market so we'd have to leave tomorrow instead and then we will be a day late.' Batist was trying his best to help.

'Majliv, could you take her to the market? Your horse can carry you both, I presume? It's not old like Blasen.' Mirini fluttered her eyelashes and gave a wide smile.

Majliv nodded indifferently and finished chewing his pancake. It annoyed me beyond measure how rude this dolt of a man was. Everyone helped clear the table and after that everyone went to their own room to pack. Only Batist and I remained in the kitchen to make elixirs.

'What you need to know about elixirs is that they don't have any effect until they've been spellbound and it's only a maker who can do that, like me.'

He stirred the cauldrons and pots while he cut and crushed herbs into a fine powder. The longer he was at it the more excited he became. I crushed fresh leaves in the mortar, but I had to peak every once in a while, at the increasing number of spoons which were stirring by themselves. The kitchen was alive with colours and shapes while the steam spread throughout the house. The smell wasn't the best since the ingredients in some of the elixirs were owls shit and werewolf sweat.

'What is all this going to become?' I asked as excitedly as I used to be on Christmas Eve when I was a child.

'This one is going to be an ointment for wounds while this one will make you smarter for a day and this last one is a love potion, but it also just lasts a day. Weirdly enough it is still very popular. The one who makes you smarter for a day has the aftereffects of making you very stupid the following day, so you must be careful with that one.'

Batist pointed while he was explaining all of this. I laughed at his expression when he was talking about the 'smarter for a day' potion since it was obvious that he had tried it himself once and became very surprised. Maybe he had made some brilliant cure for the stupidity but forgotten where he put the recipe the next day. When we were finished, we had four bottles of each elixir, and I wrapped them carefully in a blanket so they wouldn't break during our journey.

Everyone was packed and ready when Majliv entered the door wearing full winter gear. He wore a big, variegated pelt which apparently was made from various types of animals from mouse to bear and by the looks of it he added new pieces to it when needed. He came towards me and for the first time he addressed me directly.

'Are you ready?' he said and looked me straight in the eye. It was the first time our eyes met up close or for that matter the first time ever and I was caught aback by the clear dark-blue eyes looking back at me. He would have been very attractive had it not been for the rude personality. I had to collect my thoughts before I could answer. His gaze had been so surprising that I'd fallen into some kind of trance.

'Yes, the elixirs are in that bag,' I said and pointed to a rug sac next to the door.

He turned on his heel and picked up the sac before he nodded a quick goodbye to Batist. I did the same and went out to the stable at the back of the house. There I saw the biggest horse I'd ever seen. It was dark brown with white marks on the hooves and its fur was long with big hairy hoof hair and a long mane which hung down its side. The eyes were barely visible through all the hair and its tail reached almost all the way to the ground. The strangest part of it all wasn't how big it was or the thick fur but how many legs it had. The four legs which were normal for a horse was just the number of legs in the front. There were four legs attached to the back as well.

'It's.... it's.... it's got eight legs?' I said confused.

'Yes. I suppose you've heard about another horse who had just as many legs?' he said as if this was common knowledge, but it made my thoughts churn. There was something familiar about this.

'Ehm...Sleipner?' I guessed in a whisper.

'Yes, the horse of Odin.' He pointed at me and then at the horse's back to indicate that I should mount the animal.

'Am I supposed to ride it?' The words just fell out.

'Yes, unless you'd rather walk?' he asked shyly.

'No, it just surprised me a little.'

My words had started to tumble and ended up in a rush of mumbling. He bent a knee and held out a hand I could use for support when I mounted. I grabbed hold of the hand, stood on his knee while I held onto the horse's mane and swung my other leg up the best I could. I wouldn't have made it if Majliv had given me a last push with his thigh. He put his hands against the back of the horse behind me, aimed, and leapt up. I sat there studying him for a moment. He had to be strong in order to manoeuvre his body in such an easy manner. My head was buzzing with questions, but it was apparent that he wasn't the talking kind. He scootched closer to me and grabbed a hold of the reins. With a soft jolt we were on the move. The hooves hitting the ground made noise like thunder but despite the sound and being such a great animal, the horse moved with soft are careful movements.

'How far is it?'

'We probably won't get there until the afternoon,' he answered in a clipped tone.

My thin dress didn't bring much warmth and I was soon freezing. Even though I wore both stockings and shawl, I was shivering more than ever as the wind kept hitting me. Majliv must have felt it because from time to time he would grab me around the waist, pull me closer and put parts of his pelt around me. He was warm and steadfast. The calm and steadying breath made his chest move and I could feel his heartbeat towards my back. Since I wasn't cold anymore, I was enjoying the time spent travelling and it had been a while since we'd spoken when Majliv pulled the reins and the horse stopped.

'We need to get some food. Mirini prepared your lunch, and I've got it here.' He jumped down from the horse and looked up at me while holding out his arms. I grabbed hold of his shoulders and slid down the horse's side. He caught me making it a soft landing.

'Thanks,' I said but he didn't reply. He just let me go. I sighed and thought that this was going to be a long journey. I was quite disappointed that he kept giving me the cold shoulder. It wasn't that I was very interested in having a long conversation with him, but it felt a bit awkward being with someone this long without speaking. I looked around for a place to sit and chose a big rock which I cleared of snow with my shawl.

'You can't sit there. You'll get cold and sick,' he said and pulled out a knife which he used to cut two branches of a pine tree. They were full of pine needles, and he gave me one of them. I put it down on the rock and pulled out my lunch. Batist's breakfast had been just as wonderful as this lunch was boring. It was dry flatbread with brown applesauce. I ate the first half and then the second half.

'What's the name of your horse?'

'Pronto. Why?' he answered with his eyes locked on the rest of his lunch which he was now wrapping up.

'Can Pronto have the last half of my flat bread?' I asked as sweetly as I mustered.

'Yes, just ask him if he'd like it first,' Majliv answered and looked over at the horse.

'Ask him?'

'Yes, then you'll quickly find out whether he wants it or not,' Majliv said quietly.

'Hi Pronto, would you like a flat bread with applesauce?' I felt so stupid. I often talked to Tinka at home, our dog. She usually cocked her head and looked like she understood what I was saying but she always wanted food. Pronto inclined his head a couple of times so I reached out my hand with the flat bread in it. My hand seemed very small compared to Pronto's mouth. I felt quite safe around him now and laughed at little to myself when I had to extent my arms above my shoulder in order to reach his mouth.

'Are you ready?' Majliv asked and brushed a couple of pine needles off his trousers.

'Yes.' I was now looking forward to getting up on the horse and under the warm pelt. It was cold out and my cheeks were rosy as a result, besides, my dress was way too thin. For a moment it didn't matter so much to me that I was on a horse with a person who acted coolly towards me if I could lean into his warm body. We wrapped ourselves in our clothes and moved on ahead.

The journey continued in silence. I tried to start a conversation a couple of times, but my questions were answered in shortness. Majliv only answered with 'yes' and 'no' or 'I don't know.' After my last question, which was about electricity and whether that was a thing in Grimrokk, I gave up. The answer I'd received was a heavy sigh, which I felt against my neck, and a weary shake of his head.

The forest was slowly opening around us, and we could barely see a long field behind the trees. Just then it began to snow, grand, beautiful snowflakes were covering the landscape in white. At the opposite end of the field, I could just see a tiny village with a church visible above the rooftops.

'This is the city I arrived in when I first came to Grimrokk,' I said out loud to myself.

'Yes, all Grimmers enters here through Father Benedikt's mirror. It is the only mirror left for miles around after the werewolves were let loose. After that, the decision was made to separate the two worlds entirely once and for all, but they forgot about this one mirror, and it was hidden away for many years. The rumour has it that other mirrors exist too, but nobody can confirm this, or if they exist, where they are.' It was the longest sentence he'd ever spoken with me around. I was so surprised that I was unable to say anything but 'Mhm.' I hadn't expected an explanation, but his words clung to the air around me as if this was the most important thing, he'd ever tell me. The mirror was the entrance to this world, and it would be exciting to see it again. We increased our speed and soon passed over the drawbridge which led over the moat. The village was more charming during the day when people were walking the streets and people were talking at the corners. We stopped not far from the church and Majliv gave me the rucksack with elixirs.

'That's the market. You should probably go to the store first so you can try on clothes and figure out what you need. That store over there is owned by a close friend of Mirini's. You do what suits you best but I'm heading over to Father Benedikt in the meantime.' He tied Pronto to a tree and headed towards the church.

'Am I shopping alone? I don't know who these people are,' I said unsure.

'It's not dangerous. Come over to the church once you're done and don't take longer than you need. We must be on the road again before evening falls,' he said with indifference and disappeared into the church.

'Men,' I hissed to myself. He was so self-absorbed. It would have been helpful with some company since I wasn't used to the fashion around here. Come to think of it, Majliv probably didn't know that either. I took a deep breath and entered the shop across the street. It wasn't big but I believed that I'd be able to find something that would keep me warm.

'Can I help you?' I heard a voice ask from the back of the shop in a corner, however, all I could see was clothes.

'Ehm, yes please, I'm a friend of Mirini and I need some warm clothes.' I looked around but still couldn't see anybody.

'Mirini? How lovely. I haven't seen her in a long time,' the tiny voice said, and I could hear it clearer now. At least I thought it belonged to a lady.

'I am very sorry, but I can't seem to find you,' I laughed politely.

'Oh no, where are my manners?' the voice said and in between the garments a tiny lady showed up. She couldn't be any bigger than a coffee pot and she sat on a shelf right beside me and dangling her legs.

'There, much better,' the lady said smilingly. She was twiddling her thumbs feverishly while she spoke. She had long hair in braids and a round nose placed square in the middle of her face. The small round body was dressed in a red silk dress full of laze and embroidery.

Chapter 7
An awkward trace

'h, uhm, hi,' I stuttered in surprise. After having met the beautiful horse, although headless, a woman with a tail, and another creature with eight hooves you'd think that there wasn't anything left to make me speechless. You'd 'think' being the queue word.

'You're new here, aren't you?' asked the little woman. She reminded me of rays of sunshine. 'Yes, and not to be rude but...,' I stammered and was interrupted before I could finish my sentence.

'A gnome,' said the lady. 'That's what you were wondering wasn't it?'

'You're a gnome? Ok, I suppose that makes sense,' I said feeling rather awkward.

'My name is Sally,' said the little woman and reached out her tiny hand.

'Am... I mean, I am Mia,' I said and grabbed the little hand in a light handshake.

'You need clothes for the cold. I'll show you what we got.' Sally bounced from shelf to shelf and kept finding garments she believed would fit me.

'Sally? I was wondering if it is ok that I pay you in elixirs?' I'd been dreading asking.

'That's fine. What have you got?' Sally smiled.

'An ointment for wounds, a love potion, and one that makes you smarter for a day. Four bottles of each.' I was a little impressed with myself that I'd remembered all their names without flinching.

'The ointment for wounds won't give you much but the other two will give you plenty,' Sally said and laughed. Her laughter had a contagious effect. She kept looking around while I tried on whatever she found. She was obviously a person who you got to know quickly, and she also knew everybody else. The only words I was able to squeeze into the conversation were 'mhm' and 'yes' on occasion. After a while I could leave with a solid stock of clothing and instructions to send her greetings to everyone familiar.

At the church, Father Benedikt and Majliv were having a long conversation about the festival when I opened the double doors leading up to the altar. I finally felt more like myself. The clothes Sally and I had chosen were a knitted creamy white angora sweater with a wide collar. The sweater tied together at the waist with pelted leather straps. The pants were made of suede pelt in a light blue-grey colour, almost like my own eyes, and they were quite fitted around the legs. Over my shoulder I had a big white woollen robe without sleeves which reached all the way to the floor. My head was covered in a wide hood which almost covered my whole face. I had tried to find something I'd like on purpose while also finding something that was like Silva's clothing.

Majliv and Benedikt were in the first row of benches, and both turned around in my direction when they heard me enter. I had, judging by the expression on their faces, interrupted them and they remained quiet and looked at me.

'My dear child, Ame, I'm sorry, Mia,' said Father Benedikt and straightened up in order to give me a big hug. Majliv turned around quickly when he heard the name and turned back just as quickly. Was he afraid that I'd be revealed to someone?

'Father Benedikt. Now I'm finally getting the opportunity to thank you,' I smiled while holding his hands in mine.

'My dear, that was nothing. We must do what we can for each other.' He sounded as if he was completing a sermon for a congregation of Grimmers.

'So far, I think it's wonderful here,' I said. I hadn't convinced myself just yet. Majliv got up and pulled his pelt around himself.

'We must leave. It's starting to get dark, and I don't want to run into the Myrthing Clan today. Thank you for your time, Father Benedikt. I'll see you at the festival.' Suddenly he seemed to be in a hurry. Serious as always, he strode down the aisle.

'It was nice meeting you both again, especially you Mia. We didn't have the time to be introduced the first time we met.' Father Benedikt kissed my hand and waved goodbye while I hurried down the aisle to catch up with Majliv. Outside, there was now so much snow that our boots made deep footprints.

'What's going on with you?' I asked annoyed.

'Nothing. I just said we had to leave before it gets dark,' he said in his usual unattractive tone.

I shook my head and followed him. I let him help me onto the horse, he got up behind me and gave Pronto's reins a shake, so he jumped and rose on his hind legs for a second before he regained his balance and moved on in a quick canter. We kept a high pace as the snow kept coming down thicker and even though I was better dressed now I could still feel the snow and the cold. When we reached the forest road we slowed down. This man was getting on my nerves. What had I done in order to deserve this sort of attention? Maybe he had had other plans the day he saved me and was pissed off because of that? If that was the explanation, he should turn to Huldra with his grim mood not me. We rode in silence until darkness surrounded us. It was too dark to move on and Majliv was worried we'd lose the trail we were following.

'We'll camp here,' he said and jumped down from the horse. I followed, this time without help. My cold feet were numb, and pain shot through them as I landed. Silently I admitted to myself that I should have accepted help when dismounting. Majliv lit a fire and cut down branches for us to sit on. I sat by the fire and tried to get warm. The journey had been cold without the warmth of the pelt. My new clothes weren't really that warm, however, when Pronto increased his speed there was nothing that could keep me warm like Majliv's pelt. He was now mounting a resting place which looked like a one-walled-tent. He had placed it so that it would be protecting us from the wind and snow.

Majliv pulled out the food and a bag made of sheep stomach containing our water. We ate what was left and tried to get warm by the fire still without speaking more than necessary. I thought about how well I could have gotten to know somebody in the time I'd spent with Majliv. He barely said a word and appeared to be grumpy most of the time. I told myself that maybe he just had a negative way of behaving, and this idea calmed me a little.

'I'm going to bed. We must get up early tomorrow to not waste any time,' Majliv said and moved towards the tentlike construction. I didn't take long before he was asleep, but I wasn't tired and remained awake staring into the flames. It had stopped snowing, and the sky was full of stars. I glanced up towards the moon and could see the circles indicating the cold surrounding it becoming bigger and bigger. When I finally grew sleepy, I just lay down on my side while the last flames were still alive, and the embers still gave off heat. I fell asleep like that by the fire, but the deep sleep never engulfed me. I was shivering but I still didn't wake up properly. Far away I'd begun to float before it quickly became warm, and I was pulled into a deep sleep.

CR୫ଠ

It was snowing in Gaia. It was Saturday and I'd waved Will off to work. Like most brokers who took their job seriously, Will worked on the weekends. It hardly ever bothered me to be alone. I had always viewed myself as independent and preferred to do things my own way.

I went to the mailbox and found a letter addressed to me from the hospital. It contained instructions about the test tube procedure and a prescription for a nasal spray. It was to be taken four times a day and I was to start in just a couple of days. There was also a prescription for hormone injections I had to take once a day. The thought of needles made my stomach churn and I put the papers down on the living room table. During the last couple of days, I'd been so consumed by Grimrokk and the grumpy Majliv when I spent so much time there that the thought of the test tube treatment had been pushed to the back of my mind. To be honest, it had been nice to think about something else for a while. The air felt easier to breathe when my thoughts were in Grimrokk.

My experiences in Grimrokk made it difficult to sleep, especially when Will was snoring, and I often lay awake and imagined what I'd experienced. It was like a movie playing in my head. The thought about what awaited me when I woke up in Grimrokk made me excited which also prohibited sleep in Gaia.

This morning was rather normal, and I was so tired that I didn't realize that I'd awoken in my own room and not one of Mirini's or somewhere in the forest. It wasn't until I sat down by the computer to research Sleipner that I realized that I hadn't been to Grimrokk during the night. A doubt hit me straight away, had it all been a dream? I had never had very vivid dreams and they had seemed real, all of it. No, I understood that it wasn't possible. It couldn't be anything but real. I knew within me that I had been there and now, however crazy it sounded, I missed it. Not having to deal with all the attention and pity which we were drowning in from the people closest to us appeared to be addictive. I had to get back. I'd forgotten all about research and the internet while I sat there wondering and I didn't look at the website which had popped up in front of me. The search gave an overview of the gods of the Norse mythology and Sleipner was only mentioned as Odin's horse. When I finally came back to reality this didn't satisfy my curiosity. I had to go to work today in order to find out more. The library where I worked had a rather good selection of books on this topic which were often more informative than the world wide web.

The snow had fallen heavily and covered everything. It was slippery outside, and the cold was nipping at my nose. The library was almost empty, and I assumed that the weather was mostly to blame. I found a shelf containing books about religion and moved quickly through the titles. There, among hundreds of bibles, Koran's and different religious overviews I found a little brown leatherbound book. It had had better days. The title read 'Norse Mythology' and it contained verses and stories about the gods and their enemies. I went straight to the register and found Sleipner. It said:

'One myth concerns Sleipner, Odin's horse'. It had eight legs and was the fastest horse there was. A giant had made a deal with the Aesir to build them a great castle. He wasn't allowed help besides his horse and the castle had to be done by the first day of summer. In return he would be given Frøya, sun, and moon. Svadilfare, his horse, pulled an impressive number of rocks to the building site so that when the first day of summer was closing in there was only the castle gate left. Since it was Loke who had made the deal, the Aesir bid him to come, and they threatened his life so that he would end the ill-fated deal. When he heard this, Loke transformed into a mare and ravaged the stallion all night so that when the morning came there wasn't a single stone at the building site. The giant was livid with the horse. Thor, who were returning home from a journey, contributed with his hammer and killed the giant with a sloid blow. The situation was now thus that Loke had ravaged Svadilfare so badly that he had fallen pregnant. The result was a foal which had grey fur and eight legs, and a faster horse hadn't been seen in Valhall, so Odin took the horse as his own and named him Sleipner.'

⊂⋙⊃

I was lying on something soft and warm. Before I opened my eyes, I was enjoying the silence surrounding me, but I quickly remembered where this silence belonged. I was back in Grimrokk, and I wasn't alone. I opened my eyes carefully and had to think through my last night here because something seemed out of place. I had awoken next to a muscular man who had a close grip around me. A hand was stroking my lower back with small careful movements. My head was resting on his chest which moved steadily every time he breathed. Confused, I realized that it was Majliv who was holding me and touching me in this loving manner. What was going on? My body stiffened and my right arm, which I was laying on, went numb. The last thing I remembered from Grimrokk was the embers of the fire and that my teeth were clattering but I couldn't remember anything beyond that point. I needed more time to gain an understanding of the situation but ironically, I could feel a yawn making its way up my throat. The sound of this yawn would betray that I was awake, and Majliv immediately let go of me and lay there stiffly. Even if he lay still, and I covered half of him, I could feel him moving further and further away from me. My numb arm started to prickle from the blood streaming to the limb and I took the chance of leaning on said arm. I turned around but before I could turn all the way Majliv pushed himself aside, got up and left our resting place quickly. It was as if someone had set fire to him. Nothing had changed and he barely spoke a word for the rest of the morning until we were about to leave.

'We're lucky with the weather. I suspect we'll be there earlier than estimated.' This was good news. I didn't want to spend many more days around this grumpy creature.

'How wonderful.'

'We're taking a shorter route than the others. Pronto can handle a rougher terrain so we don't have to stay on the trail all the time,' he said just as serious as ever and hailed my rucksack over Pronto's back. He reached out an arm and waved me towards him without so much as looking in my direction. I walked over to him and grabbed his hand, put my foot on his leg and mounted. I'd grown used to this way of mounting the horse but this time I was surprised by the unexpected warm jolt that shot through me as his hand grabbed hold of mine. Shocked over my own reaction, I ended up sitting very still and concentrating hard on breathing normally.

I looked around and adjusted my focus solely on the idyllic environment around us. We were riding over a snow-covered field which hadn't been disturbed yet. For the first time in Grimrokk, the sun warmed my face and it felt wonderful! Pronto was moving at a steady pace without complaining. He gave off a low movement, almost like a vibration, and the result was that it felt like I was riding in a new car, except for the other movements. I was amazed that you could ride such an animal and not feel small. Majliv was quiet as usual behind me.

'Do you know Mirini's family?' I had decided to make yet an attempt to get a conversation going. If he was shy surely, he had to warm up to me soon.

'Yes, I'm a close friend of Mirini's nephew, Kian. We go hunting together.' I had not expected this amount of information. I was surprised and grasped eagerly for more.

'What sort of hunting do you do?'

'Moose, deer, anything really.' He wasn't so tense anymore. Maybe he'd gotten used to me?

We had moved to a higher point in the terrain now and the wind was picking up. I was so cold I barely managed to hold on to my cloak which was hanging over my shoulders. My fingers had turned blue, and my nails were causing me a lot of pain.

'You would have frozen to death in this world if I hadn't saved you,' Majliv said and closed the pelt around me. It felt nice. His body was warm, and he tucked me closer to him while holding the reins and keeping the arms halfway around me.

'Why would you say that?' I wasn't sure what he was talking about.

'You fell asleep last night alone by the fire. It was pure luck that I heard your teeth clattering and your lips were blue when I came to get you. You didn't wake up when I moved you either.' So that is why I'd been lying next to him.

'Thanks,' I said quietly. He had kept me warm in the night. That was the reason why we'd been so close together but why had he been caressing my back? I had been warm when he'd done so. I supposed there was a logical explanation even if I had mistaken it for a gesture of love. My conclusion was that he was trying to wake me up.

Evening was approaching and it was clear that I wasn't the only one who was hungry. Pronto had started to act fuzzy. We stopped in a forest where we were sheltered from the wind. The rays of sunlight were barely visible over the treetops and there wouldn't be light for much longer. The snow reached me to my knees now and Majliv lead Pronto in between the trees. I followed as best I could. Pronto left a makeshift trail behind which made it a bit easier for me to find my footing. I didn't care much for wading through knee deep snow. My expectations when it came to snow were to have a white Christmas and other than that I didn't really care. We hadn't moved far before Majliv found a big pine tree where the ground was bare.

'We'll make camp here. The tree will protect us from the weather. If it starts to snow, we'll keep dry.' He removed our stuff from Pronto's back and let him roam freely around the pine tree.

'I'll be back in a while. It would be good if you could find some firewood. Take whatever's dry and don't take branches of living trees.'

'What? Where are you going?' I called after his back which was quickly disappearing into the forest.

'I'm getting us food,' he said right before I lost sight of him.

'Men...this is so typical men. Let the one who's a stranger to this country carry on for herself,' I said loudly to myself but something inside me was hoping he could hear me. It was very quiet. Only the treetops made whooshing noises occasionally, and it was the only thing I could hear beside my own breath.

I wasn't very keen on attempting to find firewood, especially when this involved wading through knee-deep snow, but I had to contribute, and I did want a fire. Luckily, my tracks were clearly visible in the snow, so I had no trouble finding my way back to the camp. I waded around between the trees and found broken branches and twigs which poked out of the snow. Suddenly I heard some noises deep in the woods ahead of me. It couldn't be Majliv because he had wandered off in the other direction. I could feel my heart hammering. Then I remembered with a chill what was roaming this land. I was defenceless if Lamia showed up. I would be the easiest prey in the world. If I'd just done as Huldra had instructed then maybe I'd felt safer, however, the truth was that I hadn't even tried. I just couldn't wrap my head around it and take it seriously. I broke a branch off a pine tree and jumped when the sound was louder than I expected.

'Get it together Amelia. This is nonsense. Come on, find some of that courage now,' I instructed myself. I inhaled deeply and hummed to myself to break the silence, so it wasn't so deafening. The humming followed the scale, and I went up and down it several times. Sometimes I continued to a higher pitch and sometimes lower. No tone excelled the other.

'That's what I thought. Just nonsense.' There wasn't a pitch I hadn't tried therefore, I concluded, Huldra had to be mistaken about my so-called ability.

I decided that I'd collected enough wood for the fire, and I was also tired of noises I couldn't place. Besides, darkness had now engulfed the world. My tracks were very deep which was lucky because even if I couldn't see them, I could feel them. At the camp, Majliv still hadn't showed up but Pronto was present chewing on an elderberry bush and caring very little if he was alone or accompanied by me. No wonder when you're his size I thought.

I tried to arrange the wood in the shape of a tipi, but I lacked the training and was pretty sure Majliv would rearrange it if it wasn't good enough. I sat down under the pine tree, leaned my back against it and tried to get some rest. Why couldn't he just return? I felt a lot safer when he was close by. Far away I could hear noises which were difficult to place because the snow muted the sound, so I closed my eyes to hear better.

'I hope you like hare?' Suddenly he was right in front of me with a hare dangling from its hind legs in one hand. My heart nearly jumped out of my chest from the shock.

'Oh my god you almost scared the shit out of me,' I said and put a hand on my stomach.

'Sorry, I thought you heard me.' He shook his head and threw the hare down in the snow. Just as I'd expected he started to rearrange my tipi fire. The branches were all put into a new position and were lit by hitting two rocks towards each other. This man really was predictable.

'Don't eat all the berries Pronto. I need some of them too,' said Majliv and went over to the bush where he tore a handful of berries of. I remained seated and watched as he prepared the hare, but I had to look away when he skinned it. Even if my stomach was rumbling, I didn't feel particularly hungry while I watched Majliv cook. When he had finished the gory part however, I could feel the appetite sneaking up on me. He took out small bags containing different seasoning and smeared them on and inside the hare meat. Then he poked a stick through it which had been waiting next to the fire in the snow. Not long after he'd hung it over the fire a smell of fresh herbs started to waft around.

'It smells good,' I said.

'It will be good,' he said indifferently. It was impossible to give him a compliment without being left feeling dumb, but it was true; the meal was exquisite.

After we'd eaten, he got to work on the tiny piece of fur. It didn't take a professional to see that he'd done this before. His movements were so quick I struggled to keep up. Majliv then arranged our sleeping quarters below the pine tree and put out a woollen blanket over the brushwood he'd found.

'I'm going to bed. You should probably do that too, so you don't fall asleep by the fire again.' He lay down on the blanket and pulled the pelt over him.

'That's probably a good idea,' I said unsure and wondered if he meant that I should lay down next to him. It didn't seem natural at all but there weren't a whole lot of other places for me to lay down. I headed for the sleeping quarters where Majliv was laying on his side with one arm under his head and the other opening the pelt so I could scootch under.

'You should use that as a pillow,' he said and nodded towards the cloak still hanging over my shoulders.

'Oh right.'

I was the one who was quiet now. He had wanted me next to him. My thoughts were spinning trying to find an explanation as to why. The cold was the obvious reason after last night. Maybe he was afraid he'd freeze or maybe he had some hopes of the sexual kind, but I quickly shook that thought out of my head. The most logical explanation was that he feared that something would happen to me and that he had to protect me since Mirini and Batist had asked him to. I followed his instructions and folded my cloak in the shape of a pillow and lay down on my back.

'I don't bite,' he muttered suddenly. I had laid down so far out, almost at the edge, to make as much room as possible between us.

'No, uhm, I guess not,' I mumbled and moved closer until my shoulder touched his arm.

'Better now?' I asked sarcastically.

'You're the one who'll be cold but do as you please.' He turned around with an obvious annoyance. I didn't have any more to say so I remained on my back looking at the branches above us. I missed Will. He was rarely grumpy, rude, or cross and with that thought I fell asleep.

CB80

Even if it was Will who filled my thoughts when I fell asleep it was not him who filled them when I woke up in Gaia the next morning. It was impossible to chase Majliv out of my thoughts. His warm body, his dark-blue eyes, the muscular arms who held me in the morning. Jolts rushed through my body, and I caught myself blushing a couple times when I unintentionally speculated about what could have happened. My pulse increased and my breath caught. There was something about him I couldn't figure out and that made him both annoying and exciting at the same time.

My conscience quickly stopped this train of thought because there was no one better than Will and I wanted him just as much now as ever. I felt like my head was going to explode. There was too much to think about. The test tube trial, Will, Grimrokk, Majliv, Lamia, all this was spinning around like a crazy tornado in my thoughts. How was I supposed to keep these two worlds separated when I couldn't get Majliv out of my thoughts? Why was he even in there to begin with when he was so obnoxious? There was only one reason for me going to bed early that night, I wanted to see Majliv again.

⚬✦⚬

I felt hot flushes rushing down my back as I awoke. Before I opened my eyes, I could sense a deep breath close to my ear. The jolts on my back came from a hand caressing me softly. I opened my eyes slowly. Majliv's muscular body, his breath and his calm heartbeat were there behind me. I didn't move. For the first time I noticed how pleasant his odour was. It was a mix of rosemary and lavender mixed with fresh forest and an undertone of apple. The truth was that the most prominent and alluring smell was the familiar sent of a clean man.

I hadn't realized that I was breathing rapidly before he moved his arms away from me. My hand was resting on his chest, and I felt his heart hammer fast and steady. The time froze. Everything in me wanted this moment to last forever but Majliv knew that I was awake, and his body gave clear indications that he wanted to move.

'Good morning,' I said abruptly.

'Morning,' he replied kneeling down by the burnt-out fire. He relit it with the last few pieces of wood I'd gathered the night before. My cloak lay outside the woollen blanket, and I had to rinse it off snow. No matter how much I shook it the snow was stuck.

'We should make it to Siljan before dinner. We don't have that far left.'

'That's good.' It would be great to meet someone who was willing to engage in conversation.

We let Pronto get a solid warmup before we increased our speed but when we did his mane was billowing in the wind and the snow whipping around the hooves. The sun made the snow shine with crystals and the fields were transformed into a picture of winter wonderland.

The day felt like it lasted forever but that was probably because I was looking forward so much to arriving. My back was aching, so I stretched my arms and massaged my neck. It was easy to alter one's position while we were moving but I did my best to stretch my back. I put my hands on my lower back and leaned forward so I could reach it and massage it too. When I leaned back, with my hands still on my lower back, Majliv gave a little jolt and pushed himself backwards.

'Ops, sorry,' I said, and I could feel my cheeks heating when I turned to look at him. I hadn't thought about where my hands had been when I leaned backwards. We sat so close together that I hadn't been able to avoid touching his pants.

'It's fine,' he said with a small smile at the corner of his mouth. This made a whole lot of difference to his person, and it was like he changed in front of me. His eyes sparkled and he had perfect white teeth, and each cheek had a dimple. My eyes were glued to him for a minute, and he looked questioningly at me still with that little smile.

'What is it?'

'You're smiling?' I answered and smiled back.

'Yes?'

'It's the first time I've ever seen you smile. You should do it more often.' I turned away, shy at my own comment. Behind me I could hear him chuckle. 'It looks good on you,' I said but this time I didn't dear to look at him.

The sun was steadily moving towards dinnertime. I'd learned that by now since the sun was Grimrokk's watch.

'Do you see the farm right over there?' he said and pointed ahead of us while he leaned towards my cheek. A warm flow passed through my body and my heart rate increased.

'Yes?'

'That's where we're going. That's Siljan's farm.' His smell reached me, and I couldn't resist taking a deep breath. How had I missed out on this heavenly smell before?

'See, we made it for dinner,' he said pleased.

A small farm lay at the edge of the forest in the afternoon sunlight. Smoke erupted from a small chimney on the small white house. The roof where tall and oblique and the chimney gave the impression of serving as a big top hat on the roof making it all look like something that would fit on a Christmas card.

Chapter 8
Naked skin

e rode into the farm towards a large barn that was directly in front of the house. At the entrance stood a small, round man with grey hair and a confused expression on his face. There was no doubt, this had to be Siljan. He looked absent-minded, just like Mirini. Next to him stood a girl about my own age, with thick, dark hair in a ponytail and big, beautiful eyes. She smiled broadly and skipped down the stairs coming towards us with her father in tow.

'You must be Mia. I'm Siljan, this is Lynn, my daughter, and he with the crossbow on the horse over there is Kian.' The words came so quickly that I wasn't sure if it was my turn to say something or if he just needed to catch his breath. He pointed around and finally in the direction of a young man on a speckled horse. The man was fully occupied with his work, far out on a field near the house.

'Nice to meet you,' I said and shook hands with those closest to me.

'Excuse me, I'm a bit short on time. The pots need stirring before they burn, otherwise none of you will have dinner, and you know what Mirini's face will look like if she hears that I served you burnt food. She'll criticize me when they come on the 'morrow. It would be so typical of the stressful... always... she wants...' Siljan was already on his way in as he talked to himself.

'Aren't they alike, dad and Aunt Mirini?' Lynn smiled and shook her head.

'Yes, you're right.'

'If you ask me, I find it strange that Siljan doesn't have heart problems,' Majliv chuckled, and a smile played at the corner of his mouth.

'The others are at the lake now, so they'll probably arrive here tomorrow around lunchtime. She should have gotten herself a new horse.' Lynn was bubbly, a person you couldn't help but like. She wore a greyish-purple sweater, and on top of it, she had a rough, brown leather corset. The corset was decorated with lacing and seams all over. The pants were tight and made of light brown leather. On her feet, she had pelted brown boots that reached to her knees.

'Blasen is just as stubborn as Mirini and won't give up until he has to.' Majliv made a frustrated expression.

'How was the journey? I hope you didn't scare Mia to death?' she asked, looking at me.

'No, it went great. It was only the cold which made it a bit cumbersome,' I said. Promptly, the image of me enveloped with Majliv's arms and warm cape popped up in my mind, and I struggled to keep from blushing.

'That's good. How about you, Majliv, you great player, are you going to play war with Kian as usual? If so, I can steal Mia and show her around,' Lynn said. She patted Majliv on the shoulder and laughed.

'War, huh? We have important things to do, too,' he chuckled and went out into the field towards the young man.

'Why did you go alone though? I never got a proper answer from Mirini,' Lynn took my arm and led me around the farm.

'Have you talked to her?' I asked confused.

'Yes, in our own way. I can read thoughts just like her, and therefore we can communicate quite effectively.'

'Oh... I didn't know that. Or, I knew Mirini could read thoughts, but not you as well.'

'But why did you go separately?' She didn't give up.

'Well, I needed winter clothes, or I mean warm clothes for the Frostpace?' I wasn't sure if that was the right term, but Lynn nodded understandingly.

'So, in order to save time, Majliv took me to the small town... uh... with the church...' I couldn't remember the name of the town.

'Wargborough? Where Father Benedikt is the priest?' Lynn tried, questioningly.

'Yes, I bought clothes there, from Sally.'

'That's where I usually shop too. Sally is a funny character. She never says a bad word about anyone. What do you think about Wargborough?' Lynn and I turned the corner of the house, and she headed towards the field where Kian and Majliv were talking with expressive body language.

'To be honest, I didn't get to see much of it. It got dark pretty quickly, so Majliv wanted to leave in a hurry,' I said, surprised. Lynn stopped for a moment.

'You see, Varg, the son of Knuiw Myrthing, owned everything in that town. After his wife died, he left everything to his father and then committed suicide.

Myrthing has such high thoughts about himself that only his followers are allowed to move outdoors when it's dark. His clan keeps watch around the clock.' Lynn shook her head and sighed heavily. 'Enough about that. You have to meet my brother. Kian!' she shouted and waved the boys a little closer. Kian, who had gotten off his horse was about as tall as Majliv. He was just slightly slimmer and didn't have such distinct features. He wore a black shirt with a knot at the neck, and a white undershirt peeked out from under the shirt. The pants were made of charcoal grey linen, and he wore black, mid-height leather boots. The cape was made of suede with something that resembled rabbit fur at the edges.

'Hey. I didn't mean to be rude, but I didn't hear you come. I'm Kian, and I guess you're Mia,' he said with a charming smile and sparkling blue eyes. His hair was short, jet black, and tousled in a way that almost looked planned.

'Hey. Good guess. Or did Majliv dish?' I teased back.

'Yeah, it's possible,' he laughed and threw the edge of his cape over his shoulder, revealing his thigh and the strangest crossbow I had ever seen. It looked like it was twisted together from three branches and less powerful than I thought a regular crossbow would be. However, strangest of all, even though it was made of wood, was its colour. The whole crossbow was silver. There was no trace of any arrow.

'What's that? A crossbow?' I asked.

124

'Yes,' he replied and reached down into a sort of half-glove attached to the underside of the crossbow and pulled it up.

'This was a gift from Huldra. It was made many years ago from branches of Huldra's tree,' he said obviously proud as he showed us.

'Where do you store the arrows?' I asked, and the three others began to laugh.

'Kian doesn't need arrows. He has something else to fire with,' Lynn explained.

'What does he use to fire with?' I felt stupid but I had to know.

'Watch now,' said Kian, and turning towards an assembly of rocks protruding between some trees at the edge of the forest, he lifted the crossbow and aimed. Sparks crackled around his arm, into the branches that twisted into the crossbow, and when he triggered the shot, it flashed just like lightning. On the rocks, there was now a white scar, just like the two of them had been struck hard against each other.

'My ability is that I'm blazing hot and can use my body as a weapon. I have only one ability, but it is strong,' he laughed at his own demeanour.

'What about you, Lynn? Aren't you going to show your ability? Since your brother is boasting, you can too,' Majliv said, nudging Kian's shoulder.

'Well alright, but then I have to demonstrate it on one of you. Kian, why don't you?'

'Do I have to, or do I volunteer? You always choose me!'

'You must. Come on!'

'Fine but catch me this time. Last time, I got a concussion,' Kian said, rubbing the back of his head.

'Yeah, yeah, yeah. Cover your ears, the rest of you.' We did as she said. Lynn looked at Kian for a moment, and suddenly, he fell into Lynn's arms.

'What was that?' I was curious.

'I can make people fall asleep if they stand close enough. It's a boring ability because many can do the same. But I can read minds too so that makes up for it at least a little,' Lynn said as she leaned over Kian and gave him a little slap on the ear to wake him up.

'That was the last time I'm your volunteer for a while. It's so annoying to have to be woken up every time,' he said and yawned.

'How exciting,' I said enthusiastically.

'Can we play some other time? I think I'm going to collapse if I don't get some food very soon,' said Majliv, and everyone trooped back to the house.

I felt clammy and had been longing for a shower ever since I had taken a quick wash at Mirini's. Lynn told me they had a hot spring in the woods that I was most welcome to use. It was supposed to be a little way into the forest and surrounded by tall fir trees. I followed the directions to where a high hedge of fir trees stood in a circle. At the opening, the trees overlapped with each other, so it was impossible to see inside. I went in, stood, and surveyed the place. At the centre of the trees rose a high mountain knoll. There was a large crack a distance down from the top. Water was gushing out of the crack onto a shelf. The water filled a pond big enough to take a few swim strokes, and the pond was surrounded by fresh flowers growing close to the edge. Steam rose from the surface, and the water smelled delicious of lavender. The snow layer was thick outside the trees, but the grass was getting greener and greener towards the pond. I undressed and left my clothes on a rock nearby. The air was a bit chilly, so I sank into the warm water. I dunked my head and ran my fingers through my hair to get rid of the tangles. As I swam around a bit, I thought about my abilities. Even though I had practiced without further success in the woods, it had given me new hope to see Lynn and Kian demonstrate their abilities. I sang a little to myself and tried some notes higher than the others. The scale was the easiest way to reach all the notes, but there wasn't a distinct note that felt exactly right for my ability. The singing and humming gradually turned into the Huldra's song, and I let the notes flow as they wanted. The bath was the most delightful experience I had ever had. The water that flowed down from the mountain washed over my shoulders and down my back. I scrubbed my body with a cloth and enjoyed running my fingers over my soft skin. This body was so different from what I was used to that I found myself admiring it. Then I had a feeling that I wasn't alone. I looked around and towards the opening in the hedge.

'Oh... sorry. I didn't think anyone was here,' I heard a familiar voice say, at the same time as a figure quickly jumped back behind the hedge.

'I'll be done in a minute,' I called back. Majliv apparently also needed a bath after the journey. I quickly got to my clothes and dried off most of the water. It wasn't easy to put on such tight pants when my skin was damp, so I almost lost my balance a couple of times. Finally, the pants were on, and the sweater hung more or less on my upper body.

'Come in. I'm dressed,' I called out. He came in through the hedge with his gaze on the ground. I arranged the sweater properly and began to put on my boots. Out of the corner of my eye, I noticed that he had started to undress his upper body. My gaze was inevitably drawn to where he stood, I couldn't resist. The upper body had muscles that were toned to just the right amount. When he moved, I could see the muscles move under the golden skin. His stomach was firm with two well-trained chest muscles. The back was broad and V-shaped with a prominent neck. I tied my bootstraps without looking at them, just so I could sneak a peek.

'I'll go up to the house now. Be careful down there,' I said, pointing down to the water's edge. 'That rock is pretty slippery.' I gathered my things and walked out through the opening between the trees. There, I stopped for a moment and looked down at the new snow on the ground. I wondered how long he had been standing there. How much had he seen? The temptation was too great, and I leaned against the opening peering through the branches, just a little, just once. There, I saw him swim to the waterfall and climb up onto a rock. He stood up and leaned both hands against the rocks in the waterfall, so the water flowed over his neck and down the defined back muscles. My heart skipped a beat as he flexed his well-trained muscles. This was the body I had lain next to at night. The thought gave me butterflies in my stomach. If only I could understand the person inside that attractive body, I could like him very much. Now he had actually opened up a bit on the last day. I had already been standing there for too long when I heard voices from the farm, so I hurried away so no one would see me spying on Majliv.

Mia?' Lynn's call sounded loud, and I jogged to get further out of the woods before answering, so he wouldn't hear how close I still was to the bathing spot when I should have been at the house a long time ago.

'Mia?' she called again.

'I'm here,' I replied, waving from the edge of the trees. I realized that the whole situation was pretty stupid.

We had eaten dinner, and Lynn showed me where I was going to sleep. She had made a bed for me in her own room, and it looked very inviting. However, my whole being knew that it wasn't where I wanted to be. Nothing could be better than waking up in Majliv's arms. Now it was probably never going to happen again. Unexpectedly, something stabbed my chest. Will, the man I had promised eternal fidelity to, hadn't been in my thoughts all day, and my conscience burned.

ॐ৪০

I decided to visit work because they were probably wondering how I was doing. The visit did me wonders, and it gave me a new feeling of enthusiasm when everyone said they were looking forward to having me back at work. Those were good words to hear. When I got home, most of the day had passed, and it wasn't long before Will was due home. I decided to cook dinner, even though it was usually his job. He cooked, I did laundry, and we were both happy with that arrangement. When Will came home, the smell of food filled the whole house. I had set the table, and candles sparkled on the dining table. He was pleasantly surprised to have dinner ready when he got home, as he had been so busy at work that he was completely exhausted.

'Oh, you're so sweet. Did you cook, too? That's so nice,' Will smiled that smile which had made me fall for him so long ago, the smile I hadn't seen in ages.

I thought it was nice to do something for him too, since he had been so exceptional towards me when I was sick. It was the least I could do in return.

'It was my turn to do something nice for you,' I smiled back. Deep down, a little voice said that I was doing it out of guilt, but I shook it off pretending that I could snap the voice of conscience in half.

We had a really romantic evening. It felt good to sit close to Will, and he stroked my cheek, looked deep into my eyes and kissed me gently. For once, we sat and talked all evening like a newly in-love couple. We talked about things we hadn't talked about in a long time, completely insignificant, easy things. I felt so loved. Although, when I lay in Will's arms at night, I thought again of the arms I had slept in the last few nights. Then I fell asleep, once again with Majliv in my thoughts.

The next morning, I was woken extra early by the alarm. It was a reminder that I was supposed to start using nasal spray, which I had to take four times a day.

'Ugh. Am I going to voluntarily do this four times a day for four weeks?! I can barely wait for the effect,' I said sarcastically to myself. It said in the hospital papers that while I was on these hormones, I would go through a false menopause and might notice mood swings, sensitivity, and hot flashes. Fortunately, Will understood this, and he probably thought he could endure it anyway. All these medications made me think about how much I missed having a child. If I could just have one child, just one, it would be enough. Was it really too much to ask for? Had I done so much wrong in life that I didn't deserve a family?

CRSO

In the late morning, Batist, Mirini, and the others also arrived. This caused Siljan to stress more than ever. Everything he had done in preparation the day before was well received by Mirini, who had nothing to complain about, no matter what Siljan might think. We ate and packed the wagon. It was a pure moving load. Siljan, Mirini, Batist, and the kids sat in the wagon pulled by Siljan's big mare and Batist's old gelding. The black horse followed and would take over if one of the other horses got tired. Kian and Lynn rode on their own horses, and I, who didn't have my own, had to ride

Pronto with Majliv. We saw the farm grow smaller behind us. The old horses kept a steady pace, so it was bumpy and slow. It was nice to be back on horseback again, but if I was completely honest, it was probably the rider that pleased me more than the horse. Majliv seemed to be in a slightly better mood than usual. Not that he smiled, but at least he wasn't angry. Pronto was solid and well behaved as usual. Only the small, vibrating movements betrayed that we were moving. The landscape was enchantingly beautiful. One postcard-worthy view after another enchanted me. The branches on the trees in the forest around us intertwined around the trunks like embraces. I could never remember seeing trees grow like that before. It didn't take long before evening crept up and it got dark. We found a campsite and lit a fire. Mirini's small tent resembled a tipi and had just enough room for her and the children.

When the campsite was ready everyone gathered around the fire and drank currant and honey mead. I sat between Batist and Lynn with Majliv sitting opposite me on the other side of the fire. I couldn't help but look at him across the flames. A couple of times, I caught him staring at me for a long time. Everyone was having fun. We laughed and chuckled while Siljan told old stories, and Batist gave us riddles to solve.

'Can you guess this one? It can't kill, but if it could, it would hurt none the less? What is it?' he said, looking around at us with a sly look.

'It could be anything, like a tomato or something,' Kian joked, and everyone laughed.

'Idiot. You could choke on a tomato and die,' Lynn couldn't resist correcting him. I pondered and thought about the icy stare Majliv had given me on the first day.

'The gaze?' I said cautiously.

'Yes, that's correct,' Batist smiled in surprise, and the others looked at me with wide eyes.

'Now, try this one! What can ruin you for the rest of your life without touching you, come into a room before you, without being seen, and make you hated by some and loved by others at the same time?' He looked slyly at me again.

'That's the dumbest thing I've ever heard. There's nothing that can ruin you without touching you!' Kian couldn't help but speak up.

'If you don't know the answer, then shut up,' Lynn snapped at him.

'Gossip,' I replied quickly.

'She got it right again. Riddles seem to suit you well,' Batist laughed.

'Batist must have told them beforehand. It's unfair. No one is that clever by nature,' joked Kian.

'No, not you at least,' said Lynn playfully.

The atmosphere around the campfire was pleasantly relaxed. The children soon went to sleep in the tent, and a little bit later Mirini, Siljan, and Batist followed suit. The men had set up a sleeping area at the back of the wagon, so it looked like they had a canopy over the entire loading area. Kian had tied a hammock between two trees and lay in it with blankets around him. He chatted with the others for a little while, but it didn't take long before he fell asleep. Lynn had made a sleeping spot on the seats in front of the wagon and snored as soon as she put her head on the hard wood. I couldn't imagine that it could be comfortable or how she could fall asleep so quickly. I sat and watched the flames in the fire.

'Aren't you tired?' Majliv asked, moving over to my side of the fire.

'There are too many thoughts swirling around in my head,' I replied.

'I know the feeling,' he nodded.

'Can I ask you something?' I whispered.

'Yes, you may. Ask away,' he said.

'What were you doing in Huldra's forest?' I tried to ask cautiously.

'I was asked to keep an eye on you,' he replied.

'Why?' I wondered why I would be sent somewhere I could be in danger.

'You were supposed to meet Nicor, and he's become so unpredictable now that Lamia has been wreaking havoc for so long. Almost no one gets lost alone in the forest anymore, so it's been a while since he's managed to trick someone into coming to him. Huldra was afraid that your song wouldn't be enough,' he answered, suddenly serious as he looked into the flames.

'What did you see when you followed me?'

'I lost sight of you when you started running. It was a bit difficult to find you again, I didn't see you until you went into the water, and I was almost too late. Why did you run?' he asked, furrowing his brow.

'Something was following me. I got scared, but it wasn't dangerous,' I replied, looking down at my finger. Where I had cut myself with the stone, there was now only a small scab left.

'What did you see?' He looked at me questioningly.

'It sounds silly now, but a horse with only three legs and...'

'Without a head?' Majliv continued, his gaze back on the flames.

'Yes! What kind of animal was it?' I could have woken everyone up with my exclamation, I was so surprised.

'Shhh... it's The Hell Horse. It comes to get people when they die and rides them to the realm of death. Almost no one has seen it, but it's not known to do any harm. What did it want from you?' Majliv was obviously curious.

'It had gotten tangled in a thorn bush, so I untangled it,' I replied.

'So... what did you get?' he asked.

'Get? How do you...'

'If you help the animals in Huldra's forest, they won't let you go empty-handed. What did you get?'

'I'm not sure, but I think maybe it has made me immune to being hurt by thorns. When I helped free it, I should have gotten many cuts, but I didn't get a single mark. I tried cutting myself with a rock to see if it would heal quickly but I still have a little scab left.' I couldn't believe how stupid that sounded when I said it out loud.

'Hmm…,' he pondered. 'Have you found your tone yet?'

'No, that became quite clear in the forest. I don't understand how I'm supposed to know which tone is the right one.' Frustrated, I threw a small stick into the flames and followed it with my eyes.

'You feel it. Just wait, when you have it, you'll understand what I mean.' He stood up and looked at me.

'Now it's probably time to call it a night.' Majliv let out a small yawn.

'Yes, that's probably a good idea.' Where was I supposed to sleep? No one had told me where to set up my sleeping spot. A small thought hoped there was room at Majliv's. He had found a large conifer tree with dry brushwood underneath, and there he had laid out the large blanket we had shared the previous time. I didn't want to suggest it and thought that if there wasn't any other place to sleep, I would sleep on the ground by the fire again. I hoped it wouldn't be as cold as the night I had almost frozen to death.

'Are you coming or what?' he said softly.

'Hmm?' Did I hear right? Was I supposed to sleep with him?

'Aren't you going to bed?' The look he gave me was a little confused.

'Yes, I'm coming,' I whispered. He leaned back and put his arms under his neck. I lay down next to him and pulled the fur up under my chin.

'How many animals is it from?' The large pelt had so many different colours and textures that it almost looked like a patchwork quilt.

'I don't know. There are constantly more being added, so it's difficult to keep track,' he replied.

'Are all these from animals you've hunted?'

'Yes, we use the skins and fur of animals we eat. No one hunts for fun. It's not right.' He turned towards me and looked at me intently.

'Good to hear,' I nodded.

'Is that one of the things that's been swirling around in your head?' he chuckled softly.

'No, but right now I'm thinking it's a little strange that we're lying under the remains of animals.' What did I say? Remains! Not exactly a very smooth pick-up line.

'I think it's time for you to get some sleep,' he said, shaking his head. Then he turned his back to me and fell asleep.

CRSO

The days in Gaia disappeared in everyday chores, and I could hardly wait between each time I was going to come back to Grimrokk. It always seemed like an eternity, and it had now become quite common for there to be a day's break between each time I woke up there. Fortunately, the IVF experiment was getting closer. I had gotten my last period before the experiment and called the hospital, just as I had been instructed. It wasn't until this had happened that I was given a doctor's appointment which would take place 13 days later. When this was sorted, I showed up at the lab to get some bloodwork done since the results were needed ahead of the doctor's appointment. I was already shaking. I couldn't stand needles. Never had. The thought of daily injections scared me. We had been given tons of information, but it was always different to experience it for yourself.

CR80

I woke up feeling warm and comfortable, lying on my side with my arm under my head. As I regained my senses, I noticed that I had something around my waist. Whatever it was, it had a firm grip on me. I opened my eyes gradually and soon realized what was holding me so tightly. Just centimetres from my face were Majliv, watching me. He stiffened a bit when I opened my eyes but didn't move away. His eyes were dark blue, they glimmered like soft stars. What should I do? Would he push me away if I moved closer, or would he come even closer? My heart was pounding intensely, and a swarm of butterflies had landed in my stomach. He smelled so good. His arm was still around me, and it showed no sign of moving. The next thing that happened was a series of automatic movements. First, my free arm moved from Majliv's stomach to his neck. Then my head suddenly moved forward. And finally, two completely uncontrollable, moist lips touched Majliv's mouth. The movement that followed was determined and very controlled. The arm that held me pushed me away firmly and took a new grip around my waist.

Chapter 9
One there and one here

Come on, guys. We can't let the day slip away from us like this.'

It was Mirini who had woken up and was busy waking everyone else by drumming on a pot. Majliv looked at me quickly, then looked away. I got up, still dazed and confused from sleep, and while gathering and organizing my things, I tried to make sense of my feelings from the night before. I didn't know if I regretted revealing my desire, nor if I was relieved that nothing more happened. As I put on my coat and ran my fingers through my hair, my conscience kicked in. Will. What had I done? I just wanted to erase this episode from history. I went over to Mirini to help her with breakfast.

'Good morning,' she said, patting me on the cheek.

'Good morning,' I sighed back.

'Is something wrong? You don't look so happy.' Mirini looked at me inquisitively.

'No. I just woke up on the wrong side of the bed, I think.'

'It'll get better throughout the day, you'll see.' She looked away for a moment. It was only when I saw who her gaze met that I understood. Mirini hadn't woken up on her own. She had heard Majliv's thoughts. But then why did he hold me every night if he didn't want this as much as I did? I wasn't the one who had taken the first step. If he had any sense at all, he would have wondered if there maybe already was someone who owned my heart. Most girls in their twenties have their own family or at least a boyfriend nowadays. He knew I was from Gaia. Couldn't he have thought about that? I looked at Majliv, then at Mirini. She furrowed her brows and breathed heavily, then turned and went over to the fire with a pot. There was nothing in front of me, but I couldn't move my gaze back to him. I could catch a glimpse of his eyes from the corner of my eye. He looked towards me.

I hadn't said a word during breakfast and wasn't particularly talkative when Lynn came and sat next to me.

'Not in the mood?'

'No.' There was no point in adding anything else.

'He's not easy to deal with,' she said.

'Who?'

'Majliv,' she said, turning her head towards me. The look I got was thoughtful and understanding.

'More people have listened to his thoughts, I gather,' I couldn't believe she was aware of what I had done. It made everything so much more real, and I thought I could just put it behind me.

'It's not something I can help. It's like he talks right to me. Just like you can't help but look at something that's right in front of your eyes when they're open.'

'I would have closed them then!' I stood up and walked over to Batist who was loading our gear onto the wagon. There was nothing more to say. When everything was packed and ready, it was time to leave.

140

Sitting on the horse with Majliv now was not very tempting, but I also didn't want anyone else to find out what had happened. There would definitely be a lot of questions and whispering if I changed seats. Pronto stood a little more than an arm's length from me when Majliv mounted. I took a deep breath and glanced at him. For all I knew, maybe he didn't want me riding with him anymore? The look he gave me was questionable, but still serious. He probably also wanted us to forget what had happened. He held out his hand. I stood still for a moment, then took hold of it, and he pulled me up with both hands, so I felt like I weighed no more than a small child. As usual, we did not exchange a word, but something felt different this time around. He was not as cold as he used to be. At one point, we let Pronto run loose and rode up a steep slope, and he surprised me by putting his arm around my waist holding me tight. We had ridden up many slopes before, but he had never done that. When evening came, we stayed at an inn called The Mad Raven. The inn was a small, coal-grey hut made of grey stone and black roof tiles. Inside the door was a small foyer with a bar that served as a reception, where a small, old man greeted us. All the women were to share one room and the men another. The rooms were on the floor above and were tiny, with four hard wooden beds. Next to one of the walls there was a small iron furnace which ensured a warm and comfortable feeling in the room.

Before heading down to dinner, we all washed off the road in our rooms. In the dining room we all sat together in a big group. Everyone enjoyed themselves and it felt like we were a big happy family. My mood lifted.

'Sorry about earlier,' I said to Lynn as I sat down beside her.

'No need to apologize. Private things should stay private, I fully understand,' she whispered and playfully nudged me.

'Can we just forget the whole thing now? Like it never happened?' I asked.

'Of course. But Mia... don't think he doesn't like you. He does,' she whispered in my ear.

'He has a strange way of showing it.'

'Majliv has never had any romantic relationships here, ever.'

I couldn't imagine that was true. I couldn't be the only one who had a stroke of the butterflies when I saw him.

'What do you mean - here?' Had I missed something?

'He's a grimmer just like you. Hasn't anyone told you?' Lynn looked surprised. How could someone not tell me?

'No wonder he seems so grumpy all the time, he doesn't want to be here either.'

'Don't you like it here, Mia? You seemed so happy yesterday.' She seemed a little bit hurt.

'I do, but it's not easy. My head is filled with problems in Gaia, and now I have some here too.' It was typical of my bad luck. I was swamped with the worst possible things no matter where I ended up.

'Don't get yourself down, Mia. Just wait until the day after tomorrow. Then we will be at the Frost Festival, and it is really nice! You should really look forward to it,' Lynn put her arm around my shoulders and gave my arm a squeeze.

She kept me company during dinner and chatted so much that it would have made her father proud if he had paid attention. But no matter how hard I tried to follow the conversations around the table, I couldn't get Majliv out of my mind. I looked in his direction most of the evening and met his gaze almost every time. My cheeks flushed red, and my heart pounded. I was almost swallowed up by the shining eyes that read every move I made.

The food was consumed, and everyone retired to their rooms to sleep.

'By the way, Mia. Are you going to compete?' Lynn shouted over from her bed.

'Yes, according to Mirini, I am,' I laughed and turned towards her.

'That's fun. In what?' She was clearly curious by nature.

'You'll have to wait and see. I haven't quite decided yet.' The answer seemed satisfactory enough.

'This could be exciting,' Lynn smiled at me.

We were going to leave early in the morning. There was a knock on the door to the girls' room.

'Ladies, it's morning,' Batist's grandfather voice rumbled behind the door.

'Thanks, Batist,' Mirini replied with a creaking voice and slowly sat up in bed and smoothed her hair back. Lynn groaned from the bed she was lying in, and when she tried to sit up and swing her legs over the edge of the bed, her upper body wouldn't budge. She remained lying in bed with her legs dangling over the bedside. I brushed my hair with a brush I had borrowed from Mirini. I still wasn't used to having long hair, it was so difficult to take care of.

Everyone had finally checked out of the inn with everything that needed to be loaded onto wagons and horses. Majliv tightened some of Pronto's straps before helping me up. He walked around the horse and double-checked that everything was in place, and that nothing had been forgotten. Kian helped Batist readying the horses, while Theodor and Nette sat half asleep on the wagon seat. Mirini and Lynn said goodbye to the innkeeper and thanked him for the food and a pleasant stay.

Lynn was heading down the stairs when she got hit by a gust of wind. The day was calm without as much as a breeze, so this seemed a bit strange. Before the wind reached us, Lynn called out, 'Majliv, you're needed!' The wind tumbled around Majliv for longer than it should have, as if he was listening for something. I tried it myself and could swear I heard some foreign words whispered in the gusts of wind. When the wind died down, he quickly threw himself onto the horse and grabbed the reins.

'I have to go. Don't wait for us, we'll meet you at Rim Gorge as soon as we can.' The shocked expression on my face must have said it all, as Lynn gave me a reassuring smile and a wink. Pronto set off at maximum speed from the first leap he took off into the forest.

'What's going on?' I shouted to him.

'I got an urgent job from Huldra.'

'What is the job about?' Scare the life out of me, I thought to myself.

'A giant eagle is seriously injured at the Knight's Leap. It is important that we take care of them because there are no more than three pairs left in all of Grimrokk. If this female dies before it can produce offspring, there is no hope for the species.'

'That wasn't many for a species,' I said.

'They can't mate with family members, and that's the problem. The remaining pairs are too closely related to reproduce without this female.' His gaze sparkled. I was fascinated to see him show so much concern. I had always thought he was unusually self-absorbed, but now his true personality was showing through. A truly caring man.

We rode so quickly through the forest that I was afraid I would be hit by branches or worse fall off. This time he held the reins with both hands, with me squeezed between his arms. We rode for a couple of hours before the ground beneath us began to rise. I was amazed that the big horse could climb the steep slope, but maybe it's not so difficult when you have eight legs.

'We're almost there,' he said as the slope began to even out.

The surroundings were magical, with large trees toppled by the wind. The roots spread out in all directions and looked like scary monsters I had read about in fairy tales as a child. From what little I could see; the sky was no longer blue. The clouds formed a steady layer of grey above us, hinting about a possible snowfall. It would be just my luck if bad weather were to come when we were sleeping outside - not to mention that there was already enough snow.

Majliv pulled the reins and we stopped. He got off the horse and helped me down. We had stopped at a knoll, and all I could see over it was the sky. Majliv walked over the small embankment, and I followed. There was a large plateau in the mountain which abruptly turned into a free fall of maybe a couple of hundred meters. The plateau was surrounded by mountain walls on both sides, and behind us, there was only forest.

'We'll stay here tonight. There's plenty of firewood around in the woods for a fire, so if you ...'

'Just do what you came here for, and I'll take care of the rest,' I interrupted.

'Then you'll stay here.' He didn't say anything more, just took one of his leather bags and climbed up the mountain. When he reached the top, he looked back for a moment before he disappeared. So that was where the giant eagle was. I began to speculate on how big it really was, and my curiosity grew. If I crept up without him noticing, it couldn't hurt to just take a little peek. I grabbed hold of a crack in the rock with one hand and started climbing. It wasn't very high, but I would undoubtedly have killed myself if I were to fall down. When I reached the top, I had to step in Majliv's footprints in order to not give myself away. The footprints led me to a thicket with a small path through it. A muttering sound made me stop. It was as if the air around me was vibrating, and I could feel the hairs on my neck rise. In front of me, through the bushes, I caught glimpses of movement. I pushed aside some branches on a thorn bush right next to me and was so surprised by what I saw that I froze. At first, I was scared, but then the fear turned to wonder. It was the biggest animal I had ever seen. The eagle, standing on a crag far away, was at least double the height of Majliv. If it were a plane, it would have been a twelve-passenger aircraft!

Majliv was standing a little way off with his hands outstretched and palms facing the eagle. It stamped its feet and shook its head. Suddenly, it let out a heart-wrenching cry and I took a step back. I looked out through the branches again and saw the big tear in one of the eagle's wings. It seemed stressed and nervous. Majliv seemed unaffected by its size but respected it enough to keep his distance. I don't know what he did, but suddenly there were glowing waves of heat coming from his hands. The animal immediately calmed down and lay down on its stomach. The light in Majliv's hands disappeared and he calmly went over to the eagle and put his bag down next to him. The animal did not make a single move while Majliv inspected the open wound. What had he done? I remembered that Batist had told me that everyone in Grimrokk had an ability, but I had never found out what Majliv's ability was. It didn't look like any of the abilities I had seen so far.

It seemed like he was finishing up, and I, who was supposed to be collecting firewood, hadn't picked up a single twig. I hurried back to the campsite as fast as I could, while remembering to hide my tracks. Pronto was standing at the site, eating from a pine tree and didn't care that I was rushing towards him. Fortunately, there was a dead fir tree nearby and I jumped through the snow to grab as many branches as I could. When my hands were full, I headed back towards the site. I had barely put down the wood when Majliv climbed down from the mountain.

'Is that all you found?' he said with a furrowed brow.

'There's more, but I had to go to the bathroom. Should I get more now?' I lied. No shame whatsoever.

'I can get it later,' he said, throwing down his backpack.

'How did it go?' From what I had seen, the animal seemed to be okay, but it would have been suspicious if I didn't ask.

'It will survive. But it was badly injured. Its wing was broken, and it had a nasty wound.'

'That's good...that it will survive, I mean,' I stuttered.

The fire was lit, and Majliv had made a shelter. We ate a pigeon Majliv was lucky enough to catch while gathering firewood and watched as the snow fell.

'Lynn said that you're a grimmer too. Have you been here long?' I asked cautiously.

'Since I was seven,' he said, looking thoughtfully at the fire.

'Do you have an ability?'

'Everyone here has an ability.' That wasn't a good enough answer for me.

'What ability do you have?'

'I have the same ability as all the grange wardens have. I gather energy from my surroundings,' he said. It seemed like he didn't want to talk about it, but I was even more curious now.

'How so?'

'Is this an interrogation?!,' he said, a little irritated.

'Sorry but it seems like you know everything about me, while I don't know much about you. You're not exactly the most talkative person in the world,' I snapped back.

He went quiet and obviously had nothing to add. It would have been so nice to be with the others who were probably sitting and chatting and having fun. They had Lynn and Kian as entertainment, at least it was something. I sat here bored with a person I couldn't figure out. It was starting to get darker, and finally, the snow stopped. The view became clearer around us. 'Come,' said Majliv, standing up.

What are we doing?'

'Just come,' he repeated and walked towards the cliff.

'I'm coming,' I said, trailing behind. He stopped a distance from the edge and turned to see if I was coming. The snow was so deep it felt like walking in quicksand. I stopped next to him and gasped for breath.

'Do you see that?' he said, pointing to a small cluster of faint lights. It was quite far away, but when I focused better, I saw that it was a small town. The houses were tiny.

'What is it?' I asked.

'Rim Gorge. We're going there tomorrow.'

'It's so small.'

'It only looks that way because it's far away. It's actually quite large,' he explained. He explained where the different places were and where the roads led.

'Myrthing's castle is far behind the Rim Gorge and up towards the mountain. You can't see the castle from here, but now you have an idea of where it is. He doesn't live there anymore. He moved when his son died, and now no one knows where he is,' he explained. I thought about where I had heard about Myrthing's castle before and suddenly remembered that it was Nicor who had mentioned the place. Myrthing's family graveyard was supposed to be by his castle.

'That's where she is! Lamia! Nicor said she was at Myrthing's family cemetery,' I said.

'What?' he exclaimed, shocked. This was clearly news to Majliv.

'Yes. He said something about her sitting there and gnawing on bones.'

Majliv had a blank look in his eyes as he stared into the air in the general direction of the castle.

'If the plan is for me to 'take' her, then I need to get there,' I said, making air quotes.

'How do you know she's still there? It's been many days since you spoke with Nicor.'

'I don't, but it's the only place I can start. I don't even have an idea of what she looks like.' I was certainly not ready to meet her, but it seemed like that was the plan anyway.

'You can't go there until after the festival. You don't know the way to the cemetery, and you can't go alone. Mirini and Batist wouldn't allow it. Neither would Huldra,' he said.

'I'm not a little child who needs a babysitter. They watch over me all the time.' I felt like someone was trying to strangle me.

'No, maybe not, but it would have gone straight to hell if a certain person hadn't pulled you out of the water when you were trying to talk to Nicor.' He seemed irritated.

'Haven't I said thank you? If you weren't so damn grumpy when I tried to show my gratitude, I might have put a little more effort into it.' I heard my voice rise and blood rushed to my cheeks.

'For all we know, Lamia could show up at the festival,' he said, avoiding further comment on my statement. I took a few steps closer to him, staring him straight in the eyes. His gaze was evasive.

'What is wrong with you? I'm trying to understand you, but it's impossible. Whatever I do, it's wrong. Even thanking you for saving my life is wrong. What did you want me to do? Wasn't my reaction good enough? Should I have gotten on my knees and worshiped you? Kissed the ground you walk on?' I was so angry that I was shaking. He couldn't mean that his behaviour in the kitchen on the first day had been polite.

'That's not what it's about,' he said. Now he too was angry and met my gaze with his own.

'What is it, then? When I'm asleep, you stroke my back and hold me. But as soon as I wake up, you let go. When I try to kiss you, you scream for help.'

'I didn't scream for help!' he burst out in anger.

'It's all the same when the person you're trying to communicate with is a mind-reader'.

'I didn't scream for help,' he said, then turned his back on me and walked to the shelter.

'What was it, then?' I didn't understand anything. It took a while before he answered.

'You...tempt me,' he finally replied.

I stood there staring into space, completely stunned and unable to respond. Majliv lay down with his back to me, all the way inside the shelter. I tempted him. In what way? And if it was in the way I had wanted to tempt him, why hadn't he taken the initiative? I had shown that I wanted him. My thoughts were racing in my head. I remembered clearly when Mirini had awakened us, and he had pushed me away. And the first time he smiled at me. Then I saw him in my mind under the small waterfall at the hot springs. He had taken my breath away. I wasn't used to such drama. Will had never been difficult in that way. My stomach tightened. What was I doing? This was cheating, even if Will wasn't in Grimrokk. My heart belonged to him and no one else, I had promised him that. I sat in the shelter and warmed my hands by the fire. No matter how much I tried to persuade myself to feel what was right, I couldn't get Majliv out of my thoughts. Tears rolled down my cheek and made a cold streak down to my chin. I lay down with my back to Majliv and watched the dancing flames play around the charred branches. Finally, I closed my eyes and couldn't get out of Grimrokk fast enough.

∞

'Hi, my name is Dr. Anne Lande. You can come with me here,' the doctor said and showed us into an examination room. She flipped through a stack of papers with tables and charts.

'We'll do an internal ultrasound of your uterus and ovaries today to see how they're doing,' Dr. Lande said, pointing to a gynaecological chair in the corner. This department seemed to operate on an assembly line. It wasn't really surprising, since they didn't do anything else every day of the week. The women came in like broody hens, and everyone hoped the rooster would manage to turn the yolks into chicks.

According to the doctor's observations, everything looked good, and I received new instructions on when to start with the injections and precise times for when they should be administered. The doctor scheduled a new appointment three days later to see how the eggs were developing and how many were maturing.

Will and I left the examination full of hope. This had to work. I already dreaded the evening when I was going to take the first hormone injection. The needles were tiny and were supposed to be injected right under the skin of the abdomen. I feared I would pass out, but when the time came, I gritted my teeth and gave myself the injection without flinching.

ജ

The sound of a heartbeat was all I heard when I woke up. A warm body was breathing deeply close to my ear. I opened my eyes. The white linen shirt over the chest was almost completely open, so my palm lay flat against the smooth skin. This time he didn't stroke me but embraced me with both arms. My breath caught and it increased rapidly. He couldn't avoid noticing that I was awake, but he held me close. I took a deep breath, then I ran my hand from his stomach and slowly up the great muscles.

My fingertips glided over his chest muscles and gently up to his neck hollow. Then I turned very carefully and let my lips move along the collarbone towards his neck. From experience, I expected him to let me go at any moment, but he didn't. Instead, he held on to me tightly while his breathing increased in sync with mine. I stroked my hand down his stomach again and stopped at the belt, waiting for a reaction, but he did nothing. Was he allowing me to do this? Was he going to give in? I tested it by letting my fingertips lightly glide along his skin along the waistband. His breathing became uneven. I moved my lips in soft kisses along his neck up to the edge between the earlobe and the jaw. My lips parted for a moment. The tongue touched his skin for only a moment, and he breathed a little harder while pulling me a little closer. I let my lips slide along his jaw towards his chin, where I stopped and met his gaze. His eyes were smouldering as they moved from my eyes to my lips and back to my eyes. He moistened his lips slightly, as if to ask me to kiss them. His mouth was so close to mine that he barely brushed against my upper lip with his wet tongue. My breath trembled in my chest as I, as slowly as I could, touched his lips with mine. He took a firmer hold of my waist as he responded to the kiss. His lips felt soft and gentle against mine, as if they were familiar. My fingers were at his waistband, and I searched for the belt buckle, then loosened it. One of his hands had found its way under my shirt and stroked skin against skin over my lower back. My fingers found the lacing on his pants and loosened it. But then he froze. His head made small movements from side to side, as if he was struggling to decide whether to continue kissing me or turn away.

'No ... don't ... stop!' he exclaimed and pushed me away in a quick movement.

I sat up, and before I could think, I opened my mouth and shouted out of anger and frustration. 'What!' The sound that burst out of me was not like any sound I had heard before. It radiated out like a sharp and piercing wind and struck out in all directions. Majliv, who was still halfway beside me, was knocked to the ground with a thud. Then everything was quiet. I had found it. Somewhat shocked, I sat and stared at Majliv. His face was as shocked as mine, but then the colour began to turn more and more red. He suddenly stood up with one hand on his belt. It was not difficult to see that he was furious. The excitement I had just felt had turned into irritation, and the way he reacted made me angrier by the second. He stomped through the snow, but suddenly he stopped. It was clear that it was difficult for him to calm down. Meanwhile, I had never had so many emotions swirling around inside me - ever. A mix of desire, anger, and regret. And on top of that, a pretty big shock. Majliv turned towards me with furrowed brows.

'Do you know how angry you have to be to be able to find that specific pitch, when you've never been able to do it before?'

No,' I answered as calmly as the adrenaline in my body allowed me to.

'Hate ... disgust ... murderous desire ... anger ... should I continue?' His voice was shaking.

'Is it so strange that I react this way? You say one thing and do the opposite. Talk about sending confusing signals!'

'Think, Mia! I'm a grimmer, just like you!' That meant nothing to me. Couldn't he just spit it out?

'And so what?' My legs were shaking, and I could barely keep my balance.

'Do you have anyone in Gaia, Mia?' he almost shouted before I could finish speaking.

'YES. Yes, I do. So, this isn't as simple as you think.' As I said the words, it dawned on me more and more. He also had someone in Gaia. He felt exactly the way I did.

156

Chapter 10
A romantic walk in the city

I stared into empty space, and Majliv remained still, however, in an indeterminate way, the silence around us was not quiet in the way I had expected. A strange hum, a multi-toned, false wind made sounds around us. My body felt weird, and I felt that the calm was different from just a moment ago. Pronto began to stamp his hooves restlessly. I looked at Majliv questioningly. Suddenly, he appeared terrifyingly focused on something, but he did not look directly at me. Instead, his gaze was fixed on something behind me.

The humming grew stronger, like white noise, and it came from the forest. I turned slowly around backing closer to Majliv.

'What is it?' I whispered.

'I'm not sure, but there are no animals in this forest that make such sounds.'

'That doesn't sound very promising. Can't you make a guess?' I asked anxiously.

'If I'm right, you won't have to go to the cemetery. It has just come to you,' he said grimly.

Before I could say anything, a figure appeared in the opening of our shelter. At first glance, it looked like a colossal snake that stretched its body up from the

157

ground to intimidate, but then the upper part of the body was a naked woman. From the breasts down, the naked, olive-toned body merged into the snake-like body which coiled like the letter S. The head had big, curly hair, and the eyes were yellow with oval pupils, just like a regular snake. The teeth were long and sharp, and the canines curved into the large mouth. The tongue was split at the tip and vibrated rapidly up and down as if she was tasting the air around her.

'Lamia!' shouted Majliv, jumping backward as she lunged at him. He quickly stood up in front of me, then stood firmly with his legs apart and raised his right arm high in the air as if he was grabbing something and pulling it down.

'On the ground, Mia,' he yelled at me.

I did as he said without fuss. I looked at him in surprise and thought I saw a powerful stick made of glass in his hand, but the next moment, there was no stick to be seen. He stretched his arm back to gain momentum, then swung his arm forward in a quick motion, and something slammed so hard into the ground that there were shockwaves in the snow around us. Lamia was thrown back by the pressure, and she fell to the ground. But she stood up again, angrier than before, and lifted her whole body with her tail so that she stood face to face with Majliv.

I was still on the ground behind him. Lamia tried to attack him from the side, but he moved, lifted his arm, took another swing, and threw the stick into the ground so that snow and gravel flew everywhere. She tried to circle around him, and she tried to attack me, but I ran away from her and behind some bushes. Lamia shot herself forward at Majliv, but he beat her with the stick over her face, causing her to fall to the side.

'What should I do?' I shouted at him.

'Throw the pelt on the horse and get on,' he shouted back. I ran to the shelter and grabbed the pelt and everything I could in one sweep and threw it over Pronto's back. But I couldn't just stand there and watch Lamia attack Majliv. I looked around and saw a thorn vine that had grown up a tree trunk and grabbed it. The deep snow made it difficult to keep my balance, and I stumbled in my backpack. Something fell out of it and landed on my foot. Majliv came closer and closer to the mountainside as he struck at Lamia as hard as he could. Her agile body got away. At the same time, she managed to whip Majliv along the side with her hindquarters, causing him to fall and hit his chin on a stone, splitting his lip. At my feet lay a small bottle. It was the one that had fallen out of the backpack, the elixir I had received from Batist, the one I could use if I had to get away or hide in a hurry. Courage grew in me, and with the thorn vine in hand, I ran towards Lamia, who didn't see me coming, and whipped the vine with all my might so that one of her arms got a huge gash. Lamia let out a deafening scream, and I whipped again so that blood flowed from her skin. This time, I cut her so deeply in the throat that she fell to the side. With the thorn vine in hand, I ran to Majliv. 'Come on!' I shouted. He stood up. We ran to the horse, and I was almost thrown up on it, before Majliv mounted. I threw the bottle with the elixir backwards as hard as I could, and it formed a smog that almost engulfed us before we managed to get into the forest. Fortunately, it was enough for Lamia to lose us, but to be sure, we rode down the mountain as far as Pronto could handle. He galloped down the slope and didn't slow down until we had gotten far enough away. I couldn't see or hear anything suspicious nearby.

We arrived at snow-covered, flat ground near a frozen stream and stopped there to catch our breath. Majliv was so upset that he was shaking, but he didn't say anything, he just got off Pronto and jogged towards the stream. He lifted his right arm, grabbed something in the air, pulled his arm back, and took off. The stick was hit so hard into the ice that the water splashed around him. I got off the horse, and it staggered tiredly towards the hole in the stream and began drinking.

Majliv sat down and cleaned his face of blood. I followed him and stopped at the water's edge without saying a word. He turned around and looked up at me, but didn't lift his head completely, so he quickly turned back and rubbed the cold water on his face. Pronto drank until he was satisfied and chewed on a branch from a tree nearby. I sat down in the snow, still holding onto the thorny vine, and couldn't care less about getting wet. Majliv stood up and stared at me with a hard gaze.

'So, you can use your voice against me, but when Lamia tries to kill you, nothing happens!'

I didn't answer. My pulse was drumming in my ears and the adrenaline was almost at its peak.

'Tell me something! Who do you hate the most? Me or Lamia?' he yelled spit coming out of his mouth.

I turned around so I didn't have to look at him. 'YOU!' I screamed at the top of my lungs. And there was the pitch again, clearer and sharper than last time, and it reverberated in all directions, blowing the snow up into a huge cloud. Luckily, the biggest pressure was directed towards the stream and the snow around it, so Majliv and Pronto were only pushed back a little where they stood. I couldn't bring myself to turn my head back. It was clearly a lie. I didn't hate him at all, but there was nothing I wanted more than to hurt him as he had hurt me. He took a few steps away from me and remained silent. Guilt struck me, and I wished I could turn back time so my voice could shout Lamia's name instead of his.

'Good to see your true self. Now the temptation is gone,' he said. It felt as if he stabbed my heart. The conversation we had before Lamia had surprised us, began to come back to me. He had someone in Gaia, just like me. I had tempted him! If that had really been the case, it was clear now that this was no longer the case. I had blown my chance. Majliv stood completely still for a long time before he whistled for the horse. He took a firm grip on the reins and stood with his back to me.

'If you're not planning to walk to the festival, you'd better get up right now!' I had no idea how to answer him. My feet began to move as if obeying an order, but before I got as far as the horse, I stopped, perplexed as to how I was going to get up on the massive animal.

There was nothing indicating assistance from the dismissive male figure holding the reins. He had become such a massive support for me that it was now clear how he could venture fearlessly into these darkest forests without the fear of becoming the prey of a wolf.

Inside me, I could feel the adrenaline pumping around my body. With a deep breath, I wrapped the thorn vine around my arm, aimed, and ran towards the horse, trying to calculate the distance from where I was to where Majliv stood, and where I had to get on the horse. Fortunately, he was so close that when I jumped up to grab the horse's mane, I put one of my feet in the hook of Majliv's foot, and then kicked off.

If it weren't for the temperament that raged inside me at this moment, this overconfident act would never have been possible, but as a small reward, Majliv almost lost his balance since he was completely unprepared for my action and had to support himself. But before I could let out the devilish laughter that bubbled in my chest, he had already regained his footing.

I placed myself as far away from Majliv on the horse as possible. If I had known the way to the Rim Gorge, I would have considered walking, but I really had no choice. Majliv sat behind me and did everything he could not to touch me with so much as a hair from his pelt. The horse took off at full speed, the snow whirling around its hooves. Whether the air was cold or not, I didn't care at all. The aggression inside me warmed me up until we reached the plain outside the city, where I saw the Rim Gorge in front of us with relief. Little could have pleased me more at that moment than to get away from the grumpy beast who had been my forced companion for so long.

Pronto slowed down as we rode through the large city gate. It was well past midday, and the light in the sky was disappearing more and more. The streets were now lit with torches and lanterns. The city was larger than I had imagined, yet still intimate. It had narrow streets decorated with banners, lights, and posters on every corner, and all the small houses were made of grey stone. They had thatched roofs and tiny windows with cross braces. The streets were paved with cobblestones, and attempts had been made to shovel the snow away. It was bustling with people of all sizes and shapes who were talking, shouting, and laughing.

Regardless of how charming the city might be, I wasn't in the mood to look around. I just wanted to get off the big horse. It would be great if I could get away from the big 'baby' sitting behind me. I actually wouldn't have minded never seeing him again. Just that 'never' would have been too early. He was impossible to understand, and I felt like I had done my part. Why did I have to be the only one to take the initiative to get to know him? He didn't care one bit.

We stopped outside a small inn. Kian and Lynn were standing outside having yet another spirited discussion, but I wasn't interested. I jumped off the horse before Majliv could give me the usual hand. The jolt I felt when my feet hit the ground hurt so much that it shot up my legs, but I did not want to show weakness. No one was going to see that I was affected by the pain.

Lynn and Kian stood completely still and looked at each other confused. I ignored them completely, as if to emphasize that I was angry, and my breath came out mixed with growling noises.

'What's the....,' Lynn stopped mid-sentence and looked at me as I sent her a sharp look and thought, 'This is none of your business!' Lynn turned with a puzzled look to Majliv, who, judging by her expression, had given her the same clear 'instruction.' What was going on in his mind was the least of my concerns at the moment. I just wanted to get away from this place. It felt like ages since I had been at home with Will and Tinka. I took a deep breath and walked through the inn's door without looking back. Behind me, I could hear Lynn's desperate voice.

'What have you done?' There was no answer, and before I had reached the dining hall to look for Mirini, I heard the door open behind me. In my peripheral vision, I caught a glimpse of a fur that gave me more than enough answer as to who it was.

'In some way, I'm sure this is your fault,' I could hear Lynn say angrily from outside, and I realized she was blaming her brother for everything.

'What have I done now?' was all Kian could muster in his defence. Mirini sat at a table with Batist and Siljan, both of whom had a full and leisurely expression on their faces. With each step I took into the room, I could hear Majliv's heavy footsteps behind me. I stopped at Mirini's chair and leaned down a bit towards her.

'Do I have a room?'

164

'Yes, of course,' she replied, looking at me questioningly.

'I don't want to talk about it,' I thought, and Mirini understood the hint. She fumbled around in her pocket and pulled out a key.

'You'll be sharing a room with Lynn' she said as she handed it to me. Before letting go, she grabbed my arm firmly and didn't release it until our eyes met. She gave me a worried look full of concern, but that wasn't what I needed right now. I needed some time alone.

The crooked smile I forced out was far from honest. Even a blind person would be able to see through it. Then I went up the stairs and found the room where I would spend the next week. I couldn't close the door fast enough, so it slammed angrily as I closed it. For the first time in a long time, I was completely alone.

The small room was dimly lit, only illuminated by a small flame from an oil lamp. I turned up the flame, so the room became more visible. Two beds were placed next to each other, and the closest one seemed to be occupied by a pile of clothes. The other one was empty and was probably mine. I sat on the edge of the bed.

Then I suddenly heard a door slam from the hallway, and I was sure it was the moody idiot and that he was still angry. I lowered my head and noticed a couple of reddish-brown stains on my shirt. They were Majliv's blood. I sat there and stared at the stains. My hands were without a scratch, and the scab from the old cut had finally fallen off.

My thoughts were buzzing like bees around a hive. No matter how much I tried, I couldn't suppress the images from the morning. The feelings I had felt flowing through my body, and every picture of us where I lay in his arms, sent small shockwaves through me. I tried to shake them out of my head, but it was as if they were burned into my retinas.

It was the following images I would have done anything to bury. My chest ached. What I had done and said was so far from what I really meant. The voice hadn't come out because I hated Majliv, but because I was desperate and confused. The facade I had put up was just that, a facade. The rejection was so painful.

The adrenaline still swam in my blood, pumping with anger towards both Majliv and Lamia. How long had Lamia been lurking around us, and why didn't Majliv want me if I was so tempting? I leaned back in bed. My eyes stung making tears run down my cheeks. I closed my eyelids while longing for sleep to embrace me so I could escape Grimrokk.

☙❧

When I woke up, it was a relief to be home. I took a deep breath and felt free. But the feeling of freedom didn't last long because Will was lying next to me, sleeping. He looked peaceful where he lay. What would he have said if he had known what I had done? Would he have succumbed to temptation if he had been in my shoes?

My conscience burned in my stomach. He was unaware of my actions. He didn't know what had happened between his own wife and a wild stranger. I

166

couldn't help blushing a little as I replayed the scenes in my head.

Later that day, Will suggested we'd go shopping after the check-up we were soon to have at the hospital. My thoughts had been swirling around in my head, from one topic to another. For once, I had forgotten about the fertility treatment. I felt a stabbing sensation in my stomach and all my worries came back. Suddenly, everything else seemed insignificant.

'Babe? If you don't want to, we can do something else,' Will looked at me with a puzzled expression.

'Hmm? Yes, of course. I just started to feel a bit anxious,' I answered as honestly as I could. I was like most girls. I loved burying my sorrows in shopping.

We sat down and made a small list of things we could do to fill our day. Since we both had a rare day off from work at the same time, we also decided to treat ourselves to a nice dinner. Another facade was put up - that of a happy, carefree couple more in love than ever before.

I didn't particularly appreciate the side effects of the hormones. Hot flashes were lining up and extinguishing my body heat as fast as it happened in Grimrokk when summer arrived, or so I had heard. But Will had thankfully told a couple of friends that he didn't think I was all that bad these days, and that he had imagined it would be worse. I thought it was kind of him to say so, because I knew I hadn't been the easiest to deal with.

The guilt weighed on me, not just because of what I had done with Majliv, but because I felt that the only reason we couldn't have children was that there was something wrong with me. That it was my fault. I had a disease, not Will. He could have become a father a long time ago if he had been with someone else. When I mentioned this to him once, he became angry and said that we were a unity and that this was something I was not allowed to let spin around in my head. He had chosen me, and I him, and that was just how it was. I understood what he meant, but still, the thoughts were there gnawing at me.

After the examination on the first of December, we went into town and started our Christmas shopping. What I had thought would be a relief turned out to be more of a hassle than a pleasure. The stores were so crowded that it was impossible to get any help, and the lines at the cash registers were long. Nothing about the shopping gave me any satisfaction. My stomach was sore and swollen from the hormones, which meant that with every step I took, there was a stabbing pain in my lower abdomen.

After a couple of gifts, both Will and I had had enough of the stores, so we went to a restaurant where an acquaintance of Will's worked. The premises were beautiful and intimate, and the food was exquisite.

'Are you excited?' I asked Will during dinner.

'Of course. I have no higher wish than for this to go well. It would be an incredible Christmas present,' he said, his eyes shining with stars. He was so beautiful when he expressed his hope that this would go well. I couldn't be as positive. The impending defeat. I didn't dare allow myself to be so lucky.

'Yes. You're right. But it's important not to have too high expectations,' I switched to a slightly more serious expression.

'We'll take things as they come, I think. Then it'll probably be all right.' Will tried to smile so that the conversation wouldn't become so gloomy.

☾☽

The first day of the Frost Festival had arrived, and people were flocking to the square. I had gone back to my room after Lynn and I had something a Siljan heir rarely had, a quiet breakfast. Lynn hadn't asked a single question, but in the absence of conversation, she had instead specified the ingredients in the omelette we had for breakfast. I had decided to start this day with a clean slate, and everything that had happened on the journey here was to be left behind.

Lynn was brushing her hair when there was a knock on the door. She opened it.

'Hey, what is it?' she said indifferently. 'Mia, he wants to talk to you.' Lynn walked away from the doorway with a questioning look at me.

Who could 'he' be? What if it was Majliv? I had no idea what to say. Was he going to apologize? Should I apologize to him too? I got up from the chair by the bed and went to the door.

'Hey,' it was Kian who was standing there, smiling slightly.

'Hey. What are you doing here?' I said, surprised by the visit. Kian and I hadn't really talked much before, probably because Lynn did most of the talking when we were together.

'I thought maybe you'd like to come to the square and see what's happening. If it's convenient of course,' he said, not wanting to bother me.

I had actually wanted to see the city for a long time, and there was no point in sitting inside a small room and looking out.

'Yes, please, that sounds nice. Just let me freshen up, and I'll be down,' I smiled back.

We met at the entrance to the inn. Kian held out his arm for me to hold onto, which I did. The streets were decorated with Christmas garlands and red ribbons, and we walked through the town as Kian told me who lived where and where the different sights were. All the houses were decorated and had glittering lights in the windows.

We arrived at the square where there was music and games of all kinds. Along the houses, which formed a large, square space between them, there were small booths with all sorts of trinkets for all types of people. As we walked further, it dawned on me more and more: I hadn't seen a single child in Grimrokk yet. In the middle of the square, I stopped and turned around as I swept my gaze through the crowd. There were indeed some small people around us, but if they weren't elves, then they were dwarves. The youngest people I saw were maybe in their teens.

'What is it, Mia?' Kian's voice sounded worried.

'Kian? Are there no children left?' I asked quietly. Why hadn't I thought of this before?

'No, these are the youngest ones you see here. You always hear about those who have become pregnant and fled to avoid being found, but there are no children anywhere to be seen. Either they're well hidden, which I sincerely hope they are, or it means that... she's found them.'

The end of Kian's explanation gave me a pang in my chest. I could feel the despair, for it could not be too different from my own. Kian gave me a comforting pat on the hand and led me around the square. We stopped at a booth that sold slings in all sorts of strange shapes and colours. One of them reminded me of the material in Kian's crossbow. It shone in beautiful silver with a shiny, smooth surface.

'That one looks like your crossbow,' I said as I stroked my fingers over the sling.

'That's right. It's made from the same tree.'

'How does it work though? The stones must be quite small if they're going to fit in this little sling?'

'It's not meant to have stones. Does my crossbow use arrows?' he joked.

'No. Are there going to be those lightning-fast things in this too?'

'Haha. Exactly right. There are many here who have more or less the same ability as me, and they compete in different events. I've never been particularly good at throwing, but shooting, on the other hand...,' he laughed fondly and winked in my direction. Everything about Grimrokk was exciting and magical. It made me think back to when I was a child and saw a helium balloon for the first time. I thought it was magic.

'When do the competitions start?' I asked interested.

'They start tomorrow. You'll try your hand at it too, won't you, Mia?' he asked, looking at me. I had completely forgotten.

'I don't know. Mirini said I should compete in the sling, but I haven't practiced much,' I replied evasively. That was a genuine understatement.

'It's just for fun. Many have never even touched a sling before.' He smiled and pointed to a good example just over there. A young boy stood with a sling, and every time he tried to throw, the stone shot out to the side and almost hit a booth nearby. I laughed so loud I had to turn around so the boy wouldn't realize we were laughing at him.

'Poor guy, that's Nicolas,' Kian said, nodding gently in the direction of a man at a booth on the other side of the square. He was thin and worn with scruffy blond hair that reached his earlobes, and he reminded me of one of the local beggars in Gaia.

'What's up with him?' I asked.

'He's stuck here. His neighbour in Gaia, who turned out to be a Grimmer, happened to be in Wargborough. Nicolas, who works as a shoemaker there, saw him and recognized him. It doesn't happen often, but you can probably imagine what happened afterwards,' Kian shook his head sympathetically.

'He died in Gaia? I heard Majliv talking about him when I was with Mirini. Is it true that people attack him?' I felt sympathy for him.

'I don't know if I would call it dying exactly, but he'll never wake up there again. Unfortunately. Bardon, his neighbour, did the same thing here. Bardon has apparently always been well-liked by Myrthing's' followers, and they won't stop until they have avenged him,' Kian's gaze became stiff.

I noticed the way he phrased it, that one never wakes up again. It reminded me of how someone would explain a brain-dead person.

'So, you can't even say hello to someone you know if they're a Grimmer too? Isn't that a bit strict?' I thought the rules were a bit too harsh. The most important thing had to be that no one else found out.

'What if someone saw it and asked why he greeted Bardon? It doesn't take much to start mixing the two worlds. No, it's best to keep a strict separation. If you recognize someone and say it, you will be separated. One stays in Grimrokk and one in Gaia.'

We walked on. We had been walking for a while when we met Mirini outside a shop that sold herbs and powders. Mirini, who was always a little stressed, was standing there with her hands full of baskets and nets.

'Hey, there you are! Mia, you don't have your own sling, so I took the liberty of buying one for you, and Batist has made a surprise for you that you can get at the inn,' she said and rushed on while calling out for Teddy and Nette. I didn't get to say a word before she disappeared.

As I tried to look for her across the square, I caught a glimpse of a man in a large pelt coat who was looking in our direction, but I pretended not to see him and

173

gripped Kian's arm tighter. The desire for revenge burned inside me. In a window, I saw the reflection of Majliv looking at us for a while before he disappeared into a shop. The stabbing guilt returned. Why had I messed things up like that?

The people in the square were all kinds, shapes, and colours. Some were small and looked quite a bit like Sally, while others were larger and had tails under their skirts. One man had pointed ears and two horns on his forehead, while his lower body was fully equipped with hooves and fur, resembling the hindquarters of a goat.

'Majliv mentioned something about werewolves earlier. Do they exist here?' I asked Kian curiously.

'Yes, definitely. They were Myrthing's bitches, but the few that remain are thankfully captured. They are almost extinct,' he reassured me.

'Are there other dangerous humanlike creatures here?' I wanted to know more about everything in this strange place.

'No, not in the way you're thinking. But many hundreds of years ago, when Lamia ruled, there were some humans who were bitten by her, survived, and escaped. They eventually developed a thirst for blood that they could not control and became creatures that followed her orders,' Kian shook his head and grimaced.

'Like vampires?' I thought aloud. It would have been typical if there were such monsters here too.

'Well, you could say that. But the tales you tell in Gaia have creatures with many strange abilities. They weren't quite as romantic as that. They exist in a reality

I wouldn't wish on my worst enemy, I think,' said Kian, smiling weakly. I thought of TV shows I had seen where people did everything in their power to appear as vampires. Only now did it become clear to me how ridiculous it was. Who would want to be a half-dead body that had to drink blood, not because they wanted to live, but because they simply couldn't help it.

At the square, we saw Siljan rushing around from booth to booth, as usual. Kian laughed. 'That man never rests.'

'I've noticed. What abilities does he have?' I asked, laughing along.

'Dad? He's a wizard,' he replied simply.

'A wizard? But aren't they evil?' I looked at him, slightly shocked.

'No, not all of them. Dad isn't that powerful, but there are others, like Knuiw Myrthing. He's not quite right in the head and unfortunately has too much dark energy,' he said, shaking his head.

'Hey, guys!' It was Lynn who came towards us in a hurry.

'Can I borrow Mia? We have to pick out clothes for the dance tonight,' she said quickly.

'There's a dance tonight?' I hadn't been aware of that. Exciting, was the first thought that came to mind.

'Yes, and you don't have a dress. Come on, now,' Lynn said, pulling my arm and dragging me towards a shop.

'Mia, will you go to the dance with me tonight?' Kian called after me.

'Yes, I'd like that,' I waved back, and Lynn pulled me into a shop overflowing with the most beautiful dresses. Lynn raced around the store and pulled out all the dresses she wanted me to try on, and there were quite a few.

'But I don't have any money. These dresses must cost a fortune!' I whispered as quietly as I could.

'You can borrow from me,' she said without worry.

'And where will I get the money to pay you back?' I asked, laughing hysterically. Starting the day by getting myself into debt was not exactly a big wish.

'That's a problem we don't need to solve right now,' Lynn said, waving her arms.

'Well, then,' I shook my head, unsure if I had any choice. Not that I saw myself as a dressy type of girl, but for once, I let the little princess inside me, who had been well hidden since childhood, come out and enjoy herself. I honestly did enjoy it. We eventually found the perfect dress; it was like it was tailored to me.

Back in the inn room in the afternoon, there was a small package with a note on my bed. It said:

Dear Mia,

These can come in handy in the sling competition tomorrow. They are made of a lightweight metal with a flowing core and a hard exterior. This will cause them to push themselves as far as they can when thrown and make them easier to control.

Good luck, my girl.

Batist

I smiled to myself and looked at the small, round beads. Batist was almost like a grandfather to me, and it meant a lot that he kept an eye on me. Sitting on the edge of the bed, I ran my hands over the beautiful dress lost in deep thought. Inside me, hope sprouted that Majliv would like what he saw and maybe fix the quite unpleasant situation we were in. Even if it was only friendship, it was better than the distance between us now. My conscience was hurting me, and my heart felt like a twisted knot in my chest.

I looked over at my backpack. The thorn vine was wrapped together in a large bundle as it had been since I brought it with me from the Rim Gorge, more or less forgotten. Each branch was thin with long, narrow thorns. Even after the branches had dried, they were unusually tough and flexible. I unravelled them again so that all the branches were free. Then I took three branches and twisted them like a rope so that all the thorns pointed out and stuck evenly down the entire length. At one end, I cleared the thorns - not because I needed to be afraid of pricking myself, but because others would do it if they held it. In the end, it had become a long thorn whip that was over twice my height. I coiled it up and hung it on the bedpost.

MAGIC OF THE NIGHT

It didn't take long before Mirini pounded on the door and dragged me out to teach me how to use a sling. I had to be honest with myself, it was actually a bit of fun. In the alley behind our inn, we had enough peace and quiet to test my sling abilities without being disturbed. Mirini had fixed a target with a circle and a dot on a piece of paper. The first 20 times I tried, I certainly missed, and when I finally began to get the hang of it, there was still a long way to go. I don't know how long we stayed at it, but when it began to get darker, we finished up. The smile on my lips was a little lighter. It was fun and it occupied my thoughts from something other than worries.

Chapter 11
A naughty temptress

L ynn entered the room all dressed up and gave me a wild look.

'Aren't you ready yet? Everyone is waiting for you! We're having dinner together before the dance, hurry up!'. She left and slammed the door behind her. I laughed as I took off my clothes and threw them on the bed. Then I combed my hair and braided it in a long braid. The dress fitted me perfectly, but I struggled a bit with tightening the corset in the back on my own. I turned to the mirror to look and noticed that it was still a bit surprising to see myself. That feeling you get when you meet someone you recognize but can't immediately remember why they are familiar.

Everyone was waiting for me at the table in the dining room. Even before I rounded the corner, I heard laughter and loud conversations. Since I was late, I crept along the wall towards the table, but as soon as I took two steps into the room it fell silent. Everyone turned towards me. My cheeks turned red.

'Hi. Sorry, I'm late,' I said, embarrassed. My dress was two-piece with a light, sky-blue velvet corset and a dark blue velvet skirt. Over my shoulders, I had a white woollen scarf. Lynn smiled proudly and cleared her throat discreetly to remind people of their manners. All the men stood up and bowed. Kian pushed out the chair next to him and nodded at me to sit. I curtseyed gratefully.

On my way to the table, I looked for Majliv. At first, I didn't see him, but I soon discovered him at the end of the table. I had never seen him in formal attire before. He looked very handsome. His hair had grown much longer since the first day I saw him. It hung down a bit over his forehead, but it was still dark and tousled. Instead of a shirt, he wore a high-necked black sweater and a grey jacket with a high, stiff collar. He looked away at the same time I saw him. I sat down next to Kian and tried to look happy. Majliv's rejection had hurt my heart.

The dinner was absolutely delicious, and everyone enjoyed themselves. Almost everyone, at least. The appetizer was butter-fried brook trout with roasted cauliflower and leek tart with chervil sauce. For the main course, glazed wild boar with rosemary-baked root vegetables, accompanied by a sauce made with juniper berries and garlic. For dessert, we had a warm, bitter chocolate souffle with caramelized pumpkin seeds and jasmine-scented raspberries.

Every time I looked towards Majliv; he looked in a different direction. It wasn't accidental, but rather quite childish.

After dinner, we went out to the square. All the stalls had been removed, and long tables with roofs had been set up. Lanterns hung from the roofs and trees, and in the corners of the square, large barrels burned. It was quite chilly, but the people, the drinks, the dancing, and the live flames provided good warmth. Kian was handsomely dressed. A white shirt and a blue velvet jacket with a stiff collar which suited him perfectly, and I was pretty sure that Lynn had given him some hints on how to dress. But no matter how good he looked; he would never be more than pleasant company.

'Mia, it's time to dance,' he said, putting his arm around me and leading us onto the dance floor in the middle of the square. He twirled me around and smiled.

I enjoyed the dance and the music; it was lively and fun, and I was just one among all the others. Sometimes, I caught a glimpse of Majliv and saw him watching me while he talked to Siljan. The dance had been going on for a while when a slower melody finally came on. Lynn had brought Majliv onto the dance floor, and they were dancing just behind Kian and me. In the short break before the next dance, Lynn suddenly took hold of me, turned quickly around, and imperceptible to everyone else, we had switched dance partners. Majliv stood motionless and just looked at me. I couldn't breathe. My arms turned heavy like logs, and for the first time in a long time, I wished he would put his arms around me. His jaw tensed almost imperceptibly. I looked up into his dark blue, sparkling eyes. The music became indistinct, and I didn't notice what was going on around us. Suddenly, I got a little push in the back. Majliv quickly took hold of one of my hands and slipped an arm around my waist. My heart skipped a beat. I breathed quickly, and my knees trembled. I moved my hand up to his shoulder and waited for him to lead. He took the first dance steps but said nothing. We looked at each other seriously, and the distance between us grew. There was nothing I wanted more than to move closer, but I feared the pain of another defeat. I met his gaze again and felt my own eyes tearing up. How could things become so tense between us? Was everything really because of my pitch? I wanted to know, so I gathered the courage and moved closer cautiously. He responded by moving his hand further back on my back while looking deeply into my eyes. Now, I was sure. This was what I wanted. His warmth touched my body. The music was calm, but my heart was dancing in my chest. Majliv's gaze was fixed on mine, his jaw still tense.

The music ended, and the other couples thanked each other for the dance and left. We remained in the middle of the dance floor, completely alone, motionless, in the final dance position. The words I wanted to say swam around in my head in utter chaos. I couldn't even manage to say thank you. My hands were just as uncertain. Should I let go? Or enjoy the closeness as long as he allowed me? What was he thinking?

At that moment, he let go of me, turned around, and walked off the dance floor. I stayed put. My gaze followed his every step, hoping that he would turn around just once. But he didn't look back and I felt my heart rip apart.

The evening was over. I ran disappointed and hurt to the inn while tears streamed down my cheeks. Why did Lynn have to interfere in everything? She didn't need to get involved. Now everything was worse than before. I cursed Lynn and my own stupidity, but deep down, I knew it was all my fault.

Up the stairs and into the room, I lifted my skirt and ran. I slammed the door shut so hard and fast that a few strands of my braid got caught in the door.

'I can't take it anymore!' I screamed. In desperation, I turned to the small dressing table and pulled out the drawers in search of scissors. I undid the braid and ran my fingers through it a few times before lifting the scissors. Right behind my ear, I started cutting and moved the scissors in a straight line towards my neck. First on one side, then the other. My velvet dress became covered in hair, but I didn't care. It had to come off, and fast. I let it fall to the floor on top of the pile of hair. At the bottom of my bag, I found a shirt that was my own, and then I sat on the edge of the bed to calm down.

'Mia? It's the one who can't help but meddle... Can I come in?' It was Lynn. Now that I had calmed down, I no longer knew who I was angry at, let alone what I should do.

'Yes,' I answered quietly. I knew she would hear me regardless. She came in and looked at me with a pleading look for forgiveness which quickly turned to shock.

'What have you done?' she exclaimed as she came towards me with her hands outstretched in despair.

'I'm not used to having long hair,' I replied shortly.

'But....' She fell silent. Her gaze shifted from the tainted hair to my face, then she sighed deeply.

'I'm sorry. That was so stupid of me, but I just wanted to help.'

'You have no idea....' I wiped away my tears.

'Is it that bad? The way you two are going at it, you'd think you were mortal enemies,' Lynn shook her head.

'You could say that certain things have happened that have changed things,' I said, sighing heavily.

'What 'things' have changed 'things'?' Lynn was just as confused as ever. I slowly turned to Lynn as I replayed the scene in my mind. Majliv and I in each other's arms. Lips pressed against mine. Then I blinked and shook my head. That was enough.

'I didn't know that. So how can you go from there to here?' she asked, waving her arms.

'Let me put it this way: I've found my pitch,' I answered her.

'That's great... or is it not?' She looked at me questioningly.

'Well, in itself it is.' I shook my head in frustration.

'But...?' Lynn fished for more.

'We met Lamia.' As far as I knew, no one had found out that we had met Lamia on our way to the Rim Gorge.

'What! Are you kidding? Why didn't you say anything? What happened?' Lynn became almost hysterical, but I remained calm.

'As you can see, we got away.'

'Mia... come on. Is that how you found your pitch?' Now Lynn was really tense.

'No. Not exactly,' I replied, squeezing my eyes shut.

'You used it on her?'

'No. Not that either.' Now I regretted starting to tell the story.

'Then say it, please! Preferably before I die! Why is Majliv mad at you?' When she said it, her expression showed that she had figured it out. Her mouth gaped.

'You didn't... did you?'

'Twice,' I said, hiding my face in my hands.

'How on earth is that possible?' Lynn asked incredulously. I looked at her again and played the whole story for her. First about the kiss and the arousal, then when Majliv pushed me away and how I burst into a full-blown tantrum, and all the way to when we met Lamia. Right up to the end, when I was so angry at myself that I couldn't use the pitch on Lamia and in a fit of anger, I said that I hated Majliv more than Lamia.

'Wow... now I understand a little more. Have you talked about it afterwards?'

'No. I don't know how to proceed. Lynn, this time I have to take it at my own pace. Don't stress me out,' I said seriously.

'I respect that. I'll stay completely out of it. Don't worry.'

'Great. Thank you,' I said and hugged her. Lynn was a good friend.

CR80

The day for retrieving potential eggs had come. The room was quiet. The beds were placed along the wall, and there was only a curtain separating the patients from each other. There were low whispers between some of the patients. I lay in the hospital bed under a large, cold duvet when Will came back.

'How did it go?' I whispered as quietly as I could.

'Well, it went, literally,' he chuckled, and I couldn't help but giggle with him. It wasn't just me who had to give something today, Will's semen sample also had to be delivered.

'Godseth?' a voice said.

'Here,' Will replied, leaning forward from the curtain so the person could see where we were. A nurse smiled politely.

'Good day. I am Anette, and I work here as a nurse,' she said, reaching out her hand to me and then to Will.

'Good day. I'm Amelia and this is William,' I replied politely.

'I'm just going to put a needle on the back of your hand so you can get pain medication through it during the procedure,' she said.

'Okay. I can handle that,' I nervously smiled and watched as Anette inserted the needle into my arm.

'It's your turn right away. If you can roll the bed with me, that would be great,' she said indicating to Will.

He did as he was told, and together they rolled me out of the door and into the room across the hall. There stood a doctor I recognized. It was Dr. Anne Lande, the same doctor I had been examined by earlier. They stopped the bed right by a gynaecological chair.

'You can lie down in it, and we'll start shortly,' Dr. Lande said, pointing to the chair, then turning her head to some papers.

I lay down in the chair and put my legs in the stirrups.

'You can sit there and hold her hand,' Anette said, pointing Will towards a chair next to me.

'Then we're ready. It's important that you relax completely. If it hurts, let us know, and you'll get more pain meds,' Dr. Lande smiled encouragingly. Anette, the nurse, prepared some syringes before turning to me and soothingly stroking my hand. She injected something through the needle, and it wasn't long before everything was swimming before my eyes.

On a screen, we could follow the ultrasound image of what was being done. Well, if it hadn't been for me passing out and barely knowing what was up and down. I had enough with myself. A strange feeling suddenly came over me and I began to hiccup as if I had been crying for a long time. Soon tears streamed down my face.

'Does it hurt?' Anette asked.

'No. I... I don't know... why...,' I sobbed.

'Don't be scared, it's completely normal. It may be a side effect of the medication I'm giving you,' she said to comfort me.

I continued to cry, but I still heard what was happening. They removed six eggs from one side and seven from the other.

'This is good. Now, we just have to see how many mature and will divide,' said the doctor, smiling after examining the contents of the test tube.

'Now you can go back to bed and rest.' Will and Anette wheeled me back to the room I had been in earlier.

'You can relax for a while before you go home. Tomorrow, you call us, and we'll arrange a time for embryo transfer.' That's when they would put back fertilized eggs, and there was no day I looked forward to more than that.

The crying stopped as the medication wore off. My stomach was sore, it felt like someone was pulling on my insides, and I looked pregnant due to the hormones. The mature eggs made the ovaries the size of oranges instead of the normal size of a coin. Even though the eggs were removed, fluid accumulated in the ovaries, and it took a few days for them to return to normal.

When I called the laboratory the next day, I found out that eight eggs had divided and could be implanted, so we were scheduled to come in the following day. I was both excited and nervous. I was excited because it might result in a child, and anxious because of the alternative. It was strange to think that if there was a child, it would have spent two days of the pregnancy outside the womb. In a way, I was pregnant without an embryo inside me.

That night I slept heavily, and I didn't visit Grimrokk. I had to admit that I missed it, but it was also a relief to focus only on what was happening here in Gaia and the children I dreamed of.

It was time. The fertilized egg was going to be placed back in my uterus.

'We will put back a great embryo. We will only put back one, since you are so young, and the quality was so good. Unfortunately, you won't be able to freeze any for later attempts, as this one was the only one with good enough quality,' the doctor explained.

I was back in the gynaecologist's chair. The lab technician gave the doctor a syringe with a long, thin plastic tube that he inserted and pushed the contents out of.

'That's it then, good luck to both of you,' he said.

'Was that it?' I asked, surprised.

'Yes,' he laughed as I was wheeled out of the room again.

We were asked to relax a little before we left. I was almost too scared to move, so I lay there stiff as a board. I dared barely breathe. It was both exciting and scary to wait to find out if it would go our way.

I hadn't thought much about Grimrokk in the past few days and didn't long to go there. Especially not when I remembered my last visit.

෴

My heart leapt into my throat when there was a knock on the door around breakfast time. I quickly sat up in bed and looked over at Lynn, who was twisting around.

'Come in!' I called out, my throat dry. The door opened and Mirini peeked in.

'Good morning, girls. Today is the day of the... What have you done?!' She interrupted herself and stared at me in shock. What had surprised her so much?

'I said the same thing. I was told she was used to having it this short,' Lynn sat up and shook her head. I felt dumb. Was there something I hadn't noticed?

'You look great, but it's strange to see you with such short hair,' Mirini said. She leaned forward and ran her fingers through my hair. I had completely forgotten that I had gone crazy with the scissors the last time I was here.

'Oh, you mean my hair. I don't have the patience for braids and ponytails. Short hair is low maintenance.' I ran my fingers through my hair, made a side part, and swept it behind my right ear.

'How are you feeling today? You disappeared so quickly last night. We didn't get a chance to talk,' Mirini said, sitting on the edge of my bed.

'I don't know. I'll feel better once I'm fully awake.' I wasn't ready for intimate confessions. 'Well, there are competitions today, and you should give it a try. I have a feeling it could take your mind off things,' Mirini said encouragingly, patting me on the shoulder. 'However, if you don't get out of bed soon, there won't be any competition for either of you. Everyone else has already left.' Mirini stood up and walked to the door.

'We'll be there in a minute,' I confirmed.

'Great! I'll go down to the square in the meantime. Remember to bring everything you need,' she said and closed the door behind her.

'Are you ready to compete today?' Lynn chuckled and rubbed her eyes.

'Always!' I laughed, somewhat ironically. The truth was, I didn't have the heart to say no. Mirini and Batist had both invested time and money for me to participate, so how could I refuse now? My clothes were on the chair by the bed. I grabbed my pants and tried to scrape off the dry dirt stains, but it was useless. The wool sweater was presentable enough. It did have a few blood stains from Majliv after the unpleasant encounter with Lamia, but they weren't too noticeable. Regardless, those clothes really needed to be washed.

'You can borrow something from me,' Lynn pulled out the top drawer of the dresser and pulled out something black. 'Try this on. Here's a sweater that fits perfectly.' She dressed me up like a doll. One piece after another was buttoned, tied, or tightened. Finally, Lynn took a step back and evaluated the result.

'Almost perfect.'

'Just almost? All that, just for almost?' I chuckled.

'Yes! We have to do something with your hair.'

'What's wrong with my hair? I like it like this.' Lynn dragged me over to the mirror above the dresser.

'Whoa...' was all I could manage to say. My hair was longer on one side than the other, and Lynn said there was a big notch in the back of my neck. In addition, my hair was tousled from all the trying on.

'I can't go like this!'

'That's what I said! I'll try to fix it as much as I can.' The result wasn't too bad. Lynn managed to hide the notch and adjust the sides evenly. After having my hair fixed and dressed, I studied myself in the mirror and finally felt satisfied.

'Damn! We're going to be late!' Lynn shouted, with a hysterical look in her eyes.

'What?'

'They're gathering everyone for the welcome speech now,' she continued. I grabbed the beads, sling, and backpack before running.

The square was packed with people and a lot of other creatures. Everyone was gathered around a platform with a railing, like some sort of stage. A man went up on the platform and took the floor. Fortunately, we arrived just in time.

'Welcome, welcome, ladies and gentlemen, to the Frost Festival! Today, the tournament will begin with the following disciplines: crossbow, open combat, sling throwing, and whip. Participants can compete in as many disciplines as they wish. The tournament continues with quarter and semi-finals tomorrow. There are no competitions on Christmas Eve, and the finals will be held on the first day of Christmas. Those who do not follow the rules will be disqualified. Magic that can be performance-enhancing on weapons is prohibited. Further, it is not allowed to cut, slice, or otherwise damage opponents' crossbows, slings, wands, whips, or other equipment. Finally, anyone who does not arrive on time will be automatically disqualified. If there are no questions, those who will compete in crossbow can go to their designated places.' The man on stage was the judge, and he gestured with his arms as he explained where the different competitions would take place. As soon as he finished speaking, the crowd began to buzz as it slowly dispersed. Lynn waved me in the same direction as most others.

Now I was nervous. There were so many spectators, and I knew I was absolutely terrible at sling throwing. It didn't seem to bother Lynn much. Come to think of it, I wasn't sure what she was competing in. Hadn't I paid attention when she told me? No, she had never mentioned it.

'Lynn? What are you actually competing in?' I asked.

'Open combat,' she replied. It was probably obvious to her what open combat was, but I had never heard of it.

'What's that all about?' I asked.

'You compete with someone who has a similar ability to your own. Last time, I wasn't focused at all and fell asleep after a few minutes. It was really embarrassing.' Lynn laughed at herself and made a self-deprecating grimace.

The explanation wasn't exactly detailed, so I still felt quite ignorant. I realized I had to wait and see.

Over at the crossbow range, Kian stood with a dozen others. They all had the most peculiar crossbows. One looked like glass and used icicles as ammunition, another held a red-hot crossbow and could shoot fireballs, and a third resembled a straight twig that shot wood chips.

The tournament began with everyone shooting three shots at a target. Kian hit two targets first, but then hit the edge of the target when he was unlucky and lost his grip. He still came in third place and advanced to the quarterfinals.

Next up was the open combat event, where nineteen pairs would compete against each other. The first pair consisted of two giants who were supposed to pin one another on the back. The next pair were two wizards who turned small stones into mice. They each had their own stack of stones, and the aim was to always have the most stones while turning the opponent's stones into mice. The audience was thoroughly entertained as the little mice ran around the entire arena.

In the third pair, Lynn faced a lady, and their objective was to make the other fall asleep. The funniest part of this was that everyone in the audience had to cover their ears not to fall asleep themselves, but some forgot and collapsed. Lynn won against the lady in the first round but struggled more in the next. She then had to fight an old man who was both hard of hearing and seeing, so no matter how hard she tried, the old man remained unfazed. Eventually, she could not resist him and fell to the ground with a thump. I thought of the time when Kian had taken a similar blow and imagined the bump she was going to get on her head.

In the next event it was my turn, the sling. I regretted it sincerely. There was a crowd of people on the field, and I glimpsed an opportunity to sneak away. But Lynn had snuck up behind me and gave me a good shove in the back, and suddenly I was on the field. I really disliked being the centre of attention.

'Look at Mia, Batist,' I heard Mirini from the crowd.

'What did she do to her hair? It was so beautiful,' Batist said despairingly.

'You have to stop! She looks good. Let the girl find herself!' Lynn was clearly frustrated with the topic of conversation. I understood what the topic would be at dinner and how many times Batist would comment on the new hairstyle.

'Hey, guys. Am I late?' I turned around and looked over at Lynn and the others. Kian had just arrived.

'No. It's starting any minute now,' Lynn answered impatiently.

'Isn't Mia competing after all?'

'Yes. She's right there!' Lynn pointed at me, annoyed that he hadn't noticed me.

'Hello! Is THAT Mia? Where did she hide this cheeky minx?' Kian regarded my new style with undisguised enthusiasm.

'Cut it out!' said Lynn, pushing him.

'But look at her! If I met Mia in the dark, I don't know if I'd be scared or aroused. Those pants fit her butt like a glove and are just begging to be touched.'

Was he talking about me? What was wrong with my clothes?

'Has Majliv seen her?'

I wished he would stop saying that name in my presence. Why would Majliv be interested in seeing me, regardless of my clothing? Majliv had left the dance, and he hadn't shown himself since. I hadn't seen him either at the market or during the competitions. Unconsciously, my gaze began to search through the crowd.

'No. He just arrived. It's been years since Majliv last competed in slingshot. What made him take it up again?' answered Mirini in the background.

Was he a contestant? I hadn't thought to look for him among the competitors. Once again, I searched for him with my eyes. He stood on a field just a little further away and didn't seem to have noticed me. It felt like it had been a long time since I had seen him. My heart skipped a beat. He was so masculine and had a charisma that felt like a magnet to me. All I wanted was to keep him at a distance, but when he was near, I was irresistibly drawn to him. For a while, I just stood there paralyzed, looking at him.

He was focused, adjusting the straps on his sling to make them of equal length. He glanced at his opponents while tightening the straps. For a brief moment, he looked directly at me before moving his eyes to the next competitor. Then, he froze. Slowly, he moved his gaze back to me and held it there. I turned my head away so he wouldn't see me blush.

The organizer signalled silence. Next to me stood a gnome with a slingshot that looked like it was throwing eggs, but he was disqualified before he could throw. He had convinced a wizard to turn a chicken into a sling, and it clucked the whole time. Beyond him stood a female giant with a sling of lead solder that shot hot drops of lead.

My hands trembled as I took out the new sling that Mirini had given me. The small metal beads that Batist had given me fit perfectly in the sling. It was a glass bowl shaped like a drop, with long leather straps. When the first throw was called, I tightened the straps, aimed, and swung the sling as fast as I could.

I hit the target with the first throw. Several of the competitors had missed and left the field. The signal was given for the second throw, and everyone tightened their straps and fired again. I hit the target again. There were fewer people on the field. Not everyone hit the target; some were disqualified, and others had returned the sling and were injured on the sidelines. The third throw was called, and the remaining participants fired again. I didn't expect to make it this far, but I focused and was uplifted by performing better than expected. My throw didn't hit the bullseye, but it wasn't a miss either.

To my great surprise, I ended up as number four. I was overjoyed since it was my first time! Behind me, I heard that Majliv had become number two. I wasn't far behind. I had made it to the quarterfinals. Maybe he now understood that I didn't need a babysitter? In the crowd, I heard Mirini's cheers. She was like a whole cheering section by herself, completely ecstatic. Her thin body jumped and waved her arms and legs, so she looked like a jack-in-the-box.

'Mia! Bravo! Come, let's celebrate,' Lynn shouted while waving at me.

But I stayed put. Behind me, the organizer called the competitors for the next competition. What would Lynn and Mirini say now? The look I got from Lynn was only confused, as if she were trying to read my thoughts but couldn't grasp them. She waved at me again, but I shook my head gently and smiled crookedly, grabbed my bag, took a few steps back, then turned around and headed towards the next field.

Chapter 12
A new hope

Where is Mia going? Is something wrong?' Kian followed me with his gaze as I moved away from them.

'I have no idea. She's not saying anything,' Lynn replied, shrugging.

I turned my back to them and jogged towards the field where the next competition was going to take place. Ahead of me, I caught a glimpse of a tall, broad-shouldered figure. I picked up my pace. As I ran past him, I made sure my arm brushed against his. Out of the corner of my eye, I saw Majliv's gaze follow me.

The participants were asked to gather at the judges' table. The whips used in the competition had to be at least three meters long, so everyone's whips were measured and inspected.

Although it was not an easy task in itself, I managed to pull the thorn vine out of my backpack. Once I had unwound it, it was measured and approved with flying colours. It was just over four meters long.

This event was also to be performed in pairs. We were to face each other with three flags behind us. The goal was to knock down all the opponent's flags while protecting our own. Points were given for each flag that was knocked down and for each one we had left.

The first pair was Majliv against a small, thin guy. Majliv's whip looked like eternal grass with sharp

199

edges, woven together into a long snake. The small, thin man had a fire whip that flared up when he threw it, but why he didn't burn himself while holding it was a mystery to me. My other concern was whether Majliv's whip would catch fire if they came too close together.

Majliv knocked down two flags right away, but things looked bad after a while when they were tied. However, the little man stumbled in his eagerness and accidentally set fire to his last flag. Majliv won the match. Part of me had hoped he would lose, while another part wanted to cheer with the audience.

Then it was my turn. I was up against a huge, disgusting man who was introduced as the city's jailer. I sympathized with those who had to sit in his prison. I had no doubt that he was close to two meters tall, and his big, thick belly that hung over his belt made his leather jacket look like something that had fit him 20 years ago. His whip was something as violent as a long chain. It occurred to me how strange it was that it had been approved. What if he hit me in the head? The phrase 'knocked over the head' came to mind which often caused the victim to loose one's mind and I was not quite ready for such a literal experience.

'What is she doing? Does anyone know anything about this?' I heard Lynn confront the others.

'No. I think this is a surprise for all of us. Whip competitions are dangerous, after all.' Mirini shook her head. Typical that I would hear this now. Mirini had said that the competitions were just for fun, and now she was saying it was dangerous.

'I don't like this. The man is almost twice her size, and he's not known to be gentle,' Batist's worried words made my heart pound.

'Mia, you need to pull yourself together. Don't act like a little kid. You've been through worse than this,' I repeated the words in my head over and over again.

'Give it a rest and stop worrying. If there's one thing I know, it's that girl is determined and stubborn,' Kian emphasized before letting out a cheer.

'True enough. We've all heard how angry she can get,' Lynn laughed loudly as the game was about to begin. I took a deep breath. My whip swung through the air and tore down the first flag. If I were to have any chance of winning, I had to be quick. But the guard had the same plan. I managed to take down his second flag without losing any of my own, which made him furious, and he threw his chain at me instead of the flag. The audience booed. Fortunately, I managed to jump out of the way and seized the opportunity to rip down his last flag. My whip wrapped around the pole, and I pulled so hard that his flag landed on the ground. The spectators cheered. I couldn't believe it. Had I beaten that big bully? My body was in shock and surprise, so I remained still.

'Where did that come from?!' Lynn exclaimed and hung around my neck.

'Uh...I have no idea. I just...wanted to try,' I whispered the words. Batist was almost crying, he was so happy. Mirini had both arms around Nette and was jumping up and down.

'You really are a big surprise. But...thorns? Ouch! Where did you get that idea?' Kian asked, grabbing the whip and hurting himself.

'Long story.'

'Which you have to tell Kian later. Now you have to go to the judges' table,' Lynn patted me on the shoulder and pushed me in the right direction. I couldn't believe it. I was looking forward to the next round.

At the judges' table, Majliv was talking to a judge. He spotted me and turned his back. So, this was his true self? A selfish, conceited jerk who couldn't stand to see others succeed. With renewed courage, I stepped out onto the field, ready to fight. Three flags later, I was the one jubilantly cheering. I made it to the quarterfinals in this event too! Majliv also made it through, as expected, and kept his distance for the rest of the day until dinner. Kian sat next to me and asked me all sorts of questions about the thorns. Why didn't I feel any pain? Would I bleed if I stung myself? Did this apply to all types of thorns? My answers weren't always satisfying, so he asked the same questions multiple times.

Majliv was nowhere to be seen at breakfast. I was pretty sure he was annoyed that I had made it through in the competition. I had decided to walk around town alone after breakfast. The streets were charming, and the shop windows were beautifully decorated for Christmas Eve, which was tomorrow.

In the display window of a small candy store there were caramels and sweets in fantastic colours. They were shaped like snowmen, gifts, and snowflakes. The colours were bold and reminded me of Christmas as I knew it back home. Mom and I had always had an almost extreme Christmas spirit. It was to Will's dismay; he felt like it was almost too much Christmas decorations and flashing lights. Fortunately, we were not the worst in Duluth; there were several who had invested a lot in decorating their houses for Christmas.

I went in to look at all the candy on display. The small store was packed with all kinds of caramels and sweets. Lollipops in ten different flavours: lemon, orange, wild strawberry, blackberry, blueberry, currant, raspberry, gooseberry, cherries, and apple, which were made in all the colours of the rainbow. They had small white balls made of chocolate truffles covered with coconut and powdered sugar. It looked lovely, and even the mouth of a blind person would have watered in here. It also smelled inviting. I really wished I had brought money, but I would buy something later.

The store next door sold books and stationery. Some books flew through the room and settled on the shelves themselves. While the shop owner was busy putting ink in a variety of colours into different stands the quills wrote words on paper by themselves.

I laughed to myself and continued. In a way, I had started to get used to all the strange things in Grimrokk. The street now became narrower. I came to a little corner with a tiny shop window that was impossible to see through. Above the door hung a sign: 'FORTUNE-TELLER RAMINA VISIBLIS.' I couldn't resist the temptation. Not that I believed in such things, but it was nonetheless exciting. I went in. The small room was dark with large red pieces of cloth hanging on the walls. The smell of strong incense with some herbs I didn't recognize hung heavily in the air. In the middle of the room was a round table with a black cloth, on it was something I thought must be a dragon's claw was gripping a large orb. This place gave me an eerie feeling. Something inside me said it was best to leave, but the temptation to find out more was too great. Apart from the table, the room was practically empty. There was no one in the store either, so I turned on my heels to go.

'Oh, you can't wait. Limited patience I see. Come, come,' said a hoarse, old voice from behind the wall covering.

'Sorry. I didn't think anyone was here,' I replied. The cloth was pushed aside, and a crooked figure appeared in the semi-darkness. She really looked like the classic depiction of a fortune teller as she stood there with a large, bright blue skirt with gold fringes, a yellow cotton blouse full of embroideries in all sorts of colours, and on her head, she had a thin, yellow scarf with gold sequins hanging from the edge. The hair frizzy like grey steel wool around her wrinkled face with two yellow, piercing eyes.

'I will predict your future for you, but you must promise to share the prize with me when you win the day after tomorrow,' she said in a crackly voice. The large earrings she wore in her ears shook as she moved, and the closer she came, the clearer I could see the face, which was now clearly marked by both scars and warts.

'If I win, I can do that,' I nervously smiled.

'When, I said. Sit down, please.'

As if I had offended her, she slumped down in her chair and placed her arms on the table before pointing to the chair opposite her. She seemed a bit unpredictable and maybe a bit scary, but now that I was there, I might as well stay. I sat in the creaky chair across from her. The woman began waving her arms over the orb while uttering some words that reminded me of Latin: 'Futura ostende te...' The only word I could understand was 'futura,' which I was pretty sure meant future.

I sat completely still and watched the woman with wide eyes. This woman must have had one, if not several, loose marbles the way she was behaving. As if she were on stage with a large audience, she hummed, made faces, and continued waving her arms. It was almost enough to make me laugh.

'You have a great task ahead of you, a task you are avoiding. It will shape you if you accept that it is your future. There is much you do not know about yourself. But what do I see? Love? And uncertainty lurking.' Her eyes were like glittering embers when they opened, and I jumped. Something seemed to be moving in the orb, but I couldn't see what it was.

'Be careful, for you never know who is telling you the truth. You are going through a dark time. You must face it alone and remember - you can be heard even in the deepest of woods.'

She closed her eyes and waved her arms. When she lifted her gaze to me again, her eyes were pale and yellow, just like before. This woman must have had several marbles that weren't working properly. The things I had seen had to be some secret trick I had heard such people used to achieve drama and effect.

'Now you can go,' she said and stood up.

'Was that it? It was a lot of things without any context.' I looked dumbly at her as I stood up from the chair. She scrutinized me for a moment, and I could see the dissatisfaction radiating from her.

'You'll understand when the time comes,' she said and disappeared behind the curtain she had entered from. I stood there with a mocking expression on my face. Was this what psychics got paid for in this world? If so, I had gotten more useful things out of a game of Scrabble. I slammed the door behind me and stumbled on towards the square. None of what I had heard made any sense. She was and remained an inept, old hag. As I rounded the corner, I suddenly saw a familiar face.

'Father Benedict. Have you come to the festival too? How nice,' I smiled and gave him a hug.

'Hey, my friend. Yes, I prefer to celebrate Christmas here and be a part of the festival. Also, I've heard that you've surprised everyone and made it to two quarterfinals.' He hugged me tightly and laughed proudly.

'Yes, it seems so. I think I'm more surprised than anyone else,' I laughed at myself.

'I'm on my way to Mirini and the others to eat before the tournament. Are you going back now?' he asked.

'Yes. I'll join you; I need to get some food as well.' Lunch tasted good, as it always did. Mirini talked enough for an entire crowd, which once again lacked one, but Majliv's absence didn't bother me at all. My mood was better when he wasn't there, especially after I met Father Benedict again. He always behaved warm and inviting towards me.

'I did so well yesterday that it won't be a problem for me to make it all the way to the final,' Kian boasted to Mirini, who was sitting across from him.

'Hey! Earth to Kian, come in, Kian!' Lynn shouted. She had clearly had enough of her brother's bragging.

'You're just jealous,' he said sulkily.

'No! You're just so terribly conceited that it's a little nauseating,' she said, patting him on the shoulder.

Benedict and I sat and talked to each other. I mentioned that I had been to Ramina Visibilis and had my fortune told.

'She's good at fortune-telling, but she's in a category of her own. Many say she doesn't belong to any side and that she has been seen with Myrthing many times. I would not take everything she says too seriously,' Benedict said.

'Can I ask you something?' I asked. There were so many gaps in people's explanations, and I wanted to fill them.

'Yes, of course. What's on your mind?' he replied, putting an arm around my shoulder.

'Many have told me bits and pieces about the mirror and the werewolves who went through to the other side, but I've never heard the whole story.' I gave him a serious look. Father Benedict sighed and settled in more comfortably.

MAGIC OF THE NIGHT

'It's like this: many hundreds of years ago, ten mirrors were made, all from the same brew of an elixir. These mirrors became the portals that helped the dreamers come here. Before they got the mirrors, many arrived in the ice on the snow peak, but it was almost impossible to get there. That's why Santa gave a wizard the water from the ice as a gift and asked him to make ten mirrors out of it. The wizard's name was Ondel Myrthing, one of Knuiw Myrthing's ancestors. He was a good man who did a lot of good for the people in Grimrokk. But when Ondel died, his son, Jervh Myrthing, took the opportunity to harness the power his father had possessed and become stronger than before. He recruited werewolves to do jobs for him, and they constantly grew in number. For several generations to come, the Myrthing sons harnessed their fathers' powers on their deathbeds, which made them stronger and stronger with each generation. Knuiw was born in Grimrokk, but the other world always seemed so exciting to him, and he decided to do everything to conquer it. When he tried to go through the mirror, he was close to disappearing in the darkness. You see, the only thing that separates Grimrokk and Gaia is the darkness of eternity. Somehow it alters the time zones, so the time does not match here and there, as if time doesn't exist here when you sleep. When you come here, it's in a dream, and you come out of the mirror with a body, but Myrthing had no body to wake up in. It ended with him having to be rescued before he disappeared for good. One of his werewolves was a Grimmer, like you, and was released on the other side.

He went crazy and harmed many people. This resulted in the werewolf virus starting to ravage your world. The Grimmers here wanted to stop it before it got out of hand, so they took the lesson from here and made sure the werewolves in Gaia were eradicated. To prevent it from happening again, all the mirrors were smashed. All except one, according to the rumour. Rumours, later on, say that some mirrors were secretly moved or glued back together, but they believed for a long time that there was only one. The one in Wargborough Church was well hidden up in the ice and snow for a long, long time. It was only when things had settled down that it was moved, in secret, to the church. A spell was cast over it, so no one could disappear through it if they had evil and viruses within them, and no one gets out if evil is nearby. Myrthing has given up on Gaia, but in return, he always tries to prevent new Grimmers from coming here. Every night they come to the church to see if anyone is on their way through. Myrthing is one of the most powerful mind-readers around, and he can see through anyone. He knows if there is something going on or not.' The others stood up from the table and were about to go to the square.

'Shall we?' he asked, nodding his head towards the door. I nodded and stood up.

'Do they know who was on their way through when I arrived?' I asked as I held the door open for Father Benedikt.

'No, but Ramina probably warned him a long time ago. He does everything he can to preserve Lamia. She has contributed to him gaining even more power than before, and there are several who fear him. It's probably no secret that there is someone here who has the same ability as her. People believe it's the only way to kill her since one's strength is also one's weakness,' he replied.

'Then maybe he doesn't know that I have that ability?' I breathed a sigh of relief.

'That remains to be seen. Ramina has met you now and she probably knows more than we think,' he said, furrowing his brow.

'She said I should share the prize with her when I won. Not that I'm going to win, she can forget about that. I'm fully aware that I'm new in Grimrokk.' I shook my head. It wasn't long before we arrived at the square.

'Do what she told you to do. As I said, she's not on anyone's side. You can ask her about Myrthing's plans and see what she says. She already knows what she wants to know about you, so you have nothing to lose. Mia, listen: No matter what Ramina says or does, she's talented, but it's not always easy to understand the logic behind her words,' said Benedikt. We stopped at the courts.

'That's a good point. It sounded like meaningless nonsense, if you ask me,' I said and walked over to the other contestants. It was just my luck that I'd get hung up on such stupid nonsense. The only thing missing now was that Myrthing turned out to be Santa Claus.

It was time for the semifinals, and the signal for crossbow sounded across the square. Kian and the other contestants were ready in their places. Kian was on fire and hit the target on all three attempts. Thus, he was ready for the final on Christmas Day. Then they signalled for the slingshot competition. The competitors went out onto the field. The big 'boy,' as I thought of him, stood next to me, but didn't even glance my way. Majliv's behaviour had the same effect on me as throwing gasoline on a fire. The adrenaline in my body made me tremble, and my concentration was nowhere to be found. With the first throw, I missed the target completely, the second was too weak and didn't even make it to the target, while the last throw surprisingly did hit the target. I ended up in fourth place, while Majliv made it to the final. Without even a satisfied smile, he walked right past me as if I were invisible. My body boiled with rage. I could hardly wait for the next event so I could let out my temper. Nothing suited me better at the moment than Majliv being my next opponent. I felt like he deserved a lesson for the way he was behaving towards me.

I stood in front of my three flags. Shortly after, Majliv came out onto the field, but instead of ignoring me as he always did, he didn't take his eyes off me for a single moment. A strange feeling sprouted inside me. All the emotions I had ever had for him mixed together into a thick, messy concoction. Desire, lust, aggression, tenderness, love, hate, despair, and sorrow - I could no longer distinguish one from the other. His gaze was intense. It was as if he could see my very soul. Everything around us faded away as if we were alone in the world. Just him and me. Memories crept into my mind, and I could hear his heart, his heavy breathing.

Unconsciously, I squeezed harder around the thorn vine. The thorns didn't hurt, quite the opposite, it felt like they were a part of me. The signal was given to start. The signal was barely finished before I had the whip in the air, and I slung it so quickly over Majliv that one of his flags lay on the ground before his whip had even started to move. He slung his whip towards my flags. In the air between us, the whips hooked together for a moment. We jerked in our respective ends, and they came apart. Then his whip was quickly over my head, and he tore down one of my flags. In pure anger, I swung the whip a couple of times over my head and then the end slammed over Majliv's cheekbone so hard that the skin tore and blood trickled out. Time stood still. I held my breath. What had I done? It wasn't intentional, but it was a pretty reckless move, nonetheless. The spectators became quiet. Majliv stopped for a moment and touched his face while staring hard into my eyes. I felt like screaming. It hurt me. But in the next moment, he swung his own whip, made of grass, straight at me so I had to throw myself backwards. It was close enough that I felt the grass brush past my neck. Before he could gather his thoughts, I swung my whip towards his flags and brought down the second flag. He turned and looked at the flags behind him turning red in the face with anger. I got to my feet before he swung his whip again, and I did the same. My second flag fell to the ground, and for a brief moment, I saw a satisfied look on his face until he realized why the audience was cheering. My whip hung limp in my hand. Majliv turned around as his last flag hit the other two, which lay on the ground behind him. I gathered my whip and fastened it to my belt. There was no joy in winning this battle. Slowly but surely, my conscience began to prick at my heart.

Majliv just stood there and looked at me. I felt sick, I wanted to go home, I wanted to die. Anything but experience these feelings raging inside me. People began to congratulate me, but I didn't want to hear it. My legs had a life of their own, they ran through the crowd. Tears streamed down my cheeks as I pushed past everyone who got in my way. The cold wind made the tears icy as I ran as far as my legs could carry me. What had I done? The feeling of physically hurting Majliv was the worst I had ever felt. I reached the city gate but kept running towards the plains. I knew what I had to do. If I had come here through the mirror, I would also be able to go home that way.

Based on wild guesses, I tried to recognize the forest Majliv and I had emerged from. A thought popped up in my head, but I dismissed it. What if Lamia was out here? It meant nothing. Thoughts of everything from Majliv to Lamia felt like torture were like torture, and the images of Majliv and me in each other's arms were burned into my retina. I had whipped his beautiful face to blood.

I ran into the dense trees of the forest and finally found a rock among the spruces. Sitting down, my head fell into my hands, and tears still flowed down my pale face. Snow began to fall again as I sat there and cried. Time flew by, and it grew darker with each snowflake that hit the ground. I missed home, I missed Will and

Tinka. This place was so hopeless, cold, and loveless. The snow settled around me and stuck to my hair like tiny glittering crystals. My feet began to feel like cold blocks of ice, and my body couldn't move. The loneliness was heavy, and it felt as if life was ebbing out of me.

I slumped over in the snow so that I landed on my back and looked up at the sky, where the snowflakes came closer and closer, creating a tunnel towards the pink sky. What was it about Majliv that made me so attracted to him? Was I desperate to get him back, or had he hurt me so much that I didn't know what hate really felt like? Everything we had been through meant that there must have been some sort of emotion between us. I had to do something to get him back – if I had ever had him.

I tried to get up, but my legs gave way under me. It was no longer possible to get up as my body was almost buried in the deep snow. It was as dark as it could get when the snow created a blanket on the ground and the sky continued to release the small snowflakes. I was no longer cold, it was starting to get warm, and I was sure that no one cared where I was. My god, what a ridiculous person I was. Earlier, I had been afraid of Lamia and Myrthing, but here I lay, half frozen to death. Proud, self-centred, and arrogant. Three things that seemed meaningless now.

The snow muffled the sounds coming from the forest, but one sound stood out from the others. Some branches crackled right beside me, and I barely managed to turn my head to see what it was. For a moment, I thought my eyes were playing tricks on me, but as clear as the first time I saw it, the Hell horse stood there. Just as shiny and black as before, it approached me with small steps. The headless horse that everyone associated with death, and I suspected that the underworld had come to me. I was prepared for my last moment. The friendly creature made me feel safe in the midst of despair. It leaned down beside me, as if to say I should climb on. I gathered all the strength left in my body and pulled myself up onto the horse's back. The Hell horse rose again and carried me in between the trees. It was warm and smooth as it stepped carefully and silently. I slowly slipped into sleep, but I heard voices far away.

My body was warm when I woke up. I squinted and saw that I was lying in my bed at the inn. The sound of heavy footsteps could be heard in the room, and I turned to see who it was. There, by the window stood Majliv, leaning on the sill while looking out onto the street. His posture hinted that he was impatient. My body was stiff and sore. I tried to turn towards him, but before I could get properly settled, he turned and was immediately at the bedside to help me. There was a chair by the bed that indicated he had been sitting there earlier, and he sat down again.

'How do you feel?' he asked in a low voice.
'Terrible!'
'Are you hurt? Is there anything I can do...' I interrupted him before he could say anything more.

'No. I feel so guilty.' The cut on his cheek had been tended to and had undoubtedly been treated by Batist and his elixir skills. It didn't look so bad anymore.

'Does it hurt?' I said, reaching for his cheek.

'What? Oh...no. Batist took care of it. I barely feel anything now.' He took a deep breath. 'I've been foolish,' he continued, taking my hand. His hands were warm and tender.

'No, I was the foolish one. It's Lamia that I hate. I've never hated you! Majliv, I was just despaired and didn't fully understand what was happening. Everything happened so quickly.' My eyes let out a few tears.

'I shouldn't have said those things I said. The whole situation was completely insane. Mia, I'm usually by myself, and if I do have company, it's usually only for a day. You and I were alone for several days.'

'And I started to get on your nerves. I understand that.' I said.

'No, you didn't, but for the most part, there aren't many people around for me to talk to, and it makes me almost illiterate when it comes to communication. I have no problem talking to Kian and the others about hunting, the forest, or fishing, but I'm not good at talking about personal things.' He pulled the chair closer to the bed and rested his elbow on the edge.

'Yes, the things I brought up were perhaps too personal.'

'It's weird for me. I've never brought the romantic side of myself to Grimrokk. It's always been in Gaia.' His face was so pure and honest as he spoke, he had really thought about this.

'Well, it was that way until you came. That's why I was so dismissive. If I kept my distance, I could ignore the attraction. With a clear conscience towards... the other.' It was nice to hear him say that he had also noticed the sparks between us. I understood what he was trying to say.

'It's not easy to separate them, you and the other, but regardless of what might happen in the future, can you promise me one thing?' I asked.

'What's that?'

'Never stop talking to me again! Tell me how stupid I am or that you hate me, but don't let the silence go on this long before you talk to me again.' As I said it, I looked at our hands, which were holding onto each other tightly. I didn't have the courage to meet his gaze.

'You don't have to worry about that. The last few days have been unbearable.' He smiled for the first time in a while. It almost took my breath away, the way his dark blue eyes sparkled at me.

'What if we start fresh with a clean slate? Put everything behind us?' I asked.

'There's a lot I'd rather not forget,' he replied. I looked at him questioningly. What was it he didn't want to forget?

'What do you mean? Are there so many good memories?'

'You can say whatever you want, but for someone who spends most of his time alone, it's very nice to wake up next to someone.' For the first time, I saw Majliv blush. My heart nearly stopped, for I had never seen anything more beautiful. It wasn't like me when I blushed. My entire face became like an overripe tomato about to burst. Majliv, on the other hand, got a faint, very becoming redness on his cheeks and lips.

'You're not making this any easier when you say things like that. Don't you think I liked it? You should only know.' I felt my face turn the characteristic tomato colour.

'Give me some time,' he said. His smile faded and was replaced by an intense gaze that had an obvious effect on my pulse. My throat was dry, so I just nodded. Majliv sat holding my hand for a while longer. Several times it seemed as if he was about to ask me something, but he remained silent until there was a knock on the door.

'Come in,' he said, straightening up in his chair. His hand went limp, as if he was about to let go, but I quickly took a new, firm grip. This was the closest I had been to him in a long time, and I wasn't ready to let go just yet. He looked at me and smiled before he responded by squeezing back.

'How are you? You're awake. That's great.' It was Lynn.

'I'm doing okay now. Just a little tired.' I rubbed my eyes with my free hand.

'It's getting late, so I'll let you get some sleep,' Majliv said, getting up.

'Now that you're friends again, you can talk more tomorrow. I desperately need to sleep myself,' Lynn said with a sly smile on her face. She went over to her own bed, where she began to take off her mittens, coat, and boots. Majliv sent her an irritated glace.

'Yes, yes I just wanted to mention it,' she said. He had clearly become annoyed about something.

'See you tomorrow. Sleep well,' he smiled uncertainly at me and gave my hand a small, awkward pat before letting go. Had he really become so unsure just because Lynn came in? I sat up quickly in bed and grabbed the sleeve of his sweater. He turned with a questioning look. My heart almost jumped out of my chest, but I gathered my courage and pulled him towards me. He leaned in towards me, more than willing, and supported himself against the bed with one hand while wrapping the other securely around my waist. I put both arms around his shoulders and pulled him as close as I could. He was warm. My cheek was pressed against his shoulder, so when I took a breath, the delightful scent of him danced in my nose. For a brief moment, I envisioned when he and I were alone in the shelter. Majliv gently pulled his head back and kissed me on the cheek before letting go.

'Sleep well,' he said and walked out the door.

With my stomach full of butterflies, I fell asleep.

‰

Chapter 13
The present which
triumphs all

December 22,

The blood test had been taken, and it was finally 1:00 pm. Now, we waited for the result to be revealed. The test would tell us if the egg had been fertilized. I sat by the dining table with the paperwork in my hands, and with trembling fingers, I dialled the phone number. It started to ring, and it felt like it took ages before someone answered.

'IVF nurse, Anita,' said a sweet lady's voice on the other end.

'Hi, this is Amelia Godseth. I would like to have the results of my blood test,' I gave her all the details, as usual, and waited. My hands were sweating.

'Yes, here you are. Have you had any bleeding yet?' the voice asked softly. I hadn't, but wasn't that good? It indicated that the embryo had been fertilized, right?

'No,' I answered. I held my breath as I closed my eyes. My pulse rose, and the wait for the nurse to say more was unbearable. The seconds felt like minutes and the minutes like hours. I got hot flashes, and the sweat was pouring.

'Then unfortunately, they will probably come during the day, or possibly tomorrow,' the voice said gently.

MAGIC OF THE NIGHT

I wanted to scream in pain. My heart was about to break. I looked over at Will, who examined me closely. I shook my head. He furrowed his eyebrows, and his gaze shifted to the floor. It hurt so much. The nurse scheduled us for the next attempt before the conversation was over. I wanted to throw my phone against the wall, but it would have upset Will even more. I had to be strong.

'When can we try again?' he asked.

'In two months.' The lump in my throat grew bigger and bigger before I managed to swallow it. I could hardly breathe. My lungs just wouldn't function properly.

'Okay. Then we just have to wait.' Even though he wanted to appear strong, his eyes revealed what he really thought. They were completely blank. I didn't bother about the fact that he put on a mask. It was exactly what I did myself. None of us could bear the thought of talking to any of the other family members, because we knew they were waiting anxiously, so I sent a message to Aleksandra from my phone and summed it up briefly: 'The test result was negative. We will try again in a few months.' That evening the bleeding came.

The house was full of Christmas decorations and advent colours, but this Christmas Eve was so lacking in Christmas spirit that it might as well have been the national day, only with alternative decorations. We were going over to the neighbours with Christmas presents and greetings, something that didn't appeal to me. Aleksandra and Peter had already been informed of what had happened, or rather, what hadn't happened, the day before.

The weather was cloudy and cold, but there was no snow to be seen. Not even frost covered the trees.

'Hey, Mia,' giggled a beautiful, small voice. Christina met us at the door. She smiled widely and threw her arms around me. It felt so strange to be called Mia here in Gaia. Christina had always called me that, but she was the only one.

'Tomonnow it's Christmas. Then Santa wil come.' The little girl beamed and gave Will a hug. It was amazing what she could do to my emotions. Her big blue eyes could make anyone go to the desert for water. We took off our coats and went inside. Will carried Christina while I held the bag of gifts.

'Hey, how are you?' Aleksandra came towards me with a sympathetic look.

'I'm doing okay?' I replied with a question more directed at myself.

'Yeah. Uh...' she said back, uncomfortably, as if she really wanted to say more.

'We can't stay long, unfortunately. We have so many gifts to deliver today, and time passes so quickly,' Will said and set Christina on the floor. She ran off into the kitchen. I heard another familiar voice transformed into a childish tone. It was Peter making dinner.

'We don't even have time to eat. We have to deliver gifts to the whole family!' Peter shouted from the kitchen.

'Aren't you exaggerating a little?' Aleksandra yelled back.

'Okay, maybe a little. But we have a lot on our schedule. The food will be ready in two minutes.' There was a slightly longer silence than was normal. Maybe not what I would call awkward, but as if something was hanging in the air. I had a strange feeling. Something was different like there was a big elephant in the room.

'I'll leave the gifts here. We need to move on, and you need to get some food before the stress,' my fake laughter was uncomfortable.

'The gifts, yes, they're by the door in the hallway. Hope you have a nice Christmas. Are you going to your parents'?' Aleksandra looked at me questioningly.

'Yes, that's right. Hopefully, it will be nice.'

The atmosphere began to feel uncomfortable, but I couldn't quite put my finger on why. We wished each other a Merry Christmas and sent good wishes to our families. Christina followed us to the door, as she always did. While Will and I put on our coats, Christina fumbled with something on the table in the hall. It was a stroller board, the kind you attach to a stroller so an older sibling can stand on it while the stroller rolls.

'We're going to use this for the baby,' Christina looked up at us and laughed before quickly adding, 'Bye.'

'Goodbye.' Will waved to her and continued out the door with me following closely behind.

My thoughts raced through my head. Could Aleksandra be pregnant and not have shared the news with us? Was that why they had kept to themselves lately? Hormones from the procedure rushed through my body along with disappointment and loneliness. Once we were inside, I took out my phone and sent a message to Aleksandra.

'Are you pregnant? And if not, would you have told us if you were?' I read the message several times in a row. My heart was trembling inside me. It had a life of its own. Could the premonition be correct? It took some time before the answer came, but it couldn't have taken long enough for me. In a way, I didn't want to know it. I didn't know how to handle the answer I was expecting to get.

'Yes, I'm a little over two months pregnant. We found out a few weeks ago. I really wanted to tell you, but you were in the middle of the attempt. I was afraid it would have an impact on the result for you. If it didn't go well, I mean.'

The message was like being stabbed with a knife in the heart. It hurt more than the negative answer from the day before. It wasn't that I wasn't happy for them, but it was the feeling of being kept on the sidelines that hurt. I would have shared the joy with them as soon as I became pregnant myself. Everyone treated me with kid gloves, and I was tired of it. Why couldn't I react as I needed to?

I had no idea what to write back. My fingers did the job without me realizing it, while strange feelings flooded over me, and my eyes began to tear up. I read the message I had sent.

'You could have said something. It's good to know that others can do it. That gives us some hope. I felt it, that there was something different.'

I saw it clearly. The word that wasn't there. The word that I had completely omitted, in all my despair. CONGRATULATIONS. I really wanted to congratulate them, but I couldn't seem to write the word. It was stuck in my thoughts and wouldn't come out. You congratulate good friends if they're lucky enough to expect a baby, but I was so envious of them. They already had such a beautiful and lovely daughter, and now they were going to be so lucky to have another beautiful child, something that I was apparently not capable of. Just the joy of feeling life inside me. Everything related to pregnancy seemed so out of reach. The phone beeped with a new message. 'We were so sad when we found out it didn't work out for you. What could be nicer than being pregnant together? Sorry if you feel that way. We've just told the family, so it's not official.' I read it several times and felt the guilt creeping up my back. My body was so full of hormones that I hardly recognized myself. A sob escaped me.

'What is it?' Will stood shocked in front of me.

'Aleksandra is pregnant!' It burst out of me. He raised his eyebrows in despair and questioning. 'They're two months along. Read.' I handed him my phone. He read it and looked up at me.

'They haven't said anything. But it's nice,' he finally said.

'I would have told them right away. They've been trying for a long time, so of course it's nice. But...' I didn't know what it was, but it hurt to find out now and this way.

'It's typical that it should happen just now when we've had an attempt. But it will be us soon too. Just be patient sweetheart.' Will comforted me as best he could, and finally I calmed down. That's just the way it would always be. Friends would have children regardless of whether we succeeded or not. I reached for my phone. Will handed it back to me and stroked my hair. It wasn't easy to write anything back, but they deserved congratulations. 'It's a difficult time, so the reaction is hard. Congratulations! We are really excited for you. Wish it was us too.' I couldn't read it again. I leaned against Will's body and hugged my arms around his chest. I wasn't lonely when I held onto him. He was warm, soft, and comforting. Time could stop in Will's arms. A new notification came from the phone. 'Oh no. It wasn't supposed to be like this. But thank you so much. We love you guys.' I slowly began to understand how Aleksandra felt. We meant so much to each other, just like good friends should. This couldn't ruin such a good relationship. I replied 'Ditto.'

≪≫

I woke up to Lynn rummaging around the room as she always did.

'Merry Christmas!' she said.

'Merry Christmas!' I replied. I had completely forgotten that it was Christmas Eve. The thought gave me new energy. For once, I would start the day afresh. I had to try to leave Gaia behind today. In Grimrokk, I could be someone completely different who didn't have the same worries, and I had to seize that opportunity.

'How long until you're ready for breakfast?' Lynn said as she practically jumped around the bed to put on her pants.

'Not long. Give me two minutes so I can get dressed.'

'Shall we do some shopping after breakfast? Batist wanted you to have these. He's sold some elixirs for you.' She handed me a leather pouch with some money.

'What? Poor guy. He doesn't know the limits of his own kindness. I feel guilty,' I said, but I took the pouch with the money. Batist was truly a good man. How could I ever repay him?

'I think he sees a lot of Silva in you. You've become like a daughter to him,' Lynn tilted her head and smiled. When I finally got dressed, we went to the dining hall. There, at a table, sat Majliv and Kian with cups of Imaginari-tea. The latter was maybe not sitting so much, but rather half leaning over the table and supporting his head with his hand.

'You look alive,' Lynn said and patted her brother's shoulder.

'Unlike certain others, I was very busy not sleeping last night. I must say, Jean can be very convincing when it comes to alternative nocturnal activities, even if most of them take place under a duvet,' Kian had a smug expression on his face. He was clearly not upset about the loss of sleep.

'Kian! You pig! Mia, for you who don't know who Jean is, I can tell you she's Kian's periodic, great flirt. You'll probably meet her. She's a great girl if you like double D's and a curvy figure. And to you, dear brother, I don't need to spread my legs for everyone who passes by. But since you're so curious, you should know that Romari asked me out yesterday.'

'Congratulations! Have you finally discovered that there's something more exciting than gossip and clothes?'

'If I hadn't been interested in clothes, you would be walking around naked. You don't even know where to buy them.'

With that, they were off. Lynn and Kian knew exactly how to provoke each other, and they did it with precision. I had to laugh, because they brought up old disagreements and discussions that had nothing to do with either sleepless nights or love. Majliv gave me a frustrated look, then shook his head and rolled his eyes.

'You'd think it would disappear more with age, but with them it just gets worse,' he laughed and pushed out the chair next to him.

'I think they get some kind of pleasure out of it,' I said as we both watched the warring siblings for a while.

Majliv turned towards me. He smiled while also seeming to scrutinize me.

'You're not making it easy for me,' he said with a mischievous look.

'What do you mean?'

He reached out his hand and let a couple of fingers glide through my hair close to my ear.

'That style suits you very well.'

What did he mean? That I tempted him more now?

'You don't look so bad yourself with hair' I said, tousling his. It was almost black in the dim light, and long enough for me to run my fingers through.

'I usually don't have hair this short, as I have had it recently, but...' I hadn't noticed that it had become quiet on the other side of the table, so I jumped a little when someone suddenly laughed.

'I hope you're not going to blame me for everything again?' Kian said with a regretful expression towards Majliv. Lynn sat next to him and giggled.

'Whose fault was it otherwise?' Majliv laughed exasperatedly.

'You know you can't let me do such things. I have ten thumbs.'

'What happened then?' Apparently, it had to be something funny, as Lynn had not stopped giggling yet.

'I was going to do Siljan a favour and was stupid enough to ask Kian for help.'

'That was the last time you made that mistake,' Lynn laughed.

'You can be sure of that. As I said, Kian was supposed to help me. Siljan needed resin for incense, and I volunteered to get it for him.'

'Not to sound dumb, but what's resin?' I knew I had heard the word before, but I had no idea what it was.

'It's sap from a tree. I asked Kian to climb a branch to unhook the cup the resin was collected in, and I was supposed to catch it. I didn't want to do it alone for fear of dropping the cup, but in hindsight, it probably would have been the best idea because what happened? Kian was about to lose his balance and dropped the cup right on my head. So...' He smiled and shook his head in disbelief.

'Then there was nothing to do but shave it all off,' I concluded. 'Exactly, and if I may say so, having a completely shaved head in this season is not very practical.'

'When did this happen?' It couldn't have been long before I met him for the first time. His hair had been pretty closely shaved.

'The day before you arrived. I had been at Mirini's for three nights in a row to help you through when Kian asked me to help Majliv with his hair, but when I came home, the hair was already gone.' So, Lynn had been in the church to help me through. That was news to me. After breakfast, Kian went to bed. Majliv was going to help Mirini with a horse, so Lynn and I went to the stalls and shops to shop. We chuckled and laughed as we looked into one window after another and sniffed around all the booths presents. At one, they sold belts, buckles, and hooks. Since it was Christmas Eve, I had decided to buy a gift for Majliv. He had, after all, saved my life several times, and I had not yet done anything to repay him. The big question was: What do you give a person who is a grange warden? He appeared to have most of what he needed.

Suddenly, I saw it. A perfect gift. It was a strong cloak hook of silver with a tiny bottle as a pendant. In the bottle danced a dark red flame. I picked it up and studied it carefully.

'What is this?' I asked the man who owned the booth.

'It's an eternal flame. You can use it anytime and anywhere, but you can only use it once. Whether it's today or in a thousand years, it doesn't matter. Wet or dry, it burns just as well and warms even the coldest frost night,' he replied with some vigorous arm movements, as a true salesperson should.

'I'll take it.' He put it down in a box and wrapped it nicely in silk paper.

'If I didn't know that your cape already had a hook, I probably wouldn't have thought about it. But it's too powerful anyway. So, if I'm not entirely wrong, this is a gift?' Lynn gave me a sly look from the corner of her eye and giggled.

'So what? It's Christmas Eve. Isn't that when you should give gifts to others?'

'No. It's only Santa who does that here in Grimrokk. Of course, there's nothing wrong with others doing it too. He'll surely be delighted,' Lynn said, stroking my cheek.

At the market square, a huge spruce tree had been decorated with large glass orbs in all sorts of colours and glitter, with live candles and a big star on top. The surrounding buildings were really starting to exude the Christmas spirit, both in appearance, scent, and sound. A baker had baked something that smelled like gingerbread, a herb-shop burned incense, and on a corner stood a small group of people singing Christmas carols. I could feel the Christmas atmosphere unexpectedly creeping over me. I had the feeling that I had been sent back a couple of hundred years in time and that I was in an old English town. Not that I had ever been to England, but that was just how I thought it looked.

'You haven't seen Santa before, have you? He's absolutely fantastic!' Lynn laughed eagerly. 'No, I haven't thought about it. I'm going to meet the real Santa.' I felt like a little child.

The evening was to start early, so we began to get ready in good time. Lynn helped me get my hair in order, which had become completely frizzy in the cold weather. Then it was Lynn's turn. I put her hair up in a tight ponytail with corkscrew curls that bounced up and down as she walked. I put on my dress, the same one I had had at the dance, and then I took a look in the mirror. My cheeks were completely red and warm as if I had been embarrassed all day and the colour would now be permanent. There was only one thing that could cause this, and it was the thought of Majliv being there, and that this time we were on speaking terms.

There was a knock on the door. When I opened it, Majliv and Kian stood outside. Suddenly my cheeks got even warmer. Majliv looked handsome in a white shirt and grey velvet jacket that highlighted all his masculine features. Kian also looked nice, but I had seen the outfit before.

'May we be so lucky as to escort you m'ladies?' Kian said, bowing deeply.

'It's okay that we've dressed up for the evening, but let's not overdo it,' Majliv couldn't help but laugh.

'We are delighted with our handsome escorts,' Lynn replied in an equally affected tone as she bowed.

'Well, Majliv, let us common folk stick together, right?' I said nervously, laughing. He winked at me and took my hand. Now it wasn't just my cheeks that were warm, but my whole body.

'Shall I walk with my brother?' Lynn joked.

'You have to walk home alone, though. I have promised Jean that I will belong to her for the rest of the evening,' Kian joked.

'Don't you worry. I have my own plans,' Lynn had to assert herself.

Finally, we came out onto the street, where the cool air subdued my blush. It was almost unreal to walk hand in hand with this beautiful man. If the ladies weren't lining up to dance with him tonight, it was because they didn't have legs or had two left feet.

The square was decorated so beautifully that it resembled the inside of a palace. Where the stalls had been, there were small round tables with red tablecloths and tall, five-armed silver candelabras with white candles. The sky above us was like a ceiling, and there were red runners around the tables. Everyone had dressed in their finest clothes and looked almost like ornaments in a Christmas-decorated ballroom.

We were greeted by a young man in a white shirt, black jacket, black pants, and shiny shoes. His hair was tied tightly in a knot at the back of his neck, and he stood with his hands behind his back. He escorted us to the table. Majliv and Kian pulled out our chairs for us. This must be how the royals lived. Our glasses were filled with mead, and Kian was the first to raise his glass in a toast.

'Cheers to a lovely evening, good company, and new friends.'

'CHEERS!'

Majliv was quite quiet. It almost seemed like he was a little nervous. If he was, he wasn't the only one. I sat with the small pouch in my lap, trying to figure out how to give him the gift. Maybe he would think it was silly since it wasn't normal to give each other anything. After a little while, I took the chance.

'Here! Just wanted to say thank you for doing so much for me.' Ok. That was good. Not too much talking and not too much feeling or sentiment either.

'A gift for me?' he asked. His face sparkled a little extra as he opened it.

'I noticed that you didn't have anything to close your pelt with,' I said. Majliv's fingers admired the metal and the small pendant with the dark red flame.

'Everlasting flame,' he said. He knew what it was.

'Yes. I hope you can use it for something.'

'Most definitely.' He leaned towards me and gave me a kiss on the cheek. When he leaned back, something suddenly appeared on the plate in front of me. A tiny box.

'What's this?' I asked.

'I thought of you when I saw it. So... here you go,' he said, blushing slightly. It was enchanting how irresistible his lips became when they turned red.

I lifted the lid carefully and saw a beautiful necklace. It was a crystal with a light blue pearl inside.

'It's gorgeous.'

'Shake it.' Majliv said playfully. I took the crystal between my fingers and shook it gently. A faint light shone from it.

'It glows! Could you?' I handed him the necklace so he could put it on me. 'Thank you,' I said as I gave him a kiss on the cheek in return.

Dinner was served, and the buzzing of voices swarmed over the square, but not enough to drown out the pleasant music. The food was delicious and unfortunately disappeared too quickly. The orchestra changed the tune and played dance music, and the dance floor began to fill up. How could a world so beautiful have so much frightening and grotesque things in it? Nonetheless, this evening was more than perfect, and I enjoyed it to the fullest. A tall, handsome man came to our table and invited Lynn to dance, and without hesitation, Lynn jumped out of her chair with pure joy.

'Mia, would you like to dance?' Majliv leaned towards me and smiled crookedly.

'Maybe it'll be a bit more enjoyable this time?' I laughed.

'I don't understand what you're getting at,' he laughed ironically at himself. I laughed and took his hand as he pushed the chair forward, and we went out

235

to the dance floor. He put his arm around my waist and took a light grip of my hand with the other. Then he pulled me a little closer to him. I put my free arm around his shoulders and let him take the lead. The beautiful, soft tones of the harp, violin, and guitar sounded so clear in the evening air. I forgot all my worries as I swayed from side to side in Majliv's arms.

The music stopped. Suddenly, a faint jingling sound could be heard, and everyone began to clap. Some started to cheer and whistle. Majliv looked around with a smile on his face.

'What is it?' I asked anxiously. I had learned that anything could happen in Grimrokk.

'Santa Claus,' he said, looking me in the eyes.

A large sled with eight reindeer came rushing across the sky and descended slowly towards the square. The sled stopped behind the Christmas tree, and Santa Claus stood up, waving to everyone. He was definitely not what I had imagined. He had grey-white hair and beard and a big belly, but his pants and shirt were white, and he wore a long black cape with gold-patterned designs and grey fur trimmings. His boots were made of coarse grey fur tied around the leg. His face was sweet, with a small potato nose, red cheeks, and a big, smiling mouth that hid the corners of his thick cheeks. He sat on a large golden chair with lion feet next to the Christmas tree with a green velvet sack in his hand. A long queue of people formed, chirping with excitement. I smiled at Majliv.

'You should go and stand in line, then,' I said.

'Yes, but you should too,' he said, pulling me with him to the queue.

'I think it's a bit rude of me, he doesn't even know who I am,' I said, embarrassed.

'He knows everyone and has gifts for everyone. That's just how it is,' Majliv assured me.

Should I stand in line and ask for a gift? Talk about audacity. We got closer, and those who had already received their gifts sat at the tables and waited for the rest to get theirs.

It was Majliv's turn.

'Well, well. Here's Huldra's grange warden too. How are you doing these days, Majliv?' Nissen smiled and waited eagerly for an answer.

'I'm doing well, and how is Santa faring? Do you have a lot to do?' Majliv bowed.

'Yes, but there's nothing as fun and rewarding as giving gifts and seeing faces light up. But I miss the children,' Santa said, getting a tear in the corner of his eye.

'I have faith that things will change soon,' Majliv said optimistically. Santa gave him the gift and nodded. Majliv stepped aside, while I stood a little nervously and waited.

'Mia, don't be anxious. Come closer, please,' Santa smiled gently.

'It's nice to meet you,' I nodded shyly and curtsied.

'Is Mirini taking good care of you, and Batist?' he asked.

MAGIC OF THE NIGHT

'Yes. I couldn't have asked for better people to get to know here,' I looked over at Mirini, who was sitting at one of the nearest tables and wiping away tears.

'You've been very worried, but take hold of the opportunities with both hands, and do the best you can. No one can blame you if you've done that.'

This big, kind man made me feel warm and loved. Everyone around us smiled familiarly at me.

'There are things that have happened that I never thought would happen to me.' I managed to stop a small tear from balancing in the corner of my eye.

'There aren't many girls like you, Mia. You handle the most incredible things, and I take my hat off to you. Here is your first gift. Take good care of it.' He held out his arms and gave me a warm hug.

'Thank you, and Merry Christmas,' I waved to him. Majliv followed me to the table.

'Was he like you imagined?' he asked.

'No. He was even better,' I looked down at the gift I held in my hands. What on earth could he have given me? Santa stood up, then he waved goodbye to everyone. We stood by our tables and waved back. He sat in the sled behind the reindeer, then they floated up into the sky towards the stars and disappeared over the snow-covered peak. People sat down, and the buzzing of voices increased again. I looked around at others who sat with their gifts and unwrapped them. Their faces lit up one by one. But I couldn't open mine.

'Aren't you going to open it?' Lynn asked.

'I've been thinking all night that this is the most perfect night I could ever have dreamed of, and I know that whatever is in this, it will only make it even better. I simply don't know if I can manage to receive a gift that makes this even more perfect,' I said as I swallowed a lump in my throat.

'Mia. Santa would never hurt you. No way,' Kian said. I took off the gold-coloured ribbon and opened the green silk paper as carefully as I could. The box was made of wood and painted red with silver and gold swirls. I opened the lid and looked inside. Before I took out what I had received, I looked around at the others. Lynn had received a necklace that could be opened, and inside there was a small portrait of her mother. She hiccupped a little. Kian got a music box that played the lullaby his mother used to sing to him when he was little, and he looked down as he squeezed his eyes shut. Majliv got a red heart made of glass, but the shape of the heart was wrong. Instead of coming together to a point at the bottom, it formed two points. For once, it seemed like something was a mystery to him too, but before I could ask, all three turned to me and watched eagerly. A tear rolled down my cheek, and I let out a sob. I reached into the box and took out the object. In my hand, I held a small silver baby rattle with a blue ribbon and a note attached. 'You will someday be a great mother, so don't give up, for you have a lot of love to both give and receive.

Chapter 14
The dark room without windows

After opening my gift, I felt such a relief in my heart which I couldn't describe. As I looked around, tears were rolling down everyone's faces. How could Santa know? I hoped desperately that it would be true. Majliv looked into space with a dazed look in his eyes and took a deep breath. Something occupied his thoughts.

'Was the gift as beautiful as you had imagined?' Lynn asked. She was clearly moved too.

'It was better. It was perfect,' I said, wiping away the tears with a napkin and smiling.

Most people had received touching gifts, so the atmosphere was much calmer and content. It didn't take long before the band started playing the final dance, and everyone stood up to end the evening on the dance floor. Majliv and I danced closer than before. I rested my head on his shoulder. I didn't want this beautiful evening to be over, but what would have been perfect about it if it had lasted forever? Majliv leaned his cheek against my forehead. For a moment, I hoped it was because he wanted me closer. I closed my eyes and let the sweet music flow around me. Majliv's calm heartbeat was intoxicating. If only he knew the feelings he stirred in me!

The beautiful music stopped, and everyone in the square applauded and thanked each other for a great evening. Majliv accompanied me back to the inn. He took my hand and smiled.

'And thus, our magical evening has passed,' he said.

The streets around us were filled with laughter and pleasant greetings exchanged by happy people passing by.

'Yes, but it doesn't matter. It just gives us more to look forward to next year,' I laughed as we entered the inn's door. There were people sitting at the tables, enjoying hot toddies and good company.

'It will be an exciting day tomorrow. You're in the finals,' he said, looking at me.

'So are you,' I said, stopping outside my room. We both fell silent. My pulse raced. I looked up at him, then placed my hand on his cheek as I examined the scar I was responsible for. All that remained was a long, thin line.

'I've gone all in. You've got the next move,' I said. Not that I was a fabulous poker player, but the reference fit so well at this moment. I didn't intend to fold my cards.

'So, we're onto poker analogies now?' he asked.

'Whatever fits,' I replied.

'You'll get to play... eventually,' he said. 'There are no time limits in poker, right?' He placed his palm over mine, closed his eyes, then turned towards my hand and kissed it lightly.

We fell silent again, then Majliv opened his eyes. I felt like he was scrutinizing my soul for a moment before he slowly leaned toward me. I never thought he would take the initiative for a kiss, but there he stood just millimetres away from me. I could feel the sparks igniting my body. Majliv's lips brushed lightly against mine. This was not like the kiss we had shared once before. This time, it was convincing and tender. At the risk of going too far, I made no insinuations for anything more, even though it was all I wanted.

He pulled back gently, just an inch, and studied me. His crooked smile became visible before he gave me a small, light kiss on the tip of my nose.

'Sleep well,' he said and continued down the hallway. He stopped at his door, turned around, and winked. I entered my own room. Everything was buzzing in my head, and I was happy.

ఞౚ

Then, finally, the usual Christmas Eve arrived. The one without snow, without enchantment, without Santa Claus, and without perfection. Nothing could compare to the Christmas I had experienced in Grimrokk. No gifts were as touching, heartwarming, and tender. I longed to be back, just to be able to experience another moment of the most beautiful evening I had felt, known, seen, even experienced. But I hadn't been able to share it with Will. I almost felt guilty for leaving him out, but it had to be that way. He couldn't share it with me.

Mom and Dad's house was as it usually was during Christmas time: filled to the brim with decorations. The noble fir tree was beautifully adorned, and a multitude of gifts were placed underneath it. Pleasant Christmas music could be heard from the living room, and André, my seven-year-old little brother, sneaked around the tree to see which gifts were intended for him.

The food was good, the gifts were nice, and the company was pleasant, but I wanted nothing else but to go back to Grimrokk. The conversation never turned towards the fertility experiment. It was, in a way, taboo which actually suited me rather well. I often thought about it anyway. When the evening was over and we had returned home, Will and I sat down and we finally had a chance to relax, reflecting on the day that had passed.

It had been a long time since we had the opportunity to just sit and talk about everything and nothing. For once, I could enjoy myself. It was nice. I had never really considered how the situation had affected Will. The problem resided with me, but he felt as if it were just as much his problem. If I couldn't have children, he couldn't have children. That was his logical explanation, and it was not up for discussion. It was as simple and as difficult as that.

I was tired and longed to go back to Grimrokk. In Grimrokk, I could escape the heavy days I experienced in Gaia. Even though they were equally real, I could somehow be a different person without the problems, and all my worries disappeared. Majliv frequently crossed my mind, and I missed him. Strangely enough, I didn't feel guilty towards Will. They were two completely different parts of my life and would never know about each other.

☙❧

Morning came, and I jumped out of bed in high spirits. It was great to be back.

'My, you seem incredibly energetic today,' yawned Lynn, sitting up in bed and stretching her arms towards the ceiling.

'Don't you know the saying: Live each day as if it were your last?'

'Well, this amount of enthusiasm must be exhausting,' Lynn laughed.

'Today, I'm ready to kick someone's ass... whoever it may be,' I said and disappeared out the door to breakfast. Not many familiar faces had gotten out of bed yet, and there weren't many other guests either. But Kian and Majliv were sitting at a table, eating porridge.

'Wow, are you guys awake already?' I said, pulling up a chair.

'Nope. No one's awake here. Just two half-asleep knuckleheads,' Kian said, rubbing his eyes. 'Speak for yourself,' Majliv said, shaking his head with a smile as I sat down in the chair next to him.

'Did you sleep well?' he asked.

'Yes. You?'

'Seems like it,' he replied.

'I don't know what you guys consumed last night, but maybe share some with this poor soul so I can regain some life quality,' Kian rested his head in his hand and almost fell asleep between each spoonful of porridge.

'You have to stop flirting with the ladies so late into the night! Then maybe you'd be awake too,' Majliv laughed and nudged his elbow, causing him to jolt awake.

'Don't mind him. He's always grumpy when he wakes up early.' It was Lynn who joined us at the table.

'Said the witty...' Kian added. I was served a bowl of porridge with a cup of imaginary-tea on the side.

'How was your evening yesterday, Mia?' Lynn asked. I thought back to the boring evening I had in Gaia.

Well, it wasn't actually boring. It had been as wonderful as a Christmas Eve could be. It's just that everything had been so much better here. How could I explain to Lynn how the evening had been without revealing anything about who I was in Gaia? I thought about the monotonous atmosphere and tried to explain it in my mind as best as I could.

'STOP!' Lynn screamed at the top of her lungs. She covered her ears in a quick motion, as one does when hearing an unpleasantly loud sound. Her whole body tensed up, and she squeezed her eyes shut.

'What's wrong?' I flinched so violently that it hurt my chest.

'You can't think about Gaia to me,' Lynn said.

'I don't understand.' I had never seen Lynn react like this before. What on earth had I done wrong?

'Lynn can't hear thoughts from Gaia. Or, to put it another way... She hears them, but she doesn't understand them,' Kian said, evidently having suddenly woken up.

'Imagine a little grumpy child sitting next to you screaming into your ears at the top of their lungs then multiply that by ten,' Lynn said, breathing a little easier.

'I'm sorry. It wasn't my intention. I was just trying to answer your question.'

'I meant yesterday here, Mia. Not in Gaia.' Lynn shook her head while smiling.

'Well, then I learned something new today too.'

The competitions were set to start early, and all the finalists were supposed to gather on the field at the same time to be celebrated by the audience. The square had returned to its old self, and the beautiful decorations that had adorned the streets the night before were long gone. Majliv walked with me onto the field. I couldn't help sneaking extra glances at him and think that for the first time, he had kissed me, and not the other way around. The dream that he might become mine one day warmed my heart, even though it also scared me a bit. I couldn't be entirely sure if it would happen.

'Good luck. Imagine it's Lamia standing there,' he said, stroking my cheek.

'I'll manage this without her. Good luck to you too.'

The first event was crossbow. Kian stood ready for battle with a smug smile on his face. His opponent was none other than Jean, the young and beautiful woman he had been so preoccupied with in recent days. She had a crossbow that looked like an assembly of crystal wands, which made it shimmer in all the colours of the rainbow when the light hit it. The shots were small, sharp crystals that were highly distracting because they resembled luminous spheres in the air.

The audience fell silent. The young lady shot a perfect bullseye, but unfortunately for Kian, he was slightly off-centre. Jean shot again and hit magnificently. Kian cantered his next shot, so now he could only hope that she would miss, otherwise Kian would be out of the game, and Jean would be the winner. Once again, Jean struck a crystal right in the centre of the bullseye, and the audience cheered. Being the great flirt he was, Kian congratulated her by lifting her up in the air and celebrating with the other spectators.

Then it was the open combat finale between a wizard and the old man who had competed against Lynn. In the final, the competitors had to use their abilities to make a magnesium-filled glass sphere glow. Each sphere had been enchanted to light up whenever an ability was used within a one-meter radius. The first one to accomplish the task would win the game. And once again, it was the old, deaf man who triumphed.

Next up was slingshot. Majliv and his opponent, a small, thin man with a reed sling that threw pointed corn husks, stood next to each other on the field. Majliv seemed as calm and composed as ever. He threw and hit the target. The little man trembled so violently that I had no faith in him hitting the target, but he surprised me and hit the target. The second throw had the same outcome for both of them. The tension was high, and the silence was so great you could hear a pin needle hitting the floor.

Majliv aimed, took a deep breath, and threw. Bullseye. The audience cheered for exactly three seconds before falling silent again. The little man aimed with his trembling arm and threw. A miss. Majliv had won! I was so happy for him; he truly deserved it. Mirini ran over to him, accompanied by Teddy and Nette, jubilantly.

'That's my boy! That was magnificent!' Mirini shouted at the top of her lungs.

'Thank you,' he laughed contentedly. A voice called for the whip final, and Majliv looked at me.

'You can do this!' His shout barely made it through the crowd.

'Of course.' I wished I was as confident as I sounded.

I positioned myself for the final and looked over at the burly guy standing opposite me. Ramina's words echoed in my head. 'When you win...' If she truly was clairvoyant, this should be in the bag, but who did I think I was? This old man was intimidating, and so was his whip. He was big and strong, and he had a long, black leather whip with sharp knife blades at the end.

The battle began. Now there was only one thing I had to focus on, and that was his flags. I concentrated and swung the thorn vine over my head but missed the flag. Before I could react, I heard the crack of his whip, and my first flag lay flat. Come on, Mia, get it together. You can do this. I started getting angry with myself. I threw the whip as high as I could and swept it towards his flags, knocking one down. He threw it again and brought down another flag. I swung the whip again, but unfortunately, it got tangled in his whip. He jerked his whip, and they came loose. How could I bring down two flags before he brought down one of mine? If it had been possible to take down two flags at once, I would have done it.

Suddenly, all the sound around me disappeared. I was alone. The only thing in front of me was two flags. I had all the time in the world. A tingling sensation flowed through my body, and my hand holding the whip tingled. Something wrapped around my arm. But it didn't matter. The flags had to come down. I closed my eyes, took a deep breath, and swung the whip through the air.

In my mind, I hoped the whip was long enough to reach both of them in the same throw. It felt like hours since I had opened my eyes when I glanced over where the flags stood. They were gone. Had I brought them down? Both of them? Suddenly, the volume around me returned, and the intimidating man I had fought stood shaking his head a short distance in front of me.

There was a cheering sound from the crowd around us, and they were shouting my name. I turned abruptly to see with my own eyes that my flag was still standing. There, dancing in the wind, the flag stood just as steady as before. Had I won? Me? Yes, I'd won! I turned towards Mirini, Batist, Lynn, and the others. Majliv came running towards me, and before I knew it, he lifted me up in the air.

'You're unbelievable!' he exclaimed.

'I... I... I won!' The shock hadn't worn off. Majliv gave me a big hug before putting me down. A man approached and handed me a purse of money, congratulating me on the victory.

Mirini and Batist stood side by side, comforting each other in tears of joy. Father Benedikt looked towards the sky with folded hands, thanking God. Kian promised Majliv a jug of toddy and dragged him along. Most of the others followed in the same direction.

'This calls for a celebration. Two winners from the same group. It's almost unbelievable,' Lynn shouted as she put her arm around my shoulders and began leading me off the field. But my arm jerked as if I were stuck in something.

'Wait a moment. I'm stuck.' It was the whip that was still caught in the flags. I tried to yank the whip, but nothing happened. Something was squeezing the skin around my arm. I rolled up my sleeve and saw that the thorn vine had wrapped itself tightly around my forearm, intertwining the three branches that were braided together.

'What in the world...' I said to myself.

'Are they stuck to your arm?' Lynn asked, bewildered.

'Yes. Ugh, it's so gross. It's almost like it has grown along my arm' I twisted the branches. What kind of thorns were these? I threw the whip on the ground.

'Aren't you going to keep it?' Lynn asked.

'I don't want anything growing up my arms like a parasite. Gross! Ugh!' I shuddered a bit to emphasize the discomfort.

The inn was crowded, but Mirini had been lucky and managed to secure a long table that was now overflowing with people. It was so packed that there was no way there could be room for a single other person unless they were stacked on top of each other. Kian seemed to have already attempted that. Jean was sitting on his lap, twirling her fingertips through his hair. We stood there, looking for seats when I remembered something I had promised to do.

'I'll be right back. There's something I have to do,' I whispered to Lynn.

'What? We're supposed to celebrate! What's so important?'

'Don't worry about it. I'll be back in a bit.' I smiled and hurried out of the door again. This wasn't a visit I really wanted to make since I found her so unpleasant. It was even more repulsive that she had been right about the competition. I only remembered what Father Benedikt had said about keeping my promises. I went to the little corner where Ramina had her room and knocked.

'Just come in, Mia,' a gruff voice called from inside. I entered and saw Ramina sitting in the chair by the glass orb.

'Do you have my share of the prize?' she asked, giving me a cunning look.

'Yes, but I have a question I want an answer to before you get it. What have you told Myrthing about me?' I said firmly to show her that I was aware of what kind of person she was.

'Everything. That you possess the same gift as Lamia and that you are here to stop her,' Ramina smiled.

'And what does Myrthing plan to do about it?' I asked in an angry tone.

'You said you had one question,' Ramina snapped back.

'I'll tell you one thing. I can ask as many questions as I want, and you will answer them!' I was boiling inside. This unpleasant woman was not about to push me around.

'He has invested a lot of time in awakening Lamia again, and she has granted him a lot of power. He's not interested in letting her go so easily,' she replied, rising from her seat.

'What does he plan to do with me?' I shouted, now furious.

'He will find you,' she answered, walking towards the door.

'When did he find out about all this?' Unconsciously, my body began to tremble with anger. My gaze met hers.

'He was here a few hours ago,' she smiled, opening the door as a hint for me to leave, but at the same time blocking the exit with her arm. Her hand was extended towards me, pleading. Why should I keep this deal when she had betrayed me?

'You have such little shame that you'd take the prize money too, won't you?' I said, placing her share on the floor next to her before making my way out of the door. I thought through everything she had said as I walked back to the inn. A few hours ago. That means he had been in town during the competition. I started sprinting towards the inn. I couldn't get there fast enough. As I rounded the final corner, I saw some unfamiliar men making their way into the inn. They wore long black cloaks and were the type of people who instinctively sent shivers down my spine. Four of them stood outside, keeping watch over their horses.

I slowed my pace and turned around cautiously to avoid attracting attention. I had seen these cloaks before, a long time ago. It was when Mirini and I rode out of Wargborough with some pursuers on our tail. This was undoubtedly the same clan. If they had been with Ramina a few hours ago, they likely witnessed the tournament and undoubtedly knew who I was. What should I do now?

Through the inn's window, I could see the men talking to Mirini and Majliv. Their faces were serious, and Majliv shook his head. One of the men held a knife to Majliv's throat, pressing him against the wall.

I stood peering cautiously around the corner. I couldn't think so Mirini could hear me either. Myrthing could read thoughts too, but he was much stronger than the others. I turned to see if there were any other clan members around, but in the next moment, four men grabbed hold of me. Before I could even think, they bound my hands behind my back and slammed me hard into the stone wall behind me. I was officially scared now. I took a deep breath. The only thing to do was to scream at the top of my lungs.

'Hush,' a voice said in my ear. A figure approached us. It was a man, and he placed his index finger in front of his lips.

I opened my mouth as wide as I could and let out a massive scream, but no sound came out, only air.

'We wouldn't want you to disturb all the pleasant people around here with your screams,' he smirked creepily. He had a bluish-white complexion, green eyes, and long grey hair tied in a small braid at the nape of his neck. His body was tall and slender, resembling that of an English nobleman. He was dressed in black trousers and a knee-length cloak with a collar that almost covered half of the back of his head.

It had to be some kind of sorcery he had cast upon me. Several times I tried to scream, but no sound came out. This man couldn't be just anyone. The men around us obediently sought orders from him. The cane he had under his arm had a silver raven's head that opened wide, almost frothing at the beak. Could this be Myrthing? Something told me it was him. The repulsive and falsely polite tone of his words indicated to me that everything about this man was evil. Two of the men tied my arms behind my back and carried me towards their horses by the inn. They tossed me over a horse's back, facing the saddle. A silent cry of pain tried to escape me, but to no avail. They secured me tightly on the horse as I watched the man and the other two head towards the inn. When the door opened, I saw Majliv and Mirini still pressed against the wall. They looked towards the door and clearly recognized the man.

'Myrthing. What a surprise...' Majliv said, but the clan member holding him struck him in the stomach with his fist.

'Do you think so? I haven't been to the Rim Gorge for a while and thought this was an excellent opportunity to enjoy the entertainment. So, I suppose it's appropriate to congratulate you on your victory? If I'm lucky enough to meet some of the other winners, I'll definitely congratulate them too. By the way, it reminds me of...' He chuckled mockingly as he took a few steps aside, standing in the doorway.

'Mia! Congratulations!' he laughed. My gaze was teary, and I tried with all my might to scream, but not a sound came out. All I wanted was for them to leave Mirini and Majliv alone. If Myrthing wanted me, he could leave the others in peace.

'No! You ugly bastard! Stay the hell away from her!' Majliv shouted in anger. I had never seen him so furious. The glare he directed at Myrthing could have split the long, slender body in two if it were possible. Mirini screamed in shock.

'Please, leave her alone,' she cried as she pleaded and begged. I wished I could comfort her. Mirini's reaction took me by surprise.

'I'm sorry to say that I can't stay any longer,' Myrthing said as he walked out the door. He approached the horse standing next to the one I was tied to but stopped by me and grabbed my jaw.

'There's no point in screaming for help. Your helpless little flirt can't hear you anyway,' he said, pointing to four of his men. They were going to ride with him.

Never before had I wanted to harm someone as much as I did right now. It boiled inside me, a mixture of rage, fear, and hatred towards this man. Myrthing mounted his horse and grabbed the reins of the horse I was on. Where were they taking me? What were they going to do? I would never see the people I knew here again. But there was one person it was worse to lose than all the others—Majliv. I looked at him. There was so much I wanted to say, tell him, and show him before my time here was over. But the only words I managed to form with my silent lips were the words I never thought I would utter in Grimrokk:

'I love you.'

The horse was swiftly pulled away. I squeezed my eyes shut as tightly as I could.

'Mia!' I could hear my name being called as we rushed away into the unknown. Majliv's final words to me. I wanted to go home. Home to Gaia, our little house, William, everyday life, childless or not, our friends. Home to my mundane life.

When I opened my eyes, the Rim Gorge was just a dot on the horizon. The sky was grey and as gloomy as I felt, and snowflakes began to fall. I hung over the horse's back. All I could see were branches and trees whizzing past my face. I had never been in this part of Grimrokk before. The ground beneath me was frozen clay with thousands of hoof marks.

A man in a dark cloak holds a knife dangerously close to a restless man's throat.

'And you, don't do anything foolish. You won't find her now,' says the dark cloak before releasing his grip and leaving the room.

Close to twenty men in black cloaks stand outside the inn. They are there to prevent anyone from following Myrthing. A pair of siblings come running out of the crowd that has gathered around the inn. Kian raises his crossbow and shoots one of the clan members off his horse before firing another shot into the neck of another. Lynn throws a knife into the back of one who hasn't seen her approaching. He falls dead. Majliv grabs his staff and strikes it on the threatening man's head, causing a crunch. He grabs the staff again, slams it into the ground, causing a force with such power that some of the nearest men collapse.

Majliv mounts his eight-legged horse and disappears out of the small-town gate in search of she who had finally found her way into his heart.

We rode for a long time among trees and rocky cliffs. I was exhausted, my body ached when the hooves hit the ground beneath us. Tears streamed down into my hair. I was cold and wet. The snow that settled on my clothes melted and seeped into the leather and fabric. My feet were numb, almost lifeless. Several times, everything went black before my eyes, and it was actually liberating to escape the cold and the pain for a little while. When I woke up, everything swirled before me as the horse continued to tread on.

Sometimes when I opened my eyes, it was in the middle of bright daylight, while other times, the surroundings were dark and the sky black. I no longer had a grasp on what was reality and what were my own wandering thoughts. Gradually, the wind began to blow stronger around me, and I thought I could smell the sea.

I turned my head in the direction we were riding in and could barely see a shimmering sea illuminated by the moonlight. The sky was clear of clouds. The small stars were incredibly calming. I entered a trance-like state as I fantasized about floating out there among meteors and galaxies.

The coastline drew closer and closer. I snapped back to reality when the horse suddenly stopped. A spacious boat, big enough for at least ten people, lay by a pile of rocks at the edge of the water. Where were they planning to take me?

Suddenly, a man stood in front of me and pulled me off the horse, causing me to fall to the ground. The deep snow thankfully cushioned the fall. The man forced me to stand on my icy and numb feet. A cloth was tied over my eyes, and then I was dragged toward the boat. The boat was unsteady, which didn't help me much with my balance. We moved on the water. The waves splashed over the railing, and the water made my cold clothes feel warm again. After a while, I could hear something hard and sharp scraping along the bottom of the boat. We stopped, and several of the men disembarked. Some grabbed my arms and pushed me forward, causing me to stumble multiple times. I was shoved hard from behind, causing me to fall over the railing and land on a hard surface. I was on land, but where?

'Take off her blindfold,' I heard Myrthing say. A man leaned down towards me and ripped off the cloth as forcefully as he could. It felt like he took half my fringe along with it.

'Get up!' said another man and kicked the soles of my feet.

I tried my best, but my whole body ached. He grabbed my arms and pulled me up, and then we started walking. The little I could see were some small mountaintops that surrounded us more and more as we approached, and we slowed down. It became completely dark as we entered some kind of courtyard, but it was difficult to make out as the blindfold had been tied so tightly that my vision now was all blurred. We continued further through an opening in a stone wall. The only thing I could make out were the torches on the walls flickering in the draft.

'Move aside! You wretched woman,' one of the men shouted loudly as he pushed me from behind. I began to imagine what could be inside. All sorts of grotesque scenes from horror movies I had seen came back to me. It was always at the end of dark corridors and in cellars that there were monsters and torture chambers. I imagined myself being hung by my arms and boiled alive or trapped in an iron maiden. My feet stumbled a few steps forward in the fog while I trembled. I didn't like to admit it to myself, but now I was truly terrified. Tears streamed down my cheeks.

Myrthing led me down a long stone staircase that spiralled towards the depths of the earth. Water dripped from the ceiling and walls, and the sharp stones protruding from the walls cut my elbows and legs. The sound of our footsteps echoed far down the stairwell, making it sound like there were hundreds of us. We stopped at the bottom of the stairs, where there was a large, thick iron door with a massive iron lock that adorned half of the door with tyrannical discomfort. Myrthing opened the heavy latch, causing the door to creak, and then he threw me onto the stone floor.

'Leave us be,' he said to the others. Before he even finished speaking, they were on their way back up the stairs. He approached me and stood over me, as self-satisfied as one can be. There he stood, smiling with yellow, pointed teeth.

'Down here, no one can hear you. And you can scream as much as you want, no sound can penetrate this door. Of course, the one on guard duty is deaf, just to be safe, so neither your voice nor bribes will work here,' he smiled. 'So, the only thing you can do now is talk to yourself. Or to him over there, perhaps. Not that he's so entertaining after so many years without food. But at least you have your own company,' he laughed loudly and pointed behind me.

His laughter echoed as he walked towards the door, and before he closed it behind him, he held his hand to his mouth as if he was blowing a kiss in my direction. I realized he was teasing me and screamed as loud as I could. This time the sound reverberated from my mouth, causing the ground beneath me to shake. It was so dark. I empathized with those unfortunate enough to be blind. But what frightened me even more was the silence around me. The only thing I heard was my own breath and my heartbeat. What did Myrthing mean by saying I had company? If there was anyone else in here with me, I couldn't hear a single sound from them. I looked around, but all I could see was inky blackness.

'Hello. Is anyone here?' I hiccupped hoarsely. The only response I received was my own echo. I lay on the floor and sobbed uncontrollably. I had never been so alone, and no one would ever be able to find me here deep inside a mountain.

ରେ

Chapter 15
A rider returns to Rim Gorge

ajliv gathers his closest companions at the inn.

'Where could he have taken her?' he asks.

'I don't know. She doesn't tell me anything either. It's completely silent,' Mirini's face is furrowed by despair.

'There are probably several reasons for that,' Batist says, almost in tears. Lynn and Kian rush in through the inn's door.

'Ramina is gone!' Lynn is out of breath.

'It's useless to try to find the old witch now. If she doesn't want to be found, she's impossible to find.' Majliv is angry and shakes his head.

'What can we do?' Kian asks.

'We must search. Myrthing wouldn't take her to the castle. That would have been too easy,' Majliv paces restlessly back and forth in the room.

'We should ask Huldra for help,' Mirini suggests.

'No. It takes many days to travel there in snow this deep,' Majliv shakes his head in despair. 'Majliv! Do we have any other choice? We can't start searching under every stone. It would take forever!' Mirini stands up and places her hand on his shoulder.

'Anything could happen to her in the meantime,' he says.

'You must not underestimate Mia. Besides, there's one more thing: They would never take her with them to kill her. They want her alive,' Mirini comforts Majliv as best she can.

'So, when do we leave?' Kian asks.

'We're going to Huldra. If anyone can point us in the right direction, it's her. Pack everything you need. We leave at sunrise,' Majliv says and nods firmly.

CRSO

I opened my eyes and had no idea where I was. It must have been a nightmare. Breathing heavily, I rubbed the sleep out of my eyes, feeling like I had used every muscle in my body while sleeping.

The events of the nightmare came back to me, and I remembered it all. It wasn't a nightmare at all. I had been kidnapped by Myrthing and his clan. I sat up in bed. Would I ever escape? Was there anyone out there who would try to save me? How could I let someone know where I was when I didn't even know myself? No matter what I would think to get the attention of Lynn or Mirini, Myrthing would surely listen to my thoughts as well.

'What happened?' Will asked, bewildered, beside me.

'I... I just had a nightmare. Nothing dangerous,' I replied. Grimrokk's' little white lies was not so hard to tell anymore.

'What was the nightmare about?' he asked.

'There was a dog attacking me. Then I woke up. It's stupid, I know.' He looked at me with dark shadows under his eyes, his expression almost resigned that I had purposefully awakened him, so I turned away, slightly irritated.

The day was long, gloomy, and hardly reminiscent of the Christmas season. I tried to fill the hours with ideas about how I could escape my captivity in Grimrokk. Will took the opportunity to watch racing sports on TV, but he seemed to be lost in thought.

The following days were strange and not like the Christmas holiday used to be. I felt unusually drained of energy, so I spent my days in front of the computer and did research about Lamia, the Hulder folk, and other things usually associated with superstition. I deleted the files and search-history as quickly as possible. Will could never see them. What could happen if he did, no matter how small the chance, scared me even more than Myrthing and Lamia combined. No, I had to do everything I could to keep it hidden.

☙❧

Kian, Lynn, and Majliv leave the Rim Gorge as soon as the sun rises, riding at a fast pace until evening. Majliv doesn't say much. It's clear that he is anxious. They set up camp by the stream where Majliv and Mia had their big argument a few days earlier. Few words are exchanged around the campfire. All three of them have their own theories and helpless solutions to wrestle with.

By the time the sun rises again, the three friends are already awake, sitting by the glowing fire and eating breakfast.

'Have you heard from her?' Majliv asks Lynn.

'No. I don't think she dares. Myrthing will surely be listening and hearing every word,' Lynn looks at the boys with a worried look in her eyes.

For the first time in a while, Kian is completely silent, with an uneasy expression on his beautiful face.

CR80

I woke to the sound of someone opening the heavy iron door and throwing something on the floor before the door slammed shut. Automatically, I imagined it was something dangerous, like a rattlesnake or a bucket of widow spiders ready to slowly consume me. I remained completely still, listening for any new sounds in the cave, but it was just as silent as before. However, a new scent had emerged that reminded me of something I had smelled before. It was some type of food.

I let my fingers search along the floor to find something edible. A bread crust. That was the smell I recognized, but after a few bites, I'd had enough. It tasted like clay. Next to the crust, there was a cup of something I assumed was water, and as thirsty as I was, I took a big sip. Whatever this was meant to resemble, it certainly wasn't water. You don't need cutlery for water. The liquid was thick and lumpy. I gagged and threw both the bread and the cup against the wall, causing the cup to shatter.

The cold, damp cave made my skin wrinkled and gave me goosebumps. My clothes were full of holes from the sharp stones around the stairs and walls going down to the cave. Everything I wore was damp. I did everything I could to prevent myself from crying. I was so thirsty that my throat burned, and I knew that being without liquid, or becoming dehydrated, was the last thing I needed right now. I sat on the floor with my knees pulled up to my chest, rocking back and forth. Occasionally, I was almost overwhelmed by panic. The darkness around me made it nearly impossible to see anything, so I sat there, feverishly rubbing my eyes. I tried to pull my sweater up higher on my neck to keep warm when something small and hard brushed against my fingers. It took a moment for me to remember what it was. It was the crystal Majliv had given me.

I grabbed it and shook it as hard as I could. It began to glow, and it didn't take long before a strong light shone out of the crystal. It illuminated the entire space around me. Only then did I understand what Myrthing meant by having company. In the corner, there was a dried-up skeleton hanging from the ceiling in chains. I jerked back and screamed as loud as my lungs could manage. The sound reverberated so loudly in the small cell that the skeleton rattled where it hung.

'Majliv! Where are you?' I wanted him with me. I wanted to tell him that I wouldn't live a minute without him. Just the sound of his name echoing against the stone walls comforted me.

೦೫೪

Somewhere between the Rim Gorge and Wargborough, Mirini, Siljan, and Batist are on the move. Teddy and Nette travel together with other acquaintances to stay out of danger while the others search for Mia. The two old horses move as fast as they can to reach Wargborough. Mirini, Siljan, and Batist need to find out if there is anyone there who can provide them with information about where Myrthing takes his prisoners.

Three other brave friends have arrived at Huldra's after many long days. Huldra's younger and beautiful sister welcomes them.

'Come with me. She has been waiting for you for a few days now,' she says seriously and gestures for them to follow her.

Under the big silver tree, Huldra sits and waits but approaches them when she sees who is visiting her.

'Huldra, I hope we're not disturbing you,' says Majliv, bowing deeply.

'You are always welcome. Do you need help?' she asks.

'Myrthing has taken Mia. Do you have any idea where he takes his prisoners?' Majliv asks, shrugging his shoulders.

'Unfortunately, I don't know anything about it, but I know who we can ask. This time, I must accompany you. It has never happened before that he has targeted anyone who has been under my protection, but now he has done just that,' Huldra says, looking concerned.

'Can he help?' Lynn asks.

'That remains to be seen. He is the most reliable source we have.' Time is running out, so Huldra gestures for them to follow her. 'Majliv, there's something you should know. Mia has two abilities. One, the voice, which you have already heard, but you have mistaken the other one. The Hell Horse never granted Mia her reward. She will receive it only when she needs it most. The thorns are Mia's ability,' Huldra explains as she leads them further into the forest.

They follow the same path that Mia took when she went to Nicor, but this time it doesn't take long before the forest opens up, and a pond comes into view. They stop. Huldra sings her beautiful tunes, and the surface starts to tremble. Rings spread across the water, getting closer. The unique tunes that only Nicor can play are heard through the water. Huldra sings stronger and louder as something resembling a mass of moss emerges at the surface of the water. Nicor rises from the water and sees Huldra standing there, singing. He begins to play the same tunes as her before he lowers his fiddle.

'What do you want here, Huldra my dear?' he says rudely.

'We're looking for someone, a friend. You've met her before,' Huldra says.

'Not with me she will be.'

'You can help us find her. Myrthing has her, but perhaps you have someone with you who might have an idea of where he might have taken her?' Huldra takes a step closer to Nicor.

'Since it's Huldra who asks, let the one that dares do the task,' says Nicor, turning towards the pond.

'What do you mean? Do you want us to enter the pond?' Majliv exclaims.

'I let enter no more than one, when four days are done, stay you must since your life is now dust,' Nicor turns his head and chuckles.

'Can we trust that?' Huldra stares at him intently.

'My promise I will hold but when four days are up you must fold,' he replies before disappearing into the water again.

'Wait with Huldra until I return. I'll be quick,' Majliv says. Then he takes a leap, runs to the edge of the pond, and dives in. Nicor is already on his way down, but this time, he doesn't play his fiddle. A dim light appears beneath Majliv, revealing the outline of the surroundings. When he can no longer hold his breath, he takes a deep breath, and to his surprise, his lungs fill with air. His feet land softly on the ground beneath him, and he is dry. Nicor is nowhere to be seen. Far into the horizon, light shines like a sunset. The landscape has the underside of the mountain as its ceiling. With each step he takes, he treads over skeletons, remains, and pools of blood. He catches glimpses of figures in mountain crevices, earthy holes, and ponds, but there isn't much sensible information to be gained from half-dead pieces of flesh. Here, there are everything from malevolent goblins and trolls to werewolves gone amok, devouring themselves. Not all of them give him answers.

He cautiously asks half-dead remnants of vampires and decaying mummies of deceased murderers with gnawed-off fragments. Who knows what they are capable of! In this underworld, no one is alive, yet no one is dead either, and they will never be released. Few have had the 'honour' of coming out unscathed from Nicor's depths.

ൠ

I could no longer find any comfort in waking up in Gaia. Now, as preparation for another IVF attempt, I was once again filled with all sorts of hormones that made me almost irrational at times. It wasn't easy to think about those around me when I was feeling so miserable. Will mostly buried himself and his worries in racing sport, while I escaped into my diary.

To myself,

My reflection is just a shadow of who I once was. My hair is dull, the skin has taken on a strange shade of translucent blue, and the eyes, once so clear and sparkling, have a pale film of grey covering them. My body is merely a place to survive. It no longer belongs to me. It's stuffed with all kinds of medications, doctors examine every nook and cranny, while I lie spread out like a starfish on display. I will be pricked and cut, scratched and pained, and then wait for two weeks, waiting to see if I become pregnant—or not. And I didn't. Then there will be several more months of waiting to go through the same process again. In the meantime, one must function as if nothing is wrong, be pleasant and cheerful to everyone encountered, and be someone who thinks of others and solves their problems. Which superhero can manage that?

The following weeks didn't get much better. I felt that even in Gaia, I was becoming more and more like the lifeless person lying on the floor of the cave. But of course, everyone thought I was depressed because the IVF treatment was a long and tiring process. There was some truth to that, of course, but the worst part was going to bed at night. I was overtired and exhausted, but the last thing I wanted was to fall asleep.

The days passed like a foggy haze. What happened with the egg retrieval and test tubes disappeared in the mist around me. Was this how the rest of my life was going to be? I missed Will touching me, kissing me. It wasn't just me who had dug myself into a hole. Clearly, Will had many thoughts in his head during the day, and he didn't want to share them with me. Anyway, I didn't ask either because I had more than enough to deal with myself.

Well, the story repeated itself, and the answer was negative once again. It was far from a surprise. I didn't want this anymore; it was too tough. How could we become parents now? Will had always said he didn't think he would want to adopt, but now it seemed like the only option we had. I knew I was going against Will, but still, I started researching the adoption process and how to proceed. Was I supposed to go through life without ever becoming a mother? Nothing lasts forever and with the extra treatment my body was receiving it felt like my soul was being crushed along with my life spark. These thoughts filled my mind constantly.

CRSD

It was not easy to say how long I had been in Myrthing's prison, but every single second felt like an eternity. I could already feel my ribs due to the lack of food, but it wasn't surprising considering I was fed with mouldy bread and mud. Fortunately, water dripped from the ceiling, and the fresh water had kept me hydrated. The only solace I had was the necklace I had received from Majliv. Every time I shook it, I could, for a brief moment, envision his beautiful face.

In Wargborough, people refuse to talk. Everyone is afraid of the power Myrthing has gained, and none of the people Mirini, Siljan, and Batist tries to talk to, dare to utter a word. Lynn and Kian impatiently await Majliv's return to the surface of the pond. Lynn sits on a tree stump, picking at a branch, when Huldra approaches and sits beside her.

'What does your heart tell you?' she asks.

'That she's alive.'

'Don't worry if you can't hear her. Mia is a clever girl and probably has every reason to keep you out of it.' Huldra stands up and takes Lynn's hand. They walk towards the large silver tree standing in the middle of the clearing. It is devoid of leaves, so it appears lifeless. It shines with various shades.

'Things are not always as they seem. Looks can be deceiving.' Huldra points to the tree. 'Feel it,' she says.

Lynn places both hands on the bark.

'It's warm, and the bark is smooth.'

'It looks lifeless, but it's alive, just like you and me,' Huldra looks at her and smiles.

'What kind of tree is it?'

'Long ago, someone planted a tree as a symbol of their love for each other. They were the first Grimmers to find each other here in Grimrokk. They had a child who was born here, and this child was the first to stay. The birch they planted was planted out of love, and the day they died, something happened. The tree lost all its leaves. It became forever as you see it now. Are you good at throwing?' Huldra smiles mischievously.

'I'm average, I guess. Why?' Lynn asks, puzzled.

'Then you shall receive a gift from me.' Huldra goes to her hut and returns with something shiny in her hands.

'What is this?'

Huldra opens her hands, revealing something that resembles leather armour to wear on the forearm. It has three pockets, and in each pocket lies a round wheel. They are flat, silver-coloured, and have long prongs that all bend inwards towards the circle.

''Shuriken', throwing stars. They will come back to you when you call for them.' Huldra hands them to Lynn.

'Call them?'

'Yes. Since you have the ability to read thoughts, you also have the ability to summon them. Try it!' Huldra points at a dead tree.

Lynn aims and throws, and the star embeds itself in the trunk.

'Call it back,' encourages Huldra.

'Come here?' Lynn calls softly, a bit embarrassed.

'No. Think it. Just like you normally do. Ask it to stop in your hand!'

Lynn focuses with all her might and beckons the star back.

'Good. Keep it up!' Huldra encourages.

'I will. Thank you very much,' Lynn smiles gratefully and curtsies deeply.

Majliv has been in the underworld for several days, and time is running out. He hasn't encountered anyone who can help. The closest he has come is a siren who has been trapped by Nicor for a long time. She has seen Myrthing's boat land on an island off the coast, and he has brought prisoners with him, but what they have done there or whether the prisoners have ever left, she doesn't know. When Majliv asks where this island is, she can only explain it in images from the sea since she has never seen the inland. Majliv has no idea where it could be, but he believes there might be something to what the siren is telling him.

CRRO

The months passed slowly. Spring was in the air and in the colours outdoors, but inside me, it felt like a cold autumn. Will had finally begun to accept that we might never be able to have our own children, so when I presented all the information I had gathered about adoption, he sat awake and interested, paying attention. It was a sea of paperwork. After letting all the information sink in, Will thought it was a good idea to submit an application. However, we made an agreement that while we waited for a response, we would proceed with one last IVF attempt.

As usual, there was a long waiting period for the IVF trial, so we took the opportunity to initiate the adoption process with the Child Welfare Services. First, they had to approve that we were suitable to care for a child and provide a safe upbringing. Then we needed medical certificates, police clearances, recommendations, and other sorts of paperwork. Everything we had never thought we'd need. This process could take a whole year. Only then could it be sent to an adoption agency, which would, in turn, send the documents to the country we chose. This part of the process could take up to two years. Fantastic... If we were lucky enough to complete the entire process, we would probably be hunched-over senior citizens before we got to meet the child.

On the other hand, Aleksandra's belly grew bigger and bigger every day, and I truly didn't know how to handle my own emotions and at the same time share in their joy. I had felt the foetus kick and move, and it was so beautiful and surreal that I couldn't imagine having the same happening to me. I really couldn't comprehend that there was a real, living child inside that large belly. Will and I hadn't seen much of Aleksandra and Peter lately. It had become too difficult to talk about everything.

∞

I hadn't eaten for several days. The bread had just been lying in a pile, growing greener and greener with each passing hour. That being said I had no idea how long an hour was! My eyes could hardly open anymore. How I longed for Mirini to be with me, and the food she cooked. Or for Lynn to be here and gossip about Kian and Jean. I started fantasizing about the days I had in Grimrokk and everything I had experienced. Suddenly, the memory of Ramina Visibilis popped into my head. What she had said had been so incomprehensible. I slowly repeated her prophecy to myself:

'You have a great task ahead of you, a task you are avoiding. It will shape you if you accept that it is your future. There is much you don't know about yourself. But what do I see? Love? Yet uncertainty lurks. Tread carefully, for you never know who is telling you the truth. You have a dark time ahead, and you must face it alone, but remember, you can be heard even in the deepest forests.'

'You can be heard in the deepest forests'? Granted, I wasn't in a forest, but could it be a metaphor for being hidden away? If so, who could hear me? I gave up trying to hold on to the thread, and my thoughts wandered. The belief that someone was searching for me remained strong, but how long would they search before giving up?

What if they thought I was dead? I hadn't made a sound. Suddenly, it struck me! I could be heard from the deepest forests! Mirini and Lynn could hear me with their gifts. But what should I think? I couldn't reveal where I was, as it might result in them risking their lives to save me. Not that I had a higher wish than to be freed from this cell, but I didn't want anyone to be harmed or, worse, killed for me. I gathered my thoughts:

'Mirini? Lynn? I hope you're safe and can hear me. Myrthing has captured me. He knows about my ability, so he sees me as the weapon he can use to strangle Lamia with. You know as well as I do that he listens to our conversation. Take care of yourselves.'

What had I done? Who would save me now?

Mirini hears the tearful words crystal clear in her mind. She runs as fast as she can to Batist, Siljan, and Benedikt, who are packing the horses to go to Mirini's house.

'I just heard her! She's alive! They hold her captive, but she won't say where,' she shouts from the church steps.

'What? Is she injured? How did she sound?' Batist drops everything he has in his hands, right onto the ground.

'I don't know more than that, but the most important thing is that she's still alive,' Mirini's eyes are filled with tears.

Lynn is taking a nap on a high bed in one of the earth huts when the same words call out to her. She runs as fast as she can to Kian.

'Kian. She's alive! I heard Mia!' Kian, who is also asleep, startles and hits his head on a beam in the hut ceiling.

'What?'

'Mia. She's alive. It doesn't sound like things are going well for her.' Lynn's face is filled with despair.

'Did she say anything about where she is?' Kian asks as he tries to comfort his sister in the light of the situation.

'No, she wouldn't say. Myrthing is listening. But fortunately, she's alive.'

Majliv doesn't have much time left and desperately searches for someone who knows how he can find the island he has heard about. But there are few who will answer, and the few who do know nothing. Enchanting music can be heard in the distance. Nicor is on his way. On a sandbank, Majliv sees a figure sitting cross-legged, dressed in a black veil that covers the entire body.

'Do you know where Myrthing is holding people captive? There's an island I'm searching for,' Majliv leans down towards the figure. A crooked, white hand draws in the sand. The image that forms in front of him resembles a map, with mountains, valleys, and a coastline. The other hand lowers a string with a pendulum at the end, and it swings in a large circle over the map. The music is getting closer. The pendulum is slowly drawn towards a point and dropped into the sand.

A finger points to a small dot outside the line that represents the mainland. Majliv studies the image and nods in gratitude before the hand erases the drawing. He sprints as fast as he can towards the opening he came through.

With every step he takes, he must resist Nicor's persuasive tones. He can see the opening, but Nicor is gaining on him. Just as Nicor reaches out for him, he takes a deep breath and jumps as high as he can. The water feels like clay. His swim strokes are heavy. The beautiful tones behind him are constantly audible, clearer and closer. It feels like his lungs are burning in his chest. With the last bit of energy, he pushes himself to the surface. Kian and Lynn run into the water and grab hold of him. Nicor still sees an opportunity. Majliv's body is almost lifeless.

'Come on! You can't give up now!' Kian shakes him hard with anger. With unforeseen strength, Kian helps Majliv onto the horse's back. The mesmerizing tones are getting closer. All three of them make their way into the forest and set off towards Mirini's estate.

Siljan, Batist, and Mirini have arrived at the estate. Three horses come riding out of the forest at a high pace and up the avenue. Kian and Lynn have Majliv between them, hanging over Pronto.

'We need help!' they shout. Majliv is lifeless. Everyone gathers around to help, and they bring him inside and onto a comfortable and warm bed. If he doesn't wake up soon, all hope may be lost.

To everyone's concern, almost a day has passed, but Majliv still hasn't woken up. Kian and Lynn sit by his side, waiting patiently. Finally, he starts to regain consciousness and abruptly sits up in bed.

'I need pen and paper!' he shouts loudly.

'What do you need them for?' Kian asks.

'Something to write with... NOW!' he snaps.

Lynn immediately does as he asks and rummages through the drawers of one of the room's dressers. She finds a charcoal stick and a sheet of paper, which she hands to him. Majliv sketches the map he was shown by the figure and points to the dot where it suggests Myrthing is holding his captives.

'This island is where Myrthing keeps his prisoners, and it's our only lead. We need to leave as soon as possible.'

Lynn and Kian exchange anxious glances.

'I heard Mia. She didn't say much since Myrthing is listening, but she's not doing well. I think she's actually about to give up,' Lynn says, her eyes filled with tears.

Majliv squints his eyes and furrows his brow.

'How quickly can you two be ready to go?' he asks.

'We've been waiting for you. Everything is packed and ready,' Kian says with a faint smile.

'So why are we sitting here? Let's go!' Majliv grabs his pelt and drapes it over his shoulders.

In the stable, three horses stand well-rested and fed, ready for departure. Lynn stands at the kitchen door, talking to Mirini.

'Can you go back to Wargborough in a few days? If you can trick Father Benedikt into believing that someone is coming through the mirror, it won't be long before Myrthing finds out. Father Benedikt can't lie.'

'But there's no one coming through?' Mirini responds, bewildered.

'Father Benedikt doesn't know that. If it can lure Myrthing to Wargborough in an attempt to stop it, it means he's not on the island, and we can travel a bit safer.'

'I don't like lying to a priest,' Mirini says, crossing herself.

'That's the least of your worries right now. Mia is suffering, and you're worried about what God might think if you lie to a priest? Shame on you!' Majliv says as he passes them in the door. He turns his back on Mirini and mounts his horse. Anger boils inside him. The three friends bid farewell and ride away.

ॐ

It was only a few weeks until Aleksandra's due date, and everything was ready for the baby. Every time I thought about how happy they were, my eyes welled up. They were so proud of her big belly.

I felt like I couldn't measure up, like I wasn't normal. Elderly people who didn't have children were often seen as peculiar and unusual. As if they were less valuable, somehow inferior. I had thought the same things myself, but not anymore. Now I understood how they felt. These people said they didn't want children, probably so that everyone would stop asking or feeling sorry for them if they knew the reason. I had encountered faces full of sympathy too many times myself.

When I was little, I heard my mom talking about her uncle, who didn't have any children.

'Why don't they have children, Mom?'

'Not everyone wants to have children, my dear.'

'Are there really people who don't want children?! Are they a little strange, then?'

'No, it's not that strange. Some people want other things in life. Sometimes, there are people who can't have children even though they want many.'

'Can't they just make some though?'

'Well, it's not always that easy, you see.'

I could remember the conversation well. Later, I sat in my room and pondered what my mom had said, but how could it be that some people didn't want children? It was the most wonderful thing in the world. Imagine being old and celebrating Christmas alone. That's when I decided that I would have many children.

൦ൽൽ

MAGIC OF THE NIGHT

I lay on the floor and listened to the drops falling from the ceiling. There were never any other sounds, except when the door opened, and some bread was thrown to me. Maybe this was a dream? Was I imagining everything? Was it possible to feel so cold in a dream?

At times, it was difficult to breathe. My chest tightened, and it hurt to gather air. Several times, I considered talking to Lynn again, but it was really of no use. It wouldn't change the outcome. I was still in here, and Lynn was hopefully out there, alive. But what hurt the most was never being able to see Majliv again.

Chapter 16
One man`s despair becomes another man`s death

ays lighten and darken repeatedly as the three riders approach the coast. They stop at a mountain with a ledge, where they set up camp for the night. Majliv manages to light a fire just before the wind picks up and it starts to rain heavily.

'This is the saddest weather I know. Mud, slush, and water make me cold and dirty,' Lynn says as she looks out at the snow melting across the landscape.

'I hope the warm season comes soon. I'm tired of anything related to snow,' Kian has been surprisingly serious throughout the journey, and for once, he hasn't annoyed Lynn once.

'I hope it waits for Mia,' Majliv says without lifting his gaze from the flames as darkness begins to surround them.

The next morning is stormy and wet. The snow is gone, except for a few patches remaining in the shade of some trees. The horses struggle through mud and brush. With the thick clouds covering the sky, it quickly becomes dark.

Finally, they can hear the sound of waves crashing against the mountainside. They can see the coastline.

'Somewhere out there, Mia is waiting,' Lynn whispers just loud enough for the other two to hear.

Without saying another word, they continue riding.

'How are we going to get out there?' Kian asks.

'The Myrthing clan must use boats to go back and forth, so we'll steal one of them,' Majliv's enthusiasm has returned. A boat is moored to some rocks by the water's edge when they reach the coastline. They hide the horses in a small patch of trees and sneak down towards the cliffs.

'Where are you?' Majliv whispers to himself, looking around in the twilight for watchmen.

'Found you,' he says, pointing to a small cottage not far from the boat.

The evening has grown dark due to the trees and the forest surrounding them. It's nearly pitch black. They move cautiously toward the boat, keeping a watchful eye on the cottage above. It is occupied, and laughter and slurred singing can be heard.

Majliv reaches the boat but is interrupted before he can untie it. A man comes running out of the door and rounds the corner just in time, before he starts coughing and retching. Majliv lies flat along the rocks while Lynn and Kian squat behind a boulder. The man wipes his mouth, then chuckles to himself before going back inside to join the others.

When they finally reach the water, the sea is so fierce that rowing becomes difficult. The wind hurls droplets at them, and the waves crash splutters of water into the boat. Majliv and Kian sit with their respective oars, but it still feels like they're not making any progress.

'Majliv! This is pointless. We won't get any further in this weather,' Lynn yells between gusts of wind.

'I won't give up now!' Majliv shouts back. He stands up in the boat, raises his arm, and strikes the water's surface with his staff.

The water moves to the sides with two big splashes. Majliv sits down and continues to row.

'What's the point of that?' Kian shouts.

'Just wait and see!'

It's impossible to see anything in the storm, and the waves are becoming dangerously high.

'We're not helping anyone by disappearing at sea. We have to turn back!' Lynn is scared.

'No! We haven't come this far to turn back!' Majliv is so determined that he froths at the mouth. A tremendous splash erupts not far from the boat's side, and Lynn jumps.

'What was that?' she screams in fear.

'Hopefully, a helping hand.' Majliv stops rowing and sits there, staring straight ahead into the darkness. Something jumps in the water, and then a large, dolphin-like tail emerges.

'Sirens?' Lynn breathes a sigh of relief.

'Yes. Since the siren I encountered mentioned being here, I hoped there were more of them in the area.'

A beautiful creature with a human upper body and a dolphin-like tail emerges from the water. Majliv bows.

'Wanderers, what brings you to the sea in such weather?' A clear, melodious voice overpowers the noise of the storm.

'We're on a vital mission and need to reach Myrthing Island, which is completely impossible for us in this weather. Can we ask for your help?' Majliv tries to be as polite as possible.

'We'll gladly help you, but only until the first reef. The undercurrents there are dreadful, and many of us have lost our lives.'

Four more sirens appear. Majliv throws a rope to them, which they pull taut between them. The boat picks up speed and makes its way through the foaming waves. Kian, who has never before encountered a siren, gazes enchantingly at the beautiful creatures. Legend has it that many sailors have lost their lives to the waves, enchanted by their love of a siren. Lynn slaps Kian on the cheek to snap him out of it. Far off in the horizon, they glimpse a large, dark shadow rising from the restless sea.

'This is as far as we can take you,' the sirens bow farewell before disappearing among the waves.

'Come on, we're almost there,' Majliv says, grabbing an oar. Kian needs no further encouragement and follows his rhythm through the waves.

Small lights are visibly scattered around the island, another sign that there are people here. The waves calm around them, and it seems like the storm is subsiding. The sharp mountain ridge protrudes like a spear from the sea, surrounded by smaller rocks and islets. A kind of building is barely visible in the moonlight. There is also a dock by the mountainside, with a narrow path winding upward. To remain unseen, they moor the boat behind a small headland sheltered from the dock.

'We have to climb up here,' Majliv whispers. The slope is steep and covered with sharp rocks that make it difficult to climb. A little further up, they see another narrow path leading towards the building. It is no longer just any building; it is a fortress. The small, rocky path guides them towards a wooden door barely hanging on its hinges. This part of the fortress appears deserted and seemingly unguarded. The courtyard on the other side is a grotesque sight, adorned with chains and torture devices on walls and pillars. In the largest section of the fortress, there is a tall tower where ravens sit and peck at each other. They are also known as 'Myrthing's carrier pigeons.'

Light shines from a room in one corner. Suddenly, footsteps are heard from the main gate, and a clan member walks across the courtyard. The three friends try to make themselves as small as possible in the darkness. The man walks over to the room in the corner, and chit chat can be heard. There is no one else to be seen, but all three of them know that Myrthing would never leave a fortress like this unprotected. Somewhere in the fortress, there are more clan members who are undoubtedly ready for a fight.

There are several doors along the walls, but it's a doorless gate that catches Lynn's curiosity. Above it is an ornament of a skull impaled on a spear. She turns to the boys and points at the gate.

'Where would you have a prison cell?' she says.

'Where people dare not enter,' Majliv smiles and pulls the other two towards the opening.

A long, dark, and rocky staircase winds down into the mountain. They can only glimpse it in the faint light. Lynn stays behind to keep watch while the boys disappear down the stairs. The wet, slippery steps make it difficult to move unnoticed. Each step is either glazed with wet ice or covered in moss, making every step uncertain. Further down, Majliv stops. He has spotted a man standing guard in front of a sturdy iron door. He is dressed in black and is massive, holding a large spear with an additional curved blade protruding from one side.

Kian runs his hand down his thigh, grips the crossbow, and pulls it up. He nods to Majliv to move aside and takes aim. Without warning, a spark hits the guard's shoulder, causing him to fly straight into the heavy door. Another shot is fired, but it misses. The man gets up and grunts in annoyance. Majliv and Kian run towards him.

Lynn keeps watch. For now, it's quiet, but it shouldn't last long. One of the doors in the courtyard, a double door, leads into the part of the fortress with the most windows. Flickering lights can be seen in almost all of the windows, which can only mean one thing: There are more clan members in the fortress.

Kian strikes the guard with all his might, right in the chest, causing sparks to fly from his fists. The man staggers to the side, clutching his chest against the wall, leaving the door unprotected.

'Mia! Mia!' Majliv pounds his fists on the iron door but gets no response.

'You're probably too late. There hasn't been any sign of life in there for a while,' the guard grins, his speech slurred, as he swings around, using his spear as a scythe against Kian's legs.

Majliv grabs hold of his staff and smashes it with all his might against the hinges, causing the door to tilt to the side. One more blow, and it teeters towards him. He grabs the top and wrenches it out with his bare hands. Kian shoots the man in the side, but not before receiving a slap himself.

The room behind the door is a gloomy sight. It's cramped and damp, and the stench is unbearable. In the middle of the room, curled up on the floor, lies a figure.

'Mia!' Someone called my name from far away. I had to be dreaming again. Had I let madness win? Had I wished for it so strongly - to see him again - that I heard his voice in my own imagination?

Suddenly, I felt something touching me, something warm. It was so unfamiliar that I wasn't sure, but I didn't have the strength to move my body. If it weren't for the fact that I had to, I would have stopped breathing. My lungs felt too heavy.

'Mia, Mia? Can you hear me?' the voice said again. This time, I was convinced that someone was touching me. My whole body was turned onto my back, and my head was lifted. It had been so long since I had seen light that I no longer knew if my eyes were closed or not. The crystal felt so heavy that I couldn't bring myself to shake it.

'Mia. Are you there?' This time, the voice was clear, and a warm hand brushed my hair away from my forehead. Majliv? Could it really be him? I squeezed my eyes shut as hard as I could. Then I tried to open them again.

'Majliv?' Above me stood the most beautiful creature I had ever seen. His hair had grown so long that his bangs brushed against his nose, but his eyes, which had always been so sparkling and deep, had grown dull.

I wanted to touch him, just to make sure he was real. If I had gone mad, this could be a malicious illusion. My hand was as if glued to the floor, but something new gave me strength to lift it. For the first time in a long time, I felt joy. The feeling was so strong that it made me doubt if I had ever truly felt it before. My fingers lifted from the floor and floated towards his face. His cheek was warm and smooth.

'Everything will be fine. We'll get you out of here,' he said and lifted me in his arms. His scent was familiar and reassuring.

Majliv carried me out of the cave's door where Kian was in the midst of a fight with one of the guards. In an inattentive moment when Kian looked at me, the guard delivered a solid cut to his leg. He screamed in pain and fell to the floor. With a wicked grin, the guard turned towards Majliv, who was heading up the stairs. He took a step towards us, but suddenly the sound of sparks filled the room, and the man's chest crackled and hissed before he fell dead. Kian lay on the floor with the crossbow on his arm, red-faced with anger. He lowered his arm. His gaze met mine, and it said everything. The sight of me was clearly shocking to him.

'Mia? What have they done to you?' I couldn't find the words to respond. Grimrokk had never felt so unreal, and yet never so dangerously real. Tears streamed down my cheeks. I was saved.

'Kian! Can you walk?' Majliv interrupted while carrying me in his arms.

Kian fumbled with his belt and took it off with one hand. He tightened it around his thigh like a tourniquet, then leaned against the wall.

'Do I have a choice, mayhap? I don't plan on staying here, that's for sure,' he said, nodding towards me.

As we neared the top of the stairs, a sound resembling a mix of whistling and swooshing could be heard. The sound was followed by a thud and a shout. Majliv leaped up two or three steps at a time and arrived just in time to see Lynn throw a shuriken right between the eyes of a guard. He fell to the ground next to another guard. She extended her hand, and the shuriken's returned to her, then she turned towards us.

'There must be others who heard us. We need to go, now!' she said in a low voice. Her gaze met mine in the darkness. She shook her head in shock, wearing an angry expression on her face.

'What's happened...

'Lynn, help Kian!' Majliv interrupted her. The last thing I cared about at the moment was how I looked.

Even if I had lost an eye and become bald, I couldn't have been more relieved.

'What happened?' Lynn looked at her brother and put her arm around him.

'We'll have the questions later,' he said, looking up at a window. A man looked down at us before turning back into the room.

'Intruders!' he shouted at the top of his lungs. Majliv held me closer to him, and we quickly made our way through a gate where the door hung limp on its hinges. From the courtyard, we heard doors flying open, running feet, and voices calling out to each other. Over Majliv's shoulder, I saw Lynn pulling Kian out of the gate, but they were moving too slowly. If they didn't pick up the pace, the clan would catch up to them before they reached us. We were on a narrow path winding between rocky outcrops. About twenty guards came running out of the gate, shooting arrows at us. The guards were gaining on Kian and Lynn at an alarming speed. Majliv glanced back. 'Sit here!' he said, gently setting me down on the ground with my back against a slope.

'Go! Go!' he shouted at the siblings as he stood up, legs wide apart. They ran past us and began to climb down the mountain towards the boat. Majliv raised both hands. In the same way I had seen him do when we encountered Lamia, he grasped the invisible staff and hurled it with all his strength at the guards. It struck the first four in the stomach, throwing them backward and knocking over some of the others behind them. Majliv lifted me up again and started sliding down the mountain. Some guards had the same idea and were coming towards us from the side. Majliv glanced away for a moment just as a guard nearby drew his bow and aimed right at us. I glanced over Majliv's shoulder and panic gripped me as I saw the tip of an arrow just ten meters away. Before I could think, I placed my hands against Majliv's ears and took the deepest breath I could. I gathered all the energy I had, then opened my mouth. A scream came out that cut through everything in the guard's direction. I didn't know how long my lungs would hold, but I knew I could sustain the tone long enough. The last thing I saw was the guards nearby being knocked to the ground, blood spraying. After that, everything went black.

ↂ

We were still on the waiting list for the next IVF attempt, but I no longer cared. My own indifference made me nauseous. I was now convinced that the rescue mission in Grimrokk had happened only in my crazy imagination, and it irritated me even more. The only thing occupying my thoughts was adoption. If there was a child somewhere in the world who felt even remotely as lonely and unloved as I had felt in captivity, I would help that child. Because even though I had fabricated the story, the emotions were real and palpable. The child would have a home with boundless love, kisses, and hugs. It would never feel inferior.

While I was determined about adoption, Will was a bit hesitant. I had promised him to undergo a third and final IVF attempt for his sake. Lounging in the armchair, I was brought back to life by the sound of my mobile phone beeping. It turned out to be a message from Aleksandra. As I was about to start reading, a short video clip appeared with the sound of a baby crying in the background. Aleksandra and Peter had become parents to a little, beautiful baby boy, and they were holding him between them. How proud they were!

The image hit me so suddenly that it hurt my chest, almost like an elephant stamping all over my heart. It suddenly became so real to me that I would never have a child of my own. The realization gripped me so tightly that I stopped thinking for a moment. What did I actually feel? In a way, I was very happy, but also sad. I wanted to cry, but my heart felt empty, so I couldn't anymore. Time stood still. For a brief moment, I was back in the cave, the darkness, and the silence. I could hear my own heartbeat in the emptiness.

'Who was it?' I startled. Will had entered the living room without me noticing.

'It was Aleksandra. They've had a little baby boy,' I replied. Will's face was expressionless. He smiled, but not with his eyes. I showed him the message.

'That's great,' he said.

'Yeah,' I said and sent a congratulatory message back.

To myself

The neighbour had a son today. The most beautiful, little baby boy you can imagine. My heart breaks as I formulate the words: I envy them their child. Their faces radiated joy, as the faces of proud parents should, but it still hurts to see that it's not your own reflection you see. Life gets turned upside down, everyone says, but that's fine, turn it, then, because I want nothing more than that. I thought adoption would give me a new spark, but the news felt like getting a door slammed in my face. Nothing is happening. Still childless. My hope has vanished, the light at the end of the tunnel is extinguished, and it becomes too heavy to carry this sorrow in my heart forever.

☙☙

I woke up, opened my eyes, and looked around at my surroundings. Everything was black again, disturbingly silent, raw, and cold. Where was I? I felt the ground beneath me, rough and wet. The smell of stale air, mould, and decay hit me. I was in the cave. The last shred of doubt vanished. Everything I had believed to be a heroic rescue mission had been my own madness. I fumbled around for the crystal and shook it as hard as I could, but nothing happened. It was still so dark that I didn't know if my eyes were open or closed. Had I truly gone so mad? I started to hyperventilate while sobbing uncontrollably. Couldn't this world just let me die!

'Mia! Mia! Mia... hush,' a soft and calm voice said. I opened my eyes and looked straight into Majliv's familiar face. Around us were trees and bushes, above us a starry night sky.

'Mia, calm down. You're safe.' The reassurance didn't stop my tears.

'I... thought I was in that cave again, and that it was just a wishful dream that you came there to rescue me.' The words stumbled out of me, uncertain and stuttering. Suddenly, I noticed how warm and cozy it was around me. I was lying on Majliv's blanket with his pelt covering me, and he was beside me.

'Come here,' he said, leaning back with his arms outstretched toward me. I let myself be embraced by his strong arms, and he stroked my back. His scent was almost hypnotizing, and his breath calm and steady. I felt safe, I could trust that this was real, so I lifted my head for a moment to look into his eyes.

'Thank you,' I said before lowering my head again. It was by no means a sufficient expression of gratitude for everything he had done for me, and it made me uneasy. I would never be able to give him the thanks he deserved.

He moved one hand to my chin and lifted it towards his face. There was a relief in his gaze, almost a joy. Then he gently pressed his lips against mine and kissed me on the forehead. I fell asleep to the sound of his heart beating against my cheek. It had been a long time since I had been so relaxed.

Someone stroked my cheek as I began to wake up. 'Mia?' a voice whispered in my ear.

'Mmm...' I wanted to sleep longer. It was so delightful not to freeze in my sleep.

'You have to see this,' the voice whispered again. I peeked through my eyelids and looked up at Majliv.

'Look!' he smiled and looked away from me towards the sunrise.

'What am I supposed to see?' I yawned and stretched some muscles.

'You just have to see...' he replied.

Still with my head on Majliv's chest, I looked ahead towards the trees and the clearing. The sky was turning a light shade of blue, and the sun was slowly but surely rising. The sunbeams illuminated the treetops as before, but this time they seemed greener. Was I hallucinating again? The sunbeams glided slowly down the tree trunks in the forest, and surely enough, everything did become greener.

I didn't understand what made it so special until I saw the bushes right next to me. They first formed small buds on the branches, which grew until they opened up, revealing small green clusters. Suddenly, they exploded into leaves. On the ground, there were flowers blooming. A gust of wind brushed under my nose, carrying the scent of fresh spring. In the treetops, there were small birds chirping with ecstasy, playfully flirting with each other.

'The Long Warmth?' I said. It couldn't be anything else. The warm air was starting to make me sweaty under my thick fur.

'Mmm,' Majliv moved the fur aside but kept a firm hold on me.

'That explains everything,' I said.

'What do you mean?'

'As cruel as the evil is here, the Long Warmth must be truly beautiful.'

'I would sacrifice all of this beauty to end the evil. After all, you grow used to beauty.' Majliv thought so differently from others. There was something about everything he said that was so thoughtful and reasonable. Beauty was something one grew accustomed to. A beautiful person would eventually seem quite ordinary when seen all the time. But—even though I had seen Majliv so many times before, he was still as attractive as the first time. As I got to know him, he revealed small details about himself that made him even more inviting.

'So delightful! The perfect way to start a new day,' Lynn said, stretching her hands into the air.

'You're almost right. Without food and drink, the hero might sink,' Kian laughed as he lay on his stomach, tapping a stick against the pot hanging from his backpack.

'Was that a hint for me to prepare breakfast?' Lynn stood over him with her hands on her hips.

'Oh no, are you crazy? You're a worse cook than Mirini.'

Listening to them teasing each other like before was delightful, as if I had deleted the long time I had been away from them. However, the talk of food made the hunger gnaw at my intestines. Who knew when I had actually eaten something while in the cave?

'Hungry?' Majliv looked down at me as he loosened his grip on my shoulders.

'I feel like I could eat a horse!' We stood up.

'I'll go see if there are some Plimp Sneaks we can put on the grill,' Majliv said. 'It's a fish,' he explained with a smile on his face. He grabbed some gear from our stuff and disappeared into the trees. Oh my god, he was an amazing man! If only he would let me understand if he was willing to take the next step and give us a chance. Maybe he wasn't interested after all? Maybe it had been too long?

My guilt towards Will was almost completely erased. Grimrokk was too harsh a world for me to be lonely for the rest of my life. Nevertheless, I was determined that the next move would be Majliv's, and it would go at his pace.

It was nice to distract myself with thoughts of Majliv, as it kept me from letting all the dark shadows creep in, the ones that reminded me of Nicor, Lamia, and Myrthing's gruesome cave. Lynn brought me back.

'Mia, I brought you some clothes. You can't go around in those filthy rags,' Lynn rummaged in her bag and pulled out a burgundy, knee-length velvet skirt with a silver-grey corset-like top.

'Where...' I was about to ask, but Lynn interrupted me.

'If you go straight ahead that way, you'll come to a small river. You can take a bath there without being disturbed,' she pointed in the same direction Majliv had disappeared earlier.

'Thank you. I'm looking forward to getting rid of this nauseating smell,' I said, getting up. I was so emaciated that it wasn't easy to find my footing, but I would manage on my own. With a little help from a tree right behind me, I found my balance, took a deep breath, and managed to take a few unsteady steps. Both Kian and Lynn had stopped talking while I moved. They were sitting and waiting to help in case I fell. I gave them a proud glance.

'Mia, stay there,' commanded Kian, who suddenly stood up and approached me.

'No, Kian. You don't need to help me. I'll manage...'

'Relax. I'm just going to find some citrus heather... for you to scrub yourself with. It smells good.' Kian smiled broadly and continued past me and into the forest.

'I saw a bunch of it when we rode in here,' he called back. When he returned, his fists were full of a dark green plant with tiny yellow flowers. As I took them in my hands, I was surprised by how soft they were. The heather I was accustomed to at home was coarse, hard, and thorny, but this one was filled with small velvety leaves.

'Thank you, Kian,' I smiled back.

'Kian loves it when ladies smell like lemon and orange. He always has an ulterior motive when he does something,' Lynn laughed heartily.

'Is there something wrong with the smell of citrus maybe? Especially after not being able to take a bath for many weeks?' No! I wasn't ready to talk about this yet, my emotional state was still immense. The nightmare was over, but Myrthing was still alive, and Lamia would forever be out there somewhere - until I potentially took her out of this dreadful power struggle.

I continued further into the forest without saying anything more, but Lynn and Kian were so engrossed in their sibling banter and mockery that they didn't notice. The forest was calm. I could hear the occasional bird singing flirtatious melodies while the wind gently breathed through the treetops. If it weren't for the stench of mould and dirt emanating from myself, I might have been able to enjoy the scent of the forest and the flowers as well. It was incredible that Majliv had managed to stay so close to me all night. He clearly cared more than I had thought.

Soon, I could catch a glimpse of the clearing in the forest and hear the sound of water flowing downstream. I stopped at the clearing and looked around. The river was of moderate size, and in the middle at its widest point, a small island protruded. The riverbank was mostly rocks and cliffs, but near me, between two rocky outcrops, there was a sandy beach.

I slowly walked onto the sand, which pleasantly tickled and felt soft between my toes. The water was almost mirror-like, reflecting a blurry image of the mountain and trees on the other side. There was no one in sight, which made me wonder where Majliv had gone to fish. Not that I was shy, but I didn't want anyone to see my body as it was now. It was unrecognizable.

I placed the clothes and the citron heather on a rock and took off the remaining scraps of my sweater and pants. Then I took a deep breath and continued towards the water's edge. Before allowing my feet to touch the water, I looked out over the water one last time. Suddenly, I started to break out in a cold sweat, as if my body reacted ahead of my thoughts. The small island sticking out of the surface, the ripples spreading across the water, the sound of the forest in the background. All these things triggered my thoughts. Could Nicor be here? If not Nicor, could there be other dreadful creatures lurking beneath the surface, waiting for an opportunity to attack as soon as I dipped my feet in the water?

I stood frozen in panic. I couldn't move a muscle, there was ringing in my ears, my heart pounded in my chest, and I hyperventilated. As the ringing grew louder, it felt like knives in my ears, tears streamed down my cheeks, and my body trembled. Far away, I could hear someone calling my name. A pair of large hands grabbed me gently but firmly around my upper arms and shook me, but it seemed unreal, far away. Strong arms held onto me, and the world almost faded into blackness.

'Shhh...' The soothing sounds approached closer and closer. 'Mia. What's happening? Are you hurt?' It was Majliv's voice and Majliv's arms that pulled me out of the panic attack.

'No,' I sobbed. Even though I had regained control, the tears continued to flow. This river in this world frightened me more than Nicor's pond had ever done. I remembered being at that pond before I knew what Grimrokk actually was. Now, I'd learned the hard way, and the uncertainty of this world scared me more than anything else.

For a long while, he stood there, gently stroking my back, soothing me. I rested my cheek on his chest and listened to the steady rhythm of his heart. He felt so safe.

'Wait a moment,' he said, gently pushing me aside. He bent down and started to take off his boots first, and then his linen shirt. Majliv took my breath away. His body was incredibly beautiful, so strong, and yet so gentle and soft. But neither his appearance nor his qualities could suppress the fear I had for the surroundings, erase the experiences I had gone through, or reassure me in my ignorance of what lay beneath the surface. While I was preoccupied with the anxiety coursing through my body, he began to untie the knot of his low-hanging brown leather pants. They fell to the sand. Before I could fully take in the sight of him, he swept me up in his arms, grabbed the citron heather, and took a few steps closer to the water's edge.

'No! I don't want to. There might be something down there. Nicor or other monsters,' I sobbed, clinging to Majliv's neck.

'Mia, there's nothing dangerous down there. Just a few fish and maybe a frog or two. No monsters, no Nicor,' he whispered against my hair while holding me tight.

'How can you be so sure?' I cried even more.

'I know these forests, Mia. I'll be with you every step of the way and won't let go until you feel safe. Is that okay?' He looked into my eyes. I nodded weakly, gripping his shoulders tighter and taking shaky breaths. His feet took short, steady steps into the water. Under different circumstances, I would have been weak in the knees seeing Majliv naked and holding me so closely that I could feel his pulse. But now it was about fear and security, not about being a man and a woman. Everything that was happening was about my need to overcome the fear from what I had just gone through. The water reached his thighs which meant that it touched my feet. It was warmer than I had expected and felt delightful against my skin. He continued further into the river until everything below our shoulders was submerged before he stopped. The forest was quiet around us. I took a deep breath and gently released my grip on his shoulders. He stood completely still, watching me intently. With a trembling hand, I took a handful of heather from Majliv's hand. Carefully, I began to rub the heather over my calves and thighs. Immediately, a fresh lemon scent filled the water around us, and I continued with more determination. The heather scrubbed my skin, providing a much-needed cleansing sensation. Eager to wash every inch of my skin, I continued scrubbing my arms, shoulders, and neck. Every little spot on my body received the same treatment until only my back remained. Without either of us saying a word, Majliv took the heather out of my hands and let my feet touch the bottom of the river as he held onto my waist, drawing us closer together. He gently scrubbed my back from the nape of my neck to my lower back. When he finished, I turned around and took the heather from his hand. Majliv understood that I wanted to take control, so he released his hold on my waist, and I moved behind him. Filled with gratitude for everything he had done for me, I began scrubbing his back. His muscles contracted under my fingers as they worked across his smooth back. He was so considerate, so kind. I thought back to the first day I met him in Mirin's kitchen when I thought he was terribly arrogant, rude, and superior. How could I have misunderstood him so thoroughly? He was my guardian angel, someone who protected me no matter where I was, what I had done, or how mean I had been to him.

I wrapped my arms around his shoulders, leaned against his back, and pressed my cheek against his smooth skin. Tears rolled down my cheeks once again.

'Thank you so much, Majliv. For everything,' my voice was hoarse, but this wasn't the moment to try to hide it. I gently kissed him between the shoulder blades before releasing myself backward and submerging beneath the water's surface. It was liberating to float around and let the calmness wash over me. All the while, I was aware of Majliv's proximity, as if a magnet was drawing me towards him. He moved slowly around me in the water, never touching me.

I needed air and resurfaced again. I tried to run my fingers through my hair, but it was impossible. It was a tangled mess of hair and dirt.

'Come here,' he said and beckoned me to him. When I was close to him, he held onto my waist and leaned me backward with his other arm until the back of my head was submerged underwater. Curiously, I searched his face for an explanation of what he intended to do. Soon, he began running his fingers through my hair underwater. I could feel it as the knots loosened. For a man of his size, he was remarkably gentle in every movement he made, so comforting and soothing.

Once most of the hair was untangled, he took the heather in his hands and rubbed vigorously, spreading the scent of citrus over his fingers. Then he ran his fingers over my head several times in massaging motions. I could no longer sense the smell of mould, dirt, and decay. It was as if those painful experiences were washed away with the dirt, my shoulders felt lighter, and I could finally breathe freely.

I closed my eyes and let my senses take in everything around me. Underwater, I heard the stones shifting as fish searched for food, bubbles rising to the surface, and close by, a heart beating strong and steady. His arms pulled me close to him again, and I looked up.

'It's time for breakfast,' he said, but I couldn't read his expression. While holding me tightly against his chest, he walked up to the shore and gently set me down so I could find my footing. For a moment, he stood next to me, his hand around my waist, before catching himself and walking over to his clothes. I stood still and watched him. He shook himself off, drying most of the water in from the heat of the sun.

I didn't have a towel to dry myself with, but that was okay. It was so hot that it wouldn't take long for me to dry without struggling. As I put on my top, I observed Majliv as he put on his pants. He left his upper body bare and hung his shirt over the waistband, then he bent down and picked up his boots. I was amazed by the respect he showed me. How many men wouldn't have taken advantage of this situation to satisfy their desires? But Majliv wasn't like that. He was a grange warden, a protector, and he would never do anything to me that I didn't want.

I pulled the skirt over my head and fastened it with a button at the back. The old clothes lay at my feet, tattered, dirty, and repulsive. The last thing I wanted was to touch them; they were going to be burned before we moved on. They represented what I feared the most and the place I most wanted to forget.

I could feel Majliv's gaze on me as I bent down and picked them up between two fingers. Nausea rose in my throat. Even on an empty stomach, the smell made me sick.

'I hope I never see you in those clothes again,' he said. His beautiful face was full of concern and care.

'You don't have to worry about that. They'll be burned before we move on.' Majliv took a few steps forward, standing right in front of me.

'Are you ready? We need to keep going soon.' He gently ran his free hand along my arm. As if on cue, my stomach growled, and we both burst into laughter. It was liberating but also painful to laugh on such an empty stomach.

Majliv walked over to the rocky outcrop and grabbed a bundle of already cleaned fish he must have left there when he arrived. We walked together in silence through the forest. The whole way, he stayed close to me, not so close as to touch me, but just enough that I could barely feel his warmth.

Chapter 17
Sleeping beauty

ince Kian had been so stupid as to comment on Lynn's cooking, he was the one who had to take care of breakfast.

'Finally, you're starting to resemble your old self. Are you feeling a bit better?' Kian asked while we were eating.

'Yes. Seriously, citrus heather was not a bad choice, Kian. It really worked wonders as an odour remover.' I gave him a small smile as a way of thanks.

'There you go, Lynn. I know what women want,' Kian said, putting on a pretentious, seductive smile.

'Does anyone mind if we burn these before we leave? I never want to see these clothes again. The smell alone makes me sick.'

'Burn them. We don't want to see them again either,' Lynn nodded, indicating that she also wanted to get rid of the smell. It felt so good to be back. Everything felt so normal. The light atmosphere, Kian's funny remarks, and Lynn's quick responses. They told me how they found me, where they had searched, and who had participated in the mission. When I heard that Majliv had been with Nicor for several days, I gave him a serious accusing look. He knew how dangerous Nicor was, he even had some experience, and yet he went there anyway. I was filled with gratitude that they had made such a big deal out of rescuing me, the newcomer.

We had packed everything we needed and were ready to leave. I stood contentedly, watching the last flames consume what had once been clothes I felt comfortable in. However, seeing them turn to ashes was like letting the time in the cave and everything Myrthing had done to me go up in smoke. It gave me strength and a newfound power: the thirst for revenge.

'Myrthing! You know the old phrase is wrong...Revenge isn't sweet. It's pain!' I shouted the words loudly in my mind, wishing for him to hear every single word. Shortly after, Lynn breathed in a big gulp of air and met my gaze with a shocked expression, but I just shook my head.

We didn't ride across the plains but took the back roads, shortcuts, and ventured through thickets and mountains. The risk of someone seeing us was too great. If we were ever to reach Wargborough unharmed, we had to resort to alternative routes. Never before had I felt so strongly about my role and what needed to be done. Lamia had to be eliminated! But first on the agenda was Myrthing. He had a limited number of heartbeats left if I had it my way and he should not have any more than strictly necessary. If we were lucky, he was still in Wargborough. It was actually pointless for him to spend time and effort searching for me now that he knew I would come for revenge.

It was nighttime when I sat by the fire.

'I sense that you're very far away,' a voice behind me said. It was Lynn.

'Yes. I'm reflecting on everything that has happened. It's so unreal,' I said.

'What do you mean?' Lynn didn't understand what I was getting at.

'Isn't there any logical explanation for the time between Gaia and Grimrokk? There's so much that doesn't add up.'

'No. Many have lost their minds trying to solve that puzzle, so we just have to accept it as it is. Some things can't be explained. Just like love. You can't understand or force it,' Lynn stated level-headed.

'When I wake up here next time, only a day will have passed for you, but several days for me.' My head was getting dizzy from trying to piece together fragments that didn't fit. It was time to sleep. Majliv had long ago fallen asleep, and Kian was talking in his sleep about sugar cubes in his tea.

'Sleep well, Lynn.' I got up and went to my sleeping spot.

'Good night, sleep tight,' she whispered back.

�୨ଡ଼ଵ

'Hey, how are you guys doing?' Aleksandra smiled proudly in the visiting room at the hospital. We had bought a soft teddy bear for the little newcomer.

'Congratulations again. Look at how tiny he is!' I said. In a bed lay a well-wrapped, round bundle.

'Ian, these are your neighbours.' Aleksandra lifted him up and placed him in my arms.

'Can I? Are you sure?' He was so small in the crook of my arm. Occasionally, he made adorable little cooing sounds, bringing a smile to my face. A few dark strands of hair peeked out from under his hat. I fell completely in love with the beautiful, little creature. The way the little fingers curled into a tiny fist and the delightful soft skin smelled so good. Sitting there with the little human in my lap, it felt so right, that delightful, warm feeling. What if this had been our son. It brought tears to my eyes. Will sat next to me, equally captivated by the boy. 'He's so small,' he said, shaking his head. I lifted Ian onto his arm, and Will stiffened like a log.

'He weighs nothing, I don't even feel like I'm holding him,' said Will. The conversation between Aleksandra and the two of us was a bit strained, but I had no idea what else to talk about, apart from the little wonder in Will's arms. It was overwhelming, and it became uncomfortable, so we didn't stay long. Besides, it was mealtime for the little one, and Aleksandra walked back to the room to breastfeed.

We had arranged to meet with a social worker who was coming home to evaluate us and our home. It was terribly uncomfortable to think that someone had to approve us as acceptable parents. I thought about all the people we knew who had more children than they actually wanted but couldn't take proper care of themselves. They didn't need approval before having children just because they got pregnant on their own. It felt so unfair.

❧

We had been riding for a few days, and we were not far from Wargborough. Everyone's asses were sore from sitting on horseback when we stopped again to rest. Majliv had made a forest soup with pigeon meat that we devoured to the very last drop. We were somewhere between Siljan's farm and Wargborough, but we had remained off the usual roads just in case.

'It's been a while since I've been up here,' Lynn said, enjoying the view. There were green treetops as far as the eye could see.

'I was nearby about a year ago. At Petrusen's farm,' Majliv said, stirring the mint leaves in his toddy.

'Isn't that the grumpy old man who chased Kian all around the forest with a scythe?' Lynn burst out laughing.

'Yes! That's right, I completely forgot. What was it that you did again?' Majliv looked at Kian with a big grin.

'I stole back a pig.'

'A pig that Dad had sent for mating so there would be piglets before the Frost. But thanks to you, we didn't have ribs for Christmas, just chicken. Chicken, Kian...' Lynn said. Kian couldn't help but laugh.

'The worst part was that Mom sent me to Petrusen to buy the chicken. He chased me then too. I remember his daughter, Caroline. She was a pretty girl.' It was funny to see Kian's face as he told stories. I could imagine him as a boy, a charming little rascal.

'Caroline got married a few years ago. She also had a son, who must be a couple of years old now. They live on the Petrusen's farm.' Suddenly, it was as if Majliv realized he had spoken out of turn. He turned pale. Lynn and Kian exchanged worried looks.

'What is it?' I asked. Was there something I should have known? No one answered.

'I haven't seen them in a long time. None of them,' Lynn said after a while, looking at Majliv and shaking her head in despair.

'Now that you mention it, neither have I.' Why would it matter? Had something happened to them? My thoughts hadn't regained the same speed as before, but this made no sense. They seemed like a regular family, with a little son running around... A little son... A child...

'You don't think... Lamia...' I didn't have the courage to finish the sentence. Majliv just gave me a look, and that was answer good enough.

'Kian, you're coming with me. You two stay here.' Majliv pointed at Lynn and me. Why should we stay behind?

'Hurry!' Lynn nodded back.

'Wait! Why shouldn't we come with you?' No one answered me. The boys disappeared into the forest at full speed, while I remained behind irritated, watching them go.

'Mia, Majliv doesn't want to put your life at risk. No one knows what they'll find up there.'

'I feel so useless. If it weren't for me, all three of you would have gone. You make me feel like I'm constantly in need of a babysitter.' Hadn't I proven my self-worth?

'That may be true. But there are many reasons why Majliv doesn't want you exposed to danger. One of them is that you haven't fully recovered yet, and another is that if something were to happen to you, it would be game over for all of us. No way to get rid of Lamia.'

'I feel perfectly fine, thank you...' So, I was just a tool. Whether they were the ones using me or it was Myrthing, I was still an object. I had considered them as family, more or less, and thought they felt the same. My mind was a jumble. I needed to be alone to clear my thoughts. With a heavy, resigned sigh, I turned on my heel and walked into the forest.

'Mia, where are you going?'

'I need to be alone!' I replied and continued straight ahead.

'Let me know if you need anything.' Need anything? All I needed now was peace and quiet. As amazing as I thought The Long Warmth was these first few days, it now felt like an ordinary summer to me. The trees were green, the flowers had beautiful colours, and the insects swarmed. Nothing more magical than usual. I tried to distract my thoughts from what Kian and Majliv were doing, but it was hopeless. Images of a small farm appeared in my head. A happy and content family taking care of their animals and enjoying the sun. But as soon as the idyllic images appeared, I remembered my encounter with Lamia. I shuddered at the thought of what she was capable of.

The forest around me was warm. Occasionally, a gentle breeze carried all sorts of delightful scents past my nose. A tree was surrounded by a climbing plant with large, dark red, velvety roses. There were few leaves on the branches compared to the climbing roses I had seen in Gaia. I approached to take a closer look. There was something familiar about the plant. The thorns. I had never thought that the thorny vine I was so familiar with would be covered in roses during the Long Warmth. My fingers stroked the branches. They were slender and flexible, just like my whip had been. I had been so comfortable with that whip until it decided to go its own way. Perhaps I should take the chance and make a new one. There were more than enough branches to choose from, so I tore off enough to probably make two whips. This time, I would take my time to craft the tool evenly and make it long. I found myself a spot on a rock with a view. It wasn't too far from the campsite, and I could see Lynn throwing her Shuriken's into a tree trunk.

'I'll sit up here for a while,' I thought so she could hear me. She looked around and gave me a small, confirming wave back. It was quite convenient to communicate with Lynn this way, even though I had to be careful with my thoughts.

The boys had been gone for a few hours, and I had plucked all the roses from the branches. The leaves were more difficult. Fortunately, there were few of them, but they were tightly packed, next to each thorn all the way down. Then I heard low, indistinct chatter at the campsite. I turned my head and saw that Kian and Majliv were back. I was relieved to see that Majliv was unharmed, and my heart skipped a beat. In the past few days, I had made an effort not to get completely absorbed by him. I blushed, even though I was sitting all by myself, at the fantasies I had about him and me. Fortunately, those fantasies were mine alone, completely invisible to Lynn.

'Hey,' a deep voice sounded behind me. I startled.

'Oh. Hi! I didn't hear you coming.' Majliv approached me with a serious expression.

'I didn't mean to scare you. What are you doing?'

'Making a new whip. How did it go?' His facial expression was answer good enough. He came and sat next to me on the rock, sighing as he shook his head.

'Was everyone...?' How to put this? These were people he knew.

'No survivors!' There was both anger and pain in his voice. It became quiet for a moment. 'What happened to the old whip?' he asked, looking at the long branches, clearly determined to change the subject.

'It started acting strange. Can you hand me that one?' I pointed to one of the branches lying next to him. He reached down and took a firm hold of them, perhaps a little too firm.

'Ouch... bloody....,' he got annoyed with his own carelessness.

'Did you prick yourself?'

'Yeah, but I'll be fine. What do you mean it started acting strange?' he asked while desperately trying to pull out the thorn that had gotten stuck in his hand.

'During the finale, it grew attached to my hand. Disgusting!' I said, shuddering a bit.

'What do you know about Huldra, Mia?' He still had his gaze on the thorn, which had dug itself so deep into his skin that Majliv's strong fists couldn't pull it out.

'What do you mean?'

'Do you know, for example, that she can keep things to herself? Be terribly vengeful? And be a bit malicious at times if she doesn't get her way?'

'Yes, I've heard about that.'

'What if I told you that you don't have just one ability, but two? Would you believe me?' He stopped poking while he waited for an answer.

'I don't know. It might depend on what this ability is supposed to be. In that case, it would be something unknown to me.'

'That's not for sure. What if I say that Hell Horse's gift was something completely different than what you think? Would it still be unfamiliar to you then?' He turned his head towards me and looked at me with an investigative gaze.

'I don't know. Are you saying that the thorn thing is an ability?' I didn't quite understand where he was going with this.

'Yes. But it's more than what you think. If I'm not completely mistaken, you can manipulate them,' he said and began picking at the thorn in his hand again. It wasn't the strangest thing I had heard in this world, but... Why wouldn't Huldra have told me about it?

It was evident that when it came down to it, Majliv, like most men, was unable to ask for help. His large hands desperately tried to grasp the poor, little thorn. He didn't even have fingernails to help since he constantly bit them.

'Let me...' I said and took his hand in mine. Not far from his thumb, a small prick protruded. I tried a couple of times with my fingers and fingernails, but it was just short enough that I couldn't get a proper grip. Teeth were possibly worth a try. I brought his hand to my lips and, using the tip of my tongue, felt for the prick, and carefully bit down on it, managing to loosen it. The thorn turned out to be surprisingly longer than I had expected. I carefully examined the area with my fingers to make sure nothing was left behind. The palm of his hand was rough with coarse calluses, and the fingers were long, strong, and warm. But what irresistibly captured my attention was the smooth, sun-kissed skin sculpted over the strong muscles of his bare upper body. Being so close to him sent shivers down my spine. I may have taken a bit longer than necessary to examine the area where the thorn had been, but he was undoubtedly more than willing to let me do so. My cheeks blushed red, giving me away as I drifted off for a moment. To regain my attention, he moved his fingers slightly, and uncertainly, I pulled my hands back.

'It's gone now,' I said. The conversation we had on Christmas Eve began to creep into my thoughts. Had I given him the time he needed? I didn't want to force myself on him and risk pushing him further away.

'Mia?' Hearing him say my name sent shivers down my spine. His voice was deep and rumbling, tenderly wrapping around me.

'Yes?' I replied with a shaky voice.

'Have you folded?' His words sparked through my entire body. Did he mean what I thought he meant? What else could he be referring to? 'I've gone 'all in.' The next move is yours.' My poker analogy. I remembered the words as if it were yesterday.

'No.' My response came out as a hoarse whisper.

'I thought that with everything that has happened recently... you might have changed your mind.' Majliv looked down at the grass, but it seemed like he was trying to follow every movement I made with his peripheral vision before he continued.

'You've been a bit more distant lately, so I thought...' I interrupted him before he could say something really foolish.

'I didn't want to be pushy.' Didn't he think I was interested? Interested wasn't really a sufficient description; I was more like obsessed.

'Mia. Do you really know what it entails to enter into a relationship with a grange warden?' His voice became deeper and softer.

'What does it matter? I don't care what your job is.' Only after I said it did I realize how insensitive it was to say something like that. Majliv was someone who took his job very seriously.

'I'm sorry! That's not what I meant,' I said and placed a hand on his arm. He looked down at it and placed his free hand on mine. What was he trying to convey?

'When I became a grange warden, I had to accept certain conditions. Like I said, Huldra can be a bit

321

difficult,' He fell silent and seemed to carefully consider what he was going to say. 'As far as I'm concerned, she can demand whatever she wants, as long as it doesn't come between us.' I couldn't bear the thought of being away from him, not even a minute, and now my thoughts poured out of me.

'That's precisely the point. Can you endure going weeks without seeing me? Because I can't bear the thought of being away from you for that long.' He turned his head and looked me in the eyes. I sat there, astonished. He didn't want to be away from me? Did I hear correctly? 'From day one, I was determined that Grimrokk was a place I wouldn't let in too close, and it worked well until you came along. When I carried you in my arms, away from the pond, there was only one thing I thought about: Who are you? I really tried not to think about you, and I tried to be impersonal when I met you again, but it was you who tempted me.' He let go of my hand and stood up, took a few steps back and forth, then stopped in front of me. 'The taste of our first kiss still lingers in me.'

'The kiss you cried for help to get out of? You didn't want it!' I didn't understand. What he said didn't make sense. Majliv knelt down at my feet.

'Mia, I never cried for help. It was Mirini's way of telling me to stay away from you.'

'What? Why?'

'Believe it or not, she did it for your own good.' He placed his hands on my thighs.

'There are only two ways to break a contract with Huldra. One is if Huldra herself terminates it, and the other is the obvious one... death.' Couldn't he have a relationship while working for Huldra? Didn't she allow him to have a life outside his work? 'I can do as I please, but it cannot in any way prevent me from fulfilling my tasks for her. If I could, I would take you with me everywhere I go, but... I have to travel alone.'

'But you're not traveling alone now? What makes this different?'

'When she sent me to watch over you, when you went to Nicor, it was a task, a task which is not yet finished.'

'What! Am I a job? So, you've been playing with me all this time? Entertaining me?' I couldn't breathe. My stomach tightened, I couldn't sit and listen to this anymore, so I stood up and walked away from the stone.

'No! Mia!' Majliv grabbed my arm and held me back. 'Yes. I've been assigned to watch over you, but it has never been in my job description to hold you at night, kiss you back, or feel pain whenever we're apart.' Majliv pulled me close to him and looked into my eyes. The dark blue depths that met my gaze were filled with despair.

'When I found you on the floor in the cave, I thought we were too late, but here you are.'

'I never thought I would see you again either. I could eventually accept the wet and cold, but not being able to see you again was torture.' The feeling was still so present in my memory, and the thought made my eyes sting. It was like reliving a nightmare. My pulse became uncontrollable when he was near. His body barely touching mine made my heart pound, and my fingers longed to glide over his shoulders and pull him closer to me.

'Mia. Are you sure you're not folding?' he said as his gaze tried to read me.

'Never! It's still your move,' I replied. If I had felt desire before, this was on a whole new level. Warm waves rolled through my body, and my breath became audibly faster.

'I'm going all in' he said, slowly pulling me closer with a firm grip around my waist. I heard his breath quicken, just like mine, as a soft blush started to appear on his beautiful face. No one could be more appealing than him when he blushed. His red lips called out to me. I couldn't care less that the sun was low in the sky and the wind carried the scent of food. All that was on my mind now was Majliv, and nothing had the power to distract me.

'Lynn, whatever you do... don't come over here now!' I thought as loudly as I could without screaming at the top of my lungs. His bare chest was hypnotizing. No one could be more perfect. The smooth skin, the defined muscles, and the broad shoulders. My fingertips couldn't wait any longer to touch him. I gently trailed down his chest muscles towards his navel. Under my hands, he shivered and got goosebumps. In a swift motion, he released his grip on my waist, bent down, and lifted me up in his arms. My arms wrapped around his shoulders. One of my hands grabbed onto the soft hair at the back of his neck, while the other had a firm hold on his bicep. He sat down on his knees before gently laying me down on the grass. His amazing body made my mouth water. He leaned over me, and it felt like a jolt had ignited my thighs, sending intense tingles up my hips and to my chest.

My fingers buried themselves in his hair, and I enjoyed the reactions his face betrayed as I continued my movements. Slowly, he lowered his head towards my neck and tenderly kissed me from the collarbone up to the earlobe. My breath became a gasp. His lips tickling along my pulse made my heart pound harder and faster. He leaned more of his body weight onto me and supported his elbows on either side of my head. My fingers glided over his back, over all the defined muscles and down to his hips.

Suddenly, he lifted his head and looked me straight in the eyes. His gaze made the emotions surge inside me, and I surrendered. I lightly stroked my fingertips along the edge of his pants and towards his stomach, where the knot of his trousers was located. His lips parted for a moment. He looked down at my fingers. It was now or never. This was something I had fantasized about and longed for a long time. Here was the opportunity I had been waiting for, and I couldn't stop here; it wouldn't be possible. Between the thumb and index finger of my right hand, I held one end of the knot, ready to pull, but I wanted to know that he desired this as much as I did. His gaze moved up and met mine, and he smiled. His heavy breath tickled my face.

'What are you waiting for?' he whispered, and his smile grew wider. His eyes squinted mischievously.

'I have to make sure you haven't changed your mind,' I replied. He said nothing, just let his arm slide along my shoulder, on the outside of my chest, down and back towards my lower back.

'Still 'all in'?' he asked, his eyes sparkling. I stared intensely at his lips as his tongue sensually moistened them.

'All in,' I whispered and gently loosened the knot in his pants.

In the next second, I felt a slight tug on my lower back, and the corset loosened around my waist. Neither my breath nor my heart could maintain a steady rhythm now. My hands found their way from his abdomen to his hips, and slowly I pulled down his waistline. He moved down my body, simultaneously moving his fingertips from my lower back to my abdomen. He was nerve-rackingly slow, he pushed the top up over my stomach while kissing his way towards my breasts. Once again, my fingers found his soft hair, and I couldn't resist giving it a little tug, which rewarded me with a deep, seductive growl.

In one swift motion, the top disappeared over my head, and my breasts were engulfed by two moist lips and a tantalizingly rough palm. The intense heat spreading over my body left a moist sheen all over me.

His touching game moved towards my hip, where he found the button on my skirt that had slipped from the back to the side. Under Majli's impatient fingers, it was about to meet its end.

'Calm down now...or I won't have anything to wear tomorrow,' I whispered as I opened the button with one hand while the other still had a firm grip on his dark locks.

'If it means you would have gone naked all day, maybe I should have tugged a bit harder,' he said with a grin. He sat up on his knees, placed both hands on my hips, and gently pulled the skirt down, over my thighs, calves, and finally off my feet. When he leaned over me again, I pushed his pants down as far as the position I was lying in allowed. Not long after, my pile of clothes was in the company of a pair of pants.

This time he lowered himself onto me with a bit more weight, giving me an indescribable, intense sensation. His mouth was soft against the hollow of my neck, his lips parted, and his moist tongue glided gently up my neck towards my chin, sending shivers through my body. I wanted to give back, so I rubbed my fingertips up and down his back. I was no longer in complete control at this point. I was so caught up in the moment, and I scraped my nails from his lower back up to his shoulders. The muscles under my fingers tensed, he took a deep breath through his teeth, and then he moved his lips towards mine. The way his tongue danced with mine sent small shocks through my core muscles. I already knew that just the thought of Majliv, naked against me, made my head spin. Against my thigh, I felt the pulsation of his excitement. The breath in my ear intoxicated me even more. He gently placed his palm on the inside of the opposite thigh and slowly moved it upward between my legs.

'Man... you're all wet,' his deep voice whispered. Each touch and stroke were so marvellous that it was almost painful for my longing body, and I rose higher and higher in arousal nearing my climax before he had even entered me.

Majliv positioned himself between my legs so I could stroke them along his hips. He lifted his head and looked into my eyes.

'There's no turning back now,' he said, his eyes gleaming.

'Good,' I replied. The desire was so overwhelming that I couldn't bear to wait any longer. Carefully, he shifted more of his body weight onto me while studying every expression on my face. I twined my legs around his thighs and pulled him closer. When he gently entered me, the sensation was like silk over steel, irresistible. He was a big man in every way, strong, tall, but also attentive and considerate. A wave swept through my body, and I gasped for breath, emitting an uncontrolled moan.

Caringly, he thrust into me again. I scrutinized the expression that appeared on his face. He closed his eyes, his breathing quickened, and he furrowed his brow. His arm circled around my lower back, pulling me closer to him, and then his lips found mine in a deep, heartfelt kiss. His body matched mine perfectly. Each thrust brought me closer to ecstasy while his heart pounded hard against my chest.

'Harder!' It didn't occur to me that I had said it out loud until he responded by obeying the command. His grip on my waist tightened, and the thrusts became deeper. When the internal tremors started to quicken, I knew I was on the verge of bursting into climax. What was this man doing to me? It was as if he knew every curve of my body, every enticing spot, every line to touch for the best possible sensation.

'Ah, yes!' Those words were all I needed. Shivers shot through me like lightning from my toes up to my neck. I felt light as a feather, floating outside of my own body. Vibrations emanated from my core and spread out into my stomach. The orgasm overflowed like a broken dam, and Majliv's trembling breath told me I wasn't alone.

I had no idea how much time had passed. It had lasted both a moment and an eternity. My whole being—my body and my mind—was in a state of bliss. The sun had set, and it was now just a faint glow along the horizon, while the stars emerged more and more clearly in the sky above us. Majliv lay on his back next to me, his hands beneath his head, while I lay on my stomach, studying him in the modest twilight. He was still catching his breath, and the moist surface of his skin gave it a gentle sheen.

'What are you thinking about?' I asked. He turned towards me, resting his head on his elbow.

'You and me, and whether there's any way I can be released from my duties as a grange warden without causing problems.' He observed me for a moment, then he grabbed me around the waist and pulled me close to him. I lay on his chest with my chin in my hands as he held me.

'Did you come to any conclusions?'

'I think we'll have to take it as it comes. But the dumbest thing we can do is hide it from her.' He lifted his head slightly and kissed me. If I could stay here for the rest of my life, then life would be perfect.

'Can I ask you something?' There were so many things I wanted to know about him.

'What are you curious about?' He smiled.

'You said you were seven years old when you came here, but how old were you when you became a grange warden?'

'I don't quite remember... around sixteen, I think. Why do you ask?' His eyes scrutinized me.

'You told me that everyone here has an ability, and I know your ability is to gather energy, but you didn't get it until you started working for Huldra, right?' I hoped he wouldn't take offense at my question.

'Oh... curious, are you?'

'A little.'

'I had an ability from the very first day, but it wasn't the same as the other grange warden's,' he smiled mischievously, teasing me.

'So, what was it? Do you still have it?'

'I still have it. And if I'm not mistaken, I believe you've even seen it too.'

What did he mean? The energy ability was the only one I had seen.

'Have I? When?'

He kissed me on the tip of my nose and reached his hand towards the spot where all the leaves, thorns, and roses from the whip were. His hand grabbed something and held it out to me. It was a rosebud.

'Hold onto it,' he said.

I took the rosebud between my fingers and admired it. Majliv placed his hand over it for a brief moment, and then it seemed like the bud started to glow. But what happened before my eyes afterward was truly incredible. The bud unfolded, petal by petal, and a large burgundy velvet rose bloomed in my palm.

'Have I seen you do this before?' I couldn't remember when I might have seen something similar.

'You know... even with your small feet, you make tracks in the snow, Mia. At the Knight's Leap. The giant eagle?'

'But I thought it was part of that energy thing...' It had puzzled me back then, but I had thought it was the same ability, just in a different way.

'I can make cells grow. Don't you find it strange that Kian isn't limping from the cut he got on Myrthing's island? Maybe you don't remember?' he asked, inquiringly.

'Now that you mention it... I completely forgot. Did you fix it?'

'I can't heal something to its original state, but it heals much faster, the way it's supposed to. Also, I can't heal myself.'

Before I had time to think, we were interrupted.

'NO!' We heard a deafening scream from the campfire. Without thinking, I jumped to my feet, pulled the skirt down over my shoulders, grabbed the top in one hand and the half-finished whip in the other, and ran as fast as my legs could carry me, following Majliv's lead.

It felt like it was miles to the campsite, even though it was just down the hill.

We stopped beside each other right next to the fire. Kian was sitting with his arms around Lynn, who was sobbing and crying hysterically. There was no one else to be seen around us. What on earth had caused such a reaction?

'What happened?' Majliv asked anxiously.

'I don't know. I closed my eyes for a moment, and when I woke up, she was like this. She can't say a word!' Kian's eyes were empty as he desperately tried to explain. I pulled my top over my head, but let it hang loosely.

'Lynn, Lynn! Did something happen?' Majliv sat down in front of her feet. She responded only by nodding her head between sobs.

'You have to try to tell us what happened,' Kian said, stroking her head. Lynn had a blank and vacant look, staring at the flames in the fire. She seemed to be in shock.

'Lynn! Tell us!' Majliv shouted and shook her gently but firmly by the shoulders.

'Mirini... hasn't made a sound for several days... so... so I wanted to tell her that everything was fine and that we would meet soon. But... it was completely silent. She always responds. Even if it's just to say that she'll talk to me later.' Her sobs made it a bit difficult to decipher.

'Then maybe she's very busy, or she doesn't want to reveal anything. Don't be afraid,' Kian said, wiping away some tears from her cheek.

'I got a response...' she said. We looked at each other, confused. She had just said that Mirini didn't respond. '...from Myrthing!' Her words echoed in my ears. What had happened to Mirini, since she wasn't responding, and what did Myrthing say?

'What did he say?' Majliv shook her again.

'Mirini is dead, and if we don't bring Mia to the Wargborough within two days, Dad is next in line.'

The rage inside me was stronger than I had ever felt before. Mirini was dead! The kind-hearted, gentle, and caring woman who had welcomed me with open arms, like a daughter, was no longer here. All because of me, because Myrthing wanted me to control his monster.

I looked at them. They must hate me for being here. Many times, I had put their lives in danger, but this time life had actually been lost, and it was all my fault.

'It's my fault. Everything is my fault. I should never have come here.' I took a few steps back into the darkness. They should be spared from having me there, the troublemaker who ruined everything.

'What are you talking about? Do you think this wouldn't have happened if you weren't here? Don't be foolish, Mia. I don't think you realize how helpless we are without you.' Kian shouted the words at me. A tear balanced on his eyelashes before it fell onto his cheek.

'You are the only one who stands a chance against Lamia. With her out of the way, Myrthing can forget about gaining more power,' Majliv said, coming towards me. He put his arm around me.

'But if you had let me stay behind, Mirini...' I was interrupted.

'...probably would have suffered the same fate, and we would have lost our best and only weapon.' He leaned down and met my gaze.

'You are not only invaluable to me, Mia, but to everyone else here,' he whispered and kissed me.

Lynn had calmed down and rested her head on Kian's shoulder. Everything had become quiet. The only sound was the crackling of the dying embers.

'I can't take this anymore. It has to stop. How long are we going to let him continue like this? I don't know about you, but I'm as ready as I can be. Tomorrow, I'll slaughter some clan members and enjoy it!' Kian was so angry that he frothed at the mouth.

Had the final evening really come? We were four individuals who wanted revenge against someone no one had managed to overcome before. And everything came down to me. I looked around at the three people I had grown so fond of. Kian, always with a mischievous smile that brightened my mood. Lynn, who made witty comments and always listened when I needed her. And Majliv, who was finally mine. Was I really going to lose them already tomorrow? I thought about every word I wanted to share with Lynn while trying to act like nothing was wrong.

'Lynn, I'm going to miss all of you. You have no idea how much everything you've done has meant to me. Thank you for welcoming me so warmly, my friend.' Lynn's gaze shifted to me, but before she could say anything, I interrupted her.

'Hush! This conversation never happened. Tell him that I love him.' I let my gaze wander from the dying embers, over to Majliv, before meeting her gaze again.

Lynn quickly got up, with a serious expression on her face. She came toward me and leaned down to my ear.

'You can tell him yourself!' she whispered sternly and went to her sleeping spot.

'Mia, I don't know how much you know about wizards, but they can only maintain one enchantment at a time. Even if they're as powerful as Myrthing,' she said, lying down with her back turned to us. What did that mean? So Myrthing could only hold one enchantment at a time. What should I use this information for? I didn't know if it would come in handy, but I kept it in mind. The rest of us followed Lynn's example and went to sleep.

꩜

Chapter 18
One last gift

inally, the social worker arrived for a visit. A small, pleasant lady with her arms full of papers and files sat down on our couch. We had polished the house to the extreme; it had never been so clean and tidy before.

She asked us question after question, about religion, the values we cared about, our attitude towards alcohol, child-rearing, finances, what we found negative about each other, and what we saw as positive. I had never spoken so much about myself before. Speaking so openly about these personal matters with an outsider made me realize even more how important it was for us to have a child, and I became even more convinced that I wanted a family.

It was also good to hear Will talk about his perspectives and desires. I couldn't remember the last time he wanted to talk about how he felt. He had a glow about him as he spoke. What really surprised me was that he did so much to make me happy. I had always believed that he wasn't as invested in this as I was, but there had been numerous small incidents he had spared me from.

For nearly two hours, this woman sat taking notes in a notebook before closing it and declaring herself finished for now. Fortunately, she didn't hide her opinion; she didn't believe in any way that we needed to worry about not being approved as adoptive parents. Could it really happen? Did I dare let myself hope, risking another crushing disappointment?

Before falling asleep that evening, there was so much I thought about, everything yet nothing at the same time. Thoughts swarmed like a flock of bees in my head, merging with all the others, but the underlying constant sound was the thought of Majliv. My greatest concern was what awaited me the next time I would go to Grimrokk, what awaited us in Wargborough, and how sickened I felt at the thought of bringing my few good friends into danger.

This must be what those heading off to war felt like. A deep fear weighing heavily in the stomach, along with uncertainty about what would be encountered ahead. Would everyone come out of this unscathed? No, that wasn't the answer. We had already lost Mirini, so now the question was if she would be the only one? Majliv was a strong man, but could he still be a match for Myrthing? Or Kian, or Lynn?

I thought less about whether I would come out of this unscathed myself. I was ready to face my fate. The mission I had been given had become a part of me. I was ready. But what if I never saw Will again?

CʒꙄꙄ

Majliv studied me intently. Since an uncertain future awaited us, I wanted to savour these minutes, our last morning. Nowhere was I more content than here, in Majliv's arms. At least not on this side.

'I love you, Mia,' he said, continuing to observe me and my reaction. I felt my heart expand in my chest, simultaneously quickening its pace.

'I love you too.' I leaned towards him to give him a kiss. No matter how much we both desired to get even closer, this wasn't the day for passion and desire. There were more important matters waiting for us.

Even though all four of us probably needed it, breakfast got cancelled. The only food we consumed were some dry crackers we nibbled on along the way.

We approached Wargborough, but since we kept to the woods, I had no landmarks in my surroundings to orientate by. It was the first warm day I had experienced without sun and blue skies. A thick layer of clouds loomed above us, perfectly matching my mood.

It was afternoon when we stopped at a clearing in the woods and peered through the trees.

'We need to cross the moat to get in. There are guards everywhere,' Kian whispered, pointing towards the city gate. Four guards stood watch at the entrance, so we continued on, circling around the small town.

Suddenly, I recognized the place. Among the trees, I saw the spot where Mirini and I had ridden over the moat when Myrthing's men were chasing us which meant that we were at the narrowest point of the moat.

'We'll leave the horses here,' Majliv whispered, dismounting his horse, and then he helped me down as well.

'Well, I suppose we just have to get to it then,' Lynn said in a low voice as she took a deep breath.

MAGIC OF THE NIGHT

There we were, as prepared as we would ever be. We ran together, as silently as we could, towards the moat. Over the top, I saw the church spire and rooftops, but no people. Everything looked desolated and abandoned. A ghost town.

The water in the moat was significantly warmer this time. I had to take a few swimming strokes before finding my footing again and crawl up the other side as quietly as possible. Soon, small drops began to fall from the increasingly darkening sky. The narrow alley curved inward and led to the church and the small wooden houses tightly packed with one backyard gate after another.

With quiet steps, we tiptoed while peering into each gateway, in case someone was lying in ambush. The narrow alley led us to the square in front of the church. The last time I was in the square, it was full of carts and stalls outside the shops. At the last two houses, Kian and Majliv stopped to look around each corner.

'I don't see anyone,' Kian whispered.

'Neither do I. Neither residents nor clan members. But they're here and certainly aware that we've arrived,' Majliv whispered as he looked at us. 'Are you ready?' His words didn't quite sink in. Now, right at that moment when it mattered, I wasn't ready at all. The focus on the mission, my task, was lost in the haze that had appeared inside my head. My heart pounded hard in my chest while cold sweat ran down my back. How on earth could anyone be prepared for what awaited us?

Reluctantly, I nodded in agreement, even though it was a complete lie. We tightened our grip on our weapons.

The first steps towards the square made me feel like I was walking in a sticky substance. My body tried its best to tell me that this was dangerous, and that the wisest thing would be to hide. The rain poured down, causing water to cascade from the roofs. A little way out onto the square, Kian stopped and pointed.

'What's that?' Something hung on a tall pole in the middle of the square. It resembled a grotesque scarecrow, but Myrthing's ravens circled the pole again and again, so it didn't scare away any birds. As we took a few steps closer, it became clear what was hanging there.

'That... that's... Mirini,' I said, feeling the blood drain from my head to my stomach. I felt nauseous. Her body was barely recognizable, but I recognized the clothes.

'No!' Lynn screamed and ran towards the pole, throwing herself at its base. High up on the pole, Mirini hung by her arms, motionless and out of reach. The bloody body had been tortured before the throat had been cut. The ravens dove towards the body from time to time, pecking at the corpse. She must have been hanging there for a long time; the stench of decay filled the air, and insects crawled in the wounds.

Suddenly, I heard someone clapping their hands and turned towards the sound. It came from an alley leading out to the square.

'Look, there they are. All of them,' a voice laughed. The sound of it sent shivers down my spine.

A figure emerged from the shadows in the alley. The smirk on his face made the nausea rise in me again. A tremor ran through my knees and hands, revealing a stronger fear than I thought I could ever feel. I hated being afraid; it made me angry and vengeful.

Suddenly, it was as if clan members were sneaking out from every nook and cranny.

'Why have you done this, Myrthing? Don't you have enough power?' Lynn cried. She rose from the ground and pushed the wet hair away from her face.

'Power? I didn't do this because I wanted power. You're mistaken there. I don't like it when people lie to my face, something this lady has done on more than one occasion, and now I've had enough,' he snapped. He almost made it sound like he had done a good deed.

'Where are the townspeople?' Kian asked angrily, gripping his crossbow tighter.

'I wouldn't do that if I were you. The slightest movement from you, and you're dead,' Myrthing laughed mockingly, looking down at the crossbow as he shook his head. Kian loosened his grip.

'You wonder where the townspeople are? If you were terrified, where do you think you would hide? Perhaps in the house of higher powers?' He glanced towards the church. Three clan members stood outside the door, sealing it off with wooden beams. Only then could we hear cries for help amidst the hammering and rain.

'Mia. How nice to see you again. You look a bit weak. Poor diet, perhaps?'

'You'll never have that pleasure again!' I said through clenched teeth.

'Oh, how sweet. She thinks I plan on capturing her again. Mia, Mia, Mia. I will paint the streets with your blood tonight,' froth formed at his mouth.

'My last breaths will be spent on your death. And I will do it with a smile on my face,' I replied. The thought of standing over his lifeless body and smiling was tempting.

'Enough of that! Boys? Ready for some fun?' he shouted loudly, and the clan cheered in response. 'Let the entertainment begin!' he said, leaning against the wall with his arms crossed.

Kian, Lynn, Majliv, and I stood frozen for a brief moment, looking at each other in confusion. A discomfort came over me, like when someone is watching you and you feel monitored. A mixture of hissing and deafening screams pierced the air. I swiftly turned around while letting the end of the whip fall to the ground. There she stood. Just a few meters away from us. Uglier than ever. The figure was gaunt and emaciated. Her large, piercing, yellow eyes narrowed. Her mouth opened, revealing sharp teeth as they protruded when she leaned forward with a snake-like lower body.

Instinctively, Majliv grabbed his staff and swung it at her without thinking, but Lamia swiftly dodged it. She nearly landed on Lynn's feet, who had to jump back. Kian fired a shot into her chest, but she merely absorbed it, almost unfazed. Majliv struck the staff on the ground, causing a tremor beneath us, but it nearly made all four of us stumble, not just Lamia.

I swept the whip through the air, striking her neck just as she was about to pounce on Kian with her mouth open. Her teeth stood out like sharp daggers in her hideous face. Kian managed to throw himself aside, and she fell where he had stood. Lamia's snake tail whipped around, pushing both Majliv and me to the ground. Lynn barely managed to stay on her feet, while Kian leaped over the snake's body.

Myrthing apparently didn't find the entertainment entertaining enough and sighed loudly. Suddenly, clan members stormed in from all directions, and amidst the chaos around us, I ended up alone, standing right in front of Lamia. She circled around me, hissing and screaming. Her long claws swiped at the air, just centimetres away from me. Now, I had gained my focus. Everything happening around us became irrelevant, and I locked my gaze on Lamia, sending the whip after her. For the first time since the tournament, I felt something tightening around my arm as it tingled inside. The whip end struck her arm, and she howled. I glanced down at my forearm and saw it now surrounded by branches with green leaves protruding between the thorns. Could it be true what Majliv had said? Could I make the whip behave differently?

Lamia seized the opportunity when I looked down and lunged at me with her mouth wide open, but I threw myself to the side. Once again, I sent the whip towards her, and this time the thorns lodged into her mouth, tearing it from ear to ear. With a quick glance around me, I assessed the situation with the others. Kian was in his element as he shot down one clan member after another. Lynn had found an excellent defence; two of the stars whirled around her as a protective shield, while she hurled the remaining one. No one dared to approach her. But what had happened to Majliv? He sat on the ground, both hands clutching his throat, his face reddened.

Lamia swiftly turned, her tail spinning around her with great force directed towards me. I barely managed to leap over as the tail shot past, but I missed with the whip. Quickly, I turned around to look for Majliv again. He was still sitting there, now more purple than red. My gaze then wandered to Myrthing, and there was the solution to the mystery. He stood with both arms outstretched, hands formed as if strangling an invisible man. His gaze was fixed and directed towards Majliv.

At that moment, the world stood still. A thousand thoughts raced through my mind all at once. Myrthing could only maintain one enchantment at a time, so how could I distract him? How could I simultaneously stop Lamia?

With a deep breath, I turned towards Lamia and whipped her with all my might across her abdomen, causing her snake-like skin to tear. Then, I ran as fast as my legs could carry me, straight towards Myrthing, while shouting to Lynn in my mind: 'I'm sorry!'

I let my thoughts wander through all the noisy experiences I could think of from Gaia. If telepaths could hear screams and shouts when someone directed

Gaia thoughts at them, perhaps it would be louder and more uncomfortable if the thoughts were about something loud. Rock concerts, car alarms, sirens, feedback, all the worst sounds I could remember, I repeated them over and over in my mind as I ran towards Myrthing. After just a few steps, Lynn and a few clan members began to scream, and to my relief, Myrthing did the exact same. I ran past Majliv, who was gasping for breath. I had the whip ready.

Just as I swung the whip in the air towards Myrthing, I felt a genuine desire from the depths of my being for the whip's thorns to cut him deeply. The whip soared through the air towards him, hitting him perfectly, and he screamed in pain. Then, he suddenly fell silent. His throat had split open, and blood gushed down his chest. He collapsed lifeless to the ground. I quickly turned around and, as expected, I saw Lamia lunging towards me. With long strides, I ran a distance away from her to lure her away from the others. She made another leap towards me, missed, and allowed herself to be deceived by my movement. I stopped and turned back towards her again. I stood at the end of the square, ready with the whip. Lamia hissed and screamed as we began circling each other once more.

Now or never. As she raised her body and positioned herself towards me, I had my back against the square and threw the whip in the same motion as I rushed towards her. This time, the whip wrapped around Lamia's back but continued around me. We were locked together! Lamia screamed, twisted, and writhed. I had only one weapon left, and I had to draw strength from the deepest part of myself as I filled my lungs with all the air they could hold. Then, I screamed with all my heart. In the next moment, the scream was intensified by pain as two hands with sharp claws impaled my stomach.

My body began to shake. The sound that escaped my lips, across the square and the city, caused Lamia to grimace. It was as if the energy around us converged at a single point, sparking. Lamia's body became rigid, and her head snapped backward, facing the sky. I felt dizzy and squeezed my eyes shut as tightly as I could, as the last remnants of air escaped from my lips.

Suddenly, everything became quiet, empty, and soundless. Then came a loud, violent, and painful noise. What had been holding onto my stomach released its grip, and I felt incomprehensible pain.

I looked up and found myself in a cloud of dust, alone. The thorn whip lay on the ground beside me. The dust settled with the rain, and I saw that Lamia was gone. The pain, however, still remained, and a strange sensation came over me in addition to the agony. I tasted a nauseating flavour in my mouth. It wasn't until I placed my hands on my stomach that I understood the seriousness. The taste in my mouth was blood. Behind me, I heard cheers from familiar voices, and I turned my head slowly towards the sound. A radiant Majliv was approaching. As I tried to turn and walk towards him, I found myself unable to move, and everything went black. I heard my name in the distance as my body fell. The sounds were like echoes and reverberations. The voices turned into distant murmurs. The pain released its grip. Nothing mattered anymore, and the indifference was blissfully relaxing. I had no interest in knowing who I was, where I was, or where I was going. My skin felt like billions of particles swimming in weightless state. Tiny vibrations moved around in the numb body, especially in the stomach.

In the distance, I sensed horses moving, but my body felt too heavy to mount one. I just wanted to rest. Then, it was as if something wanted to force me to breathe, and the pain became noticeable again. The voices around me became clearer but still sounded like incomprehensible mumbling. The tingling sensation in my body grew stronger and stronger until it eventually disappeared completely.

CRSO

I opened my eyes. It was warm, the sun was shining outside the window, and a sleeping Will lay next to me as if nothing had happened. Of course, he couldn't know, but I had to. What had happened after what I remembered? Why had everything gone black? Was I dead? No, I couldn't be because then I would never have woken up in Gaia. I stood in front of the bathroom mirror, scrutinized myself, and came to the conclusion that I at least looked very much alive. The stairs creaked with familiar footsteps, and Will soon entered the bathroom.

'Hey, sweetheart,' he mumbled and did what he needed to do. It didn't seem like Will was having one of his best days. He stretched and rubbed his neck over his stiff shoulders. It was a lot for him too, I could not forget that.

He approached me after washing his hands and wrapped his arms tightly around me. It felt wonderfully good. I needed to feel him here, it was as simple as that. Even though my mind could still flutter with guilt, acceptance of the two different worlds was something I had learned over time. I just had to get used to the fact that I had two lives and that I had to make the best of both of them.

Will kissed me on the forehead, walked out of the bathroom door, and disappeared into the kitchen. He was so good. I wished all these unfair problems could be lifted from his shoulders.

As I gathered my thoughts a bit in the bathroom, I came to the conclusion that I was definitely not dead, and that was reassuring. The incident in Grimrokk had left many questions in my head. Where had Lamia gone? Was Myrthing really dead? And what had actually happened to me? Would I be whole if I woke up there again?

All these thoughts swirled around in my head as I waited for the day to pass. I longed to return to Grimrokk, so much so that I could hardly wait for the evening to come so I could go to bed. The only thing I could think about was if I would see any of them again. Especially Majliv, there was no use denying it. I came up with all sorts of things to occupy myself during the wait. Never before had I taken the initiative to start dinner so early, and I began making homemade meatballs with spaghetti and tomato sauce.

As the evening progressed, my anticipation grew so much that I spun around doing laundry and vacuuming, and in the end, I even did the dishes just to have something to do. Will didn't say anything but gave me questioning looks, wondering what on earth had gotten into me. Only after a long shower did I think that the night had finally arrived, and it was a good excuse to get into bed. But as I lay with my head on the pillow, I was far from tired enough to sleep. I stayed there for at least a couple of hours before my eyes finally started to feel heavy.

൬൭

'Mia, Mia,' whispered a clear voice. If I didn't know any better, it could have been an angel speaking to me. Someone touched my hair.

'Mia, my darling,' said the voice. The joy that spread throughout my body confirmed that I knew this voice.

'Majliv?' I said, but I didn't quite have the strength to open my eyes yet.

Suddenly, I felt a faint breath against my lips, and just inches away from them, the voice said, 'Thank God, Mia! You scared us to death.' Majliv rested his forehead against mine.

'Oh Sleeping Beauty, do I have to kiss you to wake you up?' He chuckled lightly.

'Yes, otherwise, I think I'm just dreaming,' I whispered with a smile.

There they were, the two soft lips I had longed so much for. The scent of rosemary and lavender tickled my nose, as it always did when he was near. My arms wanted to reach out for him and pull him close, but I was too sore and weak.

'I almost thought I hadn't made it,' I said as I studied his face, with all the features I found so attractive.

'You actually didn't, but thanks to someone who owed you a favour, you got a second chance,' he replied. His smile faded. The thought of almost losing me seemed painful to him, but then he smiled with his whole beautiful face.

'What? Was I... dead?' I asked.

'For a moment, you were, but we weren't ready to let go of you so easily.'

'What do you mean someone owed me a favour? Who would that be?' I hadn't done anything special for anyone, had I?

'Remember when I told you that you didn't receive a gift from the Hell Horse and that what you thought was a gift was your ability? Well, instead of carrying you to the end of your life as the legends say it does, it saved you.' He sat on the edge of the bed. Just looking at him was almost unreal.

'I've gotten used to a lot with Grimrokk, but being dead... that's a tough one to swallow,' I said, sitting up in bed, still feeling dizzy.

'Be careful now! You lost a lot of blood, and it took ages to heal your stomach.' He held his arms around my waist to steady me.

'Thank you, Majliv. I wouldn't be here if it weren't for you,' I said. There was no better man for me. William or not, this incredible person was mine, at least here. Now I could finally get answers to all my questions.

'What happened to Lamia? Is she gone?'

'Literally evaporated. It was completely incredible. You're the strongest person I know, willing to sacrifice your life like that.' He wrapped his arms around me and held me tightly. The abundance of praise made me feel uncomfortable, as I wasn't accustomed to it, and after everything he had done for me and everyone else, I wasn't prepared to receive this in return. I had never done anything significant before.

For the rest of the day, I didn't get to have Majliv to myself. Everyone wanted to thank me for my efforts, both those I knew, those I had barely met, and even those I hadn't heard of before. The room was filled with flowers by the end of the evening. Lynn and Kian had sat on either side of the bed for most of the day, telling stories and bickering about what happened when and who did what in the heat of the battle - but the story always ended with me as the great hero.

There were to be a funeral for Mirini in the next few days. I missed her. She left a huge void in our hearts. The loving, talkative, and absent-minded person she was. Even her food, which in no way deserved a place in the history books, had its charm. She was irreplaceable.

∞

Now that Grimrokk's everyday life was safe for the first time in many years, a cheerful mood spread across the landscape, reflected in the vibrant colours, and even the sun shone brighter than before. This mood also affected me in Gaia. With a brighter outlook on life, I made the everyday a little more joyful around me. Will had finally regained his smile, and it was wonderful to see.

An eagerly awaited letter unexpectedly arrived early in the mailbox. It was from the social worker. Due to the high volume of applications recently, they had assigned more staff to process cases and clear the backlog, and as a result, our application had been approved. Finally. We were going to adopt!

There was still almost a year and a half to wait, but the prospects had never been brighter. I was going to be a mom! Will was going to be a dad! With the letter in hand, I ran to Will and showered him with tears of joy. We didn't have to be sad anymore; we were going to be parents.

∞

Chapter 19
The last goodbye

The hard, cold wooden box was so impersonal that it sent shivers down my spine. Inside it lay the poor body that had once been Nikolas. Now it was just a shell. He owned nothing the day he died, so the coffin was a gift from the congregation.

It did what it always did at funerals, rained. Every drop that hit me made me sadder than before and unable to console the poor, crying guy to my right. His clothes were as cold as mine, but that wasn't why his body was shaking. From his chest came painful, deep sobs.

Batist had been deeply depressed ever since the day Mirini died. Mirini, who had always been so full of life and joy. It hadn't occurred to the rest of us the strong feelings that had existed between the two until she was gone. My mother in Grimrokk was the closest I came to a comparison. She was the one who brought me into the world and cared for me when everything was new and unfamiliar. I was in no way prepared to lose her when I did.

Father Benedict gave a short sermon at the graveside. Wargborough Church towered behind him like a lance against the sky, and the spear on the bell tower was almost invisible against the grey clouds. There was a small funeral procession around the grave, maybe about twenty people, those who were truly close friends of Nikolas. Sally, the little, bubbly lady who once dressed me warmly to protect me from the cold, stood there wiping tears with a large, purple handkerchief. Well, the handkerchief wasn't really that large when I thought about it, but Sally was so small.

Next to Sally stood Romari with his mother Rosa. Romari was Lynn's annual flirt during the Frost Festival, Kian had told me so once. He was tall and dark with eyes that almost appeared black in the dull weather. His mother, Rosa, had a small bakery in the square where she made the world's best yoghurt bread. She had taken Nikolas in since the time he had been locked in Grimrokk, the time he had accidentally encountered his neighbour from Gaia - and had his life ruined. Because unfortunately, even though one is not oneself in Grimrokk and Gaia, there can often be similarities that someone recognize.

The others around the grave were people who had greeted me in passing, even though I didn't know them. Everyone knew who I was and probably felt they knew me a little after that day in Wargborough. The day when Myrthing and Lamia had created hell for the last time, and Grimrokk had finally been freed from its monsters. Lynn had said that people were so grateful for what I had done that they might as well put me on a pedestal. There were rumours that they were actually going to elevate me. Admittedly, in the form of a bust, but I would never agree to that. There were better people out there than me, and it was those people who should be immortalized.

'Look who he's with,' Lynn said, standing on my left side. Under her large black hood, she nodded her head towards the cemetery gate. I looked up, and in that moment, my heart leaped in my chest. Two people were walking towards the funeral procession, and I knew them both. One of them could sometimes scare me more than anything in this world, now that Lamia and Myrthing were both gone. Nicor was also a frightening monster, but he wasn't a problem unless you sought him out. He was, of course, dangerous because in his mind, there was only one thing that mattered, and that was to drown you so that you would forever be his.

However, the one who occasionally scared me more was the creature walking towards us now because it was scary how much power she had over my future happiness. Huldra was capricious. Good only when she had something to gain from it, and she had the power to inflict the worst possible pain upon me. She could, rightfully so, deny my dearest the chance to ever see me again. Fortunately, I still got to see him, but only when it suited her. He was the man I wanted to spend the rest of my life with in Grimrokk, the man who was now walking alongside Huldra and looking as enchanting as the first time I saw him. Majliv was the reason for my existence, in the truest sense of the word. Without him, my life would have been over many months ago.

It had been several weeks since we last saw each other, and butterflies fluttered in my stomach as he looked at me. His gaze was filled with longing but also sadness. Nikolas had been an acquaintance, and Majliv had assisted him after one of the many attacks he had experienced. Nikolas' neighbour in Gaia had some vengeful friends here in Grimrokk, and they had attacked him several times. They might also have caused his death. After Nikolas died, they had disappeared for good. Perhaps out of fear of being arrested?

My thoughts went to the last time Majliv and I saw each other, in Huldra's forest. We stood side by side facing Huldra's council, pleading for Majliv's freedom from the contract. We had decided to be honest with her from the very start, but I feared what she would say. A grange warden's contract could only be broken on two occasions according to tradition. The first was if Huldra nullified the contract, and the second was if the grange warden died. The first was almost impossible, and the second was certainly not a desired alternative. No matter how much I had done for Grimrokk by finally dealing with Lamia once and for all, Huldra would never let Majliv go. He was too valuable to her. No one could replace Majliv without first gaining years of experience, and even then, no one could fill his place. He had pride and honour in his job that surpassed most.

The only times I would get to see him were when he didn't have assignments, but in practice, which was almost never. I couldn't travel with him on those assignments either. Huldra made sure of that as soon as she heard about our romance.

'When a grange warden has a task to fulfil, the thoughts must be on the task and not on his heart's desire,' she had made it quite clear. I couldn't be with him, and as long as she needed him, he had to follow her orders.

Although it was good to see him again, it also hurt. Funeral or not, I just wanted to run into his arms and be as close to him as I could.

'Let's bow our heads in prayer.' It was Father Benedikt who caught my attention when he spoke. Everyone bowed their heads, and reluctantly, I did the same. It felt like the prayer lasted for hours. As selfish as it was of me, I just wanted the funeral to be over so I could talk to Majliv, even if only for a moment. Surely Huldra couldn't deny us that?

Benedikt's voice continued to mumble, and finally, it ended with an 'amen.' My eyes shot up and I searched for Majliv's face, but where he had stood just minutes ago, there was nothing but empty air. Desperately, I searched through the funeral procession, but there was no sign of Majliv.

'Well, they didn't stay here long,' Lynn said as she gently nudged my side. I looked at her. She caught sight of something on the other side of the fence. My gaze followed hers. There, I caught a glimpse of Majliv's eyes before Huldra called out to him, and he followed her. In that brief moment, I could see that he was a sea of different emotions. Desperation, anger, love, and longing.

'No!' I shouted, but it was too late. They were gone.

'Mia, you'll probably see him again soon. Huldra probably just wants to see how loyal he is to her.'

'He should be loyal to me, not her.' I knew there was no logic in what I was saying. He had made all this clear to me before we became involved. Majliv and I had no obligations towards each other. We weren't married, not engaged, we could barely even call ourselves boyfriend and girlfriend considering how rarely we saw each other. In the eyes of others, we might as well have been acquaintances who had shared a night together. But the night we had shared, apart from Huldra and the two of us, only two others knew about it—our friends Kian and Lynn.

The funeral was over. Lynn, Batist, and I each placed a rose on the grave, and then we thanked Father Benedikt for a lovely eulogy.

The estate was quiet. Lynn and Batist were cooking dinner together in the kitchen without exchanging a word. Both of them were lost in thought. As for me, I mostly felt like being alone. Grimrokk could be dull when the days repeated themselves and remained the same. Especially since I couldn't see Majliv or didn't have anything else to do, like saving the world from dreadful creatures. The past few days had mostly been spent tidying up, cooking, and sitting in the rose garden, letting my thoughts wander.

The rain had subsided, and it was barely possible to glimpse the sun through the thin layer of clouds. Like the previous days this week, I ventured out into the empty rose garden. The only sound that broke the silence was the birds nesting in a tree by the edge of the woods. In the middle of the garden, the gazebo stood open, waiting for me as it had done on all the preceding days. The small, curved steps almost smiled at me as I approached. I sat down. The steps were hard and cool against my thighs. From the forest, I could hear the creaking of tree trunks leaning against each other in the breeze that rustled through the treetops. I had grown accustomed to the forest around the estate and its mysterious sounds. Often, I could hear rustling in the bushes, and other times it was the occasional crack of a branch. If it had been a year ago, I would have been terrified and run away, but now it had become part of everyday life. Everyday life without Lamia and Myrthing was supposed to be free and filled with joy. Perhaps it was for most people here in Grimrokk, but not for me.

Before the dreadful day in the square of Wargborough, my life had been much more exciting, and Majliv had been there all the time. No, that wasn't true. Not all the time. The days in Myrthing's dungeon would forever remind me of how evil this world could be. I had done everything to suppress the memories, but they kept coming back. To this day, I couldn't stand the smell of mouldy bread. In the pigsty, there were occasionally mouldy breadcrumbs. The pig, after an unpleasant encounter with me, became terrified every time I approached. Perhaps not so surprising, since the first time I brought food, I was so nauseated by the smell that I screamed and ran as fast as I could while vomiting. Poor pig.

The worst part was that every day, the same memories occupied me. The feeling of being alone in the cold darkness, completely unaware of time and whether anyone knew where I was. The difference was that with each passing day, the longing for Majliv grew stronger. I felt safe with him by my side.

Finally, I had learned to live with two separate lives. One life in Gaia and one in Grimrokk. Will and I were still waiting to adopt, but first, the final IVF attempt was scheduled. The problems in Gaia belonged there and should never cross over here. If I were to master this existence, I would have to separate them from each other.

Even though my thoughts wandered, the beauty of the rose garden kept me awake and present.

'Mia, Mia?' It was Antoinette running towards me.

'I'm here, Nette,' I said as I stood up and waved my hands.

'Look what Kian brought me!' She held a grey bundle in her hands, which shook in rhythm with her as she ran.

'What do you have there?' She was so excited that she barely had time to stop at the steps and bounced like a ball beside me.

'It's a kitten. It's adorable!' She had hearts in her eyes and stroked its soft, smooth fur.

'How kind of Kian. You're lucky.' The beautiful little creature meowed and squeaked in alarm.

'Yes. Uncle Siljan's cat had kittens a while ago, and now they were ready to live away from their mother.'

'Have you found a name for it?' I asked.

'No. Hmm...'

'It must have a name. Is it a boy or a girl?'

'A boy. It must have a grand name. Like a prince or a king,' she replied enthusiastically. It was good to finally see Nette in better spirits. She had been so down since Mirini's death that I had become worried about her. She had mostly remained in her room, day in and day out. 'Can you help me, Mia? Can you think of any names of princes and kings from fairy tales?' 'Well... I'm not sure if I remember many fairy tales, but I know the names of some real royals from Gaia.'

'Can you? Say some!' She was so bubbly that it was hard not to laugh at her.

'There's one named Prince Phillip. Would that work?' I asked.

'No! Too strange,' she said, shaking her head decisively.

'Charles, then?'

'Charles? I don't think so,' she wrinkled her nose.

'Hmm... What about Harry or William?'

'Not Harry, definitely. But William might not be a bad idea.' No, I thought to myself. William is not a bad name.

'Is William handsome?' Nette asked with more anticipation.

'Yes, he is. Many girls have him as their prince Charming.' Yes, Prince William was handsome, but he wasn't the one I thought of when I heard the name William. The prince would never be as beautiful as my William.

'Then it's settled. You shall be named William,' Nette nodded decisively as she looked down at the little bundle she held in her hands. He was falling asleep there.

'Definitely a good choice, I think,' I smiled again.

'We need to baptize him. There's a basin in the pantry where we can pour water.' Nette immediately got into the idea.

'Nette, I don't think it's very kind to William. Cats don't like being bathed.'

'But he has to be baptized, otherwise he won't have a name. What should we do then?' She was desperate.

'What if we just use a tablespoon of water? That should be enough. We can't soak the whole cat.' Poor cat, so new to the world, and now it had to keep up with Nette's enthusiasm.

'Okay. I guess we can do that instead,' she said a bit disappointed.

'We need a priest,' she said in the next moment.

'Who should it be, then? We can't ask Father Benedikt to come all the way out here to baptize a cat.' I didn't like to disappoint Nette, especially not after everything that had happened, but she needed some boundaries. She was struggling and missed her mother a lot. It was rare for me to see Nette smile like she did now.

'No, we don't need a real priest, but we need a pretend one. Hmm... Who can be a priest, I wonder?' She thought hard.

'What about Batist? I think he needs something else to think about. He's so sad these days.' I looked down at her. Her sadness wasn't far away these days either.

'Yes, he misses Mom too.' A tear welled up in the corner of Nette's eye. It hurt to see her so fragile.

'We all miss her, my dear little friend. Mirini was good through and through.' My own eyes weren't dry anymore, a couple of tears were about to spill over the edge.

'I miss her so much. It's so empty without her.' Nette's head grew heavy, and she leaned forward, resting her face in her hands. I stroked her shoulder for a while before pulling her closer to me.

'There, there, my dear. We sat in silence for a while, watching William sleep at her feet. Eventually, the scent of food started to fill the air, and not long after, we heard the kitchen bell ring.

'Shall we go inside and join the others for some food? You can tell Baptiste about the important task he's been given.' She looked up at me and wiped her tears with the sleeve of her dress.

'Yes, we can do that.' Inside, everyone had already gathered around the table. At the far end, Batist sat with his head lowered. Theodor sat to his right. Lynn poured elderflower juice into the glasses, while Kian stood by the washbasin near the back door, washing his face.

'Now we're all here,' Batist nodded and sighed heavily.

'Nette, why don't you go and ask him then,' I whispered as I kissed her on the head.

'Mia,' greeted Kian as he approached me.

'Hey, Kian. So, a kitten, huh?'

'Just had to try and get her mind off things, poor girl,' he smiled sadly and gave me a warm hug.

'You're a good boy, you know that?'

'I know. The best,' he sarcastically laughed at himself, as only Kian could do, though there wasn't as much conviction this time.

'We missed you at the funeral,' I remarked gently.

'Sorry. I didn't make it in time. The pig had gotten loose, and it's dangerous for people. Dad was afraid that if we didn't get it back inside, someone could get hurt if they were unlucky enough to encounter it.'

'Where's Siljan? Isn't he coming for dinner?' I asked.

'No. He's with some good neighbours. He needed some time for himself. Who can blame him?'

'No one,' I said, and I saw Batist waving to everyone to come to the table. Batist's cooking was, as always, exquisite, even when Lynn had helped. In the past few days, she had spent most of her time in the kitchen. Not just to cook, but to keep Batist company while he made elixirs. Lynn was the type of person who couldn't sit and mourn, she had to do something. 'Batist? We're going to baptize William. Can you be the priest?' Nette didn't bother with a further explanation of who William was.

'Who did you say? William? Do I know him? But I'm not a...'

'My kitten. His name is William, and Mia and I are going to baptize him with a tablespoon of water, but we need a man who can be the priest. So, we thought of you. It's not possible to ask Father Benedikt to come all the way here to baptize a cat, either.' Nette spoke so quickly that it was easy to hear that she was her mother's daughter.

'Oh, I see. Well, I guess I can be the priest then. When do you plan on having the ceremony?' Batist chuckled at the corner of his mouth for the first time in several days.

'Hmm... I haven't thought about that,' Nette pondered for a moment. 'Maybe after dinner?' she said excitedly.

'That sounds like a good idea,' Batist said, winking at her. He had always been like a surrogate father to both Nette and Teddy, and they both greatly appreciated him. We ate, and as often during this time, there was a heavy silence around the table. Nikolas's funeral had brought our own immense grief over Mirini back to the surface. Lynn barely touched her food, and Kian sat rolling a meatball from one edge of his plate to the other, while Teddy sat absentmindedly gazing out the window. Now, the silence needed to be broken. I couldn't let sorrow ruin more days ahead.

'I wonder when the frost will come,' I started politely. The mundane topic clearly awakened more life in the room. Kian startled so badly that he nudged his bowl a little too hard, causing a meatball to bounce across the table.

'Yeah, you're right. It's still a little while away, but now that you mention it, there's quite a bit to be done to prepare for the cold,' Kian said, desperately trying to catch the meatball and his bowl before it fell to the floor.

'How are we doing with food for us and the animals in the near future?' Lynn asked as she popped a potato into her mouth.

'The last I heard, Brina and her husband were almost done with harvesting the vegetables and fruits. John had brought in the grain, but the straw is still standing,' Batist said, suddenly engaged. Brina and her husband, John, were the parents of the farmhand Sebastian and managed the fields belonging to the estate. They were friendly but mostly kept to themselves.

'Nette and I can go visit them tomorrow and see if they need any help,' Teddy suggested. He had grown up so quickly this year. He had indeed grown almost as tall as Kian, but it was more than just height. His face was more defined, his shoulders broader, and his neck stronger. He was well on his way to becoming a man.

'Oh, do I have to? I hate dealing with farm stuff,' Nette protested, but her protest went unheard.

'We all have to pitch in now,' Teddy emphasized.

'Fine,' she said, but pouted. The rest of the dinner was spent planning for the upcoming days. It might not have been the most enjoyable conversation, but it was something. I hoped that this was the beginning of a new everyday life. One where we could let go of the heavy sorrow over Mirini but keep the memories of her.

Batist stood in the gazebo with a tablespoon between his fingers. The whole scene was actually quite comical. Nette stood next to him, clutching a startled, unruly kitten. Surrounding them were Kian, Lynn, Teddy, and me. Kian had the task of holding a small cup of water that would serve as the baptismal font.

366

'Dear congregation, we are gathered here today to baptize this cat and welcome it into our family. What shall the cat be named?' Batist spoke as if this were his most important task and the purpose of life itself.

'William,' Nette solemnly replied.

'The cup,' Batist instructed Kian, with the spoon ready. He dipped it into the water. 'William, I hereby baptize you in the name of the Father, the Son, and the Holy Spirit.' Then he poured a few drops of water over the cat's head. William was far from pleased and hissed in anger.

'Dear family, please welcome your new family member, William.' Everyone applauded. At that moment, the cat became so startled that it dug its claws into Nette, causing her to release it, and it ran off. It slipped under a bush, and all we could hear were small, somewhat desperate chirping sounds.

'I wonder if we'll see that cat again,' Kian whispered to Lynn and me.

'Poor thing, she'll be so sad if she can't catch it,' I said. But before we could worry any further, Nette had thrown herself in after it and emerged crawling with the kitten by the scruff of its neck.

'She's not a girl who lacks initiative, that's for sure. Don't know who she reminds me of,' Lynn laughed.

'You mean you?' Kian loved teasing his sister.

'Not you, that's for sure. You wouldn't even know which way was front and back on your pants if it weren't for me!' They could go on like this for hours if someone let them. Even though they acted like teenagers when they argued, it was still fun to listen to.

I felt like part of the family. They asked me for my opinions, what I wanted, and if I had any dinner preferences. I was important, even though I wasn't their flesh and blood.

Evening came quickly, and everyone was tired after a long day. It was time to go to bed. I still had the same room I'd had the first time I visited the estate and entered this world. There, the same green bed curtains with white frills hung down from the canopy. Outside the windows, it had grown dark, and cool gusts of wind came in through the open window near the bed. I walked over to it and looked out over the courtyard and the linden avenue, which had a faint blue glow from the moon. The sky was cloudless, and the stars hung like a blanket over the forest. It was like a perfect painting by Benjamin Williams Leader. This world was so beautiful that it could take my breath away at times, but Majliv was right: You get used to beauty. No matter how beautiful it still was, I had seen it before and wasn't as surprised as I had been when it was new to me. There was a calmness in Grimrokk that often reminded me of what we used to call 'the calm before the storm' in Gaia. When it was quiet, it was like a silent stillness, but when there was unrest and evil forces around, everything was untamed and dramatic.

I took off my clothes and placed them on the chair by the door. Over one armrest hung the nightshirt I used to wear. It wasn't actually a nightshirt. It was Majliv's best linen shirt, with a V-neck and a tie at the neck. I had actually been given it to wash, but I couldn't bring myself to do it. It smelled like him. Lavender, rosemary, apple, and man. Majliv had his own unique body scent. His fragrance was soft, light, and round, but at the same time raw and untamed. Falling asleep with his scent around me was a balm for the soul.

Just as I sat on the edge of the bed, there was a knock on the door. There was no doubt in my soul who it was. This wasn't the first night I had a nightly visitor. I opened the door gently, and it was exactly as I had expected. There, in the hallway, stood a familiar figure.

'Can I sleep with you?'

'Of course, you can. Come in.' Nette had been sleeping with me almost every night since Mirini died. Whether she saw me as a mother or an older sister didn't matter much. She needed someone to listen to her and give her comfort. It didn't take her long to fall asleep. Most of the time, she curled up like a ball and fell asleep while I stroked her hair and sang the song Huldra had given me to her. Deep down, I had a feeling that it was the song she wanted more than anything else. In fact, she had asked me to sing it the first night she came to me in tears.

Nette crawled into bed and curled up.

'Where is William?' I whispered.

'He fell asleep on Kian's stomach, so now they're both sleeping on the sofa in the parlour. I couldn't bring myself to wake them up,' she replied, pulling the blanket up to her shoulders. 'I can almost picture it,' I chuckled softly. 'Sleep well, Nette.'

'You too, Mia. I hope you have a nice day at home.' She said this every night. The first time she said it, it sounded a bit strange to me, but there was actually a kind thought behind it. She meant well because every morning she'd ask me how my day had been in Gaia. It didn't take long before both Nette and I were sound asleep.

MAGIC OF THE NIGHT

Chapter 20
A complete 180

aia was, as always, uneventful, monotonous, and predictable. Although, on this day, I was supposed to start the hormone injections for our final IVF attempt. Not that I saw any point in it. I had given up on becoming pregnant and was ready to adopt and be content with that. Will on the other hand had convinced me that we should give IVF one last try, and if it didn't work out, we would throw in the towel and focus on adoption instead.

I had already decided on which country we should adopt from, Colombia. The adoption agent had called its children 'Children of the rainbow' when I called and asked for information. I found that exciting. I didn't dare fantasize too much about what the child would look like or whether it would be a girl or a boy, but I was starting to feel excited. That's why, deep down, I saw these injections as a big unnecessary hassle.

One evening, Aleksandra dropped by for a cup of coffee, and we chatted about various things.

'Have you started the injections again now?' she suddenly asked, without me mentioning anything.

'Yes, how did you know?'

'I can tell by your mood. Besides, I saw the casing on the kitchen counter,' she replied.

'My mood is pretty much the same as usual, isn't it?'

371

'No. You seem more distant when you take them. Sometimes I swear you're sleeping with your eyes open. Your thoughts are in a different dimension.' I started laughing and tried to brush it off. She had no idea how accurate she was.

'It's not that I'm not interested, but they make me so darn tired.' It was only partially true, but I needed an excuse.

'Apology accepted!' Aleksandra continued with great enthusiasm, fluttering her eyelashes, and feigning a swoon.

When Will finally came home from work, I understood what Aleksandra meant by 'distant.' He was no different. We sat in our respective chairs in front of the TV, and I could swear he was staring at one of the lights on the DVD player, as if the red dot deserved his full attention. In his defence, he had been working a lot in recent weeks, and I knew he dreaded this being our last IVF attempt, but he hadn't behaved like this before. Maybe he was truly depressed?

 C&D

Nette was still asleep when I opened my eyes the next day. The corners of her eyes had traces of dried tears, and she lay with her arms around her own shoulders, as if embracing someone in her dreams. It saddened me to see her like that, but grief had to run its course. All I could do was to be there for her when she needed me.

I rose carefully and tiptoed over to the chair where my clothes were located. I quietly picked them up and headed out the door. Unsure if anyone else had woken up, I continued to walk down the stairs to the first floor as quietly as possible. Suddenly, I heard someone whistle—a whistle that resembles the sound of a hot summer day when a scantily clad woman in a short skirt bends over with a group of male spectators.

'I'll be damned. Is this what I've been missing when I've been at Dad's helping him on the farm?' Kian leaned against the doorframe of the lounge with his arms crossed.

'This is nothing. You should have seen me the other day, milking the cow in my underwear,' I quickly replied.

'Haha! You've never milked a cow in your entire life, Mia,' he retorted, winking playfully. 'Majliv should really see you now, in his shirt and all. Wasn't that the one you were supposed to wash for him?'

'Uh... well, yeah, but... No, never mind.' Now I was embarrassed. Truly embarrassed.

'Take it easy. If it were my shirt, I would just take it as a compliment, seeing how sexy you look in it,' he added jokingly. Swiftly, I threw one of my shoes right at his stomach and smirked back before continuing towards the kitchen.

The kitchen was currently empty of people. The washbasin stood by the door with a jug of water beside it. I really needed a proper bath, but a quick wash would have to do. It was one thing I missed in Grimrokk—the ability to easily take a shower whenever it suited me.

Here, there was quite a bit of planning involved, such as fetching water, heating it, and hurrying to bathe before the water turned too cold. At Siljan's farm, they had the hot spring, but there was nothing like that nearby here.

I put on my leather pants before taking off my shirt. I quickly put on my sweater and just then, the door to the hallway went up.

'Darn it, I arrived just too late,' Kian was clearly in a teasing mood this morning.

'Take it easy now. Has it been a while since you had a lady over? You seem to be attracted to anything walking on two legs,' I laughed as I grabbed my shoe from his hand.

'Not everything... just you,' he said, but his face clearly showed he was joking. Kian knew very well that I had nothing more than a friendly interest in him, and it went both ways.

'You joker. Why are you in such a good mood today?'

'Since we are speaking of lady visits, Jean is coming over.' He smiled so wide that I could count every single tooth in his mouth.

'I should have guessed. You little horny pig,' I laughed and nudged him in the stomach.

'Always,' he winked again.

The kitchen door opened again.

'It's so nice to hear some laughter in this house. Anything particularly funny?' It was Batist, entering with a slight smile on his face.

'I think Kian is in heat,' I joked and giggled a little.

'You silly girl! Well, the thing is, I'll have a visitor one of these days—Jean!' Kian didn't need to elaborate further for Batist. Jean and Kian had been a couple since the Frost Festival, and they were made for each other. She was beautiful, with long, brown hair that curled like doll hair around her face. Jean was certainly a pleasant girl, but she was well aware of her beauty and loved to receive compliments, which meant it was very difficult to give her one.

'Well, dear Kian, I assume I won't be seeing much of you once she arrives.' Batist was clearly in the mood for some joking today. It was good to see.

'I believe you hit the nail on the head there Batist,' I laughed with him.

As we set the breakfast table, Kian sang at the top of his lungs, a tune that could have scared the wits out of an entire household. It was good to see that his mood was so good and that it actually rubbed off on others. As more of us gathered in the kitchen, the atmosphere only got better. Teddy arrived first, with Nette close behind. Lynn stumbled in a few minutes later, carrying the cat in her hands.

'I think there's a little one here who's hungry, and he's not big enough to hunt mice by himself just yet,' she said, and the little kitten meowed in agreement.

'There you are, you little rascal. Was Kian nice to you last night?'

'Of course, I was. He slept on my stomach all night. I just wasn't quite ready to wake up with two little paws sharpening their claws on me.' Kian pulled up his sweater and showed us the red marks he had on his stomach. Nette laughed as she brought a bowl of milk for the cat.

There was a truly cheerful atmosphere around the breakfast table, as if the day had been sweetened by sunshine, which it actually had. I hadn't noticed before that the sun was shining through the window and brightening up the mood.

The weather hadn't been much to brag about lately. It had mostly been grey and gloomy, with many rainy days. A sunny and shining day was just what we needed, and it arrived as if on cue.

There wasn't much light coming through the small window in the kitchen, even though there was enough space for about twelve people around the table. The walls were filled with shelves and medicine cabinet drawers, and it wasn't a suitable place for a family to have a meal. As long as I had lived here, there hadn't been a single tablecloth on the table. I missed a dining room that was meant for dinners and special occasions.

As I let my thoughts wander again, they did what they always did which was filling every little corner of my mind with Majliv. I thought about the first time I saw him. He had walked through the door of this kitchen and barely glanced in my direction. Now I knew how he really felt. I had tempted him. He, who had never had any romances in Grimrokk, was tempted by me. The whole thing gave me goosebumps. If only he knew how I felt about him. The images from the first time I woke up in his arms flashed in my head. Butterflies fluttered in my stomach, and I felt a slight blush creeping in. I needed something to occupy my time so I wouldn't go crazy with these thoughts and longing for him.

I had an idea. The old dining room in the manor had not been used since Mirini's husband had tragically died there a long time ago, and even then, it hadn't been used as a dining room. It was such a shame for such a splendid room to remain unused. Not that I actually knew if it was splendid or not. I had never set foot inside, never had the opportunity to peek in, but there was no doubt in my soul. As magnificent as the rest of the house was, this room couldn't be any less. It wasn't that it wasn't pleasant to eat in the kitchen, but it was more suitable for breakfast and lunch, not for dinners with guests. The first, and when I thought about it, the only time I was a guest at the manor, we had dinner in the parlour. It had been nice, but eating in the parlour was a bit impractical. No, I was determined that this house would not deteriorate any further as long as I lived under this roof.

'Lynn! What do you think about starting to use the dining room for what it's intended for? Eating food?' I thought as loudly as I could without saying a word. Lynn looked at me and slowly her face split in a big smile. She nodded eagerly.

'It's not allowed to have secret conversations during meals,' Batist coughed curiously.

'It's not a secret conversation, Batist. We just haven't had a chance to say it out loud yet,' Lynn explained playfully.

'So, if it's not that secret, you can share it with the rest of us too.'

'Mia and I are going to clean up the dining room. Would anyone like to help?' The first one to rise with a cup of tea in hand was Batist. He headed towards the hallway before we could say another word. The one who followed right after him was Kian, who had already rolled up the sleeves of his sweater to his elbows, ready to lend a hand. Teddy and Nette were reluctantly assigned to clear the breakfast table, while the adults went to do something useful.

The tall door leading to the dining room was double with brass handles and had gold-gilded decorations on the door panels. When Kian finally managed to find a key, the double doors slid open, revealing why this room had not been used for a long time. The entire dining table, which must have been eight to ten meters long, was covered with everything from empty glass containers to mortars and bowls. It was not difficult to see that the man who had spent most of his time in this room had been an alchemist. Everything in the room was covered in dust and soot.

'Wow! I knew it was messy, but this is ridiculous,' Kian exclaimed in shock.

'Where should we start?' I asked.

'By removing all the furniture. Everything needs to be cleaned, and whatever we don't need, we can sell at the market,' Lynn said as she danced into the room and started moving all the chairs around that were stacked in one corner. I couldn't regret it now. It was my suggestion, and I was going to see it through. The once grand dining room had high ceilings and a giant plaster rosette with a slightly worn crystal chandelier hanging from it. The walls were off-white with large paintings in gold-gilded frames adorning them. There was one of Mirini as a young woman, another of her husband proudly standing in front of his estate, and a full-length portrait of both of them on their wedding day. This mansion had truly been a wealthy man's residence once upon a time, but it had been neglected for far too long. We started by carrying the chairs out into the courtyard, where they received a good wash, and we could air and beat the cushions. Lynn and I pounded away, creating clouds of dust. Nette had to clean the windows, while Batist took care of the various remedies and elixirs scattered around the room. Even Kian didn't dare touch any of it. Instead, he and Teddy carried the dining table out so that Lynn and I could clean that as well. When Batist had finished tidying up, it was the buffet's turn, so the boys carried it out. It was incredible what soap and water could do to the furniture that belonged to the mansion.

The day had turned to afternoon, so it was time for a break in the sun. We sat on the steps of the veranda, each with a cup of Imaginari tea. The furniture was clean, Batist had washed the elixir equipment, and the curtains were hanging over the veranda railing to dry.

Silence settled. My thoughts wandered again. This time, I thought back on the hot spring at Siljan's farm. There, I had stood in secret and watched Majliv bathe, admiring his fantastic, naked body. The water from the waterfall cascading down his muscular back and further down to his firm buttocks. No. The memories made the butterflies flutter in my stomach, and a blush tingled my cheeks. It was fortunate that I was a little tired from all the cleaning, so the blush could be attributed to physical exertion. I quickly glanced around, but no one had noticed my little daydreaming journey.

'Mr. Kian! Teddy! You have to come!' Everyone turned toward the sound coming from the stable. Sebastian came running, pale as a ghost.

'What is it?' Kian exclaimed in surprise.

'Blasen. He has been lying down for a long time, and I can't get him to stand up. Something must be wrong because he's only getting weaker and weaker,' Sebastian cried in despair.

Everyone hurried and ran towards the stable. The stable door was open, and I could barely make out a figure lying on the hay inside. Blasen had been Mirini's faithful horse. Granted, it wasn't very fast, but it was kind and reliable.

We stopped just inside the threshold and saw him lying limp on his side. His head was lifted, but it wobbled so much that he was about to nod off.

Batist crouched down near the horse.

'This is not good. Horses shouldn't lie down for extended periods. I've never seen him this weak before,' he said.

'I'll be right back. Maybe I can get one of the hulder folk to help us,' Kian shouted as he ran out of the door and disappeared.

'The hulder folk? Can they help?' I asked cautiously.

'Not always, but if it gets really bad, they might be able to...' Lynn looked at me with sad eyes. I understood what she meant. They could help Blasen pass away without suffering.

Tears overflowed from Teddy's eyes. He had been strong for so long, but now it was too much. Throughout these weeks, he had only shed a few tears, like many men do when they try to be strong. But this time, he couldn't hold back.

He lowered himself next to Batist, then he hugged the horse's muzzle and sobbed uncontrollably.

'We have to try to get him on his feet. Maybe then he'll regain some strength,' Lynn explained, patting Batist's back. Teddy and Batist stood up and tried to support the horse's belly, gently rocking him to help him stand. Lynn and I assisted, while Nette attempted to pull on the bridle, encouraging him to rise.

But all our efforts were in vain. We couldn't get him to budge.

Kian came running back.

'They said they would try to find someone to help, but they couldn't guarantee anything. How is he doing?' he asked.

'Not good. We've tried to lift him up, but it's not working,' Lynn replied. Right after Lynn uttered those words, Blasen rested his head against the straw-covered floor and groaned.

'No! Get up! Get up!' Teddy shouted as loudly as he could at the poor horse. Batist approached him and pulled him closer. Tears streamed profusely from his eyes. I felt so helpless. This was the day when we had all finally been in good spirits and looking forward.

Suddenly, Nette ran out of the stable.

'Nette!' Lynn ran after her. Poor thing. She was so vulnerable these days, and it had been nice to see her smile a bit in the past few days. The kitten had made things a little easier for her, but now it was just as bad as before.

Batist remained seated, comforting Teddy for the rest of the day, while Kian tried to get the horse to drink a little while it lay there on the brink of life and death. I felt powerless. I had no knowledge of horses, nor was there a need for my consolation. It was best if I left them alone until help arrived.

The sun had moved across the sky and was no longer directly above us. Now it was partially hidden behind the treetops, casting softer light than before. My steps across the courtyard felt heavy. I entered through the main door and closed it gently behind me. The long staircase to the second floor seemed longer than usual, and the hallway leading to the bedrooms felt almost endless.

From one of the doors, I could hear crying and comforting words. Lynn was doing everything she could to calm Nette, but her sobs could be heard clearly, even out in the hallway. I paused outside the door. With my hand clenched into a fist, I was about to knock, but I stopped before my knuckles touched the wood. Should I go in? Perhaps Nette needed me too. No. It was probably best to leave things as they were. Lynn was a close family member and knew Nette better than I did.

This was the first time in weeks that I felt outside of the family. I was simply useless and helpless. These children had been through so much lately that I didn't even know how I would have handled the situation if it were me.

I continued on to my own room. The door closed behind me, and I stood with my back leaning against the door panel. It was so quiet. The only thing I could hear was the pounding of my own heartbeat behind my ears, causing my head to ache. I placed one hand on the opposite shoulder and started massaging the tense muscles. Everything in my neck felt stiff and sore from all the strains I had been through in recent times.

By the chair behind the door, I took off my shoes and walked over to the bed. I pushed aside the duvet and sat in the middle of the mattress with my legs curled up under me, pulling the duvet tightly up to my chin. My thoughts began to wander, as they always did, but this time it wasn't Majliv occupying them. Instead, I started to think properly for the first time about the concern I had for the two orphaned children in the house and their future.

Mirini's husband had come from an affluent family, but Mirini herself had never been wealthy. She had done what she could with what she had. Fortunately, the farm was large enough to sustain them all and even provide some extra income. Mirini had been frugal and resourceful, making the most out of very little. Teddy had inherited some of his father's clothes, and Nette had received hand-me-downs from Lynn. That's how they managed to keep the wheels turning and hold onto the farm.

What the children had that Mirini didn't have was more people to help. Previously, it had only been Mirini, Teddy, Nette, Sebastian, and his parents. But now, we were more. Even though Batist didn't officially live on the estate, he was considered a resident now, as he hadn't spent a night away from the house since Mirini's passing. Lynn was more or less a permanent resident. I didn't have anywhere else to be, so I lived here until someone told me to move. And Kian did his best whenever he was around. Siljan had enough people on his farm and could easily spare both Lynn and Kian.

I had been sitting in bed, curled up for a long time, and it had started to get dark outside. The sun always set so quickly here. After a while, I could hear the sound of horses riding into the courtyard. The Hulderfolk must have managed to get help. I felt relieved. It annoyed me that the window faced the wrong direction, and I couldn't see the courtyard from my room. I remained seated and listened, faintly hearing a couple of murmuring male voices. Probably some kind of veterinarian and his assistant, or a nurse, or maybe an executioner? Who knew how things worked in this world. Although I was curious about who had arrived, I didn't want to go down and see. It was bad enough as it was, without me standing there and being a bother.

It was quiet for a long while. I could hear every breath I took, and my pulse throbbed behind my ears. What were they doing out there? My curiosity was getting the better of me when I heard voices in the hallway. The sound was muffled by the walls, but the voices grew louder.

'There, there. He was an old horse. These things happen when you get old, Teddy,' it was Kian's voice. He was trying to comfort Teddy, who was sobbing bitterly. So, it was the executioner who had come. Deep down, I knew that losing the horse wasn't the worst thing for the children, although it was certainly terrible enough. What was unbearably painful was that they were losing yet another being they loved.

A door in the hallway slammed shut. I squinted my eyes and rubbed my nose hard with my fingers to hold back the tears that were welling up. It hurt to know how they were feeling. I lay back on the bed and focused on not crying. This would be a long evening. I couldn't bear the thought of going down to the kitchen to look for Batist. He was probably busy in the stable, and that was the last place I wanted to be at the moment.

Suddenly, I could hear footsteps in the hallway. The footsteps passed Teddy's door and stopped outside, between Nette's door and mine. Our rooms were directly across from each other in the hallway. I thought it was probably Batist coming to Lynn and Nette with a comforting cup of Imaginari tea and cookies. But the knock came from my door.

Chapter 21
William but not the cat

I got up from the bed, wiped the tears away from my face, and tucked my hair behind my ears. Over by the door, I took a deep breath to gather the courage to open it. I grabbed the handle and pulled the door slightly towards me, allowing the light from the hallway to illuminate a strip from floor to ceiling in my room. Then I looked up, expecting to see Batist standing there, but to my surprise, it wasn't him. In the dim light, there was a tall man standing there with broad, defined shoulders. He wore a sleeveless, cream-colored shirt that clung tightly to his well-sculpted muscles, and the suede leather pants hung low on his hips.

My heart skipped a beat. I looked up in surprise at his dark blue eyes, partially shaded by his dark fringe. They sparkled at me like warm crystals.

'Majliv?' I had daydreamed about him for weeks but had only seen him briefly at Nikolas' funeral. My breath stopped, and I felt frozen in that moment.

'Mia,' he said. He just stood there, gazing intensely at me.

I wanted to reach out to him, to reassure myself that it was really him, but my muscles didn't respond. They weren't prepared for this. The day had already taken us to great heights and plunged us into the depths, and here he stood, just standing there for a long time—until he

386

finally took me in his arms. All kinds of emotions flooded over me, and I could no longer hold back the tears. I had missed him so much. He buried his face in my hair and took a deep breath. I pulled him as close to me as I could, feeling his heavy breath against my chest. My hands glided over his hair and neck; I had to feel him with my own hands to know that he was real.

'I didn't know if it was appropriate for me to come, but I just had to see you,' he said. He pulled back slightly to look at me. For a moment, his eyes grew anxious as they studied the tears gently rolling down my cheeks.

'Is something wrong?' he asked.

I couldn't bring myself to answer. Everything was wrong. Mirini was dead, Teddy and Nette were orphaned, and today, on top of it all, they had lost one of their dearest animals. And I had missed Majliv so much that it hurt to look at him.

I glanced down at my feet for a moment, trying to gather myself, but the fact that he stood there in front of me made it impossible to keep my eyes away any longer.

Majliv placed a hand on each of my cheeks, then slowly lifted my face towards his. My fingers unconsciously gripped his shirt and pulled him closer to me. He gently moved his face closer, and his lips found mine. An electric shock ran through my body. The kiss was not tender, like the time he kissed me at the door of the inn in the Rim Gorge. This kiss was intense, deep, and filled with longing. He pushed me into the room and closed the door behind us. His kiss momentarily broke, and once again, he examined my face.

'Mia, it hurts to see you like this,' he said.

'The longer you're away from me, the more it hurts,' I replied. I pulled him towards me, our lips meeting again, but he took a small step back.

'Mia? What is it?' My tears worried him.

'We won't talk about it now that you're finally here,' I said. The static sparks coursing through my body were the only thing I wanted to think about right now. The tears rolling down my cheeks were purely out of joy for having him with me again. Even though something gnawed at the back of my mind, I pushed it away. I had waited so long for him, and who knew how much time we had together. It might only be a few days, and if so, I wanted to make the best of the time we had.

With all the power I had, I pulled Majliv closer without saying another word, and eventually, he responded to my silent desire. He held me tightly in his arms before sliding them down my back. When they reached my hips and thighs, he lifted me up so I could wrap my legs around his waist. He carried me towards the bed. My heart pounded so hard in my chest that it hurt. His powerful chest rose and fell with rapid breaths.

My fingers found their way to his hair and gripped it. We were by the bed, and there was nothing I wanted more than to have him. I could feel his hardness through the clothes. Majliv was warm, and his heartbeat strongly against mine. Was I dreaming? Was he really here? Whether I cried out of joy, longing, or sadness, I couldn't judge at that moment, but our faces were moistened by tears.

He gently laid me down on the bed and moved with me. I fumbled with my sweater until I finally managed to tear it off. In my haste, I could hear a couple of threads rip. His shirt was already gone when I laid my eyes on him again. The smooth skin over his firm muscles made my pulse quicken measurably. He leaned towards me and began kissing my neck before letting his lips trail down towards the cleavage between my breasts. Then he pushed my pants down over my hips while lightly running his tongue in a zigzag pattern over my stomach. Where there had once been a large gash from my encounter with Lamia, there was now only a small scar.

My breath came out in small moans. I kicked off my pants from my feet. Majliv teasingly ran his fingers along my hips, up my waist, and towards my breasts. His touch left burning traces where his skin met mine, a warmth I longed for. Then he sat up and loosened the belt of his pants before sliding them down his legs. His naked body was perfect. The toned muscles on his upper body were like a sculpture of Adonis himself. He was chiselled from stone, defined. My mouth watered.

His pants landed on the floor. Instead of lying back down, he remained sitting upright, looking down at me. His gaze was filled with desire. Clearly, my body had been without him for far too long and had been craving him all this time. We had been apart, but now we knew what awaited and didn't hold back the desire.

My breath was uncontrollable in my chest. I rose, wrapped my arms around him, and pulled him towards me while our lips moved in sync. My legs found their way around his hips, drawing him close. His warm, sweaty body rubbed against mine in a steady rhythm while his breath tickled my cheek towards my ear. Had I forgotten how incredible Majliv was? My daydreams hadn't done him justice. He was so much more. Every movement he made resonated with me. He wasn't a stranger to my body, yet he still excited me.

'Mia, I love you,' he whispered breathlessly in my ear. Then he stood up and pulled me along with him. I straddled his lap, wrapping my arm tightly around his shoulders. 'Love' wasn't a strong enough word. It didn't come close to describing what I felt for him, but it was the most powerful word I could find. I looked into his eyes. Still teary-faced, I kissed him.

'I love you too, Majliv. You have no idea.' It was like lighting a fuse. He became rougher in everything he did, but I felt safe and enjoyed it. His moans were intoxicating.

'More!' My voice was almost hoarse. Waves of warmth flowed through my body, making me want to scream with blissful joy.

Majliv's head rested on my chest. His breath was rapid, leaving a moist film on my skin.

He kissed along a line down my stomach, over my navel, and to my vagina. His warm breath sent tantalizing shivers throughout my body. I arched my back and tilted my head back in anticipation of what was to come. Then he ran his tongue over my lips.

'Do you want me?' he asked.

'Yes, more than you know.'

'I do have a pretty good idea,' he chuckled against the inside of my thighs. There was no doubt that I was wet because of him. His words alone aroused me intensely.

'I look forward to entering you and feeling you squeeze tight around me,' his words felt like electric shocks, igniting me even more if possible.

His mouth continued to work its enchantment between my thighs as his tongue delved inside me. He eagerly moaned and gave me one final lick before kissing his way back up my stomach. He stopped at one breast, sucking the hard nipple into his mouth, and teasing it with hot, small bites. Finally, I stopped thinking during this treatment, closed my eyes, and savoured every second.

He moved to the other breast, giving it the exact same attention.

'All the days that have passed since I last saw you have been unbearable, Mia. I sleep restlessly at night, waking up as tired as when I went to bed, daydreaming about you.' He was a tender and warm man in the body of an animal on the hunt for food.

His kisses from the breast and upward turned into nibbles, and when he stopped at my shoulder, he sank his teeth into me. I arched my back and desperately grasped the sheets to keep a hold on reality.

'Oh... My God!' It was impossible to stay silent during this escapade.

Majliv lifted his head from my shoulder and stared intensely at me. He leaned down until our lips met in a deep and fiery kiss that curled my toes. His hands gripped my thighs, causing me to spread my legs and wrap them around his hips. I could feel how hard he was and the smooth droplets he left on my stomach.

'Mmm... I don't want to wait anymore, Majliv. Now!' Before I could even think about what I was asking for, he plunged into me with his massive shaft. He was a powerful man, proportionate in every way.

'Yes!!!' I felt like I had been empty for a long time, and now, in this moment, I felt complete. He was my air. Without him, I couldn't breathe. My hands stroked his naked back, and I could feel that every inch of his smooth skin was moist, just like my own. His breath grew faster and faster. Soft moans rumbled deep in his powerful chest. I was ready. The wild tremors started from my spine and spread in all directions.

'Come with me!' I shouted as his thrusts became quicker. One final, hard thrust, and Majliv's entire large body contracted, and a loud grunt was muffled into the pillow beside my head as I bit down hard on my lower lip to remain silent. His body calmed down before he rolled us to the side.

'Oh, Mia. How are we going to survive like this for a long time? I'm going crazy.' He sighed and rested his forehead against mine.

'It's just pure luck that I'm here now. I was there when news of Blasen arrived, and I was on Pronto before anyone could gather their thoughts.'

'I hate that it's so difficult.'

'I'll stay here for a couple of days. Kian wants me to help him buy a horse. We need one to fill in for Blasen, so we have to do it fairly quickly. One of the nearby farms has a couple of horses for sale, and they've promised to wait until I've seen them before selling' he explained.

'Nette is completely devastated these days. She's still deeply mourning the loss of Mirini, and now she has also lost her horse. Poor girl. Kian gave her a kitten to comfort her, but she's not doing well.' I had so much empathy for her. We lay there in silence, arms wrapped around each other. I was so tired. Everything that had happened in the past few days, not seeing Majliv as often, everything that occupied my mind in Gaia, it was all too much for me. I longed to wake up one morning to a completely ordinary, problem-free day. A simple day where life was easy to live. A day that lets you win a small prize in a lottery. A day that served you a prime steak for dinner with a glass of red wine. I just wanted one such day. As I slowly drifted into sleep with Majliv, I looked forward to Gaia's 'normal' everyday life.

CR80

Several gloomy and eventless days passed, and the days were as devoid of excitement as they could be. The day for egg retrieval was approaching, and my belly was starting to swell. I had completely lost faith in everything and saw this as utterly unnecessary and meaningless. The way things were, I would never be able to get pregnant, so for me, it was a complete waste to spend all this time on the IVF attempt when it could be used for other pleasant pursuits. Deep down, I had to admit that it was my fear that made me so negative. The fear of failing once again hung over me like a dark cloud, and it would feel like the ultimate defeat. But what wouldn't one do for their spouse.

⊂⊃

When I woke up in Grimrokk the morning after, I expected to be enveloped in Majliv's arms, but his side of the bed was cold and empty. Had he already left? I sat up on the mattress and rubbed the sleep from my eyes. There were sounds outside that piqued my curiosity. My bare feet met the warm wooden floor as I walked over to the window to look out. The sight that greeted me made my body rejoice even before it was fully awake. Majliv stood by the shed, chopping firewood shirtless. His body was sweaty, and the muscles rippled beneath the smooth skin with every swing of the axe. He was a man, in the truest sense of the word. I had never seen anything more arousing. Well, that might not be entirely true. The sight of Majliv in the hot spring at Siljan's farm had also affected me, I couldn't deny that, but there was something about seeing a sweaty man at work that appealed to me. As I stood there admiring him, he encountered a large stubborn log, but Majliv didn't give up. Eventually, he grew so frustrated that he raised his arm over his head, grabbed hold of the invisible rod of energy he possessed, and smashed the log to kindling, quite literally making splinters to start fires with. He took a deep breath, shook his head, and resumed chopping.

'William! William!' I could hear Nette shouting in the distance as I continued to stand and observe Majliv at work. Suddenly, he turned around and called out, 'Yes, what is it?' As if he suddenly realized he had done something wrong, he froze completely and looked around in despair. When he realized he was alone, he let out a deep sigh and breathed a sigh of relief. I felt a chill inside me. All the desire and passion I had just had abruptly extinguished. What had I just witnessed? Why did he respond to the name William? Perhaps that was his name in Gaia? Nette rounded the corner of the estate and ran towards Majliv.

'Have you seen my kitten? His name is William,' she asked anxiously.

'No, I haven't, Nette. Have you asked the others? Maybe Kian has seen him.'

'Thank you. I'll ask him right away,' she said and happily ran off. Meanwhile, I stood still, stunned, watching Majliv walk over to the gate and grab a piece of fabric hanging from it. He wiped his face and chest, sat on a small stool, and grabbed a pitcher of drink, which he downed in one gulp. I released myself from the frozen position I had been in and took a few steps back towards the bed to sit on the edge of the mattress. How likely was it that Majliv's name was also William? How common is that name in Gaia, aside from royal families? I shook my head. I would have to think about this more thoroughly later! Right now, I had important things to do.

William, the cat, had indeed been with Kian during the night, as Majliv suspected, and Nette was greatly relieved to have found the animal. She now sat, a bit happier, cuddling with it in front of the hearth in the kitchen while Batist brewed elixirs. Lynn continued our cleaning project in the dining room, washing walls and floors, while Kian and Teddy hung up the curtains that were finally dry. I polished silver carafes, vases, and candlesticks until they gleamed, and my fingers were blackened.

When the floor was clean, the boys started bringing in furniture while Lynn helped me finish polishing the silverware. The day went by, and when dinner was to be served, the chandelier and candelabras were lit, and the whole room sparkled. It was truly fit for royalty. Batist stood at the end of the table and tapped his spoon against the glass.

'Dear everyone. What a fantastic effort you have made, and how incredibly beautiful it has turned out. It's good to see this house return to its former glory. I wish Mirini were here today to see this.' Batist cleared his throat to rid his voice of sadness and raised his glass high for a toast.

'CHEERS!' everyone around the table exclaimed. Majliv sat next to me. He had clearly taken a bath and changed clothes, for he smelled wonderfully of clean man, rosemary, lavender, and apples. I sat and observed him for a moment before he looked at me with a smile.

'What is it?'

'Nothing special. Must there be a reason for me to look at you?' I laughed.

'Look however long you want, my girl. As long as it's me you're looking at.' He smiled back before the smile slowly faded, and he furrowed his eyebrows. Both he and I knew that it wasn't just him who received looks from me, and the same went the other way around. It was something we had to accept.

The evening was lovely, in the newly renovated dining room and with good company, but I still occasionally thought about how Majliv had turned around when Nette called her cat. It was strange that he was also named William. That had to be the reason for his spontaneous reaction.

❦

Chapter 22
The point of no return

ill and I were invited over to the neighbours for a barbecue in the summer heat, and I was looking forward to a pleasant and relaxed afternoon filled with enjoyment. Lately, it seemed like both households had been quite busy. We had finally completed our last IVF attempt a few days earlier and were now trying to set everything aside for a while. All this uncertainty was so consuming that we needed a break.

Will rang the doorbell, and not a few seconds later, we heard the sound of eager little children's feet running.

'Iam!!!' Christina shouted at the top of her lungs and threw herself at Will grabbing for his neck. She had become our little treasure, and it seemed to be mutual.

'Hey, Tinkerbell! That was quite the welcome. Have you been waiting long?' Will chuckled.

'She hasn't talked about anything else for the past five hours, so if you hadn't come now, we would have come over to get you,' Aleksandra laughed from the living room.

Will scooped Christina up in his arms, and she leaned towards me with outstretched arms.

'Mia!' She waved her arms at Will and burst into laughter as he tickled her tummy.

I kicked off my sandals, grabbed the giggling little girl, and continued into the house. I caught a glimpse of Peter through the kitchen door, marinating meat for the grill, while Aleksandra had just stepped onto the porch with a salad bowl in her hands. The baby lay on a blanket in the shade, babbling and kicking eagerly.

I set Christina down on the grass, and she dashed after her mother at full speed. Then, I helped set the table, doing my part to contribute. From the kitchen, I could hear Will chuckling at Peter's underwear humour. It was so effortless to have friends like these, so liberating to come here and just be myself.

The afternoon passed with good food and pleasant conversation. As I helped Aleksandra clear the table, Peter finished preparing dessert. Will entertained Christina, who had recently learned to write her own name.

I heard Christina spell the letters aloud as she wrote, and not long after, she ordered Will to write his name too. With a cold soda in my hand, I walked back out onto the porch just as Christina lifted up the sheet of paper with 'WILLIAM' written in block letters. The sun illuminated the paper, the letters shining through the thin sheet and fully readable from the back. MAILLIW. It was spelled backward, yet still clear and distinct. Everything came to a halt.

William spelled backward was Mailliw. I had never actually thought about how Majliv spelled his name, but this confirmed the suspicion that had been stirring within me lately. Majliv's real name was William. One thought led to another, dragging me into an emotional whirlpool. What if my Majliv was the same person as my husband William? Could something so unlikely be possible? No, I halted the train of thought before it gained control over solid reasoning. It had to be a coincidence. Gaia is full of Williamses, and the difference between them was way too significant. Or what?

For the following days, I unconsciously studied Will more than I ever had since we were newly in love. His body language, how he articulated himself, and his interests. He had always enjoyed the outdoors, and from the age of seven, he had been an enthusiastic member of the scouts - a commitment he had continued throughout his childhood. He had even become a leader of a patrol at the age of thirteen. He spoke about those experiences with a passion I rarely saw otherwise. When he eventually had to quit, he was 18 and had landed his first job.

A few days later, Will felled a couple of trees from the property line, which he then proceeded to chop into firewood. I stood by the window and watched him. It was hot in the sun, so he was only wearing a tank top as he swung the axe high above his head. He had always had a prominent V-shaped back and strong, dependable arms, and now they swelled beneath the damp, sweaty skin. There was no doubt that Will was an attractive man. While not the most muscular, he was remarkably agile and stable. Visibly strong, reliable, and not to forget; very handsome.

As I stood there lost in my own thoughts, he struggled with a large, stubborn trunk that wouldn't split. He slammed it onto the ground, cursed at it, kicked it with his right foot, and raised one arm as if reaching for something, before suddenly catching himself and quickly lowering his hand again, cautiously looking around.

Alarm bells rang in my head. What had I just seen? What was he trying to reach for? It distinctly reminded me of something, didn't it?

Suddenly, I knew. Majliv had done the same thing when he had reached for the stick and turned the trunk into kindling. Admittedly, no stick had come to Will's aid, but every movement was exactly the same.

I held my breath until I felt dizzy. Images and memories of both of my men mingled into a thick porridge in my mind. The deep, dark blue eyes, the features, and the movements, all were undoubtedly the same. How had I not seen it before?

Could I really have fallen for the same man in both worlds?

CRANGO

For each passing day, I saw more clearly what I hadn't noticed before. The way Majliv stretched his neck when he got stiff, how it was simply impossible for Will to go up a staircase without taking two steps at a time, or how both of them took off their sweaters by first grabbing the neckline with one hand and then pulling it forward over their heads - these were precise similarities, among dozens of other small things.

With each day, I also became more aware of what I had learned about the Grimrokk curse. Suddenly, it was more real to me than ever before, even though I had seen what had happened to Nikolas. Every second, fear clung to me, the dread that the Grimrokk curse would strike us.

Majliv had been away from the estate for a long time, but this time I hadn't missed him like before. Despite the fear, there was also comfort in thinking that Will and Majliv were most likely the same person. Because it meant that not a single day went by without seeing him, and absurd as it was, I had begun to accept it. Anything was better than living with the intense longing day after day.

This evening was like any other evening. Batist, Lynn, and I were in the lounge playing cards, Kian was on a sofa with his feet on the coffee table, small electric sparks dancing between his fingertips. Teddy and Nette were lying on the floor with a ball of yarn rolling between them, playing with the kitten that bounced back and forth in its playful hunt for its now quite frayed prey.

It was getting quite late, so the last thing any of us expected was for the doorbell to ring.

'Well... that's strange. Who could that be at this hour?' Batist got up and went to answer it.

A short while later, he returned with a smile and a familiar figure in tow.

Majliv radiated toward me. I always felt a bit safer when he was nearby, and I sensed my body releasing muscle tension I didn't know I had.

He came over to me, bent down, and gave me a kiss.

'What are you doing here so late? Don't think I'm not happy you're coming, but you usually don't come here so late in the evening,' I smiled at him.

'Believe it or not, it was Huldra herself who said I needed a few days to attend to my dearest treasure. So here I am,' he said. His voice was gentle, but the smile on his lips didn't quite reach his eyes. Huldra was rarely so gracious as to give Majliv time off without ulterior motives. It had never happened before, and what was with the cryptic message about taking care of the dearest thing he had?

Everything had a purpose when it came from Huldra.

'Hmm... that's strange. Has she ever given you time off like that before?' I had to ask, even if I might not want to know.

'No. Never before have I been told to take a few days off. It has only happened when I've been between missions, waiting for a new task, but never time off like this.' He shook his head as if to clear his thoughts and returned with a broad smile that sparkled in his eyes. His hands snaked around my waist. I rested my head against his chest and filled my nose with his delightful scent.

'Get a room, you two!' Kian shouted and flicked a spark that gave me a jolt right on my backside.

Everyone laughed as Batist cleared the table of glasses and games. The children were sent to bed, and the adults bid each other goodnight and went their separate ways.

On the way up the stairs, I grabbed Majliv's hand and eagerly pulled him with me towards my room.

'Oh, really? Is there something special on your mind that you're so eager to have me alone?' I could hear his laughter in my ear and felt his breath against my cheek.

'You would probably like to know,' I chuckled with a mischievous smile on my lips. He grabbed my shoulder, leaned down, and lifted me effortlessly, simultaneously kicking open the door to my room.

'Shh! The walls are thin,' I whispered, a bit too loudly and with laughter in my voice. Majliv entered my room with me in his arms, pushed the door back with one foot, and leaned against it, letting it close with a thud.

It was so delightful when he was playful like he was now. He was rarely this relaxed; he usually carried the world's weight on his shoulders. My heart pounded with eager longing to have a whole night with him again.

He set me down on the floor and his hands travelled from my waist, up my chest, to my neck as his mouth met my neck. His lips were warm and soft, kissing their way up from the collarbone to the earlobe. My pulse raced through my entire body as he teased every inch of skin on the slow journey to my lips. My own lips, on the other hand, were impatiently waiting for his, and I eagerly contributed to meet him. Soft, tender lips met each other.

'Oh my God, how I've longed for this.' He grabbed behind my thighs and lifted me until I could wrap my legs around his hips. I laughed in surprise as I was lowered onto the bed, and nimble hands untied the knot at my waist. With my fingertips, I frantically searched for smooth skin, tugging at every piece of clothing that stood in their way.

'I've longed for you so intensely. It feels like an eternity since we were together like this.' I understood so deeply what he meant. It hadn't really been that long since we had time to ourselves, but we would never know how long we'd have to wait until the next time. Our only thought was to seize the opportunity now, as it came so eagerly.

'Give me everything you've got!' The words came out with a moan from my lips. I started tugging at his shirt, the soft fabric sliding up the hard, muscular body. I wanted to lick every inch of the perfect, masculine sculpture that loomed over me with strong arms. Majliv kissed my stomach and slowly pushed my top upward. He licked my breasts and teased me with the tip of his tongue along my ribs. It tickled so intensely that I didn't know what to make of myself, and I laughed hysterically.

'No! It tickles! William, STOP!' It slipped out of my mouth. He laughed and withdrew.

I looked up. The laughter subsided, and the big smile faded little by little.

The silence made me uncertain. What was it? Had I done something wrong? Will liked to be playful in bed.

Will? No, Majliv!

It was as if a huge stone landed right in my stomach. All my senses locked, and echoes roared inside my head.

Majliv's gaze became utterly frantic. The whole man froze in his place.

'No! No! That's not what I meant! I just misspoke!' I shouted, now hysterical.

It was completely silent around us. We dared hardly to breathe. Time didn't exist, or it mocked us. We were surrounded by a compact silence, like before a storm or in the minute before the guillotine falls. But no storm surged in. No guillotine fell.

'It can't be possible!' Majliv's words were barely palpable breath against my cheek. Had we escaped? If so, how? Why?

I felt relief pull the corners of my mouth into a smile, just as my body became heavy. The image in front of my eyes began to lose focus. Numbness prickled through my whole body, and slowly but surely, I drifted away from the world. The sounds that enveloped me felt like being wrapped in down, and gradually, Majliv's hysterical expression also disappeared, which I managed to see darken before it vanished into a mist.

The curse swallowed me. Everything turned black. Empty. Lonely. My brain ceased to absorb anything from the surroundings. And where was Majliv?

CR&CO

I slowly opened my eyes. Above me was just a white ceiling. I was breathing as if I had run a marathon. The relief was immense; I had awakened from that dreadful dream!

'It was just a dream,' I sighed half aloud. A dream. But Grimmers didn't dream. I looked around, turned to Will's side of the bed. Sweet Will, he was sleeping peacefully next to me. My breathing calmed. It could and had to have been a dream because I was in Gaia.

I moved closer to him to soothe my restless heart. His skin was soft and warm, and his breathing was deep and tranquil. I rested my head against his chest and waited for the arms that were supposed to hold me tightly, while I listened to the steady, reassuring thump of his heart.

But there were no arms. No one pulled me close. No change in pulse or breath told me he had registered my presence.

Quickly, I sat up on my knees and looked down at Will. If I hadn't seen his chest rise and fall, or just heard his pulse beat, I would have thought he was dead. My own heart pounded desperately as I firmly grabbed his shoulders and shook him, hard. No reaction. Not even an irritated grunt.

Panic hit me full force because I understood what had actually happened. The Grimrokk curse had struck us after all.

Chapter 23
There's no reassurance
in good news

rey, sombre clouds blanketed the dark sky. Rain had poured down for fourteen consecutive days, and the prospects ahead didn't look any brighter.

The chair I sat on was as hard as the first time I had sat on it, and it wasn't designed for prolonged sitting. But prolonged sitting was exactly what I had been doing.

Exactly six weeks had passed since my existence had been turned upside down and the other world had been closed off. My tears had dried up several days ago, and every second felt unbearably long.

Exactly six weeks ago, Will had left me, forever, and I knew there was no way back. The curse was final, and it was because of me, my recklessness – my foolish, thoughtless mouth – that it had struck us. Between us now and forever was an insurmountable wall.

Six weeks had passed since I had last been in Grimrokk. I sighed, remembering the memories from a world I could never have imagined I would come to love so deeply when I was there for the first time. I had left those who became my family there. My faithful friends. And I had left Majliv.

My Majliv. My William, who now lay here, still. Immovable, except for the rise and fall of his chest with each breath. No, he wasn't sleeping. I knew he was alive, just not here. It felt like it had been months since I woke up with Will lying lifeless next to me, and at the same time, it felt like it had been just a few moments. The ambulance personnel had rushed through our door with bags full of life-saving equipment. Equipment that I already knew couldn't do anything to bring my Will back to me, but that I still desperately begged them to use while I hysterically followed every move. Every time I looked back, it stung in my dried-out eyes.

At the hospital, they had conducted countless tests without getting any results that could explain anything, let alone bringing Will back to me. I stood my ground and tearfully begged for more and more examinations, but all came back with negative results.

It had now been an hour since the last doctor had left our room after showing me the inactive results the tests had yielded yet again. His words carved into my mind, hurting more and more with every breath I took. Words that were decisive for whether Majliv would continue to live. The doctor said that Will was BRAIN DEAD!

On the table next to me was a brochure explaining how wonderful it was that people who had chosen to sign up for the donor registry had saved the lives of several others after their passing. How many people with life-threatening diagnoses could one patient save? I flipped through the brochure, but I knew with all my being that it was completely out of the question to donate even a fingernail-sized part from William's perfect body. How could I make the doctors understand that no one could, no one should end William's life? After all, there was no medical reason to continue this battle for someone diagnosed as brain dead.

Never before had I been so lonely. Never before so utterly, completely alone in an overcrowded world. No one could understand the impossible situation I was in. My own family had supported me for a while, until the doctor had concluded that there was no brain activity. At this point, they had gently started to say things like I 'should let him go,' and that it would be the best for me too.

Even his parents, a few days ago, had seen the brochure lying on the table like an executioner's axe. They hadn't said anything, but I knew what they were thinking. They had given up too.

So here I sat, alone like the moon behind the clouds, knowing that they were right, and yet fundamentally wrong. I was helplessly excluded, not just from Majliv, but from all the abilities and strengths I had shared with him. Everything we had shared was becoming increasingly vague memories, like distant shadows. And like the memories, I too was fading. I was nothing without him, and he was nothing without me. I remained by his bedside, and I was all he had left. We were like night and day; could only meet in the twilight, but never fully.

One evening, after I had sat still for a long while and, as always, looked at the heart monitor with a foolish hope for movement, I felt like stretching my legs a bit.

It was strange that these chairs hadn't left any marks on my bottom given me open sores, as hard as they were. I stood up and decided to go to the ward's coffee machine to buy myself a simple latte. It wasn't a long walk; it was just down the hallway. The door to Will's room was visible from where the coffee machine stood, and I pressed the button so the light brown, warm drink filled the paper cup.

As I stood there, focused on the sound of the machine and the smell of coffee, I caught something in my peripheral vision, without fully grasping where or what was moving. Three spoons of sugar into the cup, energy for another session of doing nothing, before I shuffled back towards Will's room. When I was five doors away from Will's door – I always had to count, one of the simple routines that kept the grief and anxiety in check – I saw a man in a white lab coat coming out of Will's door. He turned his head towards me but quickly turned in the opposite direction and disappeared down the corridor.

'Hey, who are you?' I called out. The only reaction I got was the man increasing his pace and vanishing around a corner. What on earth was that? There had indeed been many doctors in and out of his room, but after such a long time, I recognized all the faces.

After standing there and looking perplexedly after the man for a couple of minutes, I shook my head and went into Will's room. There, I noticed that his medical chart was open on the bed, not where it had been when I left. It wasn't really unusual for a doctor to visit his room, but after the last test results had come in, it was mostly just the occasional nurse who had been stopping by. The doctors seemed to have given up on coming.

So why had this doctor visited him now, and why did he disappear so quickly when I called out to him?

I looked at Will. He lay as peacefully as always. Then I glanced up at his monitor, which displayed the same steady rhythm it had shown for the past few weeks. My curiosity had to be satisfied, so I went to the nurse's station to talk to Annika, the nurse on duty at the time.

'Hey, Annika. Do you know who the new doctor was that just visited Will? I haven't seen him before and didn't get a chance to talk to him before he disappeared.'

'New doctor? We don't have any new doctors on the ward right now. Especially not anyone who needs to see Will,' she replied, puzzled.

'A man just came out of Will's room, wearing a white lab coat. I didn't see his name tag, but he must have been a doctor?' I asked again, this time a bit anxious about who the person might be.

'Hmm... strange! There's definitely no one who's supposed to see Will right now. All the hallways and doors here look so similar, he probably got confused and thought Will was his patient but realized his mistake and moved on. It can happen occasionally, and they tend to rush when someone catches them making a mistake,' Annika chuckled. Her explanation made sense when I thought about it, and I reassured myself with the answer I got. I thanked her and walked back down the corridor. Anyone could make a mistake, and he might have been in a hurry with a waiting patient he couldn't find.

Two nights later, I sat half-asleep between two chairs in the dimmed night lighting of Will's room when I was awakened by a sound. Since the nurses were constantly coming in to check on Will during the nights, something I had actually started to understand was an excuse to check on me a little extra, I rarely paid attention to the sounds anymore. But this time, when I cracked my eyes open, it wasn't a nurse I saw, but the doctor in the white coat, the one who didn't belong to the ward. Why was he here again?

Before I did anything, I stayed completely still and watched him. All he seemed to be doing were routine doctor procedures. He looked at the monitor, which beeped in its regular rhythm, flipped through the chart, and before I could comprehend what he was doing, he picked up a phone and took a picture of a report. Doctors never did that.

'Hey, you! What are you doing?' I asked irritably, but before I could even get up from the chair, the man was out of the room, without a sound. The blanket I had in my lap had wrapped around my foot, so when I finally managed to extricate myself from the tangle and get out into the corridor, the man was already out of sight.

I went back and looked at the papers he had been reading. It was the latest conclusive report we had received just a few days earlier, the one that stated they hadn't found anything directly wrong with him, but they also couldn't find any brain activity. What did this man want with these papers, to consider them important enough to photograph?

A possible explanation grew inside me with intense discomfort. This man must be an organ harvester, scouting for suitable and available organs from patients for his high-paying clients. I had heard of them. Sleazy and sinister people on the dark side of the law. I wasn't going to stand for it. Regardless, Will couldn't die, and certainly not to donate organs to a black market! He had to live as long as he could. No one would end his life before his time. Deep down, I was starting to realize that it could be a matter of days before it was too late, but I was going to fight tooth and nail to prevent it from happening.

Panic set in, and my feet raced towards the room where the night nurses had their office. I pounded frantically on the door while keeping an eye on the door I had come from. A young nurse emerged from the room, surprised, and before she could say anything, the words spilled out of me.

'A man was in our room again, and I'm sure it was the same man as last time. He didn't act like he had walked in by mistake; on the contrary, he took pictures of Will's chart and then ran out of the room when he realized I was awake. You have to call the police or a security guard! They might want to steal his body!' Only when the words left my mouth and the surprised expression turned into alarm on her face did I realize how insane I must have sounded. The gaping mouth, which - I noticed - matched well with her large, round eyes, closed and opened as if she was searching for words.

'Amelia, I think you need to get some proper sleep. You don't need to sit here all the time. We'll take care of your William,' she tried to reassure me, but I felt far from calm. When had I last slept properly? Could it have been a hallucination caused by my lack of sleep? I couldn't answer that for certain. Stranger things had happened to me before. All I had now were dark, empty hours without dreams. Never an uplifting, good dream. The dreams had ceased when I first arrived in Grimrokk. Was I simply losing my mind? Had I started seeing visions?

I forced a smile and attempted a dry laugh.

'I guess I've been awake a bit too much. You're probably right, it's maybe time to go home and take a shower. Change clothes.' I looked down at myself and realized that the latter was certainly true. Embarrassed, I waved my fingers as I took a few steps backward. She smiled back, but her smile didn't erase the concern in her eyes.

I took a deep breath and headed towards the exit. These cold corridors were oppressive and harsh against a grieving soul. Anyone could go mad walking here every day without purpose or meaning.

In Will's room, it was as quiet as ever. Only the hum of the machines caused his chest to rise and fall. I stood and looked at him for a while, thinking about all the plans we had made. All the days we had believed we would share, everything we wanted to do, experience, and most importantly, the family we were going to create together. It was almost certain that we would have children someday; it was just a matter of how, despite all the adversity. We had discussed the method of becoming parents, not whether we would be. I placed my hand on my stomach, and the realization that I would never feel it filled with life and kicks forced itself upon me. The hand on my belly vaguely reminded me that I had forgotten something, and it gnawed at my thoughts until I suddenly remembered. The blood test!

I had completely forgotten to take the blood test after the last trial with the test tube. I was supposed to have done it weeks ago. My life had been filled with everything else these past few weeks. All my energy had gone into keeping Will alive, keeping the doctors away from the organ donation plan. So here I stood, realizing that I didn't know the result. I grabbed the bag hanging from the arm of my chair, went over to Will, kissed him gently on the cheek, and then rushed out of the room. Now there was only one thing to do, and that was to find the nearest pharmacy.

At home in the empty house, there was a strong smell of old garbage. The house had hardly been visited for a week, except for that one time I had stopped by to change clothes. The neighbour had taken care of Tinka and everything else for me, like an angel, ever since Will had been taken away by the ambulance that dreadful morning. They had offered to help, these wonderful neighbours we were so blessed with.

They had truly done everything they could to take good care of me. The first evening, Aleksandra had come over with a pot of stew. She had placed the pot on the doorstep as I opened the door and had simply wrapped her arms around me without a word. It was exactly what I needed. An unspoken understanding. Today, a bag of fruits and energy bars hung on the doorknob.

But now, I stood here with a week-old garbage, and when I opened the refrigerator, it was clear that the milk was about to sprout legs and walk away. The cucumber had turned to mush. After disposing of all the old and rotten items and cleaning the refrigerator with soap, I left the windows ajar to let out the odorous air. Then, I went into the bathroom and turned on the water in the shower. In the mirror, I was confronted with a pale reflection of the person I knew as myself. Heavy bags under my eyes, greasy hair, and my skin had an almost translucent quality. Was this my new self? Would nothing ever get better? Will was my life, and in this house, he was missing everywhere. How could I possibly live without him? What had been a cliché before, when other people said it, had become a question that hit the mark.

I stepped under the warm droplets and let the water flow over the tense muscles in my neck and back. The water was scalding hot, but I welcomed the burning heat. I savoured the cleansing sensation until the water turned lukewarm, signalling it was time to finish up.

The towel was cold over my shoulders. I had thought that after a long shower, I would feel a bit better, but no such luck. A lump in my stomach made me feel nauseous. I closed my eyes and tried to calm my breath, hoping the nausea would subside. It took a while, but it gradually got better.

I opened my eyes, focused my gaze, and found my balance. There, on the sink, lay the little box. I hated those boxes. There had always been so many disappointments inside them. The contents were supposed to give me the answer I didn't know if I dared to see. If the answer was positive, I would have created a family, but without Will. If it was negative, Will and I would never have children. Not that he would ever see it, but the thought of having children with the man I loved more than anything meant so much to me. Almost more than before now that I had lost him.

I took a deep breath and pulled the stick out of the box, sat down on the toilet seat, and let the stick receive its required drops as I had done so many times before. I felt like vomiting. My stomach wasn't cooperating anymore and set off contractions that pulled at my abdominal muscles.

With a jump, and just in time, I sprang up from the seat and turned around. The contents of my stomach spluttered down into the toilet bowl, and I realized how little I had eaten that day. I struggled over to the sink, splashed water on my face, and filled my mouth with water that I spit out again. After several rounds of rinsing and a couple more mouthfuls of water that I swallowed down, I dried my face with the edge of the towel that still hung around me from the shower. The bloodshot eyes in the mirror had long, wet eyelashes and were set in a red-flushed face.

I pushed myself away from the sink with my hands when I felt something on the floor with my foot. It was the test that I had almost forgotten, which had ended up on the floor when other needs had taken over. I slowly squatted down, picked it up, and turned it around so I could see the little window.

Alone, nauseous, and dizzy, I remained squatting, staring at the test window, but unable to see what it showed. My fate was about to reveal itself, and I wasn't ready. It was clear that Will should have been here, holding my hand comfortingly. A couple of tears rolled down my cheek, so I wiped them away angrily with the back of my hand to see what it actually said. 'PREGNANT' was written in large letters in the window. Time had stopped. My breath had stopped. A pang in my chest. I had done this countless times before, but I had never seen that word before. Now was when Will should have been here. Because this was what he was supposed to see. We should have been so happy, embraced each other with tears in our eyes and joyful smiles. We should have called everyone in the family and our friends to share the amazing news, and they would have been happy with us. But here I stood, sobbing, with tears streaming down my face and the pregnancy test pressed close to my chest. We managed it in the end, but too late for Will. What should I do now?

An hour later, I had finally put on a tracksuit and made myself a large glass of chocolate milk. Food wasn't tempting, but an empty stomach, which had just emptied itself, was also not a good thing.

Morning came before I finally took out my phone and found my mom's number.

'Hello,' came the voice on the other end. She was trying her best to sound positive, I could tell.

'Mom, I'm pregnant,' I hiccupped with a shaky voice.

'Oh, my dear! That's such good news, isn't it?' she said gently.

'I honestly don't know how I feel. Will isn't here. He was supposed to be here to experience this wonderful news, just as excited as me. We were always supposed to be together!'

We talked for over an hour, and if anyone could make the day a bit better, it was my mom. She always seemed to find a way to see things in a brighter light. She suggested that she would call the rest of the family and my in-laws with the good news and wanted me to go back to the hospital, to Will.

So, with a slightly lighter heart, I entered Will's room and sat down on the chair as I had done so many times before. I hung my jacket and bag on their usual spot over the chair, then took steps toward Will. I leaned down, kissed his forehead, and whispered the words he would never hear:

'You're going to be a dad.'

Chapter 24
I you listen you might just hear something

A few days later, I sat by Will's bed, dazed, holding an ultrasound image between my fingers. Twins! There were two tiny children growing inside me. Two little copies of Will, who would make their entrance into my life in seven months. It was unbelievable.

I closed my eyes and tried to imagine how Will would have reacted to the news if he could. He would have undoubtedly burst with joy, shouting to everyone who passed by that he was going to be a father of two. I could picture it vividly, and tears welled up in my eyes. Here he lay, motionless, just inches away from me, completely unaware of the children we were expecting, and it would continue to stay that way. I wished he knew how much I needed him now.

After weeks of no appetite, things were different considering I knew that I was eating for three. My body was prepared on a deeper level than I could control, and the cravings overcame the mild nausea. After a visit to the cafeteria and one of my many trips to the restroom that day, I lay down in bed, right next to Will, and held him close. I was tired and needed to be close to him. Just hearing him breathe, feeling his warmth, and knowing he was alive in there somewhere was a resource of comfort. I knew that closeness could be deceptive, but it was much better than letting go of hope. Grimrokk had become like a distant dream to me, as if I had only imagined everything. It seemed so far away.

My eyelids grew heavier, and in the comforting closeness, I fell asleep. Deeper than I had in a long time. Darkness. This darkness I hadn't seen in a while. My dreams, which had previously shown me the portal to Grimrokk, hadn't been visible to me in any way since the day I fell through the mirror. However, this darkness had also been absent from me. My nights had just been empty and blank. Nothing to see, hear, or remember, just emptiness. So, what was drawing me back into the darkness now? Granted, I was all alone, no hands through mirrors or flashes of light to be seen. Everything was dark and silent, but I felt no fear. The feeling that enveloped me was warmth and safety. I was familiar with this darkness, and the feeling of being a little closer to all those I missed was strong. How much I wished to tell them what had happened! They would never be able to answer me with words, but if there was even a glimmer of a chance that someone was listening, I would seize it.

'Majliv! My Majliv. You have no idea how much I miss you. The world is so empty without you! I wish you were here to share this new life with me. This was supposed to be the greatest joy for us.'

ങ൙ഞ

MAGIC OF THE NIGHT

In Grimrokk, a grieving man sits by his beloved who is lost. She will never wake up again. Her breath and her pounding heart are all he has left of her.

The warm cloth he holds in his hands glides gently over her beautiful face and down her smooth neck. A tear falls onto the lovely dress she rests in. Her hands are folded on her abdomen, cradling a red rose. The thorns will never hurt her. Not even now in this state.

He sets the cloth aside and takes a seat in the chair beside the bed, positioned close to it. Her hand fits perfectly in his. He closes his fingers tightly around her soft ones. He lifts the back of her hand to his cheek, and he closes his eyes. He is tired, disheartened, and filled with sorrow. He sits like this until his breath calms, and he falls asleep close to her side, in an empty, dreamless state.

'Majliv! My Majliv!' The words ring in his ears. Each word feels like it's shouted directly at him with a force that hits his heart. Mia is somewhere in there! He hasn't had a single dream since he was a child. This is no dream; he knows it.

'It should have been the greatest joy for us to become parents. But how will you ever know? You are not with me, and I cannot reach you in any way. Dearest, beautiful Majliv, my William, you are going to be a father!' Her words are swallowed by tears, and then everything grows silent. Could it still be a dream? If this was the only time he heard her voice again, it would be infinitely better than nothing, even if it was only in a dream.

423

A door slams open, and a woman stands in shock in the doorway.

'Majliv! Did you hear her? Did you?' Lynn shouts.

'What? Did you hear her too?' Majliv can't believe his ears. Did they really both hear Mia? 'Yes!'

'You can hear dreams now too?' He can't comprehend how that could be possible.

'No, Majliv. You know very well that grimmers cannot dream. Regardless of what just happened, it wasn't a dream. It was Mia I'm sure of it.' He couldn't believe it. This wasn't possible; he had lived here for a long time and knew the rules.

'You must be mistaken. We are destined to be apart. That's how it is and always has been.' 'No! It's physically impossible for a grimmer to dream because the dream is the key to this place. They are in the mirror if they dream in Gaia. But Mia is lying here, so she can't be dreaming. This must be something else, but I don't know what,' she explains firmly. Majliv ponders everything Mia has said. Could it really be true? Was it her he had heard? Most importantly, he thinks about what he heard. Is Mia really pregnant?

CR80

Aleksandra and Petter had been at the hospital visiting me when one of the doctors had started talking about organ donation again. It had become clear that this topic affected more people than me on a deeper level, so now I didn't know what to do anymore. How long could I keep the vultures at bay? Aleksandra was, as usual, comforting, but it helped little when I couldn't tell her the truth about why I was so distressed. Visiting hours were over, and they both hugged me goodbye.

After a long explanation from the doctor, I was exhausted, angry, and scared. This couldn't happen. I had to save Will's life. The hospital corridor seemed narrower than ever as I hurried to reach the exit. Just as I stepped out, I saw a familiar person entering. He looked at me as I brushed against his arm, and I turned to apologize. It was only then that I saw who it was. It was the man who had looked at Will's medical records. The man I initially thought was a doctor and then suspected of being an organ thief.

When I turned around, he stopped, changed direction, and came towards me. I felt my heart in my throat and sprinted toward the parking lot where the car was parked. Behind me, I heard running footsteps.

'Amelia!' a male voice shouted.

Oh my God, he knew my name. After all the dangers I had faced, as I was being pursued by an unknown man, I was more terrified than ever.

'Amelia! Wait!' he called out again. I didn't stop. The car was only a few meters in front of me.

'Grimrokk!' The word made me stop abruptly with the key in the air just before it went into the lock. I stood completely still. The word I longed to hear more than anything came from a total stranger's lips. I would never be able to explain how it made me feel. I collapsed on the ground with the car keys in hand. Everything that had kept me standing crumbled within me, and the tears flowed. Hearing the forbidden 'Grimrokk' was an indescribable relief. At the same time, reality hung over me like a heavy cloud. I heard the footsteps approaching slowly, but this time, I didn't have the energy to move. It was too much. I could no longer keep up the façade.

'There, there. It's going to be okay. We'll help you as best we can,' said a voice belonging to a hand which gently stroked up and down my arm. I turned my head and looked up at the man crouched beside me.

'Who are you? And how do you know who I am?' I sobbed.

'I'm Andrew. I've also been a grimmer' the words he spoke initially frightened me, but it was the old fear of being exposed that still lingered within me.

'Been?' I asked.

'Yes. I was exposed when I started university. On my first day of school, I ran into a teacher I had seen almost daily. He recognized me immediately and greeted me by name. Fabian, my grimmer name.'

'How long did it take for him to disappear?' I inquired.

'It happened a second or two later. Everyone thought it was a heart attack.' I pictured the scenario. It must have been shocking, much like what I had experienced.

'Did you lose anyone close to you?' I had to know if this grief would ever fade.

'Yes. Family and friends.' I stared at him from where I sat across him, a thousand questions were hanging in the air.

426

'Can we get a coffee? I can tell you a bit about what I do here.' It wasn't a difficult decision to make. I had many questions that needed answers.

Across the street from the hospital was a small, quiet café. We found a table tucked away in the back. It was the type of café where you ordered at the counter and then brought it to your chosen table. Undisturbed, we sat with our respective cups of coffee and croissants in front of us.

'Are you going to tell me how you know about me? And why you've been lurking around Will?' I asked. Perhaps he had answers to the Grimrokk mystery or clues we could use.

'We don't know much about Will and you in particular, but whenever there is an undiagnosed patient with inexplicable cause, reports are sent to certain authorities where we have our contacts. Therefore, when the doctor...'

'Wait, wait... who are 'we'? Are there more of you?' I interrupted him.

'We are an order that has existed for many centuries. 'Noctis Onus' is a secret order that gathers all the data we can find about Grimrokk. An even larger part of our work is to find grimmers who have been exposed and help their bodies to survive for as long as possible. We know there is a life for them in Grimrokk when they seem to be in a coma here, but the doctors don't know this. Since organ donation became more common, we have had significant difficulties in being able to help in time. That's why several fake clinics have been established worldwide. Or fake, we say that because they appear to be care facilities for coma patients, but they are indeed real since we only care for grimmers and keep their bodies alive with vital supplements, making sure they don't deteriorate. There aren't many grimmers in the world, and fortunately, very few have been exposed, but we constantly keep an eye on things.' He took a sip of his hot coffee, but I sat with a piece of croissant halfway to my mouth, where I had forgotten it.

'Do you have any questions?' he asked.

'I... I don't know.' Where should I even begin? 'How could you know that I was also a grimmer? I could have just been a regular spouse,' I said. It was a chance he had taken. Such a significant secret isn't casually revealed to a stranger.

'It was a chance to take, but I've been snooping around for so long that I felt I had enough clues to suggest you were a grimmer. You had refused to decide about organ donation for so long that the doctor was actually considering having you examined after speaking with Will's parents. Maybe you didn't know that? Don't worry, they ultimately supported you, and that's what matters. If you hadn't reacted when I called Grimrokk after you, I would never have mentioned the word again and just pretended I thought you were someone I knew from elementary school. It's very rare for us to encounter spouses who expose each other. Did you only see each other in passing perhaps?'

Hearing what the doctors had considered was frightening, and the fact that Will's parents had doubted me, and my decision terrified me. I was disappointed by the lack of support but also relieved that they had changed their minds. His explanation was otherwise logical and made sense. But did I want him to know that Majliv was mine in both of these realities?

'William is my husband, but he is also mine as Majliv. We didn't know about each other until certain things suddenly fell into place. I believe we both eventually knew, but we had to hide it. One day, I accidentally shouted the wrong name, and that was it. All of this is my fault.' The weight on my shoulders felt heavier. Once again, the painful emotions surfaced.

'Wait a minute. Majliv? The Grange Warden? He looked surprised, as if the name frightened him.

'Yes. That's right,' I furrowed my brows.

'Amelia, are you Mia? Are you the woman who killed Lamia?' His eyes were wide, and his mouth was open in astonishment. Had people in Gaia really heard this story too? Perhaps he was from Wargborough or thereabouts.

'Yes, it's me. Or it was me,' I said, watching his facial expression change.

'You will never stop being Mia, remember that. Your abilities have been talked about in every corner of Grimrokk since it happened. I had already been exposed before it occurred, but for every grimmer we find, we note as much of their story as we can, so it doesn't get lost to us. Lamia has been the eternal death for everyone in Grimrokk, and she taught us not to have hope for the future. What's truly incredible is that never before, not since the dawn of time, have two people found each other in both Gaia and Grimrokk. That must have been special.'

'It was a dreadful time, and I will never think about the things I experienced with Knuiw Myrthing and Lamia again. I can't stand sadism or torture, and they revelled in both.'

'I take the hint. Let's change the subject. The order wants to initiate immediate measures to have Will moved to one of our facilities for care and treatment. You don't need to worry about what the hospital or anyone else might say; we have good lawyers who handle the bureaucratic side of things, and we have wealthy sponsors who have donated millions to keep these clinics running. You don't have to think about the money.' I was starting to feel dizzy from all of this. It was too much to take in, and it almost seemed too good to be true.

'This needs to sink in. I'm so exhausted and have so much to think about that I feel like the whole world is spinning. Do you have a number I can call?' Nausea welled up in me again, and it felt like the earth was moving backwards against its axes.

'Here's my card. We'll start a patient transfer immediately, so he receives the proper treatment. You don't need to worry about it anymore' he reassured me.

'That's good. Incredibly good.' Then it felt as if the chair disappeared from under me, and I was about to crash onto the floor. Fortunately, Andrew managed to catch me just in time.

'You're not in good shape, Amelia. Let me drive you home. You can't drive in this condition!' I was sceptical about giving my personal information to someone I had just met, and I was about to protest, but before I could start the sentence, he said:

'We already have all your and Will's information, so you don't need to worry about protecting yourself from me. Let me help you. In your condition, you should be careful not to overexert yourself.'

'You seem to know everything apparently. Fine, you can drive me home, but you'll drop me off at the curb.' He smiled and nodded before helping me up from the floor.

The ride home was silent. I was too dizzy and nauseous to engage in any conversation whatsoever.

As promised, Andrew stopped at the curb and thanked me for the chat. He let me walk the last few meters to the door by myself before he drove away.

Once inside, I curled up on the couch with a blanket and a large glass of chocolate milk while I pondered everything Andrew had told me. I still had thousands of questions, but I was relieved and grateful to know that Will would be saved. It made me curious that they apparently had so much information about Grimrokk. What if it had been possible to go back through history to stop this curse? No one deserved to live forever apart from someone they loved. One world or two didn't change that.

Chapter 25
Noctis onus

It had been a few days since my surprising encounter with Andrew, and I had come to terms with the idea that there was an organization, Noctis Onus, secretly assisting revealed grimmers. With so many strange things existing in Grimrokk, some of the peculiarities surely had to contaminate Gaia as well. I had decided to contact Andrew again to inquire about what would happen to Will next. The hospital's doctor still left what seemed like random 'Become an organ donor' brochures round Will's room, which I found frightening. How far were they willing to go to convince me that it was the right choice? With my phone to my ear, I listened to the ringtone while doodling with a pen on a notepad on the coffee table.

'Hello, it's Andrew,' said the voice on the other end.

'Hello, it's Amelia, Amelia Godseth. I was calling to see if there was any news about Will's relocation. The doctors are still pushing for organs, and I'm getting more and more scared.' 'We have two lawyers on the case. They are facing opposition from Will's parents, who say their son would want it and that they believe it's a dignified way to let go.'

'What! But they can't do that. Will would never have accepted it. Especially not while he's alive. They're going behind my back,' I seethed with anger and just wanted to confront them and tell them what I thought about their interference.

'Take it easy. We encounter such people all the time. There are always ways to handle this. You can reassure yourself that as long as this becomes a case, the hospital isn't allowed to initiate the donation. Not until the matter is resolved, and even then, there are other avenues to explore.' As Andrew spoke, the doodles grew larger and spread in all directions. I began to trace some of the lines repeatedly. They formed a pattern.

'How certain are we that this won't become a problem? And what should I tell my in-laws?' My fingers continued to chase the lines with the pen.

'Pretend like nothing for now. But there's actually a lot of information out there about people who have woken up after several years in a coma. Maybe it's worth trying to convince them that way?' I saw this as a challenge and decided that I'd face it head-on. I didn't give up so easily when I was convinced about something.

'I'll definitely do that. I've heard of such stories!' Andrew provided me with more information and said he would call me as soon as there was any news.

The call ended, and I looked down at the sea of doodles in front of me. It was a jumble although suddenly, I noticed a systematic path the pen had taken several times. Two lines curved upward, and where the tips of the curves met, they pointed downward. The edges of the curves descended and met. It resembled a heart, but instead of meeting in the middle, the heart had two tips at the bottom, right next to each other. I looked at the sheet for a long time before it dawned on me why I recognized the peculiar heart shape. Christmas Eve in the Rim Gorge. Majliv had received a gift from Santa Claus that he had never fully understood. It was a heart with two tips. I tore off the top sheet from the notepad and began to draw again on a fresh sheet. This time, I was more precise while drawing, trying to recreate it from memory. Maybe Andrew and his written stories could provide me with answers about what this meant. So, impatiently, I decided to snap a picture and send it right away. I wanted to ask if he was familiar with this particular heart shape and tell him about when Majliv received one.

A few minutes later, I received a response that he had never seen it before but that gifts from Santa Claus were often of great significance. I thought I should settle for the answer I got, and it was probably futile to inquire if it held any meaning where I was.

The phone pinged again.

'We have someone in the order who I believe can answer your questions. He's called the 'Librarian.' An older guy who lives in England.' Andrew suggested that we should research as much information as possible about secret symbols. He would discuss it with one of his experienced order members and get back in touch.

The darkness I had felt before entering Grimrokk had been absent since the night at the hospital when I surprisingly had run into Andrew. I sat in the chair, leaning my head on Will's hand, and there, darkness came with the comfort that gently hugged me. In darkness, there was hope. But was it hope for the future, or was I stuck in what I had lost? I knew it was impossible to go through the mirror again. My body was already in Grimrokk, and it could not be recreated. I leaned into the darkness, into my futile, naive little hope. I called out for Majliv. My heart shattered in the desperate gap between longing and the hope that he could hear me. He had never had the ability to hear me in there. It was only Lynn who could.

I called out for Lynn, but it was in vain. Once again, I shouted into the darkness that Majliv was going to be a father to twins. I told him I missed them and explained that there was now an organization helping me protect his body in Gaia. Every word I uttered was like an endless story I couldn't stop – a one-sided conversation that lit a tiny flame in my heart and, after a while, soothed my soul.

⚘

Twins! The word rings in Majliv's ears like a beautiful melody. He is ecstatically happy, but at the same time, it feels like the worst torture. He knows he will never see the children. But it is a great comfort to hear Mia's voice telling him about what she has been doing in the past few days. That she visits him every day and that an organization helps her keep him alive in Gaia. She tells him about Andrew, who has been of great assistance. Majliv can feel a pang of jealousy in his stomach, but what good is it? She needs to rely on someone for help.

The tones of her voice bring tears to his eyes, and there is an immense relief in his chest to hear her and to be a tiny part of her life again.

After a while, it becomes quiet, and Majliv desperately calls out for Mia, as if he fears that she will disappear again for good.

'Majliv! Majliv! Wake up!' Lynn stands over Majliv and shakes him. Tears flow, and he struggles to breathe.

'There, there. We will figure this out. There must be a special reason why we can hear her. You can hear her too, and that is entirely unique.' Lynn comforts him as best as she can and cradles him in her arms like a child. He needs it. Right here and now, he needs, with all his masculinity, to be comforted by someone who understands.

'I can't live without her. She was my life, is my life, wherever I may be. We are intertwined. I admire her, I love her for who she is. What am I going to do without her?'

'You...' Lynn says. She places her hands on his cheeks and waits until he meets her gaze.

'First, we will find out what is happening. It's something new, and we will figure it out. Then we will take things from there. Okay?' Majliv breathes heavily and nods deeply.

This unexpected turn of events brings something good with it. Now he has something to grasp. Something to figure out.

Lynn searches through all the books in Wargborough's library but doesn't discover any clues. She is determined to find out why she suddenly hears Mia again and, most astonishingly of all, why Majliv hears her too.

One day, Lynn goes to visit a friend she hasn't seen in a long time. At the door, she is greeted by a heartwarming surprise. Her friend is pregnant. No news could be happier after all the years of Lamia's havoc.

'What an incredibly pleasant surprise. When did this happen?' Lynn asks.

'I'm only about 150 days along, but it's already showing very well. We're so happy that it finally happened to us. We didn't dare to try for a child before; it was far too dangerous. Thanks to Mia's courage and all of you who were with her, those times are over, and the world is filling with life again.'

Lynn is both proud of the kind words her friend says about Mia and, at the same time, very sad. With everything Mia sacrificed for everyone in Grimrokk it just makes her disappearance profoundly sad. It was truly unfair. The one person who should have been spared this terrible curse was Mia. She had saved everyone from a cruel future.

The conversation continues casually about the wind, weather, and the latest news. Suddenly, her friend starts to hiccup, and the little coffee table rises. The table hovers steadily above the floor, and Lynn has never seen anything like it.

'Uh...? What's happening?' Lynn stammers in shock.

'Oh... it's just the baby. It seems this one's abilities are showing early,' her friend laughs. 'This happens from time to time.'

On her way home, Lynn's thoughts race through her mind. She's heard about this before. More often than not pregnant women are more receptive to the supernatural. Could this be happening to Mia as well? Are the children doing something to her? Could they open a communication channel that allows them to hear her between worlds? Or is it something else? But what could it be, if not that? The questions only multiply as she ponders the possibility further.

 infinity

I had never even been to Canada, but here I was, on the flight from Duluth to England, sitting next to Andrew. It was quite crazy, but I couldn't resist investigating this double-tipped heart. I needed to know if it had any magical abilities, because what if it could help Will in some way? If it turned out to be a dead end, at least I had tried to do something.

Andrew shared everything he could about the order and the various facilities they had for those who had to leave their bodies in Gaia.

The long journey was exhausting. My back ached, and it was difficult to get enough sleep. When the plane landed at London Heathrow, we quickly retrieved our luggage. The rumours about the English weather proved to be true as the sky was gloomy and dark with grey clouds and rain greeting us outside. In a somewhat comical way, it suited my mood perfectly. Andrew arranged for a taxi that would take us to Manchester. It felt like the trip took several hours, as I was already exhausted before it had even begun, so I eventually fell asleep with my cheek against the cool windowpane.

'Amelia? We've arrived,' Andrew gently tapped my shoulder to wake me up.

'Sorry, I needed to rest. This has been a long journey.'

'I completely understand. It's already quite late, so we'll check in at the inn run by the order here. You'll get a room to rest and have something to eat before we head to the library tomorrow. Does that sound okay?'

I looked out of the window at a well-preserved old stone building with small, checkered windows. In a flash, I had the feeling of being back in Grimrokk. These were the kinds of houses you found in most places. Not that it was surprising, as this was the order's own inn. They probably carried the architectural style from one place to another.

'Yes, please, I could use a snack. Can't say that the food on the airplane was a culinary epiphany, to be honest.'

'I'm not going to argue with you on that. Luckily, the food here is really good. They may not have Imaginari-tea, but the hot cocoa is excellent.' Andrew circled around the taxi and opened the door for me. We got our

439

luggage placed on the sidewalk by the taxi driver before we hurried out into the rain.

It was warm and cozy inside, with soft, intimate lighting and candles on the tables in the dining room close to the lobby. We checked in and received our keys.

The rooms were on the second floor, one at each end of the corridor.

'You can order food to your room if you prefer. Just charge it to the bill. I think we should try to leave by nine in the morning. Chetham's Library isn't far from here. Agaton is waiting for us,' Andrew instructed. I was terribly excited; I could hardly wait to explore this library.

'Agaton? Is that the Librarian?'

'Yes. He's an odd character but he is like a living encyclopaedia when it comes to Grimrokk,' he told me.

'It could be exciting. Is it a public library we're going to, or is it exclusive to Noctis Onus?'

'It's a public library, England's oldest. It was established in 1653 by Humphrey Chetham. He was a grimmer.' Meeting Agaton and seeing the ancient works that must be there sounded exciting.

'I can hardly contain my excitement for tomorrow!'

'Try to get a good night's sleep, and we'll see each other early tomorrow morning.' Andrew smiled and nodded a goodnight as he walked down the hallway to his door.

'Goodnight, Andrew!' I called after him.

With a deep sigh, I entered my own room. The room had a warm, inviting atmosphere. It was old but well-maintained. There was no doubt about the similarities between Grimrokk and the inn. An open redstone fireplace stood in one corner, and right in front of it was a large, sturdy armchair with a heavy, patterned blanket draped over the armrest. Against the wall on the opposite side was a simple bed, and above it hung a large painting. The subject was a pond and a forest. I furrowed my brow and took a few steps closer. It couldn't possibly be...? I'd been there. It was a painting of Nicor's pond. A chill ran through me at first, before being replaced by a good feeling. Majliv. The first time I met him was there. My life would have been over if he hadn't watched over me back then. I couldn't remember much of it, but the memory brought a warm feeling to my heart.

I heard a pendulum clock striking faintly in the distance, and automatically, I pulled out my phone and checked the time. 11:00 PM. Exhausted from the journey and several sleepless nights, I unpacked my toiletries and prepared for bed. It would be a few long days if I didn't get some rest.

As I rested my head on the pillow, I felt a sensation I hadn't experienced in a long time and had thought I would never feel again: the feeling of being close to Grimrokk.

Chapter 26
The librarian

The phone vibrated, and the alarm chimed at half-past seven the next morning. I must have been incredibly tired after everything that had happened during the recent weeks, as I had slept so deeply. To use the word 'refreshed' would be an exaggeration, but I was more alert than I had been in a while. After a long, hot shower and a bit of makeup to make myself look more presentable, I was ready for breakfast.

As I locked the door to my room, I noticed a sign with the room's name on the old wooden door. My room was called 'The Mad Raven.' I stood there, puzzled, and looked down the hallway at the other doors, recognizing several names adorning them, including The Long Warmth, the Frost, the Rim Gorge, and some other names I wasn't familiar with, like Thistle Valley, Wanderer Bay, and Rider's Peak. Places I would never get to see. All these places were now locked away. No matter how much I wished to go there, it was like a legend to me, something belonging to a previous life.

I had to put these thoughts behind me if I were to accomplish what I needed to do today. We were going to find all the information that Agaton might have available. This was where we had to start.

In the staircase leading down to the first floor, I could hear the faint murmur of other guests having breakfast. The scent of bacon and freshly baked goods crept into my nose, tempting my appetite, and my stomach began to rumble. I continued around the corner into a cozy sitting room with small tables adorned with quaint, flowery plates and lit candles. Along one wall was a small buffet with an array of temptations. As I had felt on the way down, there was bacon, fresh rolls and bread, but also fried eggs, pancakes, and slices of meat. With a plate in hand, I helped myself to a generous amount of food before preparing a cup of tea.

Balancing towards the tables with my hands full, I found a table by the fireplace. The atmosphere settled over my worries like a comfortable veil. Everything reminded me of Grimrokk and how it had been at the inn close to Rim Gorge or at The Mad Raven. In this brief moment, I was allowed to feel like I was there again.

A hand tapped me on the shoulder, and I jumped slightly.

'I didn't mean to startle you. I'm sorry.' It was Andrew, looking slightly startled himself for having startled me.

'It's okay. I was just daydreaming about distant places,' I smiled back.

'The first time I was here at the inn, I had the same experience. It felt like being back. I think that's why they built it this way, once upon a time. This way, all those who could no longer return could find a hint of Grimrokk here. Many come to the inn, but all of them are grimmers.' Andrew took a seat in the chair on the other side of the table.

'It gives me a good feeling to be here. I feel a bit closer. Until I realize that I'm still locked in Gaia, then it hurts again.' I sighed deeply as I stirred my tea dreamily. I really wished it were Imaginari-tea, and I thought about hot chocolate. Nothing happened, but the dream of sitting in Batist's living room with a cup of Imaginari-tea was worth a try.

We ate most of our food without speaking further, except for some polite phrases here and there. With two full and content stomachs, we walked out together, ready to meet Agaton. The grey English autumn weather still hung over the city, but it didn't matter. This time, I had a goal, and that was to find out what Agaton could tell me about a strange double tipped heart.

The taxi ride to the library wasn't long. After just ten minutes, we stopped in front of a large, old stone building. With its arched windows and doors, it somewhat resembled a church but with a lot of charm and character. It gave me a welcoming sense of knowledge and wisdom and piqued my curiosity.

'Come on! Agaton is waiting for us,' Andrew led me further through an arched gate in the stone wall and into a courtyard. I started walking toward what seemed to be the entrance door, where several students were coming and going, but Andrew stopped me with a hand on my arm.

'This way,' he said, pointing to a small, black wrought-iron door set slightly back. So, we wouldn't be entering the same way as ordinary people. This could be interesting.

The door was heavy and creaked on its hinges as the unlubricated metal surfaces scraped against each other. Inside, there was an old stairwell that greeted us. We climbed the stairs a couple of floors before we encountered another door. Andrew knocked, and shortly after, we heard a bolt being pushed aside, and the door opened. In the dim lighting from the room inside, I could barely make out a figure before he stepped into the light from the hallway.

'Andrew,' he muttered with a sour expression, and his gaze completely avoided me.

'Good morning, Agaton. This is Amelia Godseth,' Andrew tried to introduce me, and I extended my hand, but I received no other reaction than a grunt.

'This way. This is a restricted area for library staff and faculty, but the truth is, it's hardly ever used. The books I need to retrieve to search for answers to your questions are not accessible to everyone.' His English was cultivated, and a hint of a rather snobbish tone dripped from his words. Agaton appeared to be a 70-year-old, learned librarian from the upper class with little social grace.

'What a great start to the day,' I thought as we followed Agaton through a corridor into a new room. The door was locked behind us after all three had entered. The room was situated in the corner of the building, and the built-in bench beneath the windows was shaped like a horseshoe with a table in the centre. The rest of the room was filled with books, and I assumed they must be the oldest books in the library. The dark woodwork created a cool atmosphere around us, and the grey English weather intensified the impression.

'Have a seat,' he grunted, pointing to the bench in the corner. We sat down while Agaton remained standing at the end of the table.

'So, what are we looking for? A symbol? An object? A name?'

'It's a heart shaped object,' I explained.

'That doesn't help me at all. I need details about where you've seen this heart, who has it, where it came from, things like that,' Agaton shook his head. If he was going to be like this, I thought ironically, this could be a long and delightful day.

'If you give me some time to elaborate, you'll get to know everything I know,' I snapped back before I had a chance to think it through. Andrew emitted a small grunt of laughter that he tried to stifle before it eventually ended in a strained cough. He smiled slightly and shook his head.

Agaton stared at me with squinted eyes before bursting into laughter.

'I like this one. A lady with spirit. What was your name, you said?'

'Amelia Gods...'

'This is Mia. You've perhaps heard of the grimmer who finally managed to take La...' Andrew was interrupted by Agaton, who looked at me with wide eyes.

'Lamia!' he said.

How had people found out about this? Were there so many locked out of Grimrokk that our story had already reached Gaia?

'How did you know about it?' I looked at him in astonishment.

'I collect all information that comes from Grimrokk, and everything related to Lamia is a top priority. Now, I don't know if Andrew here has had the chance to interview you properly yet, as it hasn't been that long since you were locked out, but we try to gather updated information from all the exiled ones. What you did with Lamia, I would say, is one of the most significant events in our history.'

I should have probably felt proud of the praise, but I couldn't. I couldn't take credit for it alone. There were several of us who had fought and sacrificed in that battle, and the others were no longer close to me.

'An event I can't take all the credit for. Without my family, I wouldn't be here today.'

'Well, that's another story, and I want to hear all about it when we have time for all the details. Right now, we have a heart to find. What set this apart from other hearts since you remember it so well?'

'It was really the whole event that was special. We were in the Rim Gorge, and it was Christmas Eve. My first Christmas in Grimrokk and my first encounter with Santa Claus. He was handing out Christmas presents to everyone, and Majliv received his gift. William was my husband in Gaia and became my Majliv in Grimrokk. We didn't know it then, not until much later. It wasn't until long after Lamia had died, and everyday life returned to normal that it dawned on me that the two were the same person.'

I thought back to that day, and a lump tightened in my chest. I blinked and turned away. I needed to set this aside now and shift my focus to what was important.

'That may not be important. The heart that Majliv received from Santa Claus was made of red glass. It had two arches like regular hearts at the top, but instead of one point downward, it had two. If you have pen and paper, I can try to draw it.'

Agaton handed me a notebook he had in his pocket and a pen from the table. With my tongue sticking out of my mouth, I tried to sketch the heart as I remembered it from the Christmas celebration. Since I had seen it only once, there wasn't much to go on. When the sketch was ready, I handed the paper to Agaton, who examined it carefully while grunting and mumbling to himself. He stood there for a moment, then took a few steps toward the table and placed the sketch down before retrieving a ladder he had leaned against a shelf. His old body climbed up the narrow steps. When he nearly had reached the ceiling, he removed some old books, which he absentmindedly held out to Andrew. Behind the books, there must have been a hidden door because he pushed something aside before pulling out a massive leather-bound book. Carefully, he descended the ladder with the book against his chest.

'Now, let's see what we can find,' he said, placing the book on the table before climbing the ladder once more.

In the end, we had three equally large books on the table. Each of us had our noses buried in our respective books, examining page after page as we flipped through them. The books contained information ranging from who ruled over the various cities and at what times, to when the churches had been built, and tragic events that had befallen the people of Grimrokk. It hurt to see all this in black and white in front of us and to know that we truly belonged to this universe. It felt like living in an incomplete reality. It would never be whole again, and I knew this, but I would do my utmost to find a solution if possible.

We sat in silence around the table, fingers moving up and down the fragile and ancient pages before us. Occasionally, one of us would come across something that seemed interesting, only to shake our heads and continue scrutinizing the records.

It was approaching late afternoon, and I could feel my neck getting stiffer by the minute. Several hours had already passed since Andrew had bought lunch at a nearby cafe, and my stomach was ready for dinner. I got up to stretch my body for a while. I left the book on the table in front of me. Agaton sat almost motionless, concentrating on the pages beneath his fingertips, while Andrew leaned over his book with his chin resting on his palm, yawning.

What were we really doing here? It was not even like trying to find a needle in a haystack, but rather the thread the needle had once sewn with. First of all, we were searching for something that didn't exist in this world, and secondly, nobody knew what it was or had ever heard of it.

I closed my eyes and rubbed them with my fingers. My patience had run out, I was too tired. Just as I was about to suggest we call it a day; Agaton sprang up from his chair.

'I've got it!' he exclaimed. I rushed the short distance and looked down at the page in front of us, while Andrew stumbled over a low stool in his eagerness to see.

Sure enough, at the bottom of the page, there was a small, faded illustration of a heart with two points facing downward. Next to it was a text that Agaton read aloud:

'The Marked Souls' Heart. An unbreakable bond between two of the same will lead the marked souls to themselves. No other heart can unlock sealed doors. Only this heart can unlock sealed doors. Only then can the first pure ones of each world begin their existence as two.' He looked up at me with a beaming, satisfied expression, while I stood there like a question mark. This was like Latin to me.

'Am I supposed to understand what that means?' I asked, looking at Andrew, who appeared just as puzzled as me.

'No, but I think I do,' Agaton commented, a tad more arrogantly than necessary.

'Yes, and that is?' Andrew asked, full of anticipation.

'I think it means that the unbreakable bond is the strong love two people have for each other. Two of the same kind could mean that they share something, have something in common, or are meant for each other. Marked souls might be another word for the chosen or unique ones. But regardless of what all this means, I'm pretty sure that the heart you saw is the same as the one you see here in the book, and that it is a key to some kind of hypothetical door.'

'Hypothetical door? And what could that be?' Andrew echoed my words.

'Well... it could be many things. As you probably understand, it's not a physical object, as we usually associate with a key, so it must be for something else. A path between two places, or perhaps a portal,' Agaton spoke aloud as he let his thoughts wander.

'The last part of the text must mean that only when this door is opened can they be together again,' Andrew said. As soon as he said those words, we all turned to each other. We had solved the riddle.

'The mirror is the portal!' we said simultaneously.

Night eventually fell, and we spent the whole evening discussing keys, mirrors, and hearts, but when it came down to it, we weren't much wiser than before. What good was all this information to us if no one in Grimrokk understood what we had found? The heart was not with us; it was with them, and they were there without the knowledge we now possessed.

Andrew and I had thanked Agaton for all his help and promised to provide him with any information we might come across in the future.

When I finally found the bed at the inn, I was exhausted in both body and mind. We had spent the entire day and evening examining and analysing, and there was a lot of mental activity for a tired soul. Before I knew it, I had fallen asleep and found myself in the darkness once again. However, this time, I wasn't as troubled by where I was. After having been there several times without making any contact, I had given up the idea that anyone could hear me. What occupied my mind now were hearts and mirrors, keys and doors, all in a jumble of thoughts. I chatted with myself there in my dream darkness, and of all the things to process after today, the biggest was that, according to the legend, the gate between Gaia and Grimrokk could be opened. Eventually, my brain gave up, and all thoughts let go. I was truly tired, so deep sleep embraced me.

ⱭᏕᏠ

While Majliv, in his sleep, tries to keep up with all the twists and turns he hears in Mia's thoughts, he picks up on a few words like heart, mirror, portal, and finally, legend. Frustrated by not being able to grasp what she's saying, he shouts out as he wakes up, 'Mia!'

As on the other nights, Lynn rushes in through the door, alarmed and curious.

'What was all that about? I didn't understand anything. It was like she was talking to herself,' Lynn exclaims.

'I don't know. But it seems like she stumbled upon a legend, and if I heard correctly, it involves a portal,'

Majliv's heart races. 'What would you be looking for if you were locked out of here, Lynn?'

'A way back. A portal back,' Lynn smiles cautiously, trying to avoid getting caught up in the excitement that would end in disappointment.

'That's exactly what I was thinking. But we don't have enough to go on. Do we know anyone who knows about legends?'

'Of course, we do. Batist! Legends and magic go hand in hand. We might be lucky. Come on!' They rush out and find Batist stirring pots in the kitchen, illuminated by the flames in the fireplace.

'I hope I haven't kept you awake, but I couldn't sleep any longer. Nightmares come and go.' He looks at them questioningly, for the expressions on the other side of the kitchen table are unexpectedly expectant.

'You didn't wake us up. Quite the opposite! We're so glad you're awake! We heard from Mia again, and this time she was talking about a legend. But we only caught some keywords,' Lynn's words rush out.

'Yes, and we hope you can help us,' Majliv adds.

'I have many legends written down in my old books, but you might need to give me more to go on. What did she say that put you on this track?'

'She mentioned something about a portal and a mirror,' Lynn explains.

'And a heart, and something about keys. Have you ever heard of anything like this?' Majliv can hardly stand still.

'Come with me, and we'll see,' says Batist as he lifts one of the pots off the heat.

453

They enter the library and follow Batist to the bookshelf. He retrieves an ancient book where the pages have come loose and are stacked between the covers.

'I believe I've read something about a heart once, but it's been so long that I don't remember much else,' Batist begins.

Seconds feel like hours for the two friends.

'Let's see... Here it mentions something about a mirror, but it was used in a formula,' he mumbles and continues to flip through the pages. His fingers slide down one side and then up the other before he turns the page and repeats the motion on the next spread.

'This might take a little time, as I don't know where to start, but... wait a moment here...' He reads something without saying it aloud, then looks up at them and smiles.

'Here it is. This is the legend you're looking for.'

'What does it say?' Lynn asks eagerly, becoming very impatient.

Batist reads aloud now: 'The hearts of the marked souls. An unbreakable bond between two alike will lead the marked souls back to themselves. Only the heart can unlock closed doors. Not until then can the first pure ones of each world begin their existence as two.'

'But what does this mean?' Majliv despairs.

'It's dawning on me that this is the legend of the Mirror to Grimrokk. As you know, there were once many mirrors, but as far as we know, Wargborough's mirror is the only one left now. Long ago, when the mirror was created to be the portal here, a key was made. This key allowed us to keep Grimrokk closed and therefore safe from intruders, ensuring that we wouldn't be discovered.

It's said that the key was a heart, but no one has ever seen it, and no one knows where it is either. For all I know, the whole story could be fiction, but I don't really believe that. In short, it means that two people who share a unique connection with each other are the ones who can unlock the mirror with this heart. So, as you can understand, it's quite a complex task to undertake.'

'So what we know is that there's a heart out there somewhere, but no one knows what it's made of, what it looks like, or where it is?' Majliv, who had a moment of renewed hope, becomes disheartened once again. 'This didn't help us at all!' he shouts in disappointment and storms out of the kitchen.

ଔଠ

Chapter 27
The marked souls heart

I was on the plane on my way back to Duluth again, tired of my thoughts running in circles around the same scenarios and problems. The answer was there, right in front of us, but what good would it do if we couldn't tell those who really needed to know? Something else I had been thinking a lot about was who these chosen people could be. Would the key work if someone else tried to use it, or would someone magically appear when the key was supposed to be used?

A thousand thoughts swirled in my head, making me even more frustrated which could not be good in my condition. Lately, I haven't had much time to think about the two tiny heartbeats beating below my own heart. No matter how challenging the puzzles I struggled with were, I had that to look forward to, but it wasn't the same without Will. If the answers and solutions were with the people in Grimrokk, I had to accept that there wasn't much more to do from here. The only thing I could contribute now was taking care of Will and looking after myself for the children's sake.

CR⁂SO

Majliv becomes more and more desperate as the days go by. He's searching for something that's impossible to find, and he has no idea where to begin. He sits in the rose garden, letting his thoughts wander when suddenly the leaves start falling from the trees. The Long Warmth is over, and the chill of Frostpace is creeping in with its cold, heavy dread over the garden. He has never cared so much before, never noticed the gloomy effect it can have on the body and mind, but now it feels like snowflakes pricking his skin, as the temperature noticeably drops – and quickly.

He looks around as lilac leaves fall in thick layers around his feet. With his eyes, he follows some beautiful, perfect hearts as they descend and softly rest on the yellowing grass. Two of the leaves lie on top of each other but are not quite aligned. One lands with its tip slightly to the side. Majliv remembers seeing this peculiar shape before but can't recall where or when. He examines the leaves more closely and lifts them between his fingers. He trims the stems to preserve the shape he remembers. As he holds the leaves in his hands the way they had settled, forming a heart with the slight offset that created two tips pointing downward, the leaves change colour from green to yellow and then to a deep red before turning brown and disintegrating between his fingers.

A red heart with two points. He can see it so clearly in his mind, but where has he seen it before? The heart in his memory couldn't have been made of leaves, he's sure of that, but he feels the red colour is right. Hearts are usually red, after all. Could it have been made of metal since the legend mentioned it should be a key? Keys are typically made of metal to maintain their shape over time, but what kind of metal is red? Could it have been made of stone, perhaps? But still, the heart should be red, and only gemstones come in a clear red colour, and they are very rare and fragile like glass.

Glass!

Finally, he connects the information from the moment and the past, and he runs, without thinking of anything else, to the room where he has gathered all his belongings. With hands trembling with excitement, he frantically pulls one thing after another from his backpack. In the end, at the bottom, with all his possessions strewn across the floor, his fingers find the small box. There it is, and there it has been ever since he received it from Santa in the Rim Gorge, without Santa explaining to him what he was actually receiving. He lifts the box and carefully opens the lid. So, the heart has been a clue all along, but Majliv had never dreamed it would contain something so fantastic, something so crucial. With tears in his eyes, he takes out the fragile heart and holds it up to the light from the window. The red core looks almost liquid. Could this really be a key to the mirror and the portal between Gaia and Grimrokk? Could it be the one solution they had found in an ancient legend, with the help of Santa himself? With the heart safely back in the box, he rushes out of the room and calls for Lynn with both his most powerful voice and the full force of his thoughts. He must find her right away; they have no time to lose. When he reaches the exit door, Lynn is there, and despite the urgency, she needs an explanation.

'What's happening? Is something wrong?' she asks anxiously.

'No, no, nothing is wrong, but look here!' He pulls the small box out of his pocket, lifts the lid, and shows the heart to Lynn.

She looks down at it in amazement, and then she looks at him with eyes that widen and an open mouth.

'Is this... where... when?' She can't find the right words.

'This is the gift Santa gave me on Christmas Eve in the Rim Gorge. I never understood what it was for and had long forgotten it, but I was reminded of it when I saw some fallen leaves in the garden, and when I recognized the shape, everything fell into place. It must be this heart the legend talks about! You know how Santa is, no gifts come from him without a greater purpose behind them.'

'We can't be certain that it's exactly this heart, Majliv, but we need to go to Wargborough right away. The only way to find out is to try,' Lynn grabs her winter coat and hurriedly dresses. She rushes out the door with Majliv following.

In the stable, he wraps the fur around his shoulders and saddles the horses. Once everything is in order, they set off towards Wargborough and the church where the mirror is located. Small snowflakes fall like dots in the air and sting their cheeks as they ride as fast as the horses can run.

When they finally arrive, the snow has already covered the landscape in a soft white blanket. At the church, Majliv dismounts and rushes up the stairs, taking two steps at a time, before he swings the door open forcefully. Lynn hurries behind him. The church is dark except for a few living candles around the altar where the mirror stands.

The aisle seems infinitely long. They take it slow to avoid stumbling in the darkness and stop when they stand at the foot of the mirror. Lynn turns to Majliv.

'Yes, what now? There's no keyhole to place the heart into.'

'The mirror looks completely ordinary. You'd think it would change when the portal was closed,' Majliv muses and reaches out his hand to let his fingers glide into the surface as they have done so many times before. But this time, it's as if the liquid surface freezes into ice where he touches it.

'What in the world?' he says.

'That's strange, isn't it? I've never experienced that happening before,' Lynn wonders, her astonishment evident as she watches the surface melt and clear up as soon as Majliv stops touching it.

Majliv takes a step back and retrieves the box from his pocket. With the heart out of the box and a soft yet firm grip on it in his right hand, he tries to touch the mirror again, but the same thing happens once more. Wherever he touches the mirror, it stiffens.

'What's happening? I thought this was supposed to be the key! I thought I had found the solution!' he exclaims in frustration.

'Could it be because you're a Grimmer? Let me try,' Lynn says and extends her hand. She takes the heart and approaches the mirror. She takes a deep breath and then moves her hand toward the surface. As soon as she gets close, the surface stiffens and becomes impenetrable.

'But... this is really strange!' Lynn hands the heart back to Majliv. She tries again, and now the mirror behaves as usual, with her hand dissolving into it as it always has before.

'This can't be true! We weren't supposed to succeed. I've been deceived! The heart wasn't the key at all!' A rage unlike anything he has ever experienced sweeps over Majliv. The pain of crushed false hopes and the realization that he has lost Mia forever shatter him completely. He feels his chest explode, and his heart literally breaks.

He turns around and grabs a massive candelabrum, about the size of a small man, and starts swinging it in the air around him before attacking the mirror. The mirror stands there, unbroken and unmoved, fuelling his frustration and pain even more. Tears stream down Majliv's cheeks. He drops the candelabrum, takes a deep breath, and looks down in disgust at what he still holds in his hand. Then, he squeezes the glass heart with all his might before, with a piercing roar, he hurls it into the mirror. Exhausted and without the strength to attempt or damage anything further, he watches the mirror's surface engulf the heart, but he barely glimpses it. The heart hovers beneath the surface, enveloped by the mirror's liquid substance.

Majliv looks over at Lynn, who is shocked and stares back at him. She understands neither what she sees in the mirror nor in Majliv. Before they can compose themselves, the church floor begins to tremble beneath them, and a deep rumble rolls through the stone walls. They hold each other's startled gaze, ready to flee, but as quickly as the rumbling started, it stops. Before the silence settles in, another sound takes over. Now, Majliv is truly frightened. It sounds like ice cracking, like when The Long Warmth comes to the lakes. They turn toward the sound and see that the entire mirror has frozen over, and cracks have begun to form from the bottom, spreading rapidly across the surface.

'No! What have I done?' Majliv becomes completely hysterical and desperately tries to put his fingers into the cracks to prevent the mirror from shattering, but to no avail. Slowly but all too surely, the mirror crumbles under his touch. When the crack reaches the top edge of the mirror, a high-frequency squeal pierces their ears, and right before their eyes, Majliv sees the little heart explode into millions of tiny shards of glass. Shortly thereafter, the same happens to the mirror. All resistance is exhausted, and as the glass heart shatters, Majliv loses consciousness.

CⱤ80

It was getting late, and I was tired. The past few days had demanded a lot of energy, and I simply needed to sleep. I turned off the TV, kissed Tinka on the nose, and went to bed.

Sleep enveloped me almost immediately, but then something strange happened. I felt like waking up, even though I had just fallen asleep, so I lay there and squirmed a bit. The soft mattress felt hard, like when I woke up after lying in the same position for too long. I surrendered, sat up, and rubbed my eyes. It was only when I opened my eyes that I realized I wasn't at home. This wasn't mine and Will's bedroom, not my bed, and not my soft mattress. It took exactly one heartbeat before I understood where I was. I was back in Grimrokk.

Adrenaline surged through my veins, and whether I was dreaming or really in Grimrokk, I had to find people and get answers. Without thinking, I ran on unsteady legs out of the room and shouted at the top of my lungs, 'Majliv! Lynn! Batist! Is anyone here?'

As I came down the stairs, I met Sebastian, who couldn't get a word out. He looked like he had seen a ghost.

'Sebastian! I'm so glad to see you,' I said, ran toward him, and gave him a big hug. He wasn't the one I had missed the most, but I had an overwhelming need to touch and feel what I saw. Was he real? Was this true?

'Miss Mia? Am I seeing things, or are you actually awake, for real?' His big, beautiful, green eyes gazed at me.

'It's absolutely amazing; I'm back without being able to explain exactly how it happened. Do you know where Majliv is or Lynn?'

'No, unfortunately. All I know is they took the horses out of the stable and rode off hastily earlier today, but I have no idea where they went,' he explained disappointingly.

'I'll have to go and look for them.' I thanked Sebastian and continued outside to see if I could find anyone. I wasn't patient enough to sit and wait, but there were many places to search since they had been riding. Suddenly, I remembered Lynn's ability to hear thoughts and immediately called out to her with all my mind, 'I'm back! I'm here!'

☙❧

Not many words had been exchanged between Lynn and Majliv since they left the church. The horses moved slowly forward while both contemplated in silence. Without saying anything, Lynn pulled the reins, causing the horse to stop and stand completely still.

'What's going on?' Majliv asked impatiently.

She looked him straight in the eyes, tears streaming down her cheeks, flowing from radiant eyes.

'Ride home! As fast as you can!'

'What's happening at home?' He looked at her suspiciously.

'RIDE! NOW!' she shouted. She couldn't waste time explaining what she didn't understand.

A spark of hope ignited in Majliv, and at his command Pronto picked up his speed. No horse could run like Pronto, but even so, it wasn't fast enough.

☙❧

Chapter 28
The meeting of the marked souls

I had neither the strength to search nor the patience to sit, so I wandered aimlessly away from the estate and down the linden alley. Over my shoulders, I had a cloak I'd found on a hook in the hallway to keep me warm, and I had also found a pair of warm boots, which, judging by their size, must have belonged to Lynn. The cold weather nipped at my nose, but my body was warm from the inside. I felt immense joy at being back in Grimrokk.

In the distance, a rumbling sound could be heard. At first, I didn't quite recognize it, but as the sound drew nearer, I knew exactly what it was. That sound could only belong to one. It was undoubtedly the sound of Pronto in full speed!

In a rush of joy, I ran as far as my body could carry me, down the alley and toward the open gate. There, in the distance, a rider was approaching at a tremendous speed, raising a cloud of snow.

A distance away from me, the rider dismounted and ran toward me with outstretched arms.

I saw that his eyes were bloodshot as he wrapped his arms around me and pulled me tightly against him. His lips met mine with an intensity that took my breath away. All the emotions that sparked between us in that moment were unleashed by a long-held longing.

'I'm dreaming! This can't be possible!' he repeated it over and over. 'We actually thought we had misunderstood and ruined everything forever.' I felt his warmth, his scent, and his strength, and it was intoxicating. For the past few months, I hadn't been living, but merely existing. Here I was, finally in the arms of the man I loved above all else, and I got to have him with me again.

'Sorry! Sorry for exposing us. Can you forgive me?' I said between sobs.

'Mia, it wasn't your fault. I was on the verge of doing it myself several times. The feeling I had when I realized you were you in both worlds, I can never explain. Relief, joy, horror, fear, yes, all of that and probably a thousand more because it was so overwhelming, all while knowing what it meant.'

'When did you realize that I was Amelia?'

'The first time I got suspicious was when we visited Benedikt in the church, on our way to the Rim Gorge. He was about to slip up but corrected himself at the last moment. After that, I scrutinized you more closely but couldn't quite find an explanation for what had caught my attention. What made me certain was when you unconsciously hummed Huldra's song for a long time after the operation. There was no other explanation then, and it scared me tremendously. You can never imagine how scared I was.'

'Did I sing that in Gaia? I've never noticed that I did. But it was the same for me too; there were several small things about you that gave me hints. Like when Christina asked you to write your name, that time we had a barbecue at their place. Your name, William, shone through the sheet, and I read your name backwards from the back. That's when I understood that Majliv's spelling wasn't what I thought.'

'I was a little boy when I came here, and like many children, I found it fun to play with words backward, so I took that name.'

'Then there was that time you were chopping wood in Gaia and reached for your stick when you needed more power. But what ultimately made all the pieces fit was when you answered back when Nette called for little William that time. I watched you in secret from my window on the estate. You looked around in shock, and you looked terrified and clearly relieved that no one had heard you. After that, I understood that I had to be on guard. I still can't believe how foolish I was to expose us. A big part of me died that day.'

'I don't remember anything from that day, but Lynn has told me that she found me screaming with you lifeless in my arms. The day after, I woke up without a voice and refused to speak to anyone. Every day after that, I took care of you.'

'I think I know how you felt. It didn't take long for the hospital staff to start talking about organ donation, and I was terrified. Thankfully, I've received good help. You wouldn't exist anymore if it weren't for them.'

'Who are 'they'?' he asked bewildered.

'Noctis Onus. An order of exiled grimmers. I'll tell you everything, but can we go inside before my teeth start chattering?' I laughed.

'We can, but first, I just have to ask: Is it true? Are you pregnant with twins? Are we...?' His smile spread across his whole face.

'Yes, William, I'm pregnant with twins. But how can you know that?' I sobbed. I radiated with happiness, but the tears welled up; there were so many emotions and rapid changes.

'I heard every word you said through the darkness, every tear you shed, and every despair you expressed. I still can't believe it's really true,' he said, holding me with outstretched arms to examine me closely.

'It's so unreal that you're here, alive in front of me. How did you learn about the legend, the special heart, and the key with the mirror?'

'It was Noctis Onus. They are historians in Gaia who gather and record everything they can remember and come across in terms of information about Grimrokk. They also have clinics for the outcasts' bodies, where they can be cared for in safety. Otherwise, they would either have been extinguished, and their organs passed on, or without proper care, they would have wasted away and died.'

'You have to tell me more, but let's go inside. I'm going to feed you until you burst and warm you by the fireplace.' Majliv kissed me on the lips, hard and long, like he wanted to make absolutely sure that I was there.

That evening, everyone gathered around the fireplace, and I told them about Noctis Onus, Agaton, and the inn, and about the library with all the information he had collected over time. They listened and clearly showed relief that there were people taking care of grimmers in Gaia as well.

Majliv told me that he no longer worked for Huldra, as she believed he had become entirely useless from the day I was banished. It was painful to hear what he had been through after I had exposed us and disappeared.

'Mia, would you like a cup of Imaginari-tea?' Nette asked eagerly.

'Oh, yes! You wouldn't believe how many times I thought I was sitting with Imaginari-tea in my hands and was disappointed when I took a sip.'

She handed me a cup, and I immediately thought of hot, bitter chocolate with a pinch of salt and cream on top. I brought the cup to my lips and blew on the drink before taking my first sip in a long time. As expected, it tasted absolutely fantastic.

'I've missed this,' I said, closed my eyes, and savoured it. Majliv's breath brushed against my neck as he leaned in close to my ear and whispered as softly as he could, his lips barely touching my earlobe.

'Have you missed anything else?' I turned around and looked him deep into the eyes before I gave a sigh so loud that everyone could hear.

'Thank you for the wonderful welcome, everybody. I'd love to continue this conversation, but it's been a long day and it's time to get some sleep, don't you think Majliv?' I said. Some chuckled and laughed softly to themselves. Majliv got up and held his hand out to me. Hand in hand we walked up the stairs to my room. It felt so safe to have him there close by me again. He held the door open for me and closed it behind him. I looked him over for a long time. His hair had grown long and hung down into his eyes, his broad shoulders had lost a little of their prominent appearance, but he could still be called a great, handsome-looking man with a body worth kissing the darkness for.

'Mia, kiss me. It really hasn't dawned on me that you're back yet. You're here! I just want to touch you and kiss you all the time, so you don't disappear again.'

'Then do it! You have no idea how intensely I've longed for you. Having you here, within reach, but still at a distance is almost torture. I want to be next to you can kiss every centimetre....' Before I could finish, he was in my arms kissing my lips. From there he moved on to my neck while his hands started working on undressing me. My fingers did the same to him. I found the edge of his shirt and moved my hands under it until I found soft skin and the toned muscles I knew so well. I'd missed this more than I thought. The closeness and the warmth were what I needed in order to breathe normally. When Majliv's shirt was on the floor I stroked my fingers on the inside of his waistband along his waist and I pushed his pants further down over his toned buttocks. He drew his breath deeply and pulled my dress over my head. He turned me around and kissed my neck, my breasts, and my stomach. His lips and tongue played from side to side at the same time as his hands massaged my butt and my thighs. He moved a step back and looked at me with a playful smile crinkling his mouth.

'Welcome home' he beamed at me, and his strong arms lifted me up and placed me on the bed. I was on my back and studied him in the same way he had studied me. His facial expression gradually changed from playful and excited to scrutinizing and bemused.

'Majliv, what is it?' I giggled. I wasn't following the mood change at all.

'I just... don't know how to say this without you taking it the wrong way. But as you know, I've been taking care of you and tending to your needs since we were locked out from each other, and that also includes nourishing you. But it's not an easy task to feed someone who neither chews nor swallows. Most people tend to lose... a lot of body mass, and I feel like you've also gotten thinner, but...' He stuttered and stumbled over his words, which I couldn't quite follow as I was still a bit dazed from the happiness.

'What are you trying to say?' I asked, sitting up in bed.

'I just find it a bit strange that you... seem to have become... fuller, especially there...' he said, nodding towards my belly, which had developed a quite noticeable round shape, clearly visible as I sat there.

I, too, was puzzled by the fact that my belly had grown much larger than before, and since the rest of me had become leaner, it did look odd. I grabbed the duvet beside me, poorly concealing my annoyance, and pulled it over me.

'No, Mia, that's not what I meant. I was actually thinking along completely different lines. You don't think... I mean, how far along are you with the twins in Gaia?' The more he spoke, the more offended I felt. How big was I? If he was fixating on whether my belly was big or not, he could forget about any intimacy. But slowly, his question began to sink in. Now that he mentioned it, I saw it too. I had almost the same size in Gaia. Majliv crouched down in front of me, his hands on my knees.

'I really messed this up. It was just my mind wandering, I should have thought before I spoke. There's nothing about you, that's not exactly how I want you to be. Please forget that I said anything, can you forgive me, please?' he pleaded.

But what he had said had put my thoughts into overdrive. Was it possible to be pregnant simultaneously in two worlds?

'I am about this size. I am almost done with my first trimester, so my stomach is this visible since I'm carrying twins.' I got up from the bed and stood in front of the mirror, letting the duvet fall to the floor. I could see it myself now, there was no doubt. Without saying anything I turned towards the side. Majliv sat quietly following my movements without saying a word. From the side it became even more visible. There was no doubt a tummy there which hadn't been there before. With my fingers I carefully applied a little pressure to get a sense of whether it was firm like it had been in Gaia. It was surprisingly firm all over. My doubt faded away like a curtain being drawn from a window. There were too many similarities for it to be anything but a pregnancy.

'I believe you're right,' I smiled at Majliv in the mirror. He moved up behind me and held me. He put both his arms around me cupping my stomach.

'This day is most definitely the best day of my life. First you come back to me, and now this,' he said and stroked the bump with both hands. Again, he leaned in and kissed my neck. His hands wandered up towards my breasts. It tickled me and I turned towards him. I could feel how willing he was against my hip and how willing I was myself, in my heart. The whole of him was perfect and we were together. I pushed myself harder against him and with a small sigh of pleasure he grasped my thighs once more, lifted me up and turned me so my back was against the wall. I held him close to me and in small movements he moved inside me. My feet locked around him and I held fast onto his shoulders. It was so freeing to feel him inside me again and to know that we fit together like a heart, a sign that we belonged together. His breath grew quicker, and his pace fastened. My nails made red marks down his wide back. I leaned my head against the wall and let go while breathing his name between my clenched teeth. Majliv put his face against the nape of my neck and hissed as he released himself. After taking some deep breaths, we lifted our heads and gazed into each other's eyes for a long time. Our lips met, and his tongue gently slipped between mine. All the painful experiences, all the nightmares were washed away with that kiss.

He carried me in his arms to the bed and lay down beside me.

'I've believed for so long that you were gone forever. It's so incredible that you're here. I love you so incredibly much, sweetheart' his words touched my heart.

'I love you in this world and the next and the next and all that may come after. You will always be the one for me,' I felt myself falling asleep, and suddenly panic came over me. Would we both wake up in Gaia now?

∞

I opened my eyes and realized that I was back home. The space next to me in bed was empty. No matter how much I wished for it, I knew it couldn't be a dream. I hadn't dreamt since the first time I came to Grimrokk.

With my phone in hand, I rushed downstairs to let Tinka out while frantically trying to call the clinic where Will had been admitted. It took a while before someone finally answered the phone.

'Good morning, this is Amelia Godseth. Has my husband woken up?' I didn't have time for pleasantries, and a perplexed voice replied just as briefly, asking if I had dialled the right number.

'Yes, I have. Can I speak with the doctor in charge right away, please?' She transferred me, and once again, I had to wait for a long time, repeating the question without any small talk.

'This is Amelia Godseth. Has my husband woken up?' The woman who had answered the phone remained silent for an uncomfortably long time.

'He probably has. Everyone has woken up, in fact! It would be nice if you could come here. Unfortunately, we can't answer questions over the phone.' She hung up.

Everyone had woken up! I knew I should go to Will immediately, but I also had to take in what she had said. So, we hadn't just opened the portal for the two of us, but for all the others as well. My legs gave way, and I ended up sitting on the kitchen floor filled with joy I had never experienced before. Soon, the phone rang again, and this time it was a voice I had longed to hear.

'My Amelia! I've had the surprise of my life, and a confused nurse told me that you already heard about it? It took a while before I understood where I was, in an unfamiliar house and a world I thought I had left behind forever. But now, I'm just relieved, it's so good and safe to know that I'm here with you.' It wasn't difficult to hear the relief in the voice on the other end. Majliv was here in Gaia too, as my Will.

'You can call me whatever you want now, William. There's no longer any danger of us being locked out from each other. You're my William in Gaia and in Grimrokk.'

'I feel the same as you, Amelia. I must say I like Mia as a pet name, though. It has a certain charm,' he added with a teasing tone that excited me.

'Call me whatever you want, husband, or you can stick to those two names, that's enough,' I laughed back. I jogged to the car with the phone in my hand while sending Snapchat messages with joyful news to everyone in Gaia who could possibly understand. Then,

I called Will's parents and shared the miracle they had stopped believing in. My mother-in-law was overwhelmed with happiness and kept apologizing for not supporting me in the decision to decline organ donation. She thanked me for having faith that it would turn out well and for standing my ground despite facing so much opposition. She and Will's father would come to visit their son as soon as we got home.

'Mom, he's awake!' I shouted when my mom answered the phone. It was so great to say it over and over again and to be part of the reactions of those who received the unexpected, good news.

'No, it can't be true! Is it true? Thank God!' My mom immediately started planning a grand celebration. The families would gather and celebrate life, as miraculous as it had turned out for us, with Will waking up and the pregnancy we hadn't fully enjoyed in all the excitement.

When I arrived at the clinic, Will was already packed, and had undergone a comprehensive health check. The doctors were busy and clearly had neither the opportunity nor the desire to keep anyone there longer than necessary.

In the car on the way home, Will stared out the window.

'What are you smiling about?' I asked.

'I'm just thinking about how long it's been since I saw this. I never thought that this landscape would be something I'd miss, and here I am, looking around at everything I took for granted,' he said with a peaceful look on his face.

'I recognize that feeling. I felt that way when I got to see Grimrokk again. All the emotions that resurfaced, which I had never realized I had,' I replied.

Will looked at the radio and smiled.

'I've missed this too,' he laughed and turned up the volume. The song filling the car was entirely irrelevant to me, but I would never forget his face at that moment.

On the steps at home, we were greeted by Aleksandra holding Ian in her arms, and Peter presenting a massive bouquet of flowers. Christina jumped up and down, shouting for William. Tinka understood it was a big moment and circled around the rest of the family, wagging her tail against the adults' thighs and the face of little Christina, who reached her arms up.

'Iam! Iam! Wher've you ben?' she asked Will when he lifted her in his arms, a big smile on his face.

'I've been sleeping very well, for a very long time. But now it was time to wake up, don't you think?' he laughed at the little one.

'Yes, t'was time,' she nodded with a grown-up expression.

Tearful hugs were exchanged between the neighbours and us. They had been invaluable support for me throughout the difficult time, even though they might have lost hope of ever talking to Will again.

A few days later, I got to share the joy of the pregnancy with Will for the first time, as it should be, when we had an appointment for an ultrasound examination. We saw the two small foetuses on the screen while the doctor examined them carefully. He probably believed we were overwhelmed by emotions since we were pregnant with twins.

CRESO

As the months passed, my belly grew to enormous proportions, something Lynn and Kian found quite amusing.

'Look at her. She's about to tip over... forward,' Kian chuckled, and the rest of us joined in the laughter.

'You've been mistaken for a different mammal, Mia. It looks like you're in your eighteenth month,' Lynn burst into laughter.

No one had ever been pregnant simultaneously with the same man in both worlds. Agaton had searched both the library in Manchester and in Dahlera, where Grimrokk's largest library was located. After all, he was a grimmer too, and a dedicated librarian through and through. The question everyone discussed was, of course, whether it was the same children in Grimrokk as in Gaia. In other words, were our Grimrokk children and two other children in Gaia, or were these the same? Since the pregnancy in Gaia was most likely the result of the IVF experiment, we had a fairly accurate due date. But did that also apply in Grimrokk? And were these also twins? That's how it looked, at least from Mia's perspective.

We could only wait until the children were old enough to communicate before we got answers to all our questions. How we would explain to others if two children began to talk about fantasy creatures was something we would have to figure out if it actually became a problem.

Fortunately, the mirror in Wargborough had not been shattered during Majliv's rage. However, the red heart and the ice it had formed on the surface of the mirror had completely dissolved, so thankfully, Benedikt and Lynn could continue receiving new travellers who arrived in Grimrokk, just like before. Even though there was no curse over Grimrokk, it didn't mean that anonymity was no longer important. Grimrokk's world was accustomed to the supernatural and the grimmers who arrived, but Gaia was a sceptical world that could just as easily pose a threat to the travellers. No one believed Gaia would readily accept a magical world.

∞

One day I woke up feeling unwell, and intuitively, I understood that something was not right, so we drove to the hospital where they conducted an urgent examination. Everything happened quickly because it turned out I had pre-eclampsia and needed to undergo an emergency C-section. Will was with me during the C-section, holding my hand faithfully. When they administered anaesthesia, I drifted off.

∞

Lynn shook me urgently until I woke up in Grimrokk. I was lying on a table.

'Lynn? What are you doing?' I mumbled groggily, trying to push her away.

'Thank God! Mia, the baby is coming, and I can't give birth for you while you're asleep. I'm not a doctor. You need to help as well!' she cried desperately.

So, the babies were really going to be born on the same day. We weren't completely sure, of course, but all signs pointed to twins being born in Grimrokk as well – the unusually large belly and the wise woman who had 'definitely' heard two sets of fast heartbeats in addition to mine when she examined me.

Before I could think more about it, I felt a strong contraction tighten over my belly. It hurt! The pressure intensified as I took a breath, and at the same time, something moved down in my lower abdomen. Even amid the newfound pain, thoughts raced through my mind like fleeting flashes I just managed to glimpse before they disappeared. Where was Majliv? Was he in Gaia helping me with the C-section? Was it over there? Was he taking care of the babies? Once again, there was a push over my belly, and something moved even further down. Lynn stood at my feet, which I had instinctively pulled up to make more room. Suddenly, Batist rushed in with his arms full of blankets and various bottles.

'She has finally woken up. But I sincerely hope she stays here long enough for us to complete the birth, because either this baby is gigantic, or there are two coming out,' Lynn struggled, and sweat dripped from her temples.

'That's good, that's very good. Mia! You need to work as efficiently as you can in case you fall asleep again. None of us have any experience with this, so even though you're here now and can help, we have to be prepared for anything,' Batist put down everything he was carrying, came over to me, and kissed my forehead.

It didn't take many contractions before a little fellow came into the world. He was far from a giant, just small and incredibly beautiful. Lynn washed him gently and placed him in my arms. He had porcelain skin, short light locks of hair, and a tiny voice that chirped.

'Marcus. His name shall be Marcus Godseth.' I had chosen the names long ago, and as soon as I held this beautiful creature in my arms, I knew the name was right.

After only a short pause, new contractions started. Batist lifted Marcus gently from my hands.

'You'll have him back soon. We need to welcome the next one as well, you know,' he beamed and winked at me.

This time, it went even faster, thankfully, as I had become terribly tired. My strength was nearly spent, and my energy was draining from me. When my second child was placed in my arms, I saw that he had dark and lustrous hair, velvety, round cheeks, and large, dark blue eyes. So different from his brother but equally beautiful. 'His name shall be Oliver Godseth.'

Both boys were placed in my arms. It felt perfectly right. Even as tired as I was, I looked up at Batist and Lynn, and four shining eyes looked back at me. The moment was filled with gratitude, the hard work was over, and it became difficult to stay awake.

'We'll take care of you, Mia. Just sleep,' Batist said as he wiped a damp cloth over my forehead.

🙰🙵

Will stands with his first son in his arms while the doctors deliver the second. Both are breathing, both are crying, they come with ten fingers each and ten toes. They are absolutely perfect. He can't even try to hold back the tears; he has waited so long and held back so much. He knew he had given up; he had lost faith that he would ever experience fatherhood. He had never thought he would see these children. What a woman he has, so strong, so enduring. Without her, he wouldn't be here.

He looks down at the child in his arms and murmurs a promise into the tiny ear. He promises the little one to be there for the rest of his life, to protect him forever and always. The other little bundle is placed on Amelia's chest and settles down at the sound of his mother's beating heart.

Will's reassuring voice woke me with sweet, whispered words in my ear.

'Amelia, look at these beautiful little beings we've created.'

The voice was a welcome intruder in my senses. I turned my head towards the sound and saw my husband with a little bundle in each arm. He leaned down so I could get a closer look at the little ones. One had light locks, and the other had dark velvety hair. They were so beautiful! He placed one of the children in my arms. I smelled the light locks, and motherly love spread through my entire body.

'You must also see the adorable little creatures that Lynn and Batist are taking care of now,' I whispered, making sure only he could hear.

He looked at me with wide eyes, and his smile grew even bigger than it already was.

'Now? At the same time?'

'Yes. Marcus and Oliver are there waiting for us when we get back,' I smiled.

'Marcus. Oliver. Do they resemble these two?' he asks, furrowing his brows slightly. For a long time, it had been a concern for us whether there would be two different sets of twins. In that case, we might have to leave two small children at night to care for and attend to the other two, and it wouldn't be easy for either of us. 'They are exactly like themselves. This is Marcus, and that's Oliver. Such a strong resemblance can't be a coincidence.' We smiled happily at each other. Finally, we were together. Finally, we were a family.

'Is it really true? We worried so much. You've thought about it, too, haven't you, that these children are entirely unique? No one has ever been born in two worlds like these boys. They'll never have to be alone like I was when I arrived there,' said William. It was true. They were truly one of a kind, our two little, world's most beautiful creations.

MAGIC OF THE NIGHT

Family and friends came and showered the small world citizens with kisses and gifts. Tiny fingers were examined, small heads were caressed, and tiny toes were tickled. Could one be happier? This thought rested in me several times a day, and it was hard not to look back on how all of this could have gone, painful as it was. Life was smiling at us now, and we knew it wasn't a given. We had fought, and we had won, everything we had dreamed of. Nothing could separate us anymore.

CRES

We believed that. We lived each day as if it were the end of the adventure, until one day a beautiful creature, a magnificent man, stood on the estate's steps and asked us to bring the children forward for Huldra. No one said no to Huldra. I would have preferred to take both boys and run away to hide them, but it would have been futile, I knew that.

We had no choice. We bundled up the boys to keep them warm and carried one child each under our clothes, close to us, before we followed the man from the Hulderfolk. The forest was winter-clad with white tufts on the trees and a thick, white carpet on the ground. The crisp snow crunched under our boots.

At the boundary of Huldra's forest, the forest changed its identity and became colder. It had icicles instead of soft tufts, and the snow crackled like ice under our shoes.

The colder it got, the more my nerves crackled, and I had a stomachache. Facing Huldra with the children scared me much more than when I was alone.

We arrived at the circle where all the earth houses were located. Everyone from the Hulderfolk was gathered there, with Huldra herself in the front and centre. We stopped in front of them and were about to bow and kneel to show humility. Before we could gather ourselves, Huldra knelt down and bowed her head all the way to the ground. Around her, everyone else did the same, until they all knelt on the ground with bowed heads. We stood there utterly bewildered, not understanding what was happening at all.

Finally, everyone rose, and Huldra took a few steps closer to us.

'We all wanted to welcome your children into the world. As you may have understood, these two are not like the rest of us. They are the first of their kind and will have great significance in both worlds.' She placed both hands on the boys' foreheads, and of all the astonishing things: Huldra smiled.

'As you have understood along the way, there has been a lot at stake and many decisive events this year. Although you have uncovered the story bit by bit, it has not been a matter of chance. The legend reached people's ears several hundred years ago, but as the years passed without it being fulfilled, it eventually faded into old scriptures and was forgotten. Grimrokk was a gloomy and desperate place for far too long, longing for rescue. Who would have thought that a young woman, for strange reasons not arriving here until adulthood, would be the one to set things in motion by fulfilling an ancient legend she had never heard?

The day you entered our world, the wind told me that you were not an ordinary woman and that you were important. At our first meeting, I strongly felt that you were special, but it wasn't until you were banished that I understood who you were and the mission you had been assigned. You were one part of the marked souls. It was also unknown to me that Majliv had received the heart; it was Santa's secret.' She stood before us, more open than ever, and now we saw that she had a warm presence.

'The hearts of the marked souls. Your hearts. What you two may not know about the legend is that it tells that this heart, with its two tips, will guide these unique beings. They are the first of their kind, the two heart children. These hearts will acquire special abilities as they grow.' We had already learned a lot, but before we could digest it, Huldra continued her speech, and the continuation was no less surprising.

'This one will have the ability to see the truth in what is said, like a good leader should.' She drew a circle over Marcus' forehead and then leaned over to kiss it.

'This one will have the ability to crack nuts; he will be a problem solver and give good advice, like a good leader should.' She drew another circle, this time over Oliver's forehead, and also kissed him.

'Heart children Marcus and Oliver will grow up to be the leaders of the future. They will contribute to Grimrokk's people and creatures living in harmony, something that has been missing in this world for several hundred years. With good leadership, Grimrokk will flourish. These are the past, the future, and the present.'

Majliv and I looked at each other. I felt both pride and fear for everything that would come in the future, but together we would be there for them and guide them every step of the way. A heavy responsibility had been placed on their young shoulders, but together we would help them grow into their roles, lead them in the right direction, and teach them to be good people, people who would be loved. Not just by us, but by many. Just as good leaders should be.'

9 788269 349917